Shojo Beat

VAMPIRE KNIGHT

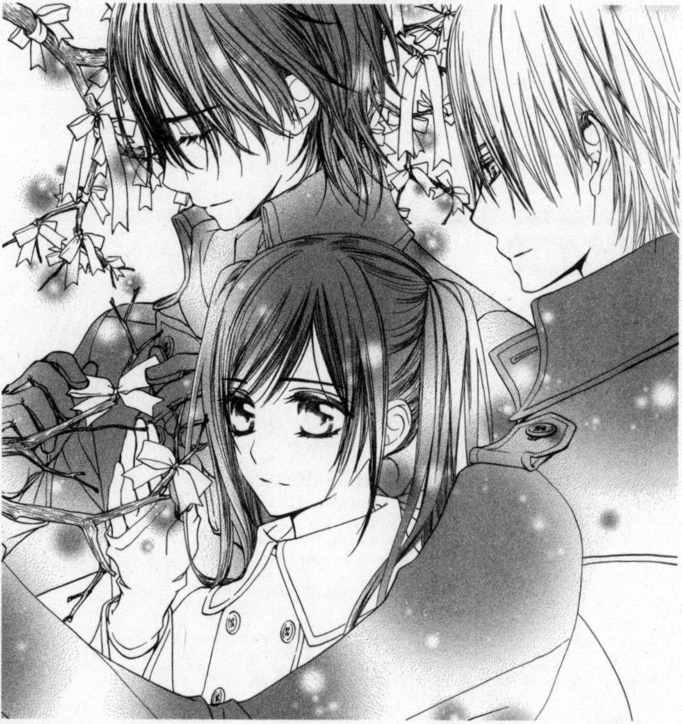

Story & Art by
Matsuri Hino

Vol. 16

The Story of VAMPIRE KNIGHT

1 Cross Academy, a private boarding school, is where the Day Class and the Night Class coexist. The Night Class—a group of beautiful elite students—are all vampires!

2 Four years ago, after turning his twin brother Ichiru against him, the pureblood Shizuka Hio bit Zero and turned him into a vampire. Kaname kills Shizuka, but the source may still exist. Meanwhile, Yuki suffers from lost memories. When Kaname sinks his fangs into her neck, her memories return!

3 Yuki is the princess of the Kuran family—and a pureblood vampire!! Ten years ago, her mother exchanged her life to seal away Yuki's vampire nature. Yuki's Uncle Rido killed her father. Rido takes over Shiki's body and arrives at the Academy. He targets Yuki for her blood, so Kaname gives his own blood to resurrect Rido. Kaname confesses that he is the progenitor of the Kurans, and that Rido is the master who awakened him!

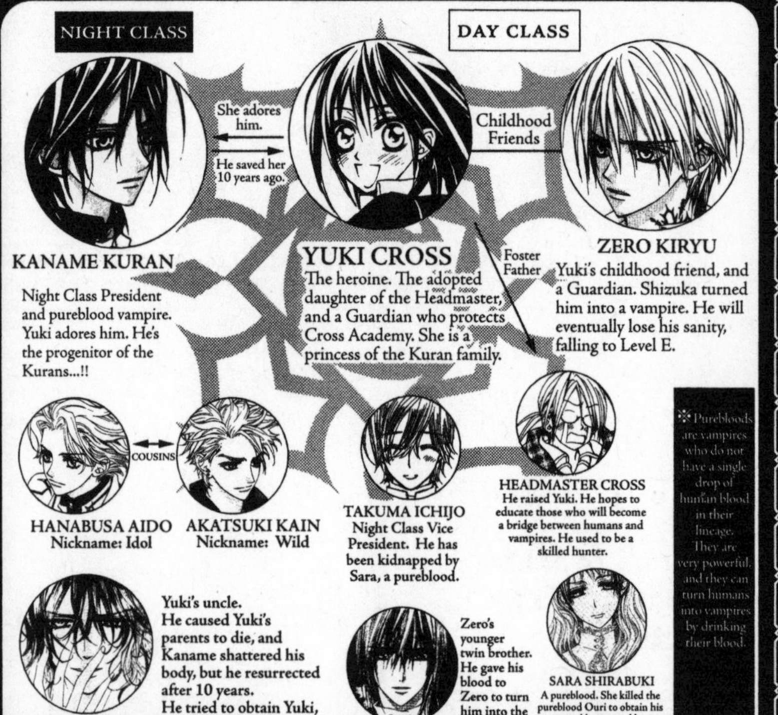

NIGHT CLASS

DAY CLASS

She adores him.

He saved her 10 years ago.

Childhood Friends

KANAME KURAN

Night Class President and pureblood vampire. Yuki adores him. He's the progenitor of the Kurans...!!

YUKI CROSS
The heroine. The adopted daughter of the Headmaster, and a Guardian who protects Cross Academy. She is a princess of the Kuran family.

Foster Father

ZERO KIRYU
Yuki's childhood friend, and a Guardian. Shizuka turned him into a vampire. He will eventually lose his sanity, falling to Level E.

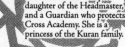

←COUSINS→

HANABUSA AIDO
Nickname: Idol

AKATSUKI KAIN
Nickname: Wild

TAKUMA ICHIJO
Night Class Vice President. He has been kidnapped by Sara, a pureblood.

HEADMASTER CROSS
He raised Yuki. He hopes to educate those who will become a bridge between humans and vampires. He used to be a skilled hunter.

❈ Purebloods are vampires who do not have a single drop of human blood in their lineage. They are very powerful, and they can turn humans into vampires by drinking their blood.

RIDO KURAN

Yuki's uncle. He caused Yuki's parents to die, and Kaname shattered his body, but he resurrected him after 10 years. He tried to obtain Yuki, but Yuki and Zero killed him.

Zero's younger twin brother. He gave his blood to Zero to turn him into the strongest hunter.

ICHIRU

SARA SHIRABUKI
A pureblood. She killed the pureblood Ouri to obtain his power, and has turned human girls into vampires. She claims she wants to become a "Queen," but what does she mean?!

4 Cross Academy turns into a battlefield. After fierce fighting, Yuki and Zero succeed in defeating Rido, but right after Zero points his gun at Yuki. No matter what their feelings are, their fates will never intertwine. Yuki leaves the Academy with Kaname, and the Night Class at Cross Academy is no more.

5 A year has passed since Yuki and Zero's parting. Sara Shirabuki begins making suspicious moves by creating more servants of her own. Kaname gives Yuki his blood to show her his memories of the time the progenitors existed. Yuki sees a woman with whom Kaname shared a strong bond in the past. Distressed at how vampires were preying on humans, the woman gave up her life to cast her heart into a furnace, creating weapons humans could use to kill vampires. The resulting substance became the base of vampire hunter weapons.

6 Yuki tries to live together with Kaname, but Kaname slays Aido's father then disappears. Yuki is taken captive by the Hunter Society and restarts the Night Class at Cross Academy to help maintain order. Even Sara joins the academy. Now Zero has persuaded Yuki to drink his blood to quench her thirst?!

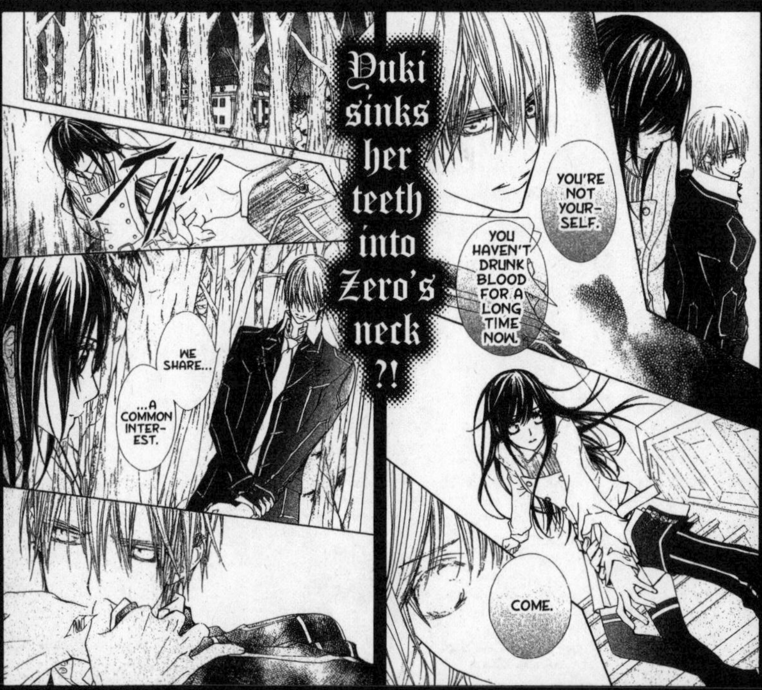
Yuki sinks her teeth into Zero's neck ?!
YOU'RE NOT YOURSELF.
YOU HAVEN'T DRUNK BLOOD FOR A LONG TIME NOW.
COME.
WE SHARE...
...A COMMON INTEREST.

VAMPIRE KNIGHT

Contents

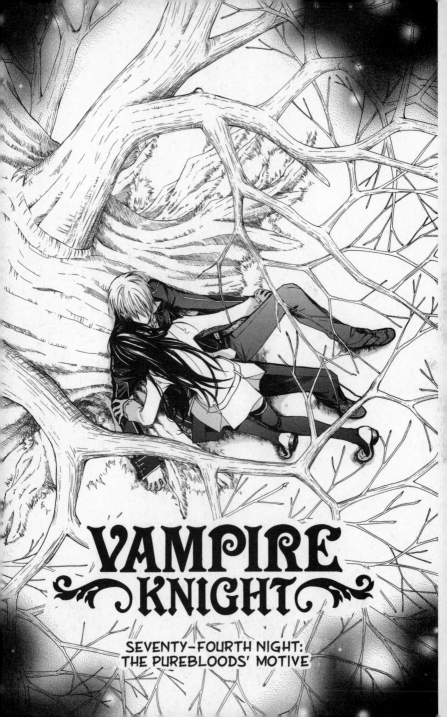

VAMPIRE KNIGHT

SEVENTY-FOURTH NIGHT: THE PUREBLOODS' MOTIVE

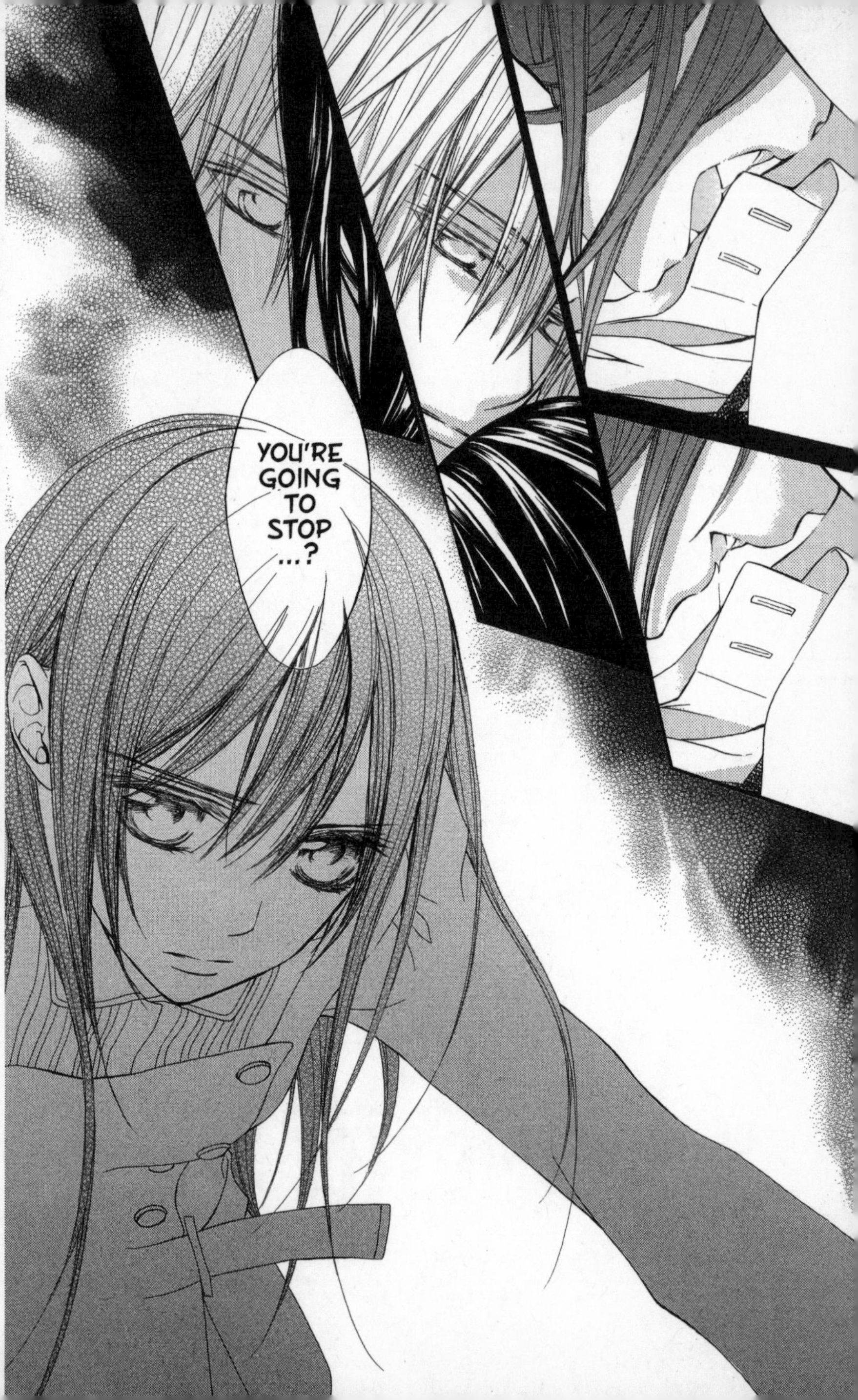
YOU'RE GOING TO STOP ...?

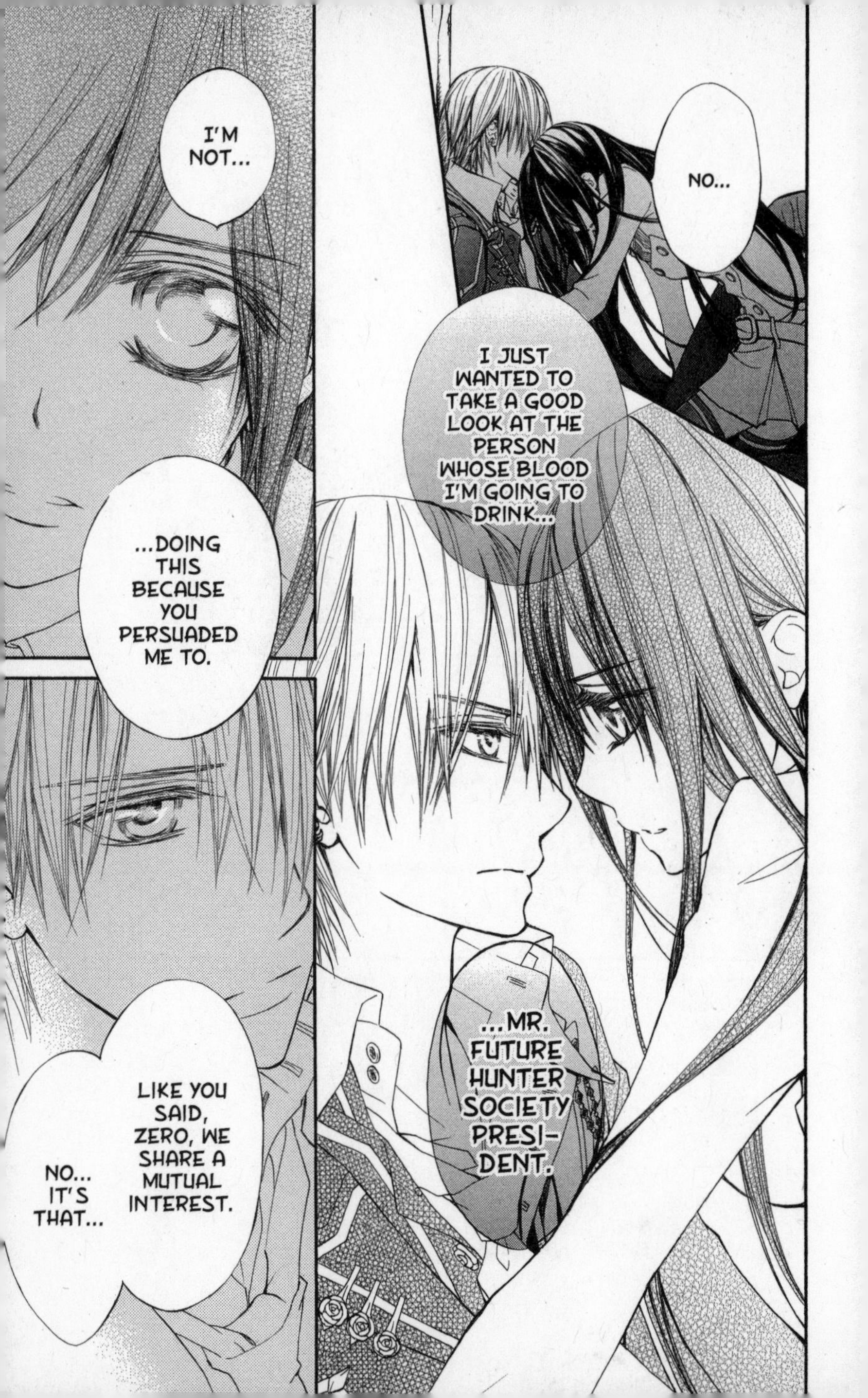
I'M NOT...
...DOING THIS BECAUSE YOU PERSUADED ME TO.
LIKE YOU SAID, ZERO, WE SHARE A MUTUAL INTEREST.
NO... IT'S THAT...
NO...
I JUST WANTED TO TAKE A GOOD LOOK AT THE PERSON WHOSE BLOOD I'M GOING TO DRINK...
...MR. FUTURE HUNTER SOCIETY PRESI-DENT.

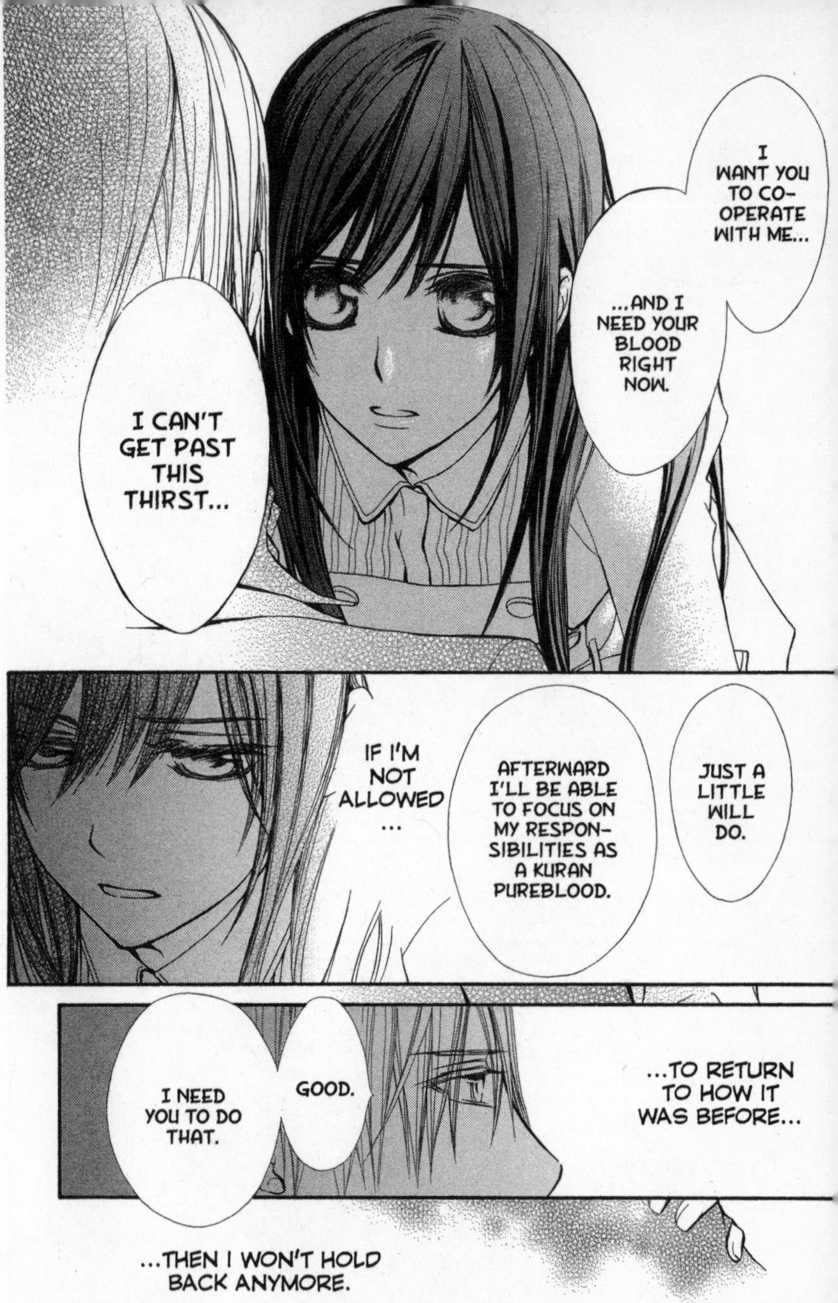
I WANT YOU TO CO-OPERATE WITH ME...
...AND I NEED YOUR BLOOD RIGHT NOW.
I CAN'T GET PAST THIS THIRST...
JUST A LITTLE WILL DO.
AFTERWARD I'LL BE ABLE TO FOCUS ON MY RESPON-SIBILITIES AS A KURAN PUREBLOOD.
IF I'M NOT ALLOWED ...
...TO RETURN TO HOW IT WAS BEFORE...
GOOD.
I NEED YOU TO DO THAT.
...THEN I WON'T HOLD BACK ANYMORE.

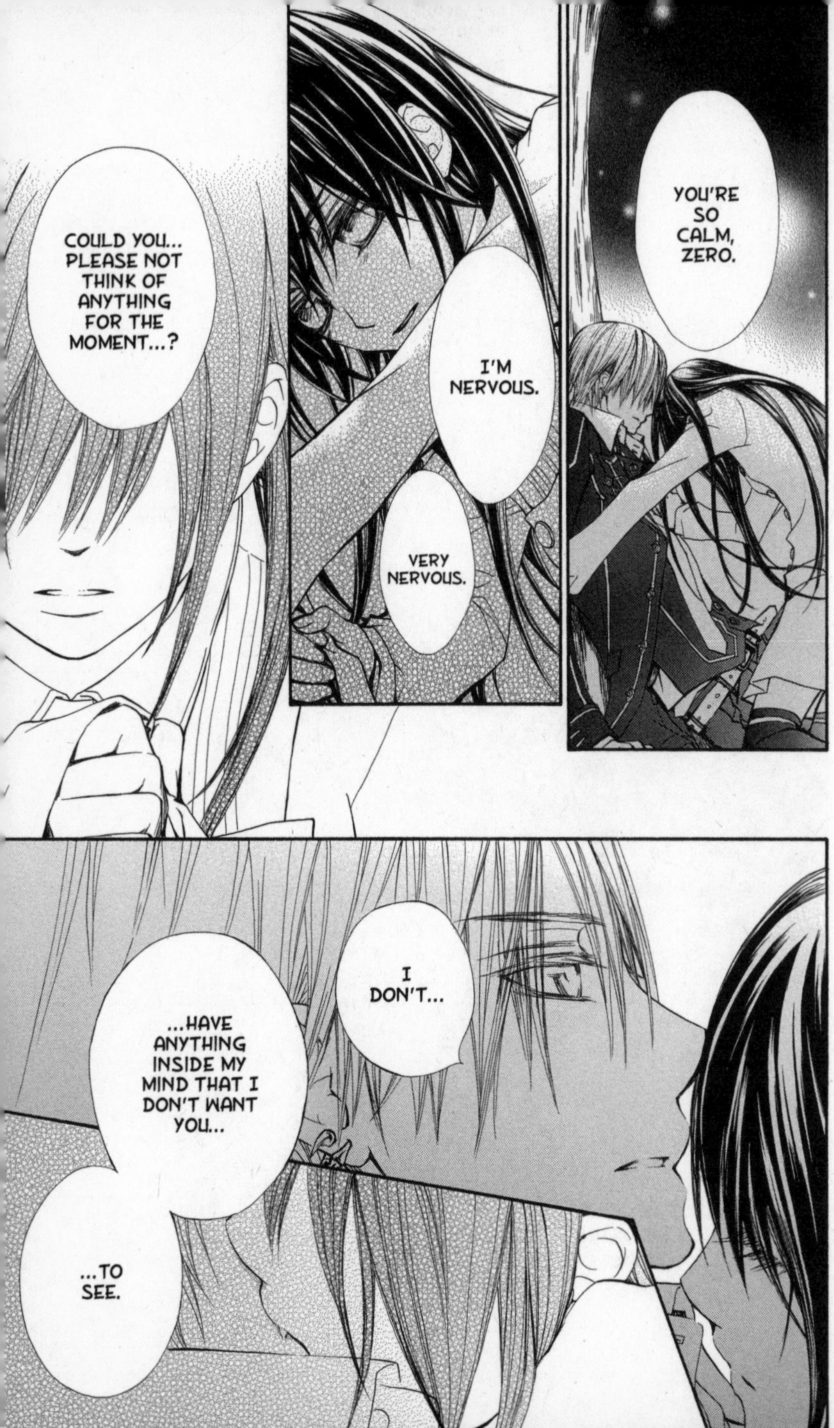
YOU'RE SO CALM, ZERO.
I'M NERVOUS.
VERY NERVOUS.
COULD YOU... PLEASE NOT THINK OF ANYTHING FOR THE MOMENT...?
I DON'T...
...HAVE ANYTHING INSIDE MY MIND THAT I DON'T WANT YOU...
...TO SEE.

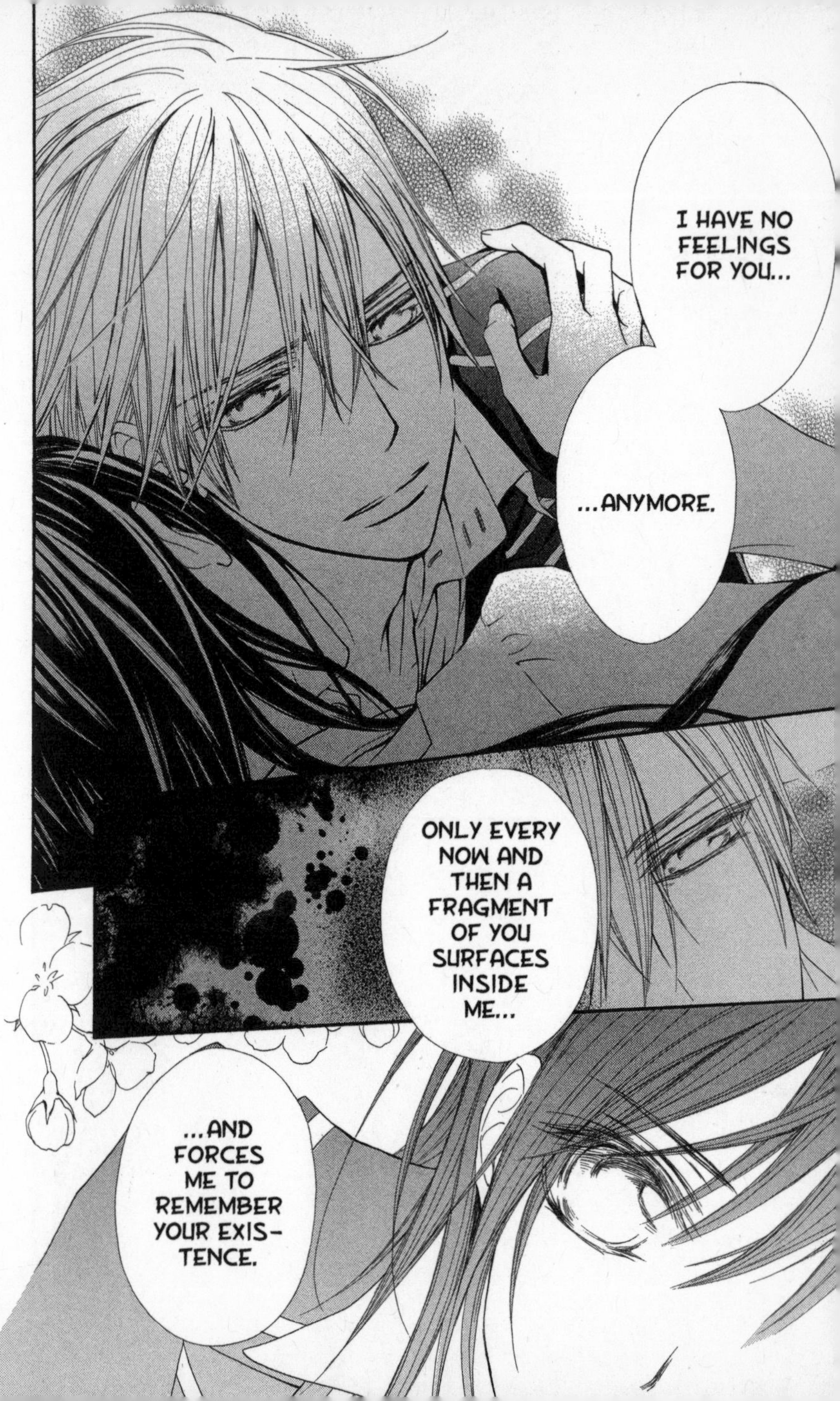
I HAVE NO FEELINGS FOR YOU...
...ANYMORE.
ONLY EVERY NOW AND THEN A FRAGMENT OF YOU SURFACES INSIDE ME...
...AND FORCES ME TO REMEMBER YOUR EXIS-TENCE.

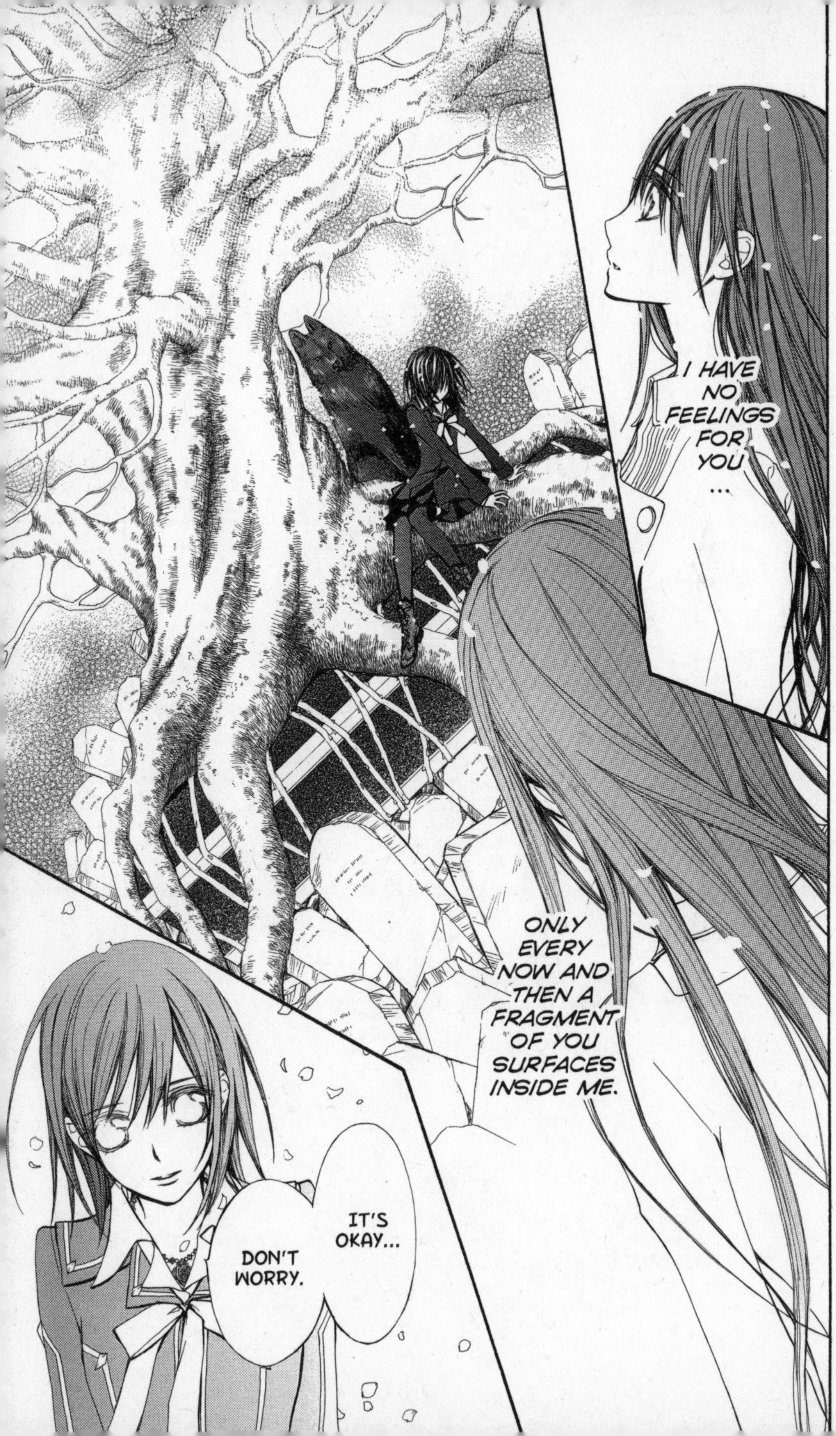
I HAVE NO FEELINGS FOR YOU ...
ONLY EVERY NOW AND THEN A FRAGMENT OF YOU SURFACES INSIDE ME.
IT'S OKAY...
DON'T WORRY.

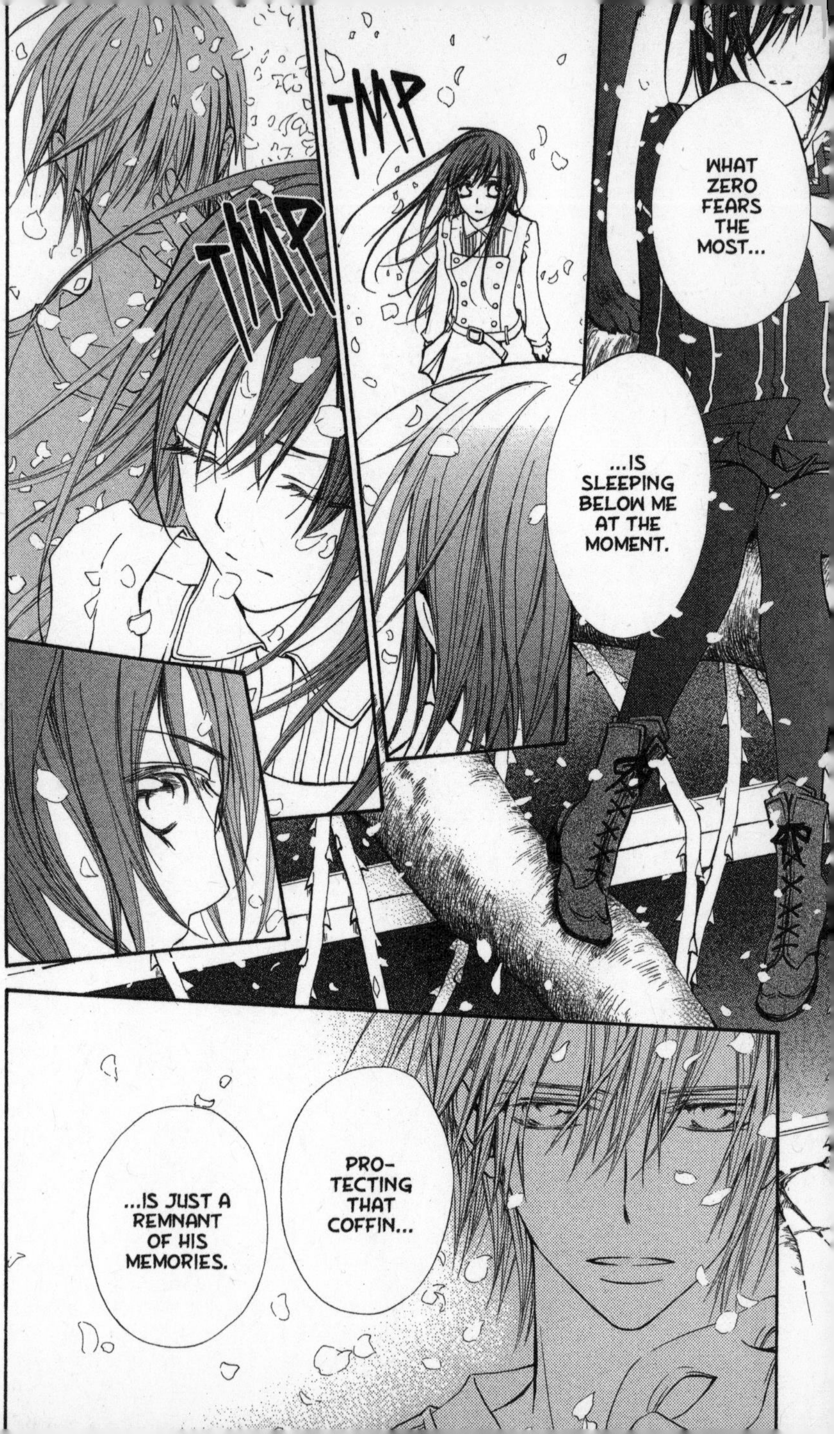
WHAT ZERO FEARS THE MOST...
...IS SLEEPING BELOW ME AT THE MOMENT.
TMP
TMP
PRO-TECTING THAT COFFIN...
...IS JUST A REMNANT OF HIS MEMORIES.

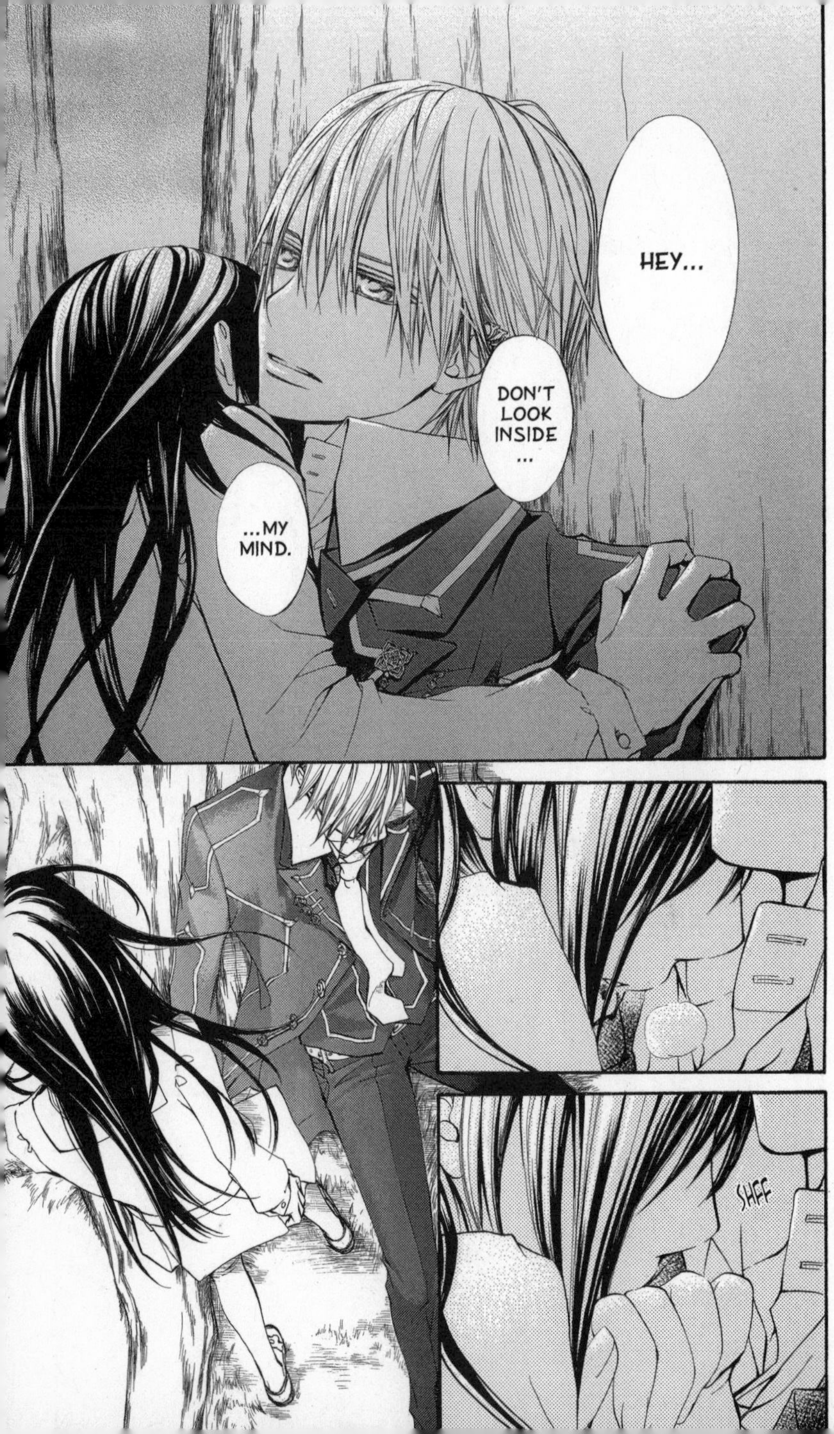
HEY...
DON'T LOOK INSIDE ...
...MY MIND.
SHFF

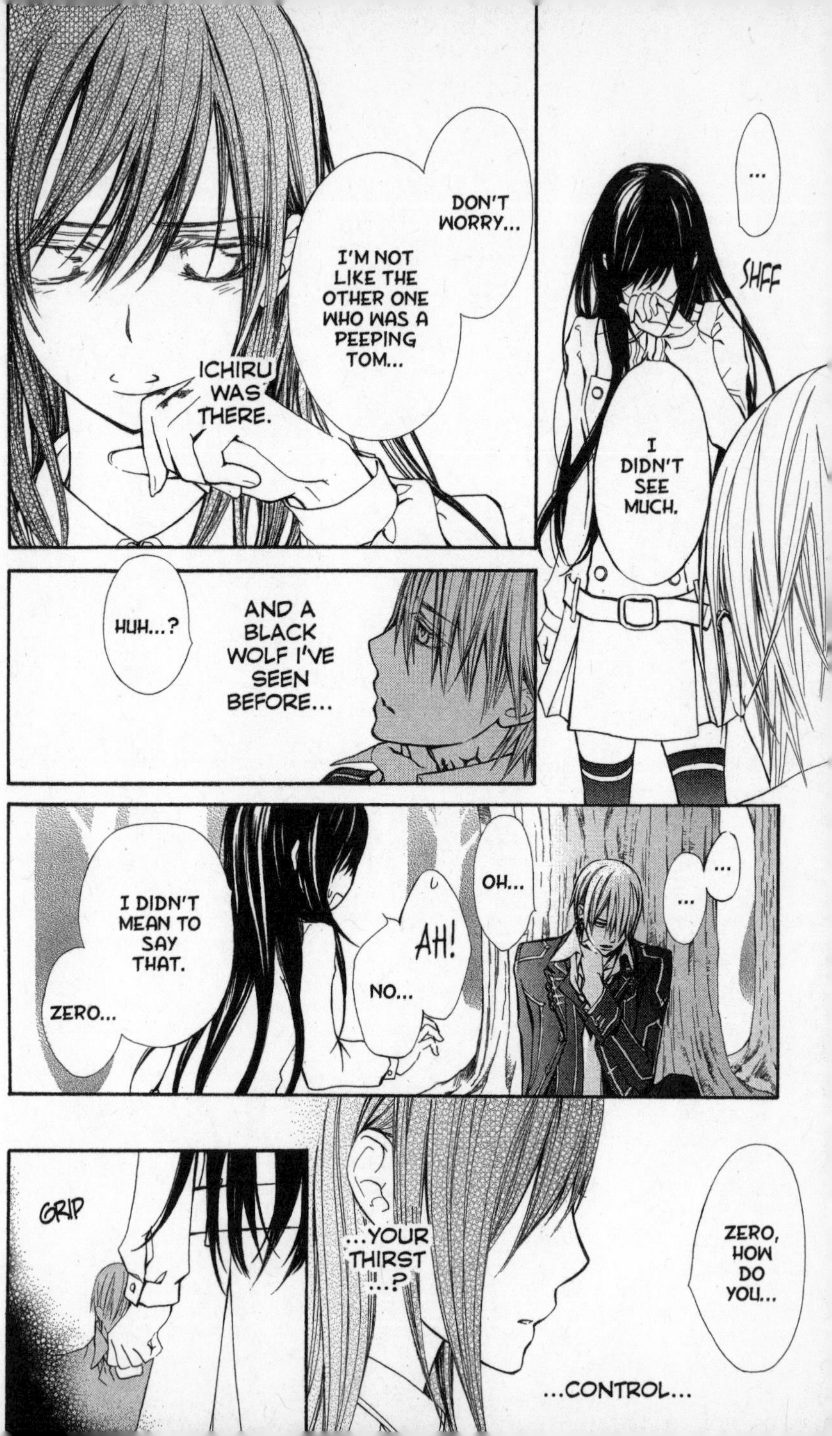
...
SHFF
I DIDN'T SEE MUCH.
DON'T WORRY...
I'M NOT LIKE THE OTHER ONE WHO WAS A PEEPING TOM...
ICHIRU WAS THERE.
AND A BLACK WOLF I'VE SEEN BEFORE...
HUH...?
...
...
OH...
AH!
NO...
I DIDN'T MEAN TO SAY THAT.
ZERO...
ZERO, HOW DO YOU...
...CONTROL...
...YOUR THIRST...?
GRIP

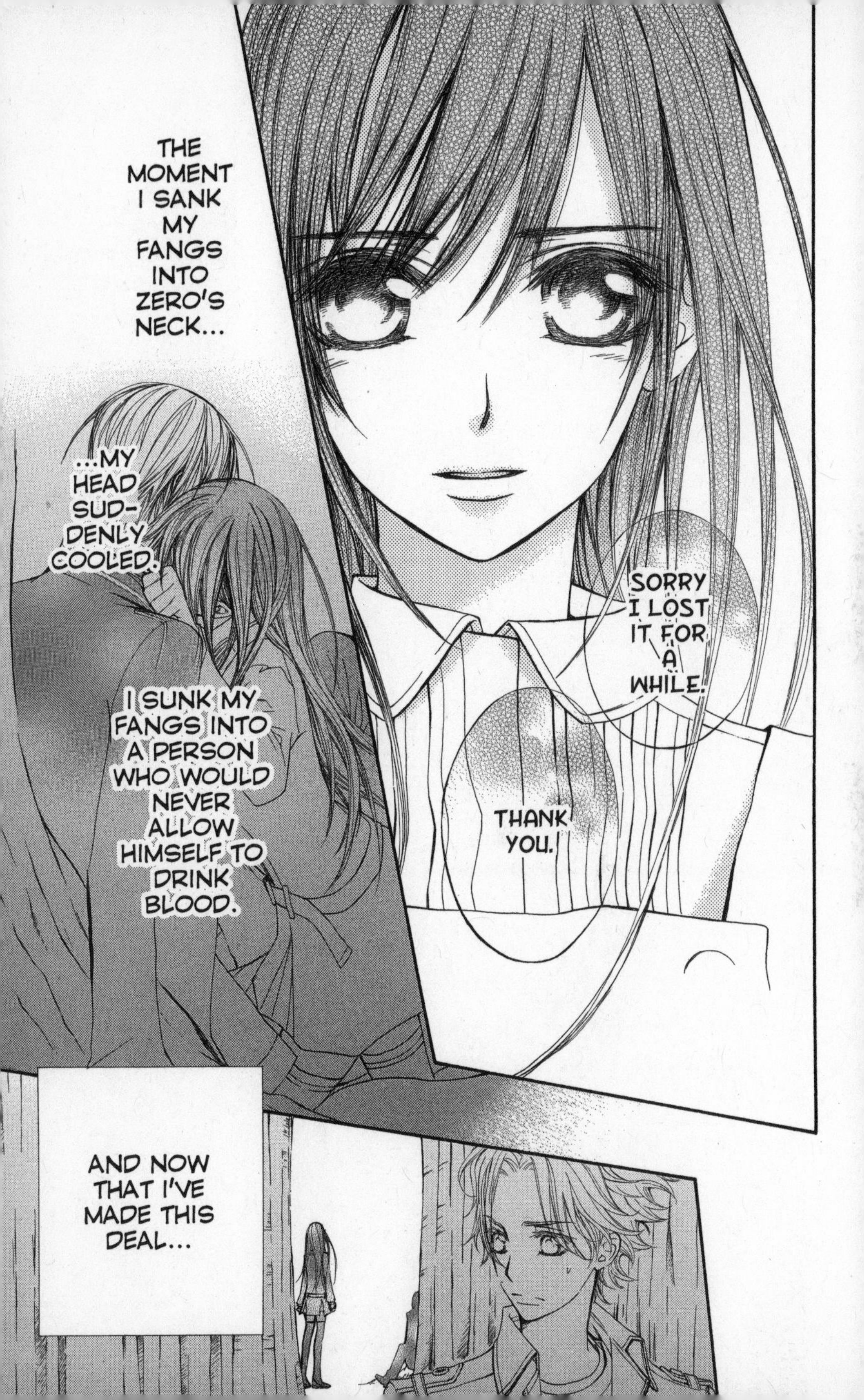
SORRY I LOST IT FOR A WHILE.
THANK YOU.
THE MOMENT I SANK MY FANGS INTO ZERO'S NECK...
...MY HEAD SUD-DENLY COOLED.
I SUNK MY FANGS INTO A PERSON WHO WOULD NEVER ALLOW HIMSELF TO DRINK BLOOD.
AND NOW THAT I'VE MADE THIS DEAL...

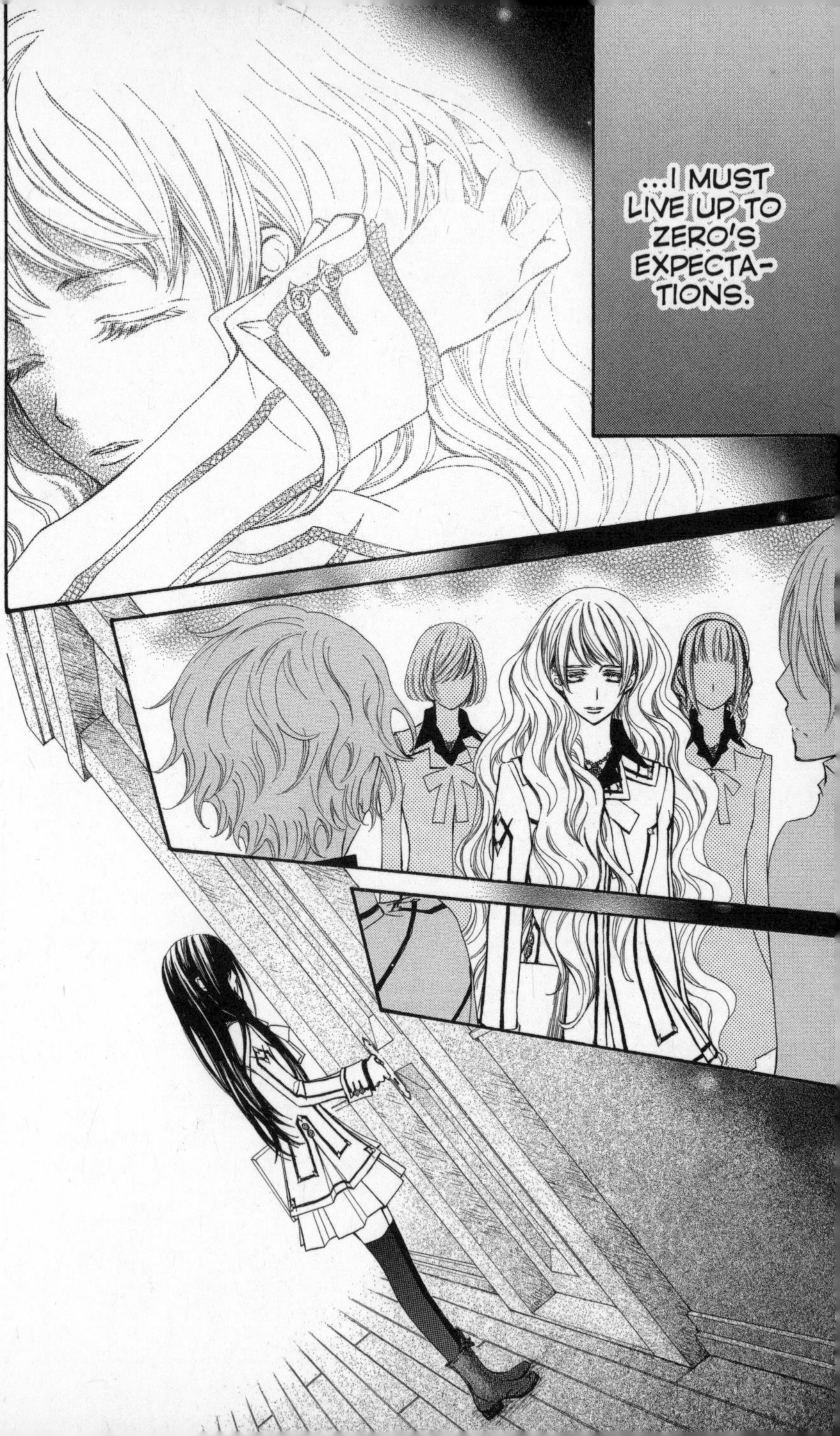
...I MUST LIVE UP TO ZERO'S EXPECTA-TIONS.

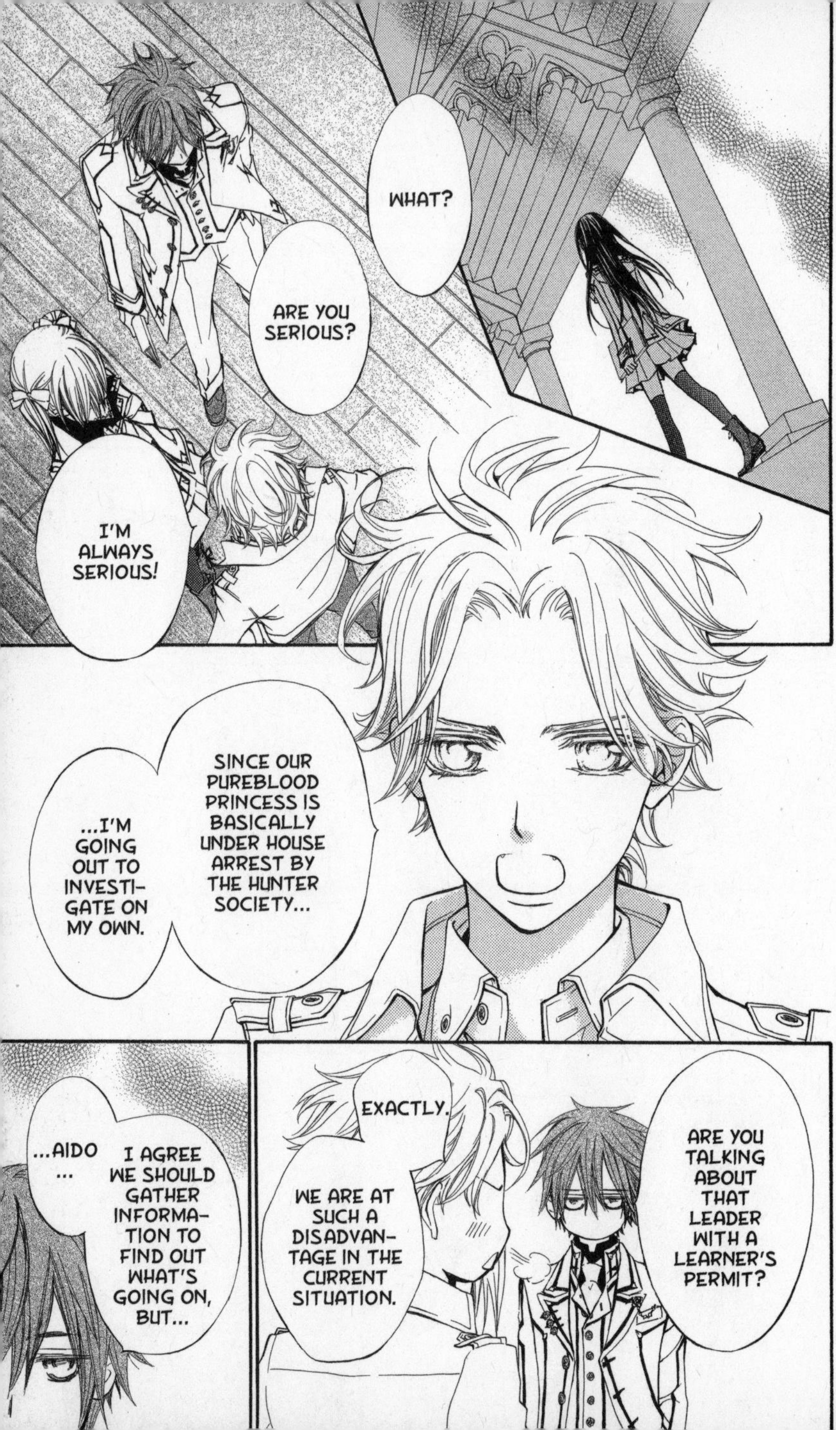
WHAT?
ARE YOU SERIOUS?
I'M ALWAYS SERIOUS!
SINCE OUR PUREBLOOD PRINCESS IS BASICALLY UNDER HOUSE ARREST BY THE HUNTER SOCIETY...
...I'M GOING OUT TO INVESTI-GATE ON MY OWN.
ARE YOU TALKING ABOUT THAT LEADER WITH A LEARNER'S PERMIT?
EXACTLY.
WE ARE AT SUCH A DISADVAN-TAGE IN THE CURRENT SITUATION.
...AIDO ...
I AGREE WE SHOULD GATHER INFORMA-TION TO FIND OUT WHAT'S GOING ON, BUT...

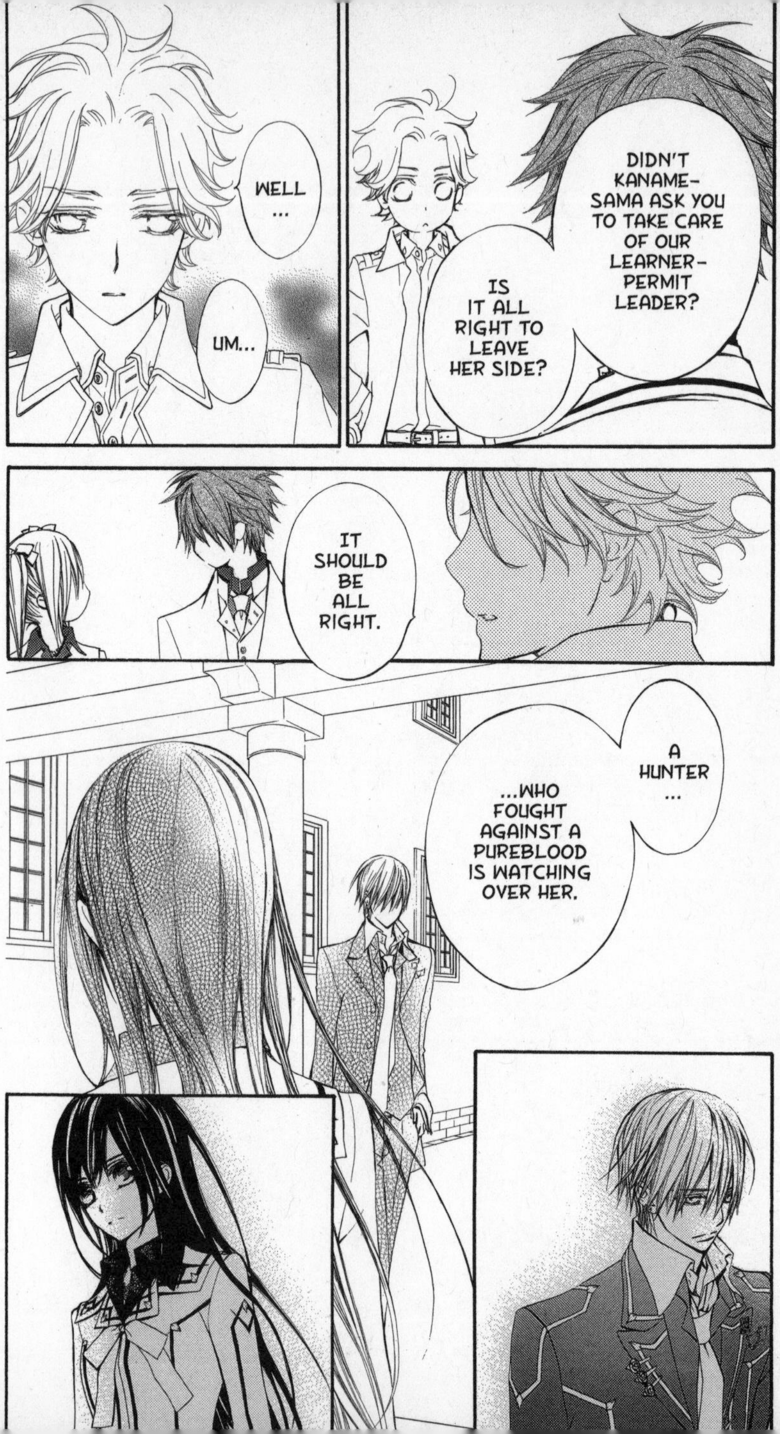
DIDN'T KANAME-SAMA ASK YOU TO TAKE CARE OF OUR LEARNER-PERMIT LEADER?
IS IT ALL RIGHT TO LEAVE HER SIDE?
WELL ...
UM...
IT SHOULD BE ALL RIGHT.
A HUNTER ...
...WHO FOUGHT AGAINST A PUREBLOOD IS WATCHING OVER HER.

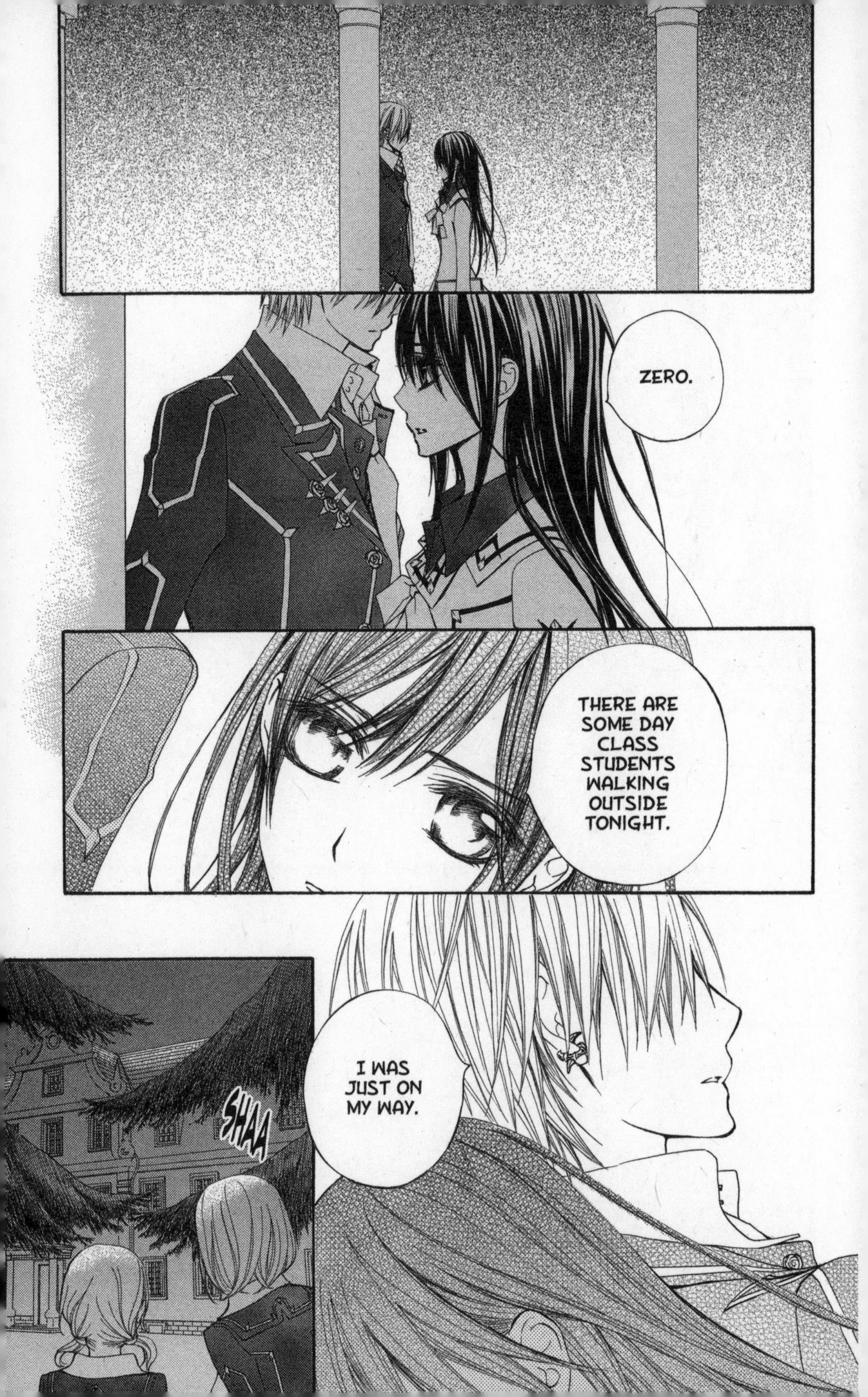
ZERO.
THERE ARE SOME DAY CLASS STUDENTS WALKING OUTSIDE TONIGHT.
I WAS JUST ON MY WAY.
SHAA

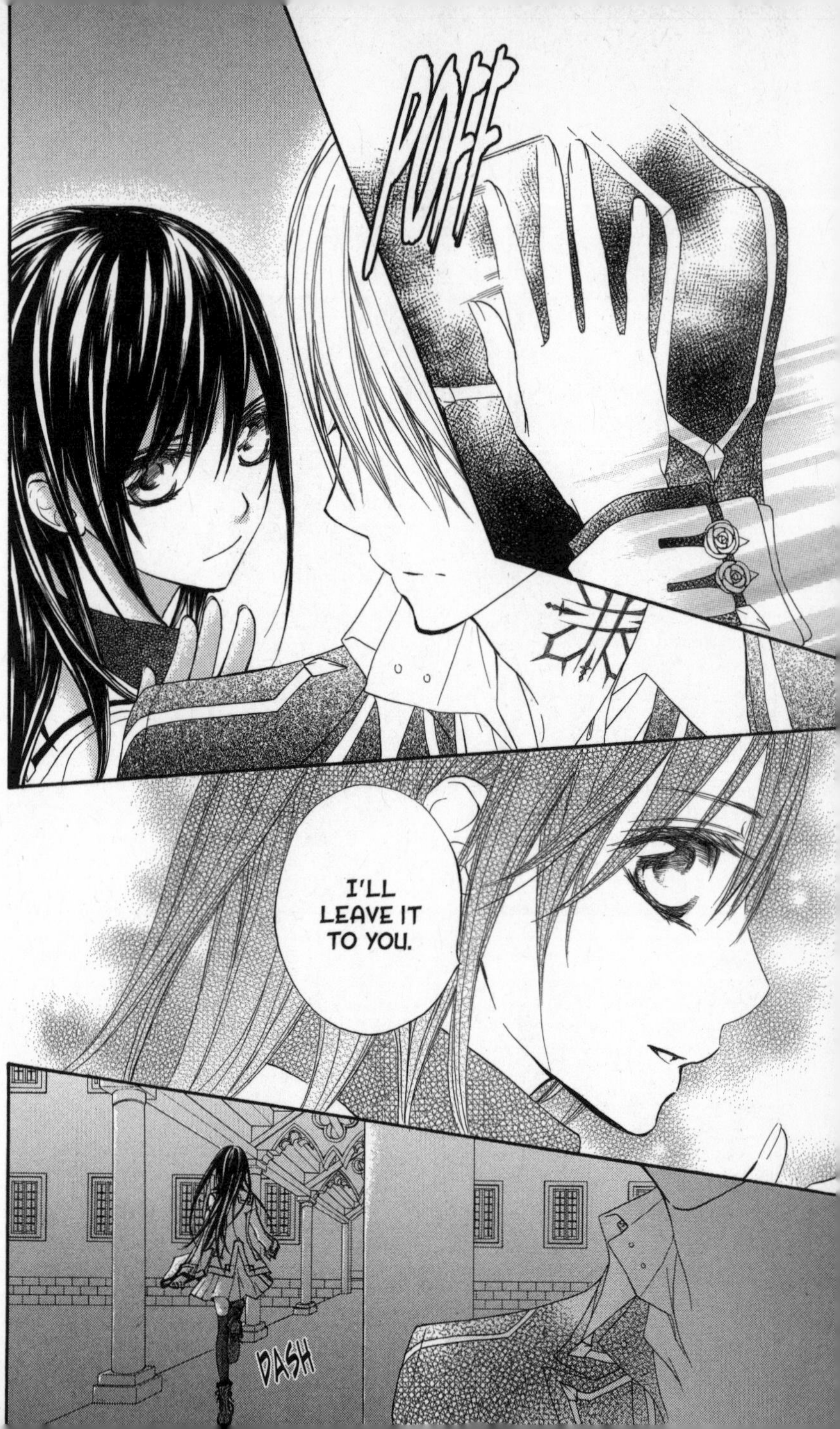
POFF
I'LL LEAVE IT TO YOU.
DASH

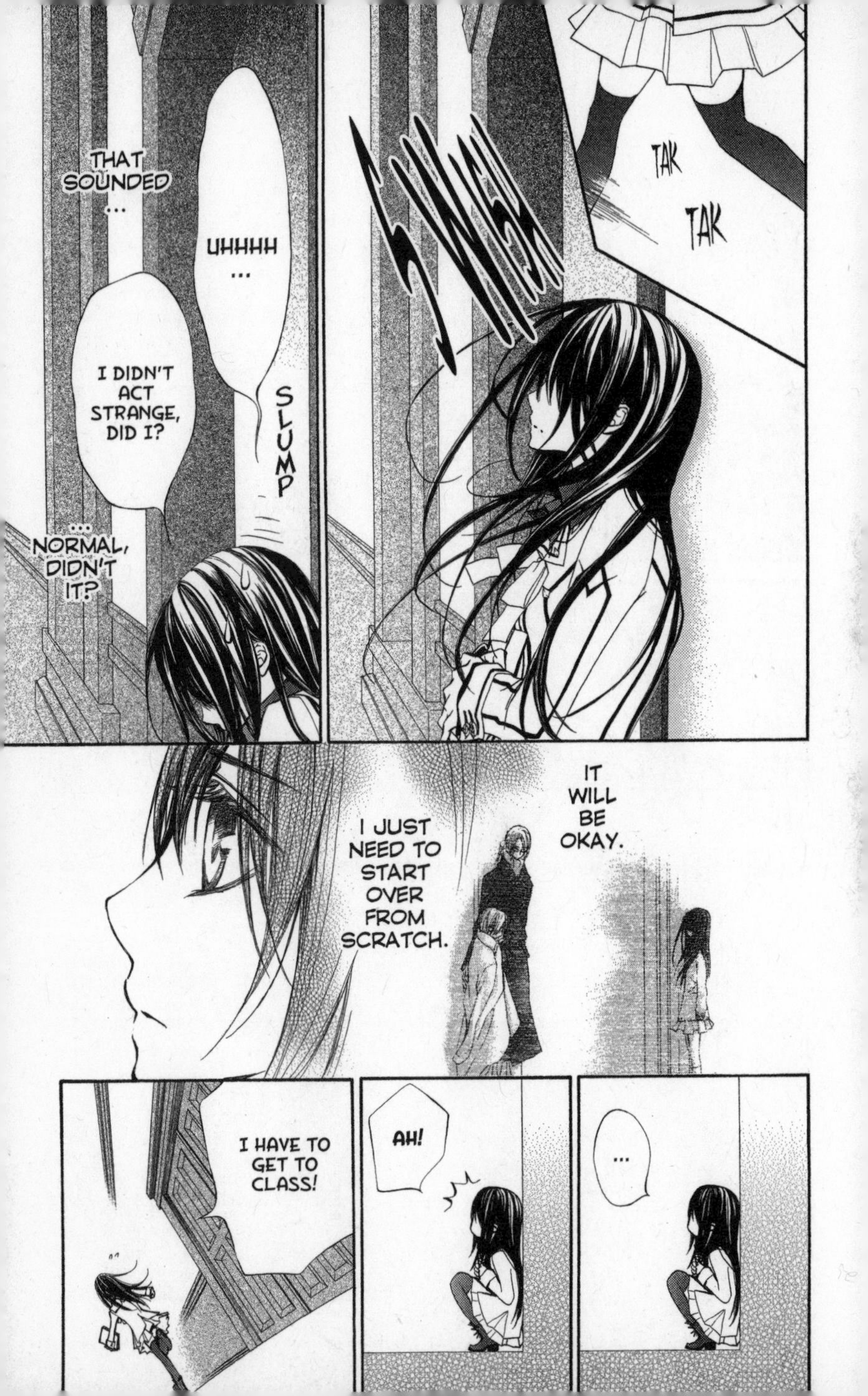
TAK
TAK
SWISH
UHHHH...
SLUMP
I DIDN'T ACT STRANGE, DID I?
THAT SOUNDED...
...NORMAL, DIDN'T IT?
IT WILL BE OKAY.
I JUST NEED TO START OVER FROM SCRATCH.
...
AH!
I HAVE TO GET TO CLASS!

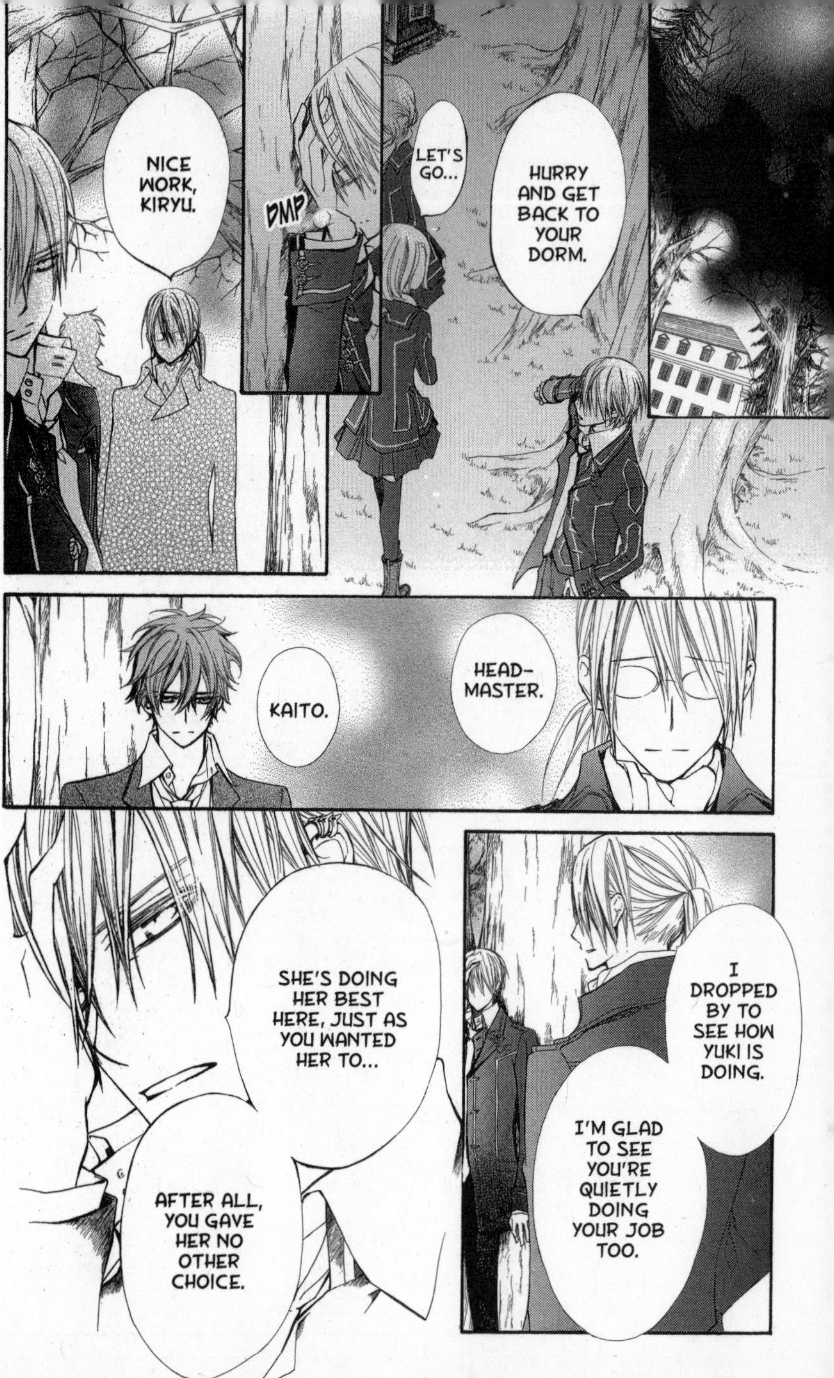
HURRY AND GET BACK TO YOUR DORM.
LET'S GO...
DMP
NICE WORK, KIRYU.
HEAD-MASTER.
KAITO.
I DROPPED BY TO SEE HOW YUKI IS DOING.
I'M GLAD TO SEE YOU'RE QUIETLY DOING YOUR JOB TOO.
SHE'S DOING HER BEST HERE, JUST AS YOU WANTED HER TO...
AFTER ALL, YOU GAVE HER NO OTHER CHOICE.

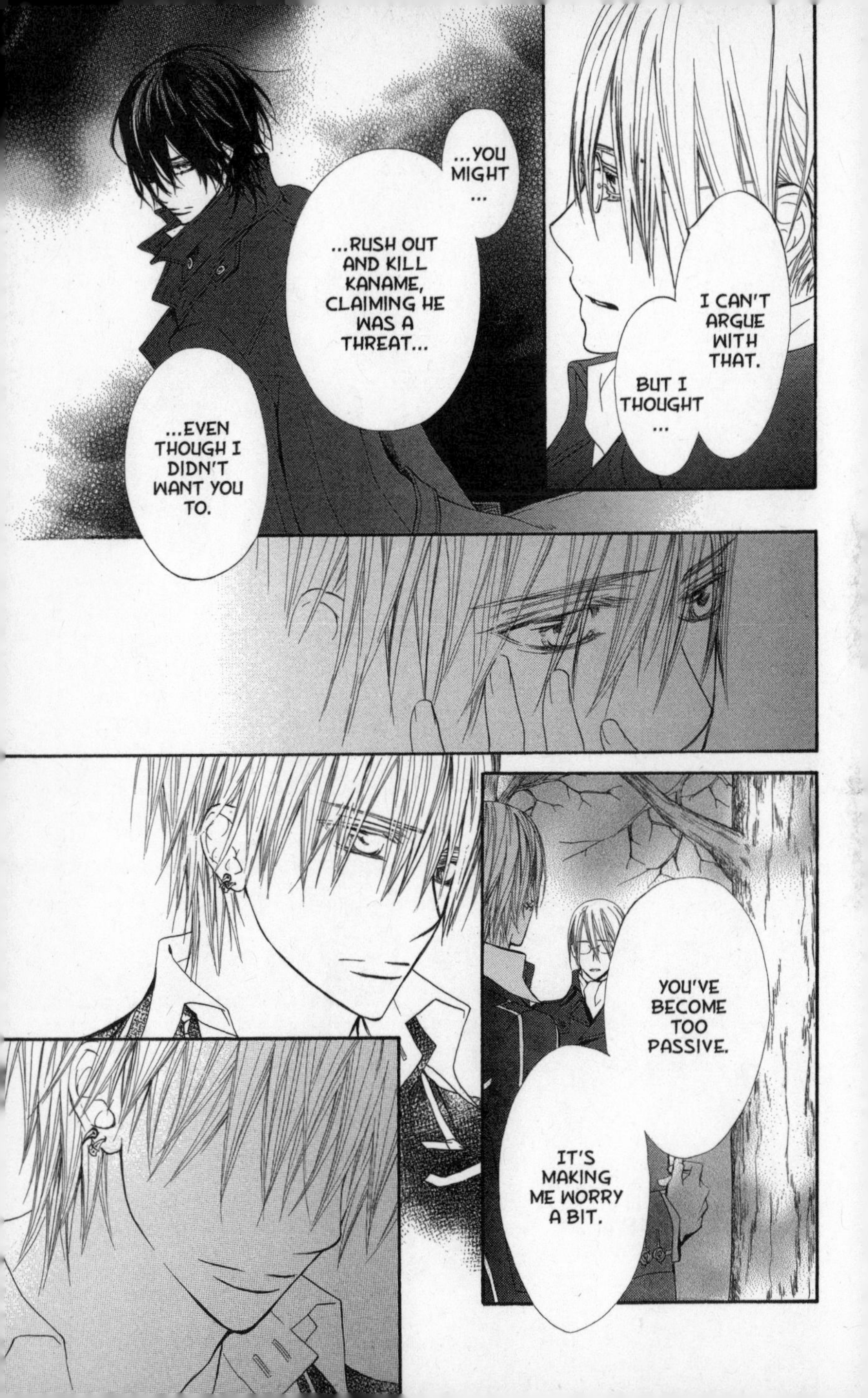
I CAN'T ARGUE WITH THAT.
BUT I THOUGHT...
...YOU MIGHT...
...RUSH OUT AND KILL KANAME, CLAIMING HE WAS A THREAT...
...EVEN THOUGH I DIDN'T WANT YOU TO.
YOU'VE BECOME TOO PASSIVE.
IT'S MAKING ME WORRY A BIT.

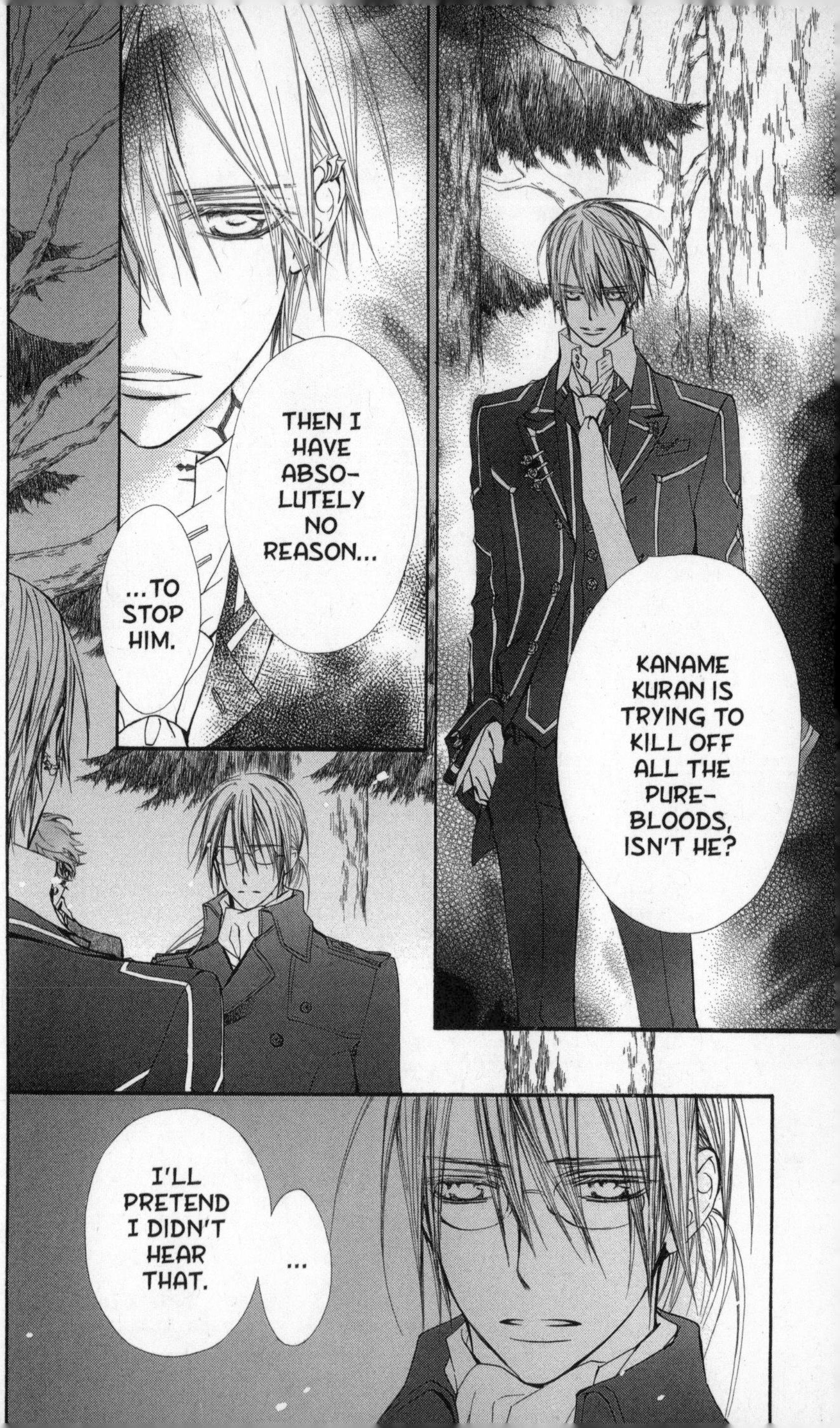
KANAME KURAN IS TRYING TO KILL OFF ALL THE PURE-BLOODS, ISN'T HE?
THEN I HAVE ABSO-LUTELY NO REASON...
...TO STOP HIM.
...
I'LL PRETEND I DIDN'T HEAR THAT.

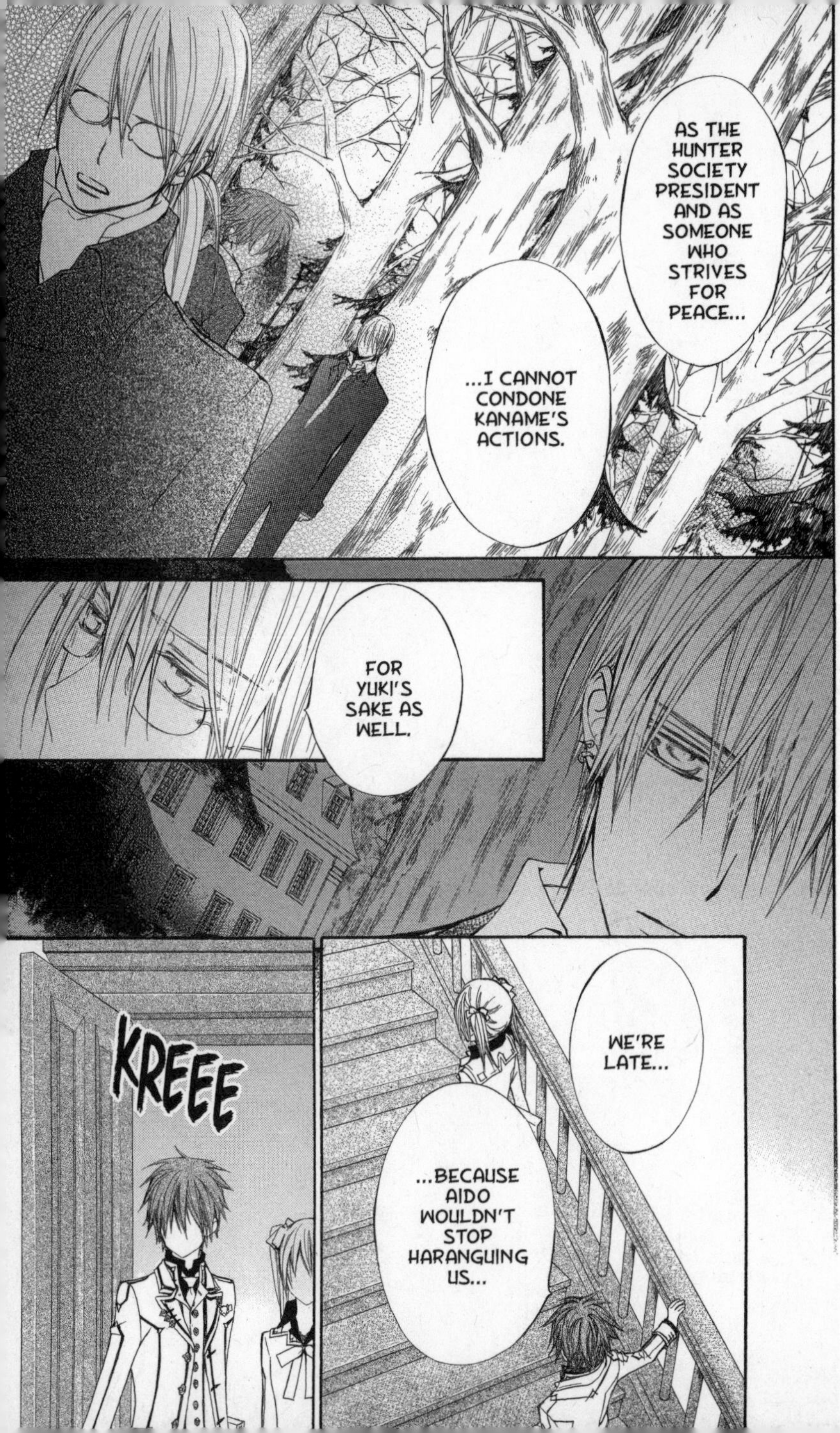
AS THE HUNTER SOCIETY PRESIDENT AND AS SOMEONE WHO STRIVES FOR PEACE...
...I CANNOT CONDONE KANAME'S ACTIONS.
FOR YUKI'S SAKE AS WELL.
WE'RE LATE...
...BECAUSE AIDO WOULDN'T STOP HARANGUING US...
KREEE

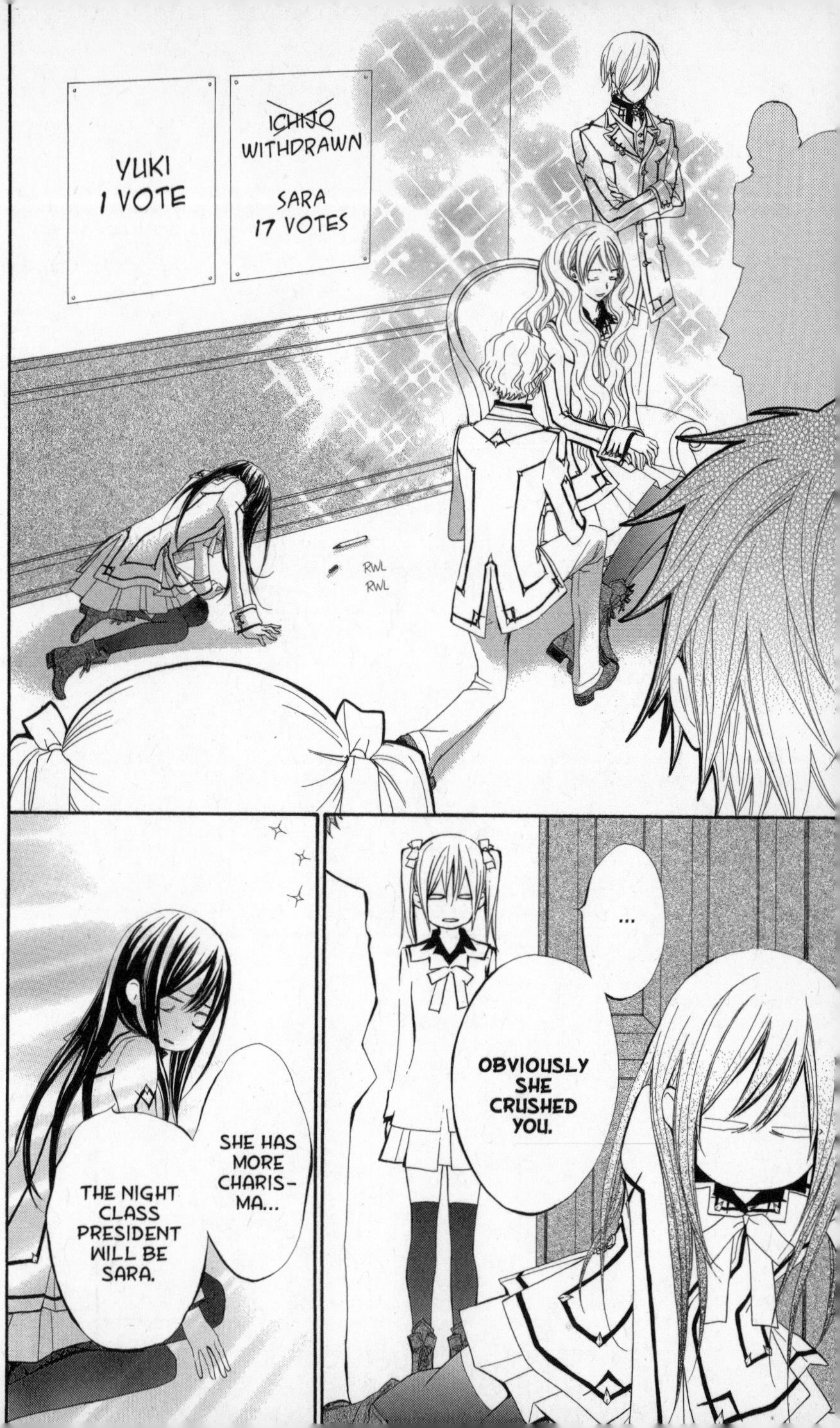
ICHIJO WITHDRAWN
SARA 17 VOTES
YUKI 1 VOTE
RWL RWL
...
OBVIOUSLY SHE CRUSHED YOU.
SHE HAS MORE CHARIS-MA...
THE NIGHT CLASS PRESIDENT WILL BE SARA.

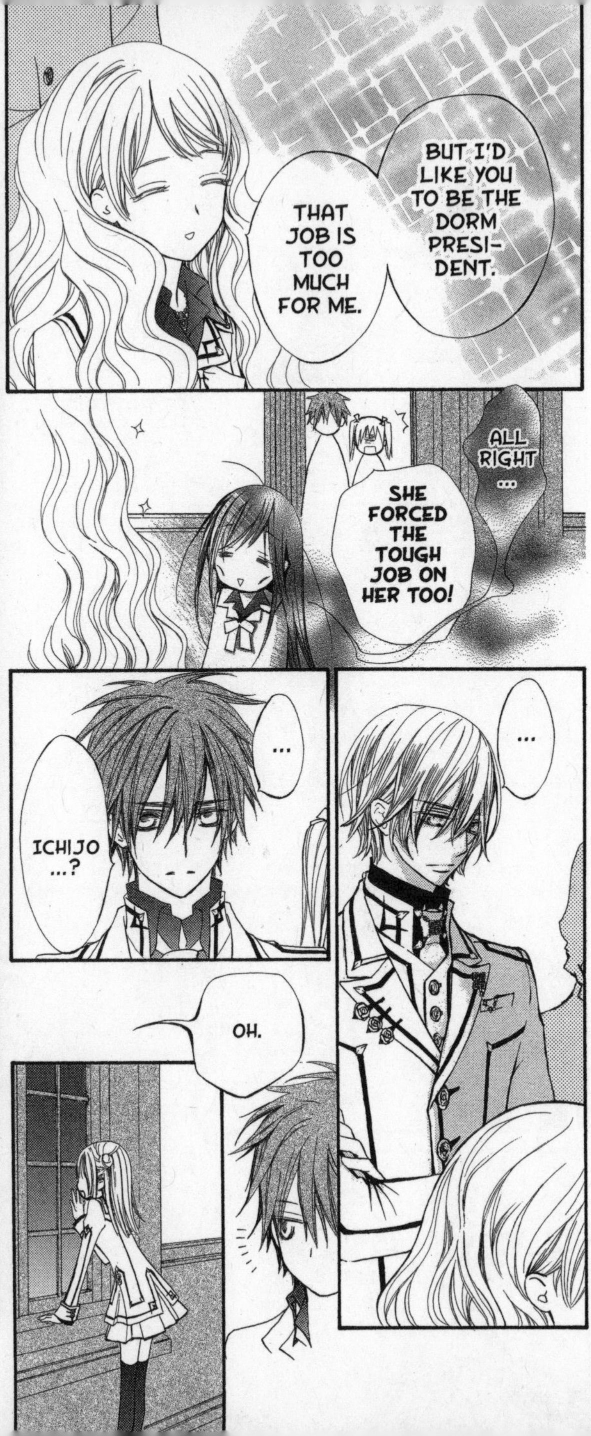
BUT I'D LIKE YOU TO BE THE DORM PRESI- DENT.
THAT JOB IS TOO MUCH FOR ME.
ALL RIGHT ...
SHE FORCED THE TOUGH JOB ON HER TOO!
...
...
ICHIJO ...?
OH.

I

Volume 16 is here! I've gotten this far without my series being cancelled. It is all thanks to the people who have bought this series. I truly thank you from the bottom of my heart. At this moment I know how many volumes are left in this series. I am starting to see the goal, so I have newly resolved to use all my effort to keep moving forward.

My editor with whom I have been working all this time got married, and my situation has changed too. This series has gone on long enough for the readers to have moved on to higher education, be employed, or to have gotten married during it. And I hope that the end of this series will turn out to be something worth all the time I've spent... (I'm trying to pressure myself...)

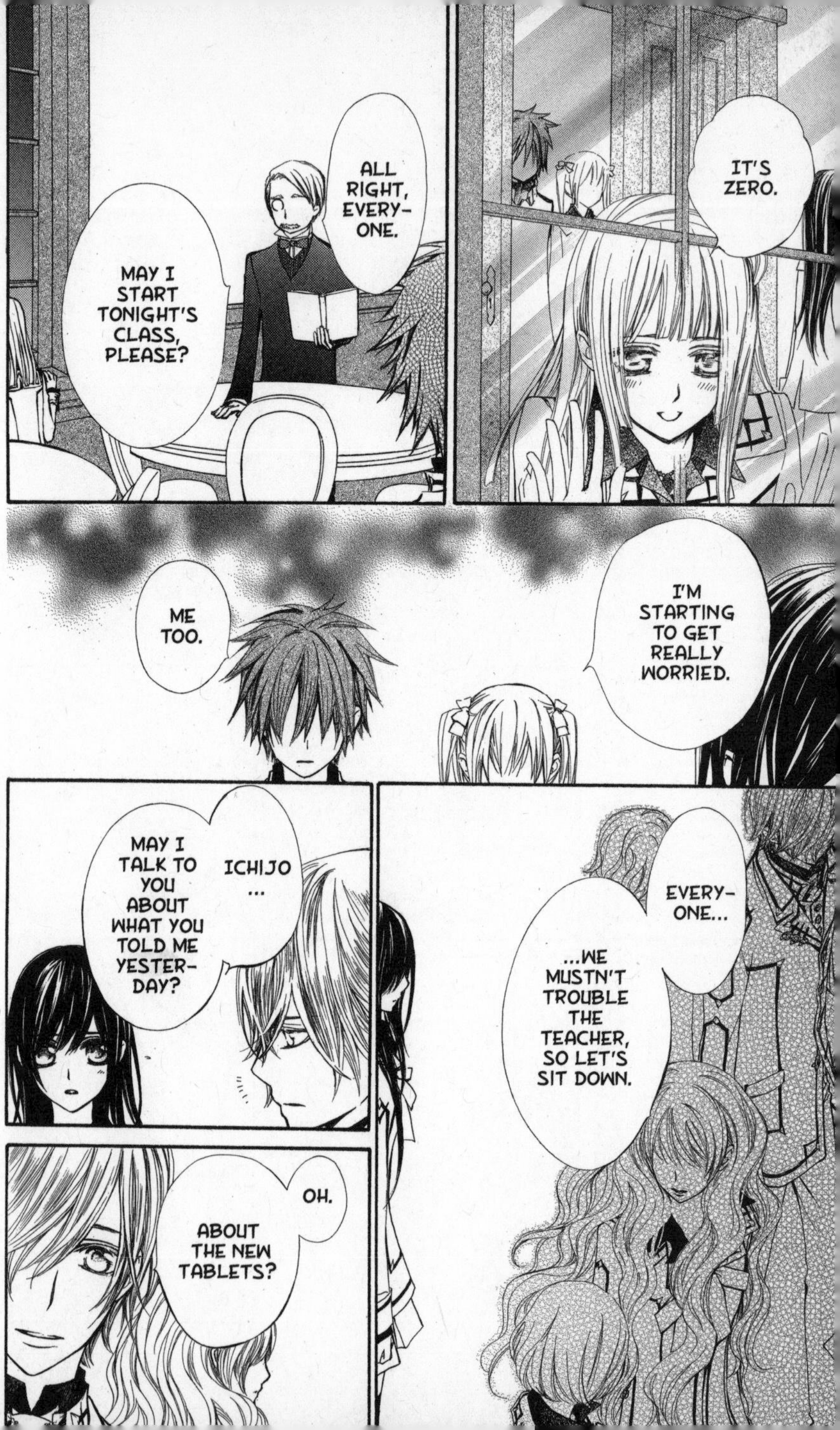
IT'S ZERO.
ALL RIGHT, EVERYONE.
MAY I START TONIGHT'S CLASS, PLEASE?
I'M STARTING TO GET REALLY WORRIED.
ME TOO.
EVERYONE...
...WE MUSTN'T TROUBLE THE TEACHER, SO LET'S SIT DOWN.
ICHIJO...
MAY I TALK TO YOU ABOUT WHAT YOU TOLD ME YESTERDAY?
OH.
ABOUT THE NEW TABLETS?

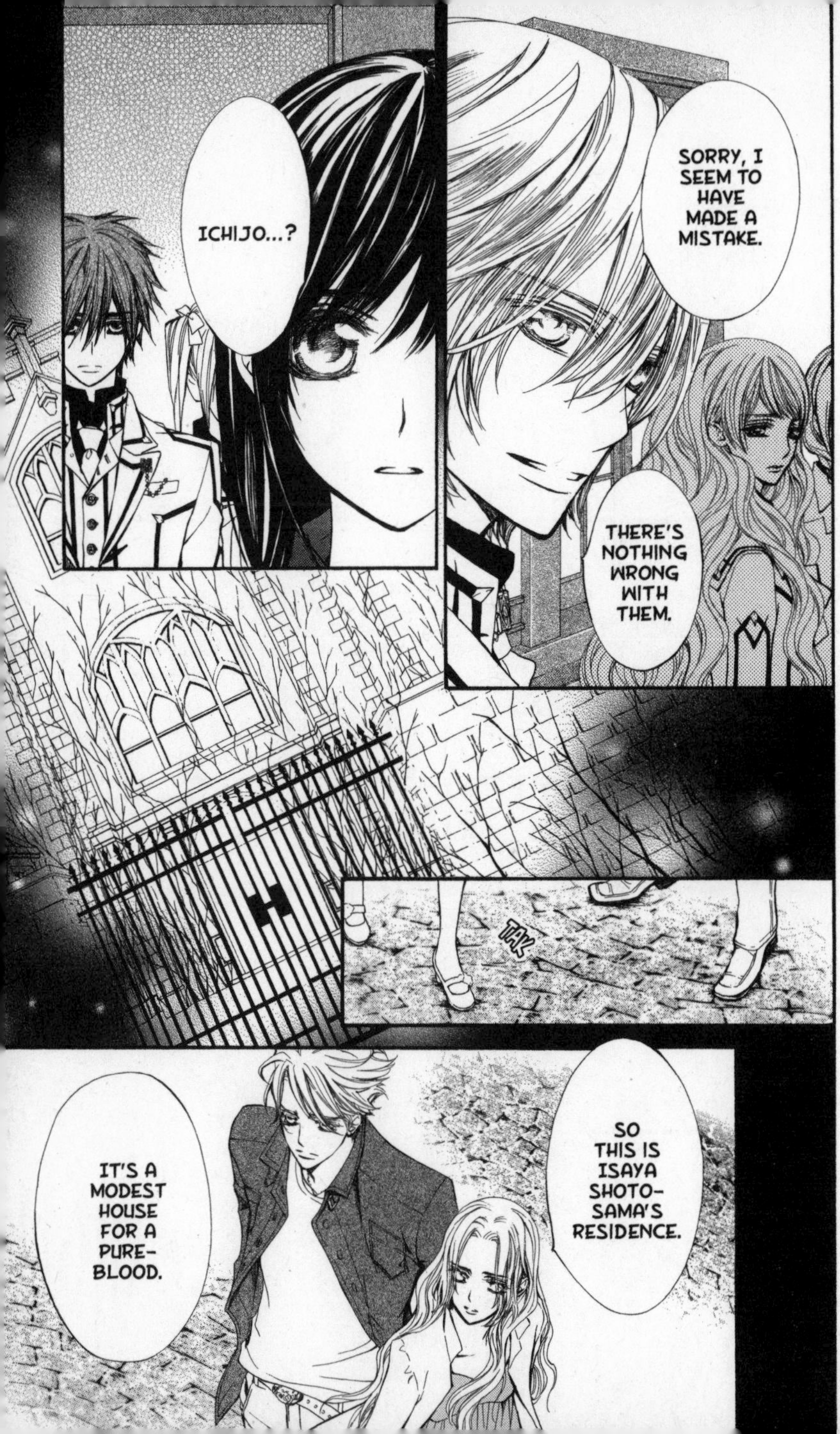
SORRY, I SEEM TO HAVE MADE A MISTAKE.
THERE'S NOTHING WRONG WITH THEM.
ICHIJO...?
TAK
SO THIS IS ISAYA SHOTO-SAMA'S RESIDENCE.
IT'S A MODEST HOUSE FOR A PURE-BLOOD.

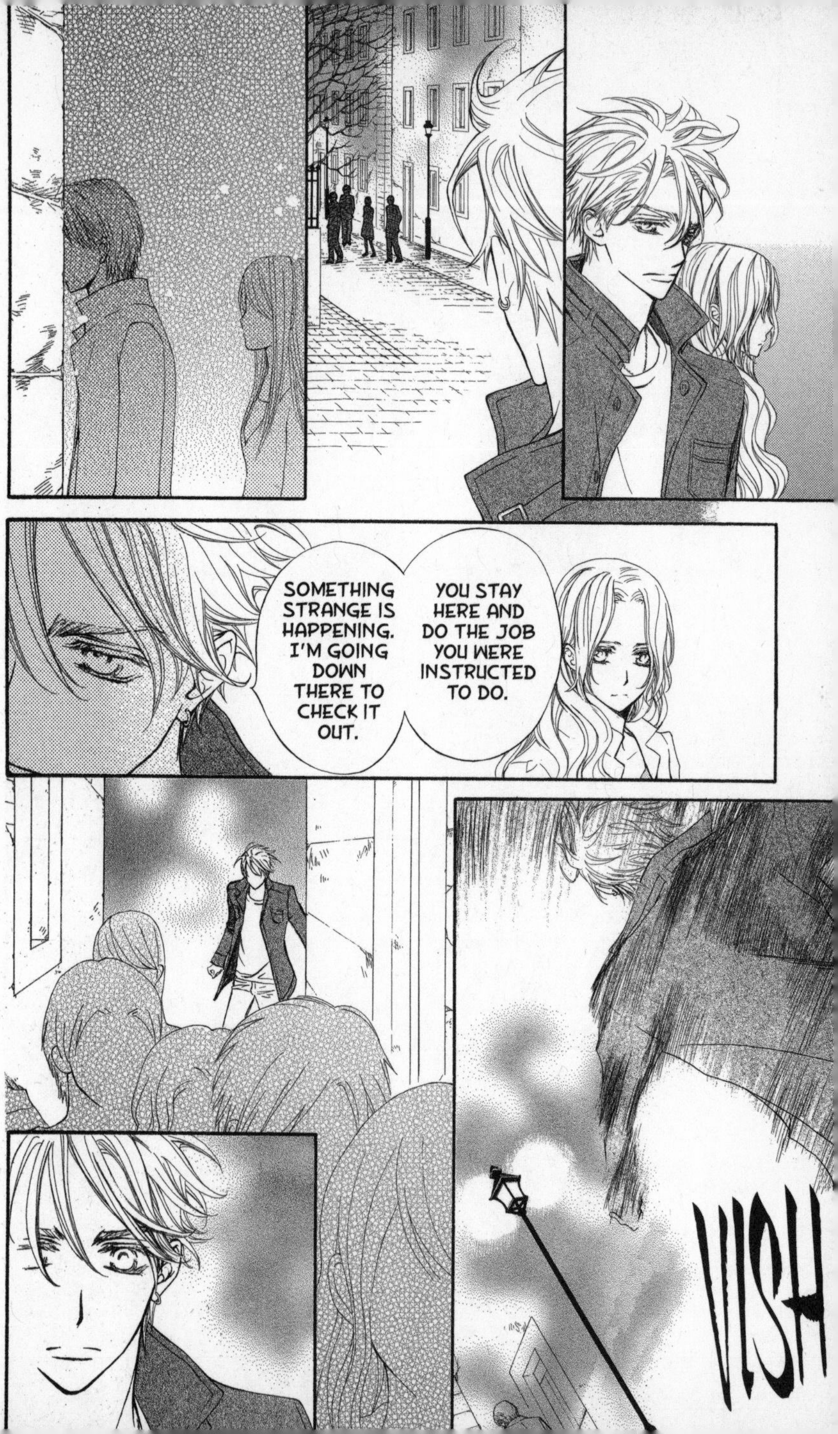
SOMETHING STRANGE IS HAPPENING. I'M GOING DOWN THERE TO CHECK IT OUT.
YOU STAY HERE AND DO THE JOB YOU WERE INSTRUCTED TO DO.
VISH

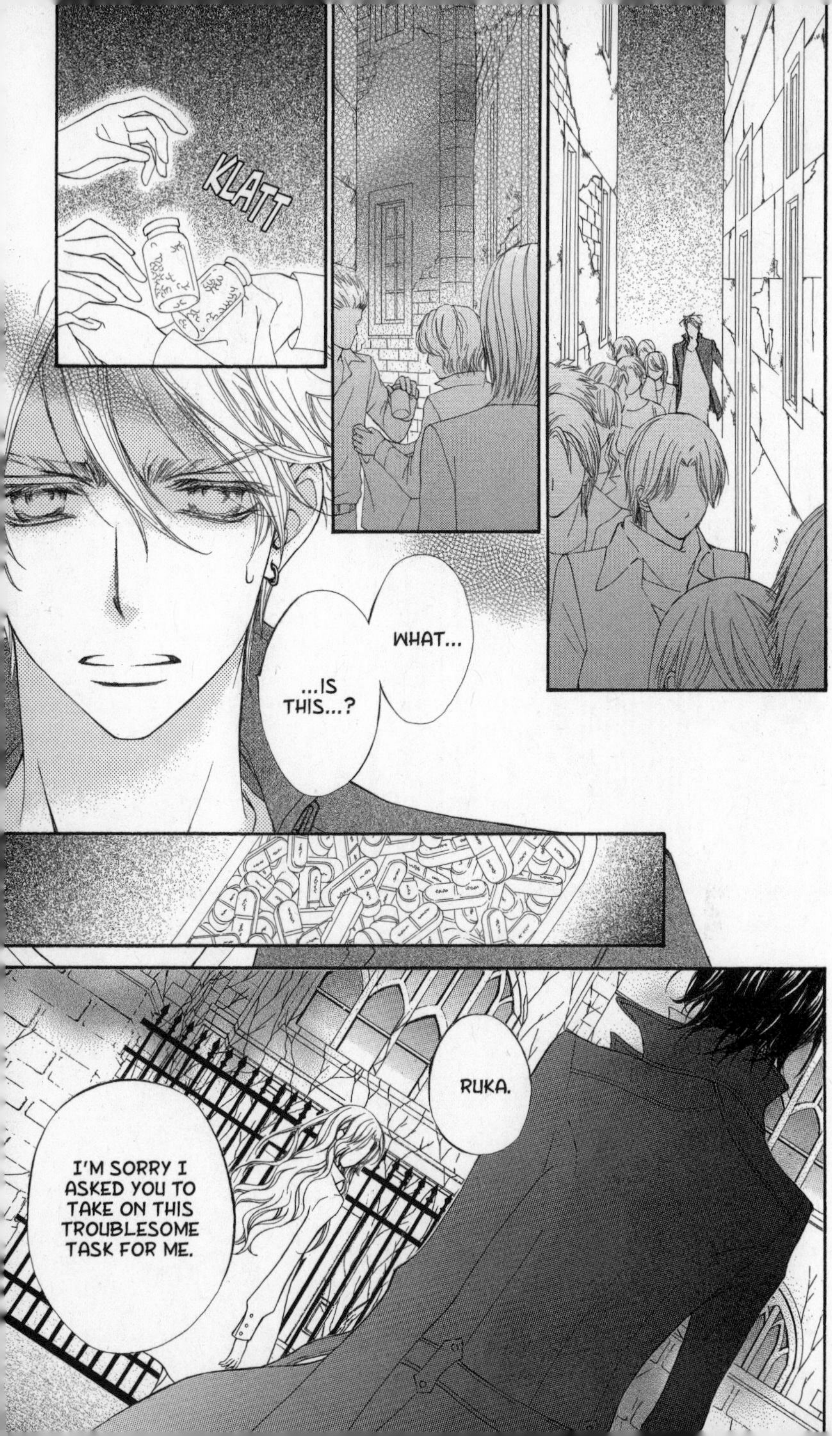
KLATT
WHAT...
...IS THIS...?
RUKA.
I'M SORRY I ASKED YOU TO TAKE ON THIS TROUBLESOME TASK FOR ME.

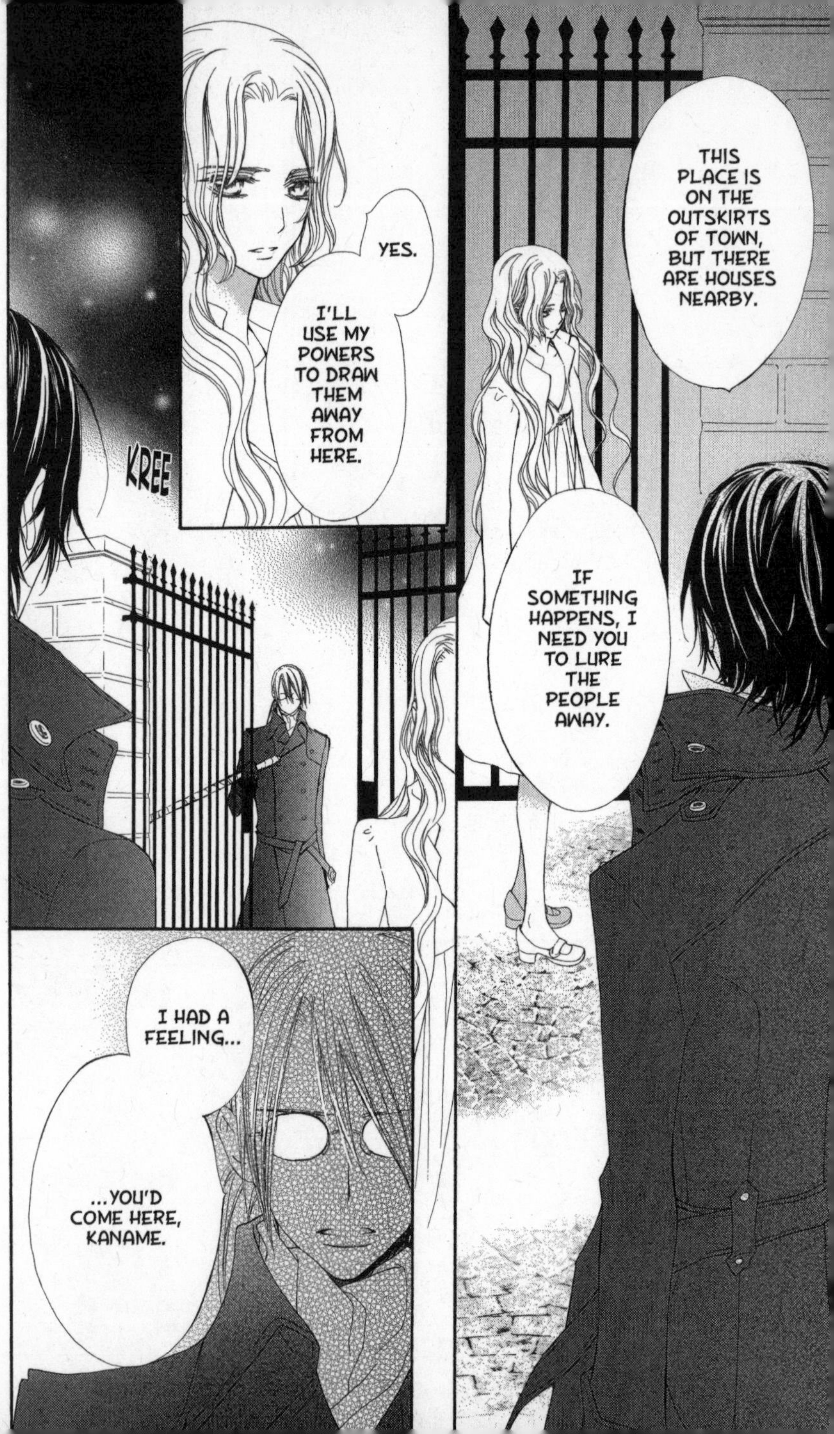
THIS PLACE IS ON THE OUTSKIRTS OF TOWN, BUT THERE ARE HOUSES NEARBY.
IF SOMETHING HAPPENS, I NEED YOU TO LURE THE PEOPLE AWAY.
YES.
I'LL USE MY POWERS TO DRAW THEM AWAY FROM HERE.
KREE
I HAD A FEELING...
...YOU'D COME HERE, KANAME.

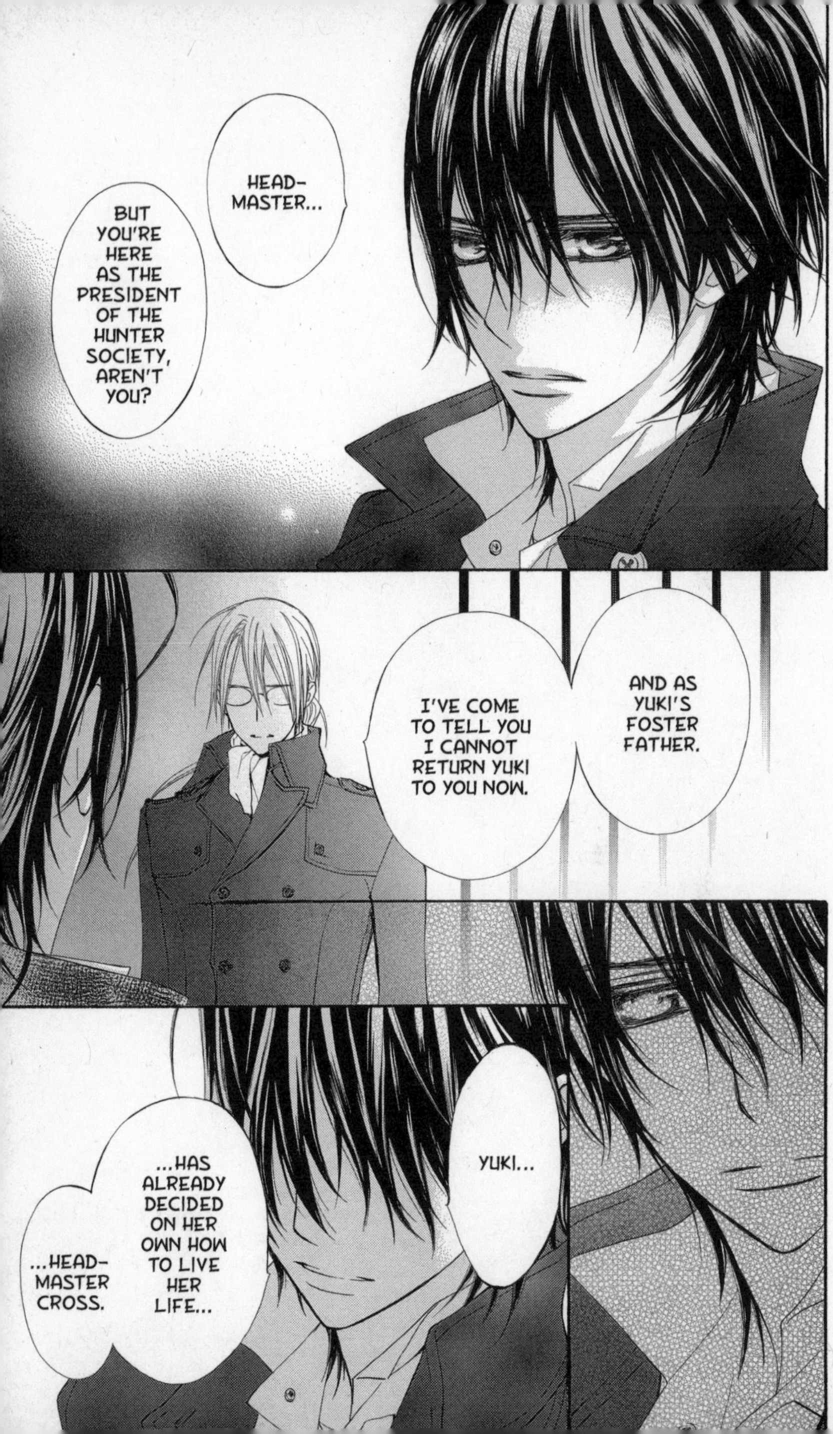
HEAD-MASTER...
BUT YOU'RE HERE AS THE PRESIDENT OF THE HUNTER SOCIETY, AREN'T YOU?
AND AS YUKI'S FOSTER FATHER.
I'VE COME TO TELL YOU I CANNOT RETURN YUKI TO YOU NOW.
YUKI...
...HAS ALREADY DECIDED ON HER OWN HOW TO LIVE HER LIFE...
...HEAD-MASTER CROSS.

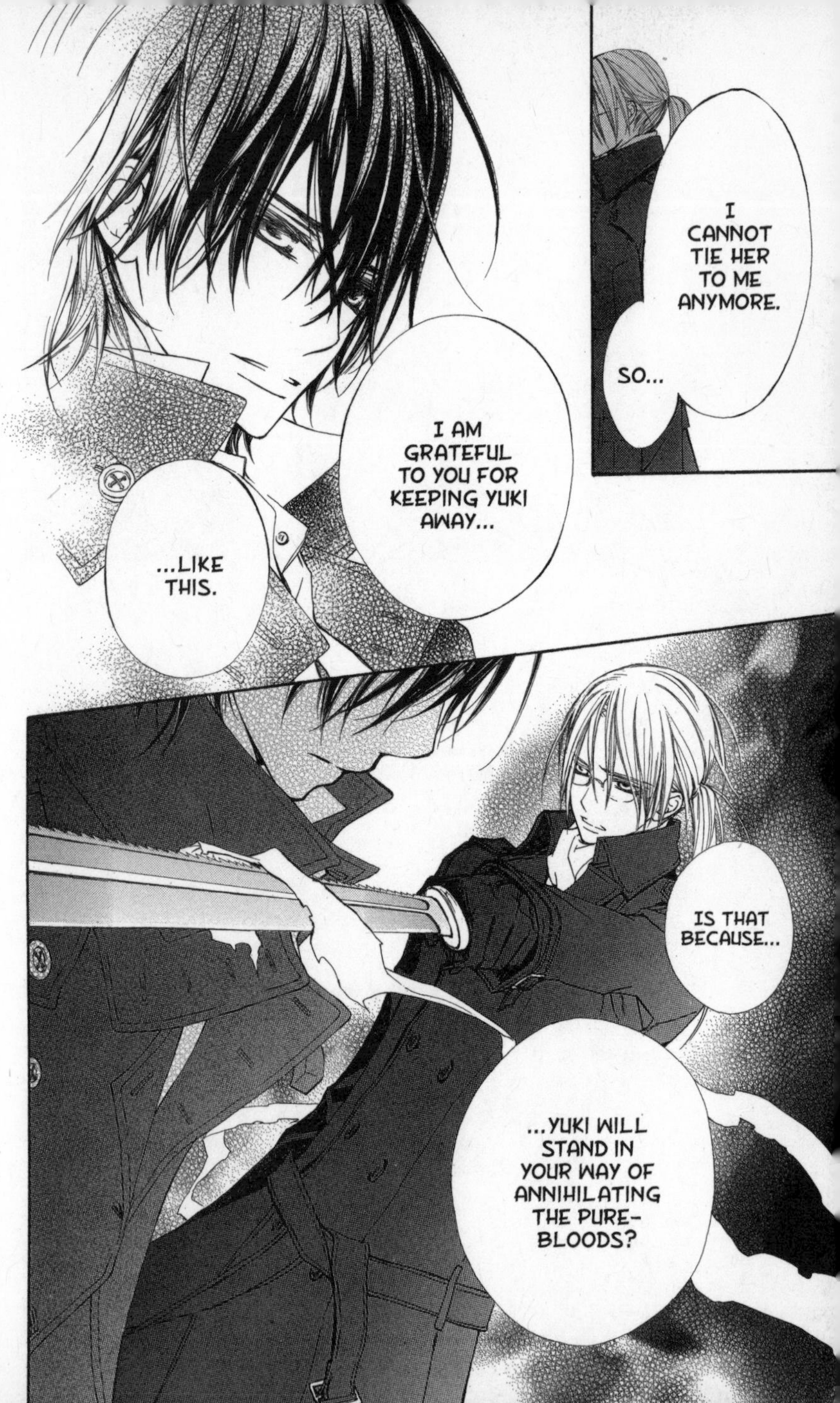
I CANNOT TIE HER TO ME ANYMORE.
SO...
I AM GRATEFUL TO YOU FOR KEEPING YUKI AWAY...
...LIKE THIS.
IS THAT BECAUSE...
...YUKI WILL STAND IN YOUR WAY OF ANNIHILATING THE PURE-BLOODS?

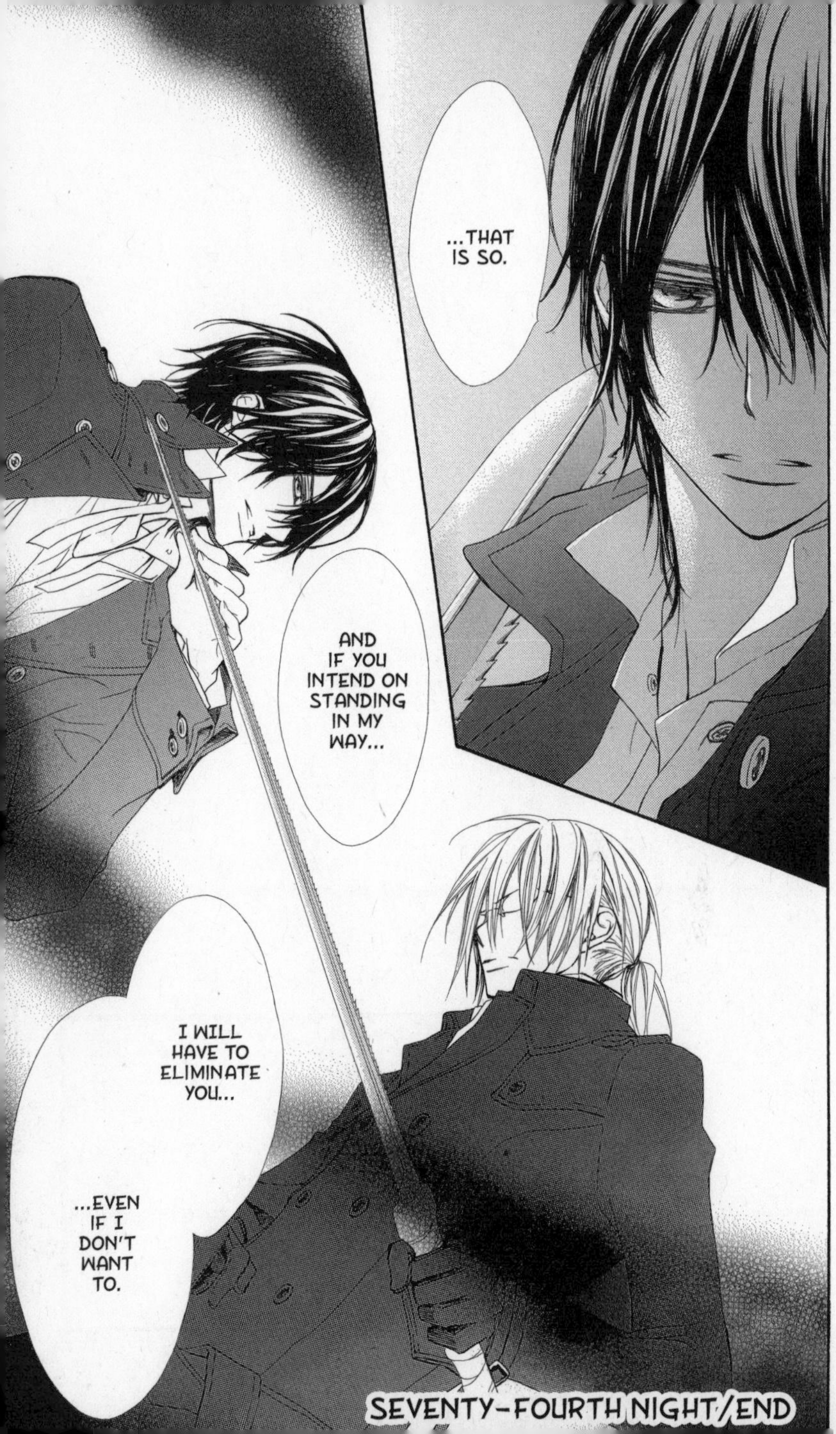
...THAT IS SO.
AND IF YOU INTEND ON STANDING IN MY WAY...
I WILL HAVE TO ELIMINATE YOU...
...EVEN IF I DON'T WANT TO.
SEVENTY-FOURTH NIGHT/END

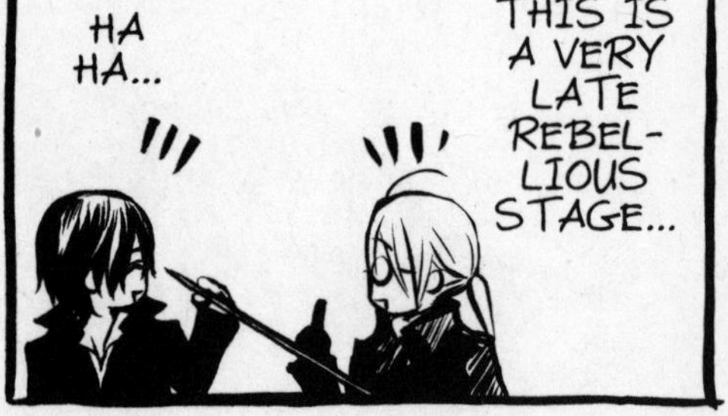
MAYBE THIS IS A VERY LATE REBEL-LIOUS STAGE...
HA HA...

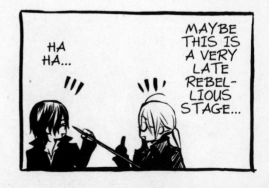

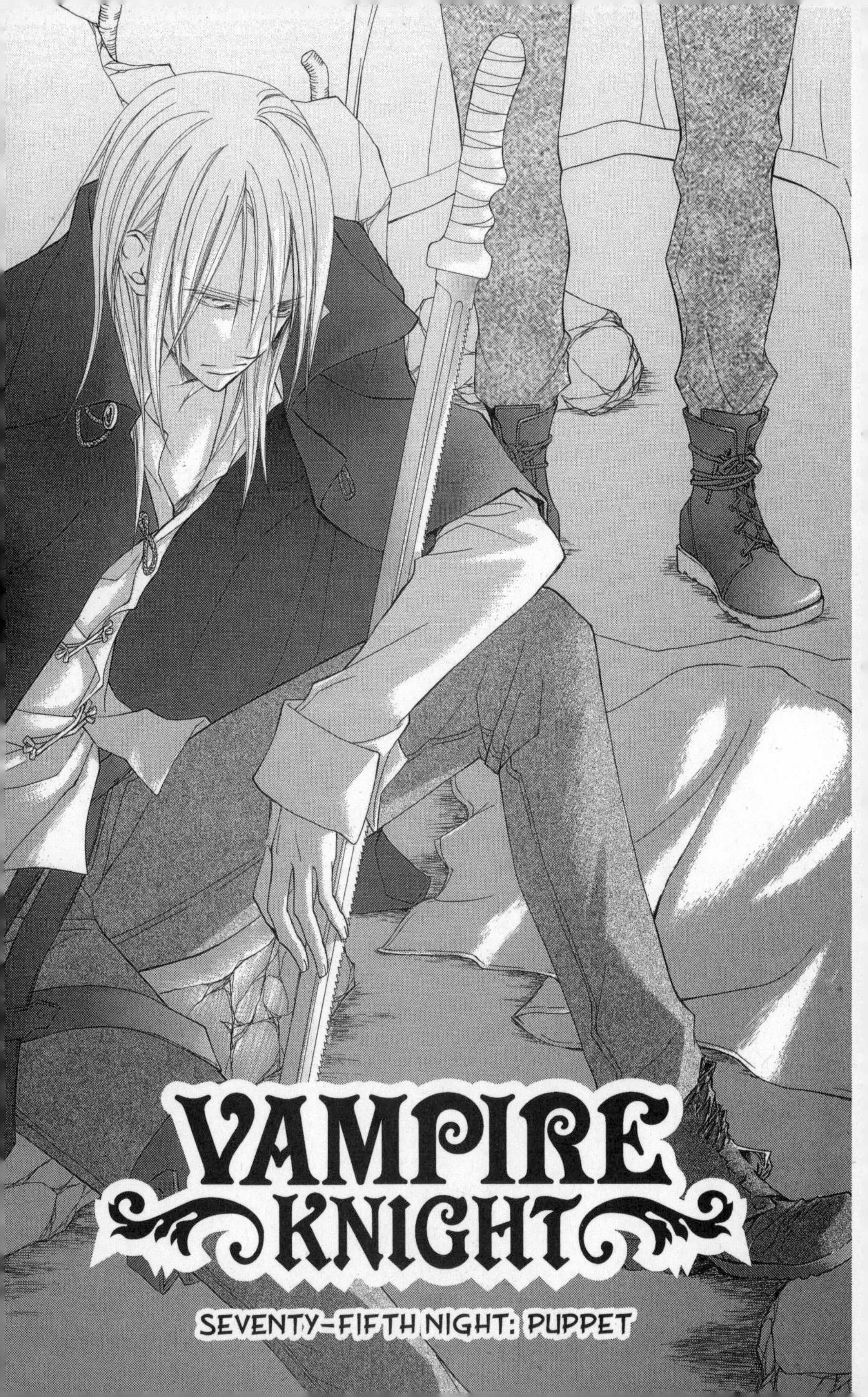
VAMPIRE KNIGHT
SEVENTY-FIFTH NIGHT: PUPPET

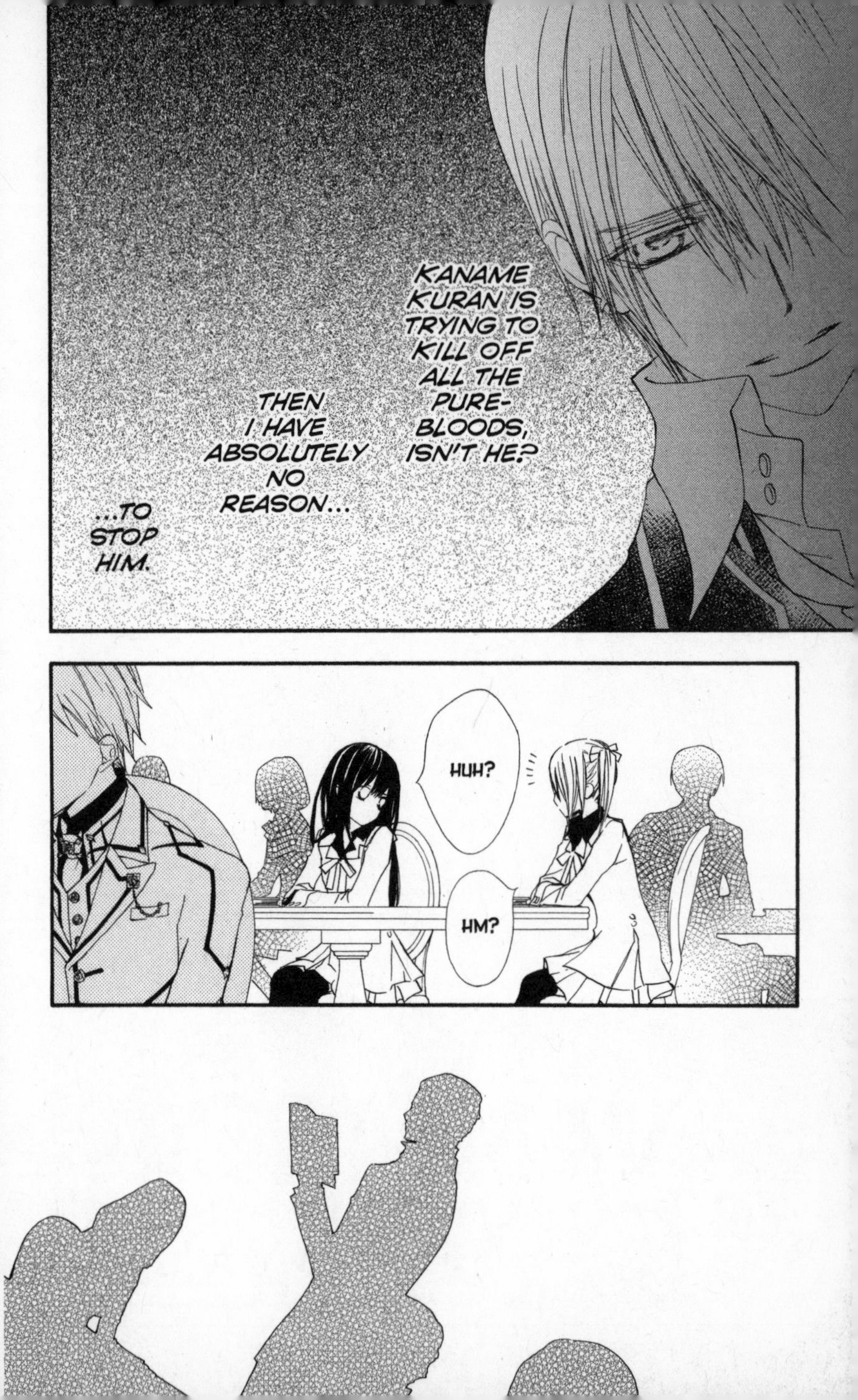
KANAME KURAN IS TRYING TO KILL OFF ALL THE PURE-BLOODS, ISN'T HE?
THEN I HAVE ABSOLUTELY NO REASON...
...TO STOP HIM.
HUH?
HM?

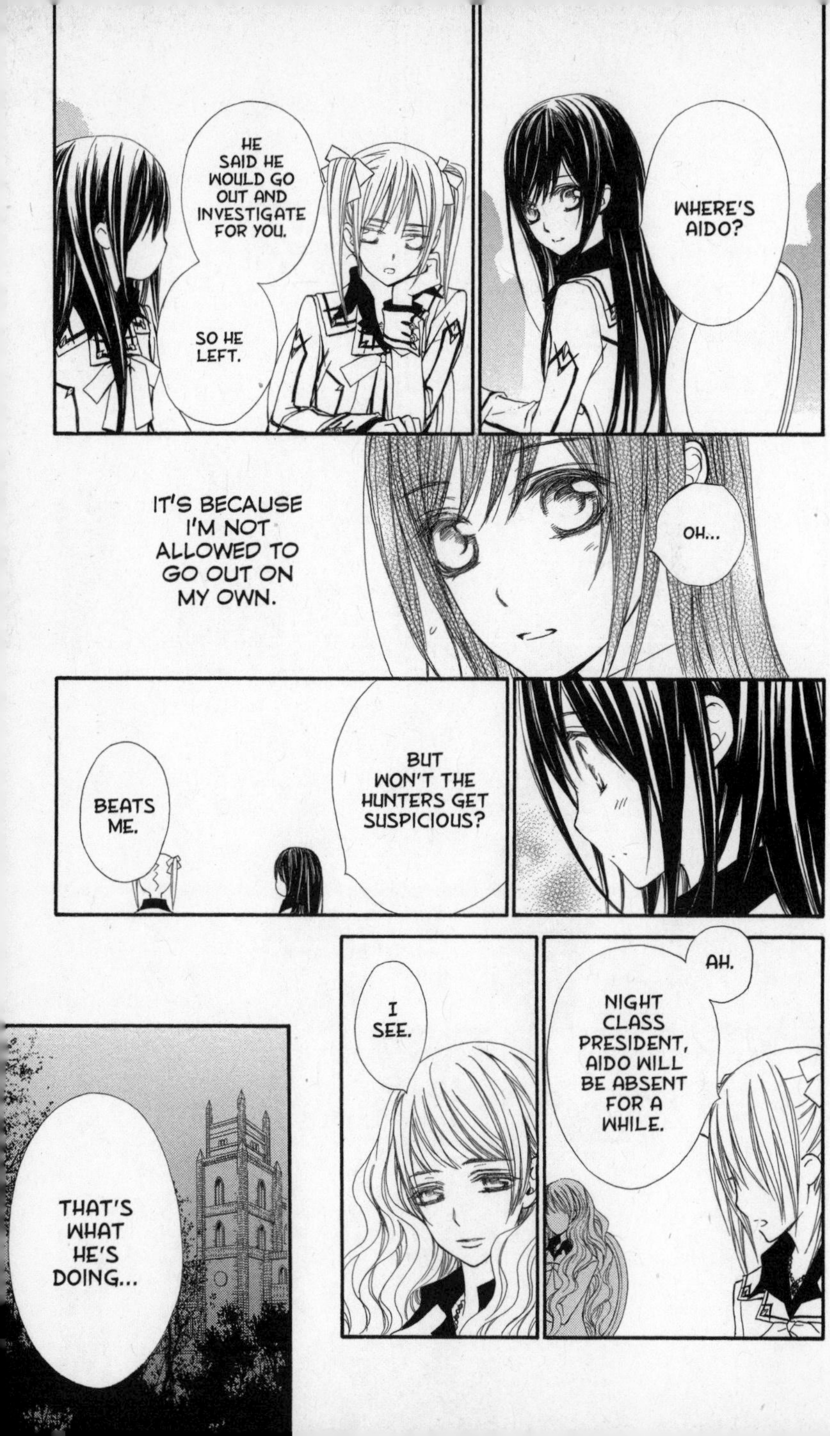
WHERE'S AIDO?
HE SAID HE WOULD GO OUT AND INVESTIGATE FOR YOU.
SO HE LEFT.
OH...
IT'S BECAUSE I'M NOT ALLOWED TO GO OUT ON MY OWN.
BUT WON'T THE HUNTERS GET SUSPICIOUS?
BEATS ME.
AH.
NIGHT CLASS PRESIDENT, AIDO WILL BE ABSENT FOR A WHILE.
I SEE.
THAT'S WHAT HE'S DOING...

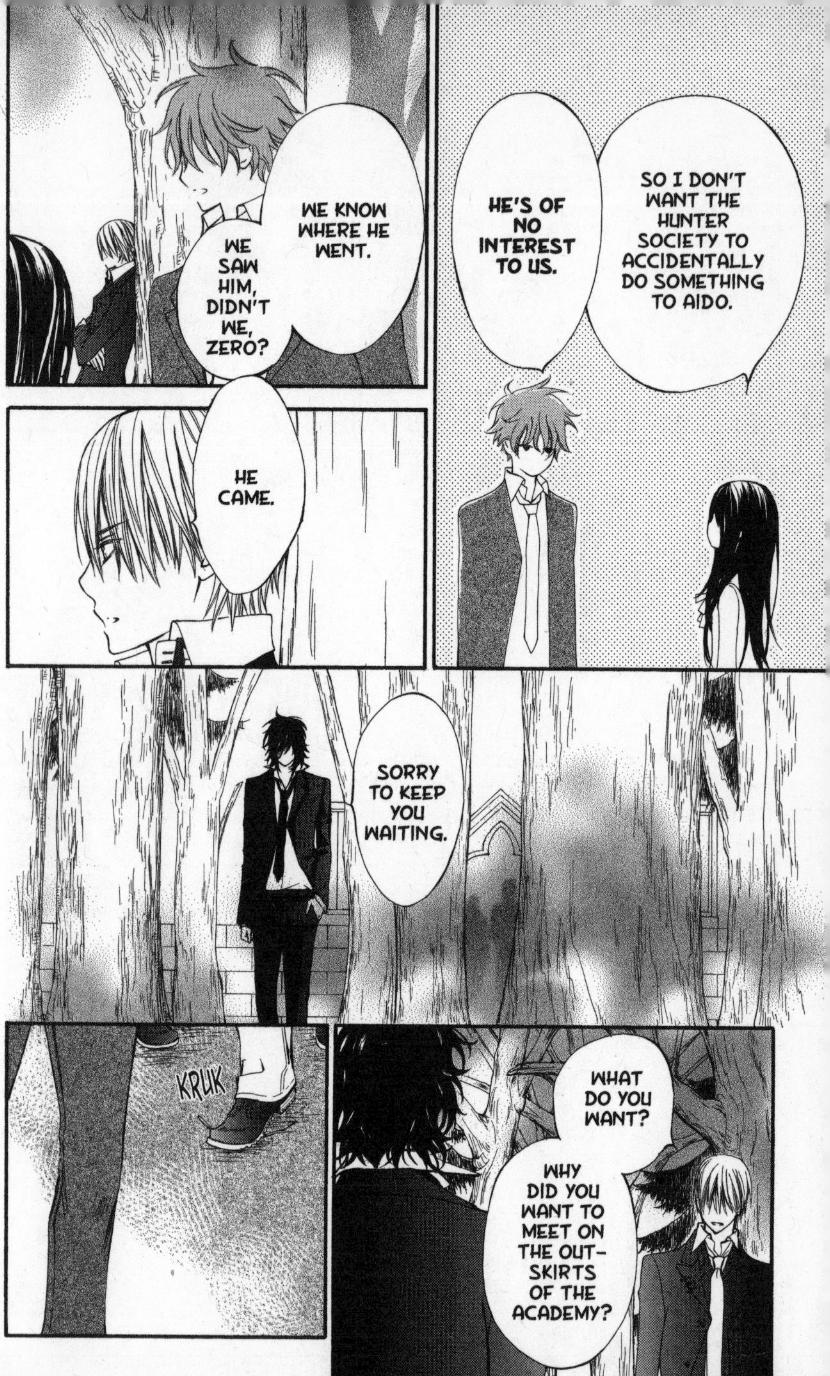
HE'S OF NO INTEREST TO US.
SO I DON'T WANT THE HUNTER SOCIETY TO ACCIDENTALLY DO SOMETHING TO AIDO.
WE KNOW WHERE HE WENT.
WE SAW HIM, DIDN'T WE, ZERO?
HE CAME.
SORRY TO KEEP YOU WAITING.
WHAT DO YOU WANT?
WHY DID YOU WANT TO MEET ON THE OUT-SKIRTS OF THE ACADEMY?
KRUK

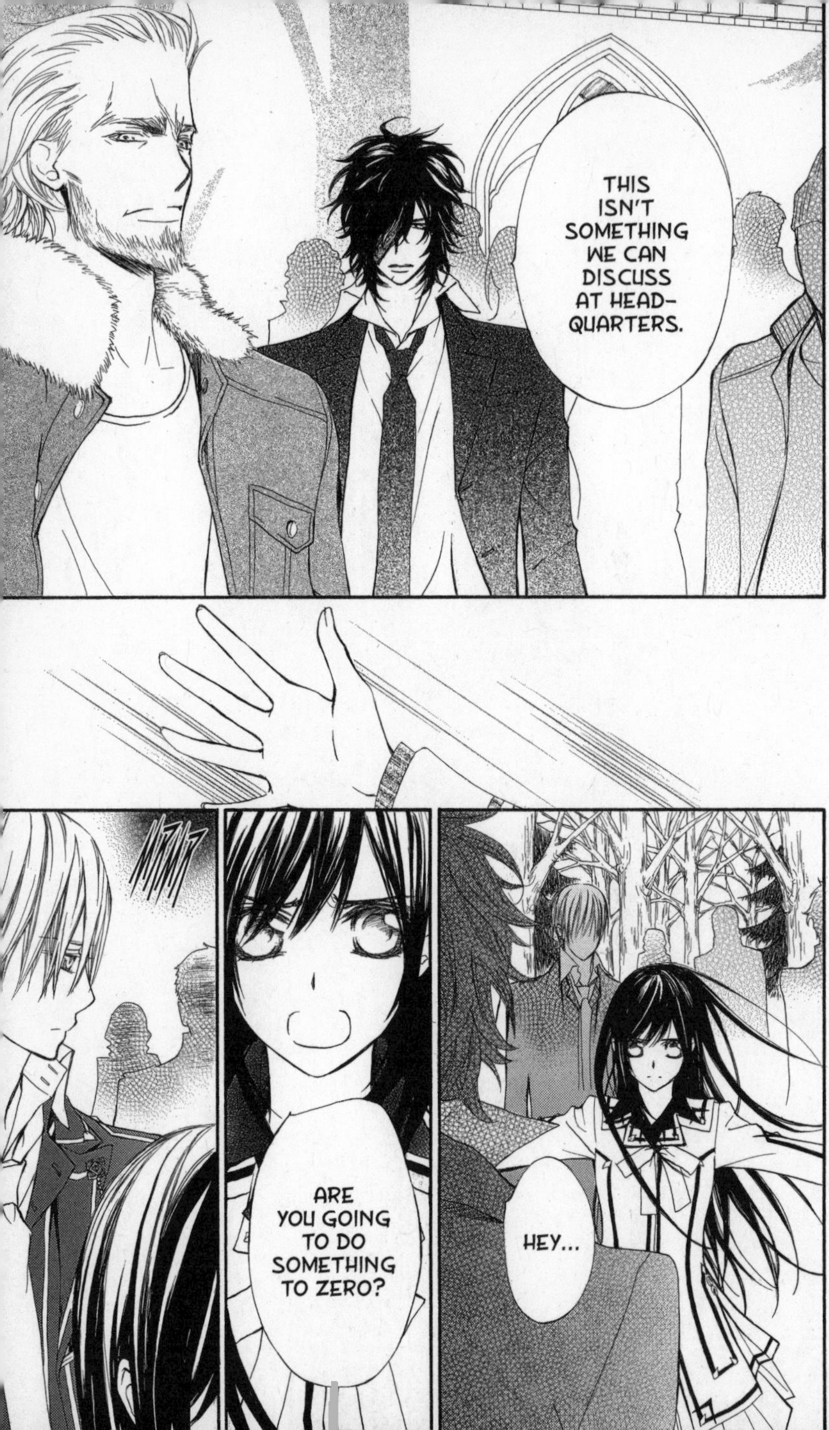
THIS ISN'T SOMETHING WE CAN DISCUSS AT HEAD-QUARTERS.
HEY...
ARE YOU GOING TO DO SOMETHING TO ZERO?

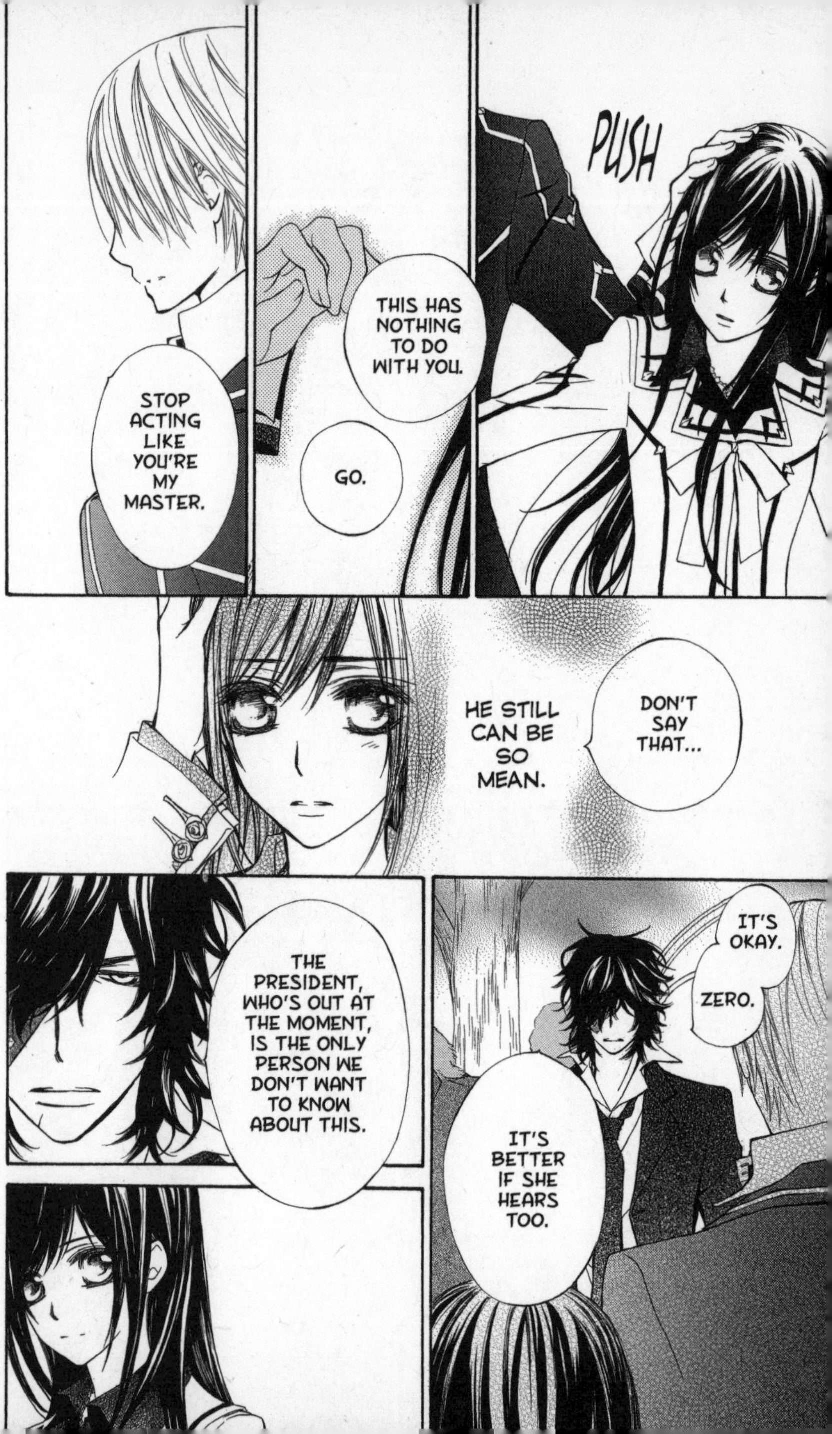
PUSH
THIS HAS NOTHING TO DO WITH YOU.
GO.
STOP ACTING LIKE YOU'RE MY MASTER.
DON'T SAY THAT...
HE STILL CAN BE SO MEAN.
IT'S OKAY.
ZERO.
IT'S BETTER IF SHE HEARS TOO.
THE PRESIDENT, WHO'S OUT AT THE MOMENT, IS THE ONLY PERSON WE DON'T WANT TO KNOW ABOUT THIS.

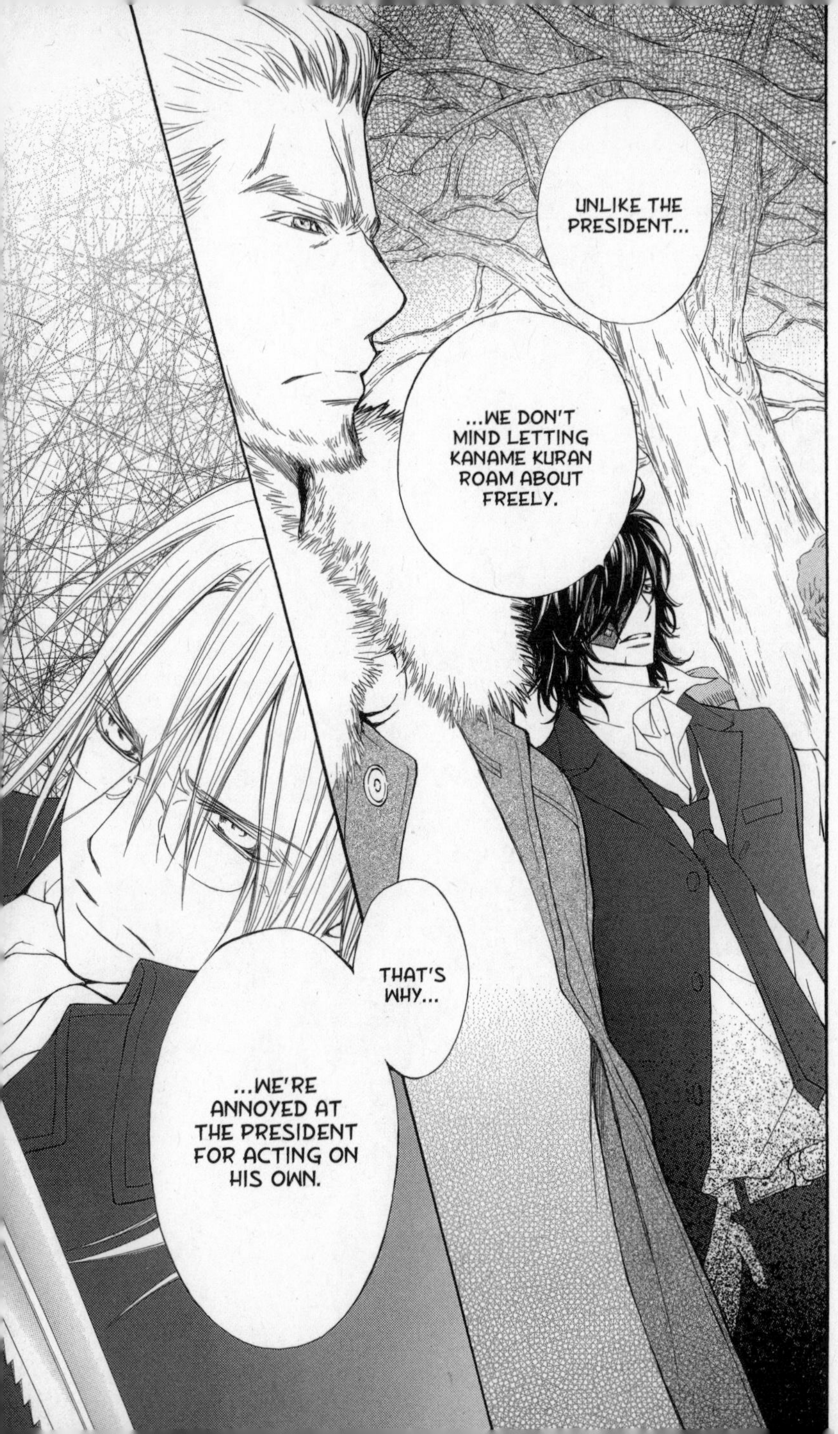
UNLIKE THE PRESIDENT...
...WE DON'T MIND LETTING KANAME KURAN ROAM ABOUT FREELY.
THAT'S WHY...
...WE'RE ANNOYED AT THE PRESIDENT FOR ACTING ON HIS OWN.

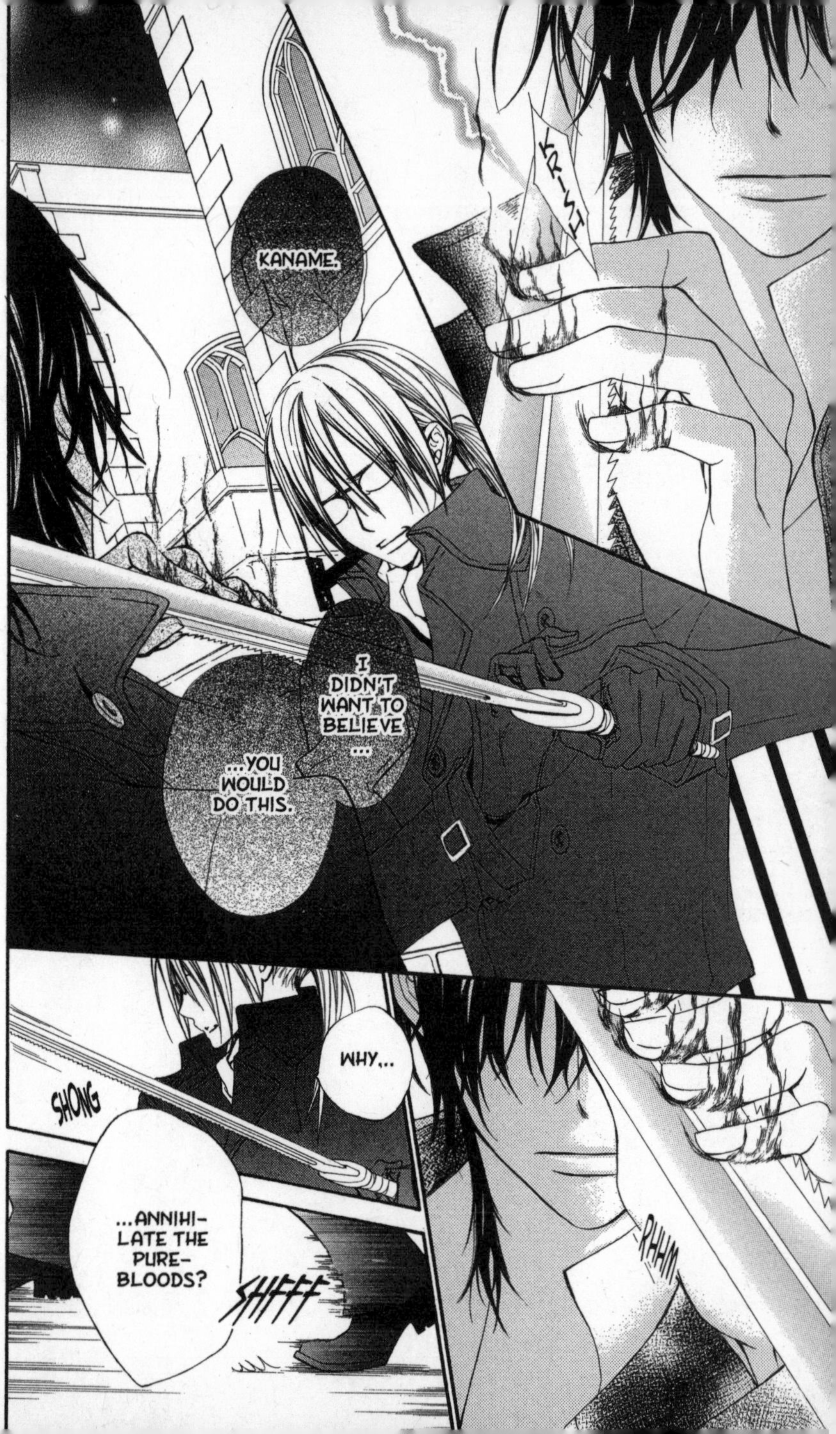
KR-ISH
KANAME.
I DIDN'T WANT TO BELIEVE...
...YOU WOULD DO THIS.
RHHM
WHY...
SHONG
...ANNIHILATE THE PURE-BLOODS?
SHFFF

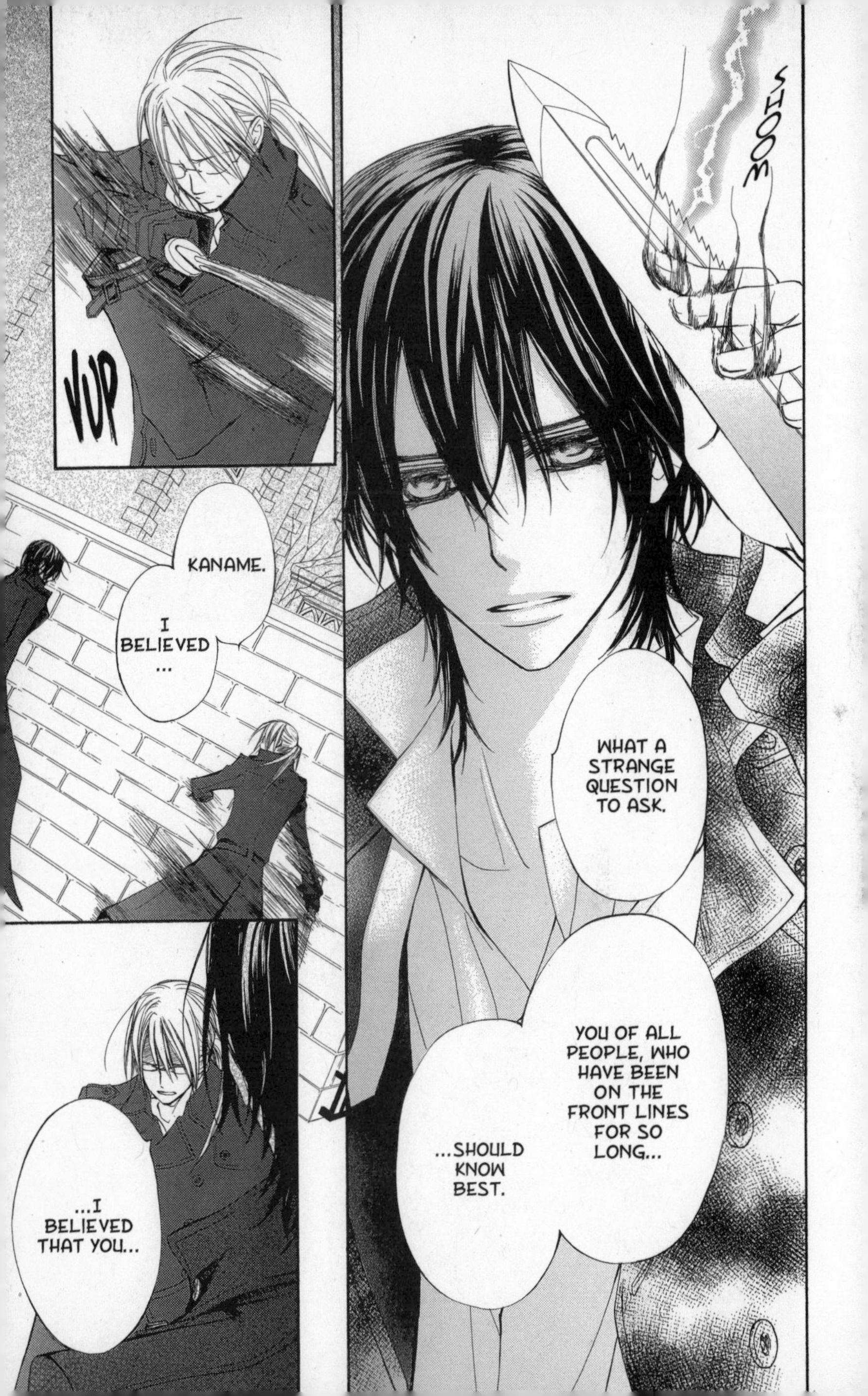
SHOOM
WHAT A STRANGE QUESTION TO ASK.
YOU OF ALL PEOPLE, WHO HAVE BEEN ON THE FRONT LINES FOR SO LONG...
...SHOULD KNOW BEST.
VUP
KANAME.
I BELIEVED ...
...I BELIEVED THAT YOU...

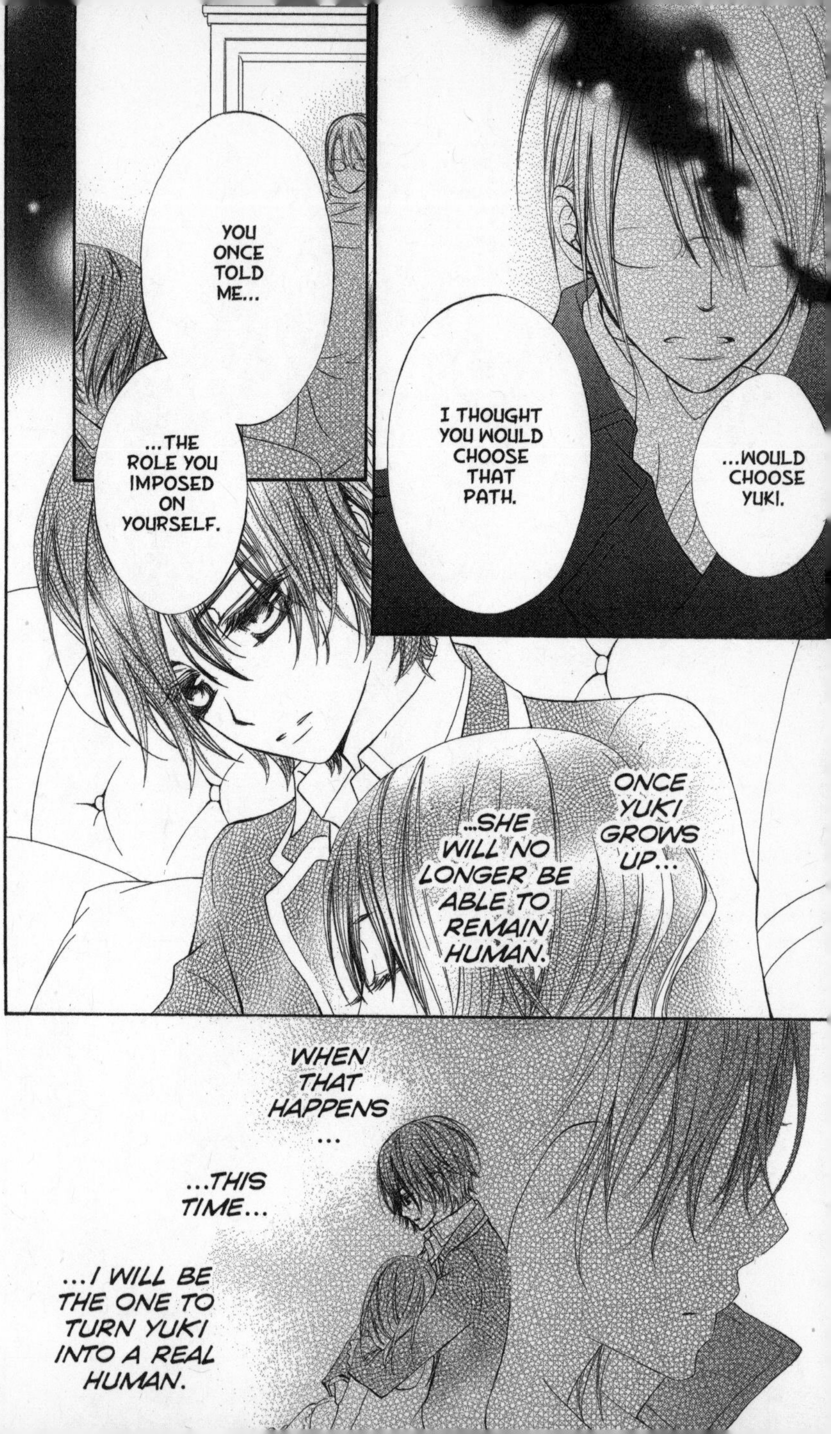
YOU ONCE TOLD ME...
...THE ROLE YOU IMPOSED ON YOURSELF.
I THOUGHT YOU WOULD CHOOSE THAT PATH.
...WOULD CHOOSE YUKI.
ONCE YUKI GROWS UP...
...SHE WILL NO LONGER BE ABLE TO REMAIN HUMAN.
WHEN THAT HAPPENS...
...THIS TIME...
...I WILL BE THE ONE TO TURN YUKI INTO A REAL HUMAN.

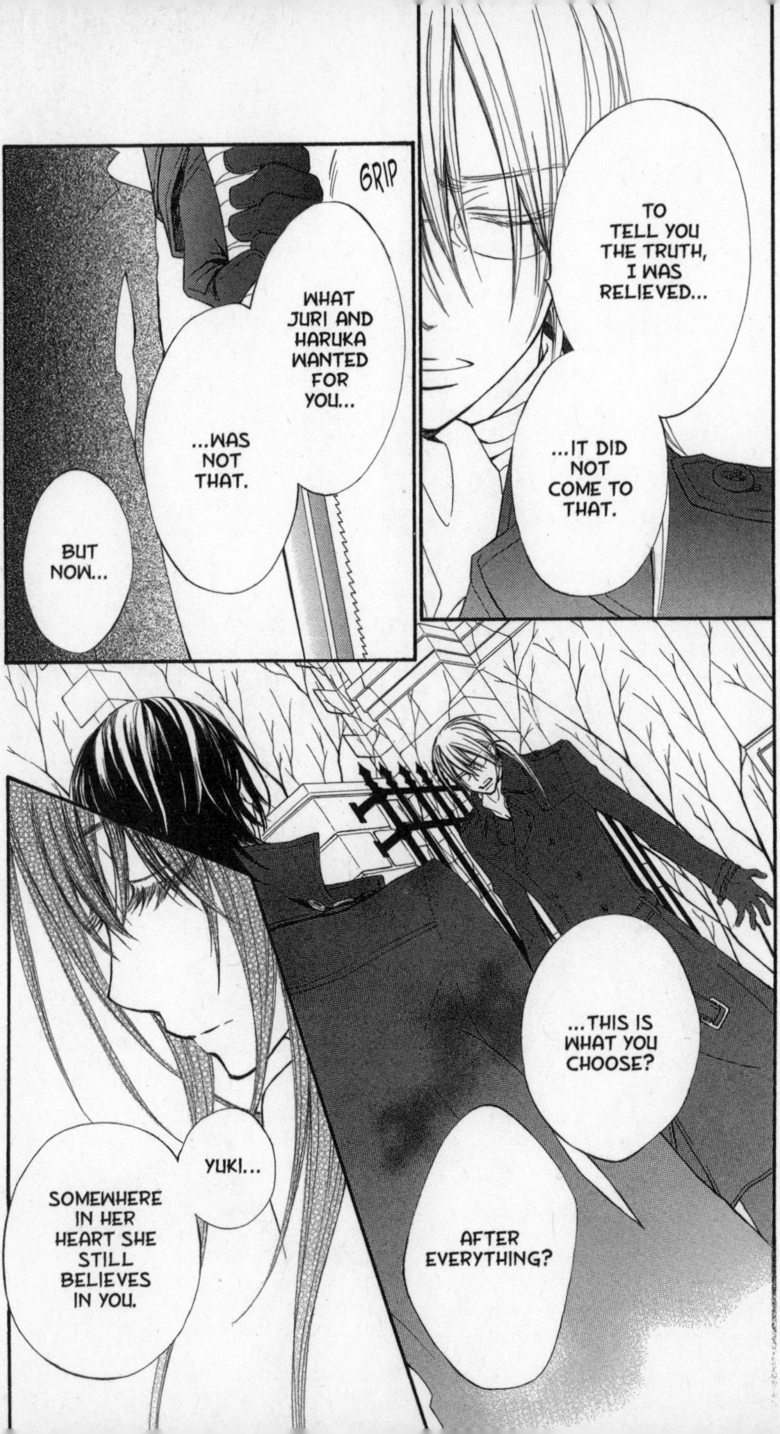
TO TELL YOU THE TRUTH, I WAS RELIEVED...
...IT DID NOT COME TO THAT.
GRIP
WHAT JURI AND HARUKA WANTED FOR YOU...
...WAS NOT THAT.
BUT NOW...
...THIS IS WHAT YOU CHOOSE?
AFTER EVERYTHING?
YUKI...
SOMEWHERE IN HER HEART SHE STILL BELIEVES IN YOU.

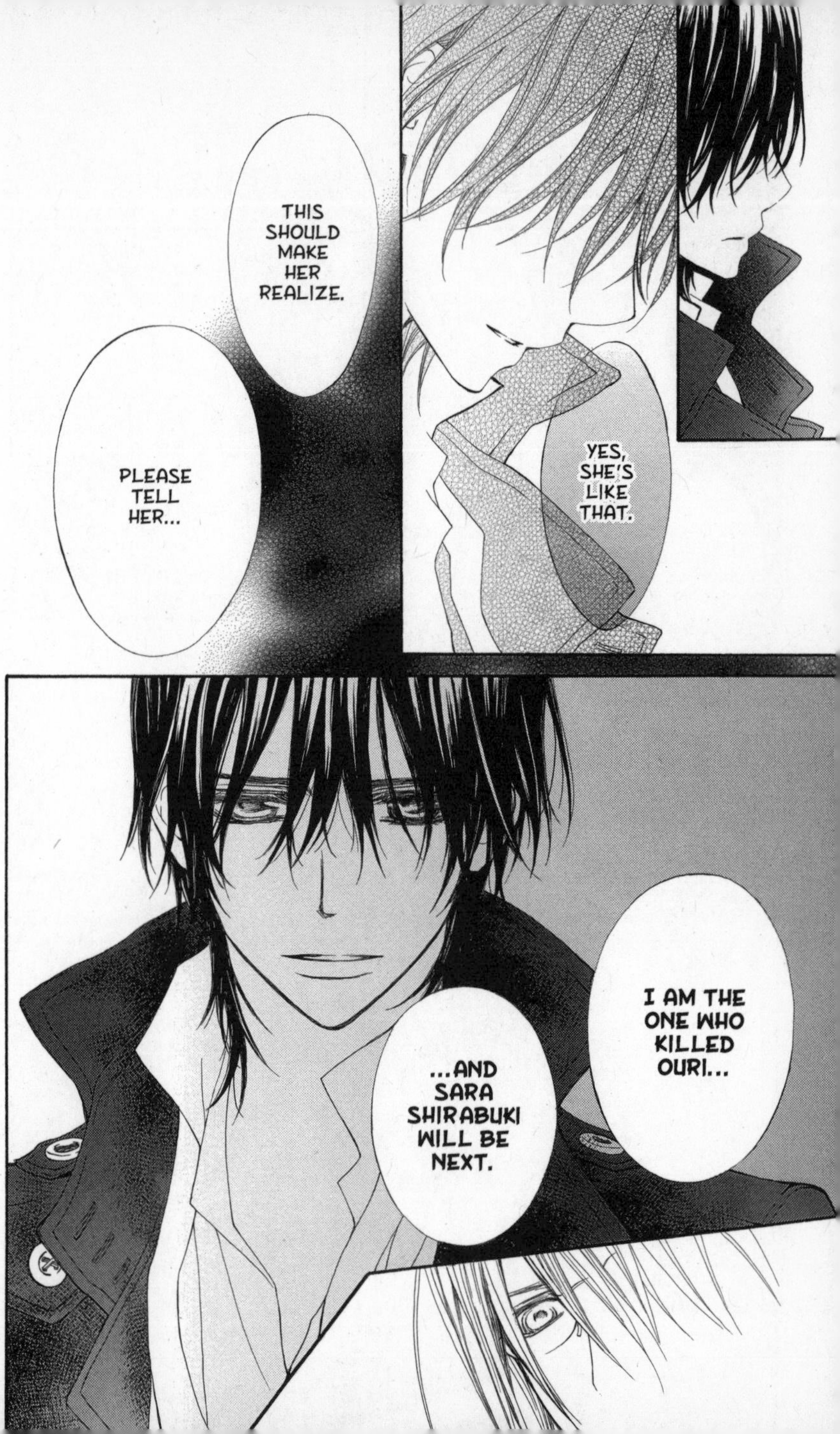
YES, SHE'S LIKE THAT.
THIS SHOULD MAKE HER REALIZE.
PLEASE TELL HER...
I AM THE ONE WHO KILLED OURI...
...AND SARA SHIRABUKI WILL BE NEXT.

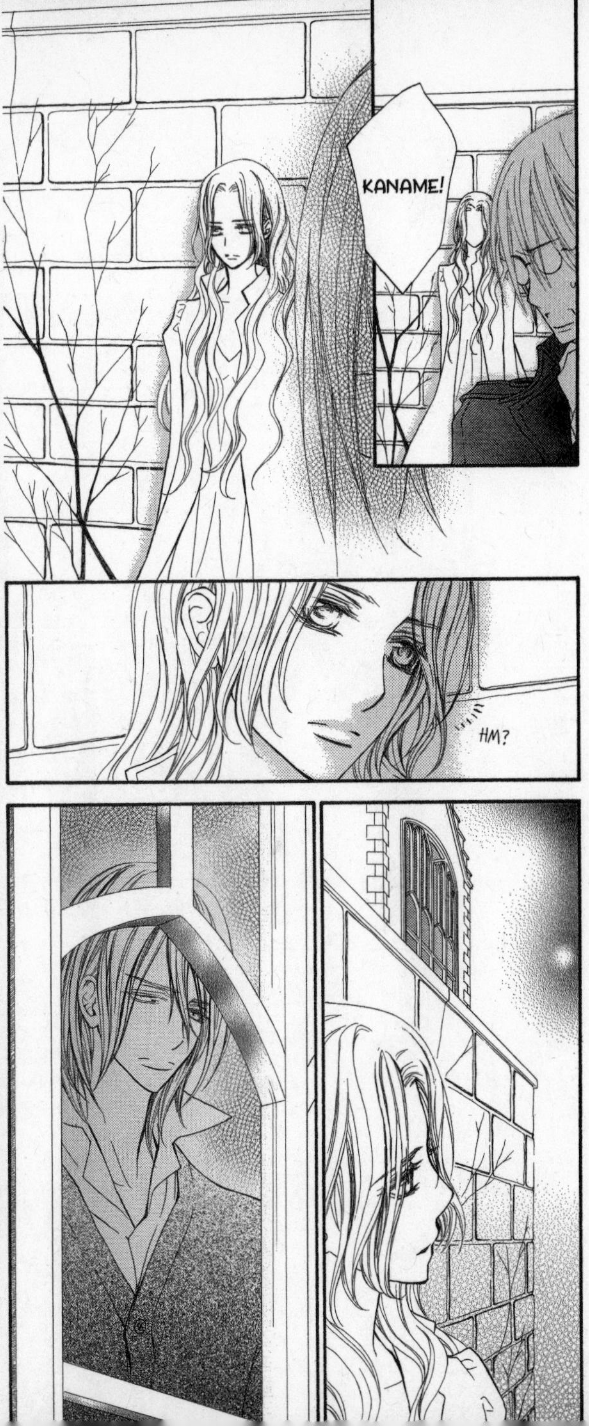
KANAME!
HM?

II

It is up to my editor to decide what to put on the paper band around each Japanese volume, so I really look forward to seeing them. I even look forward to the magazine. I like to read the lead-ins on the chapter title page and on the Vampire Knight fan pages. This isn't in every issue, but I love the introduction and conversation among the characters on the fan page. Of course these are written by my editor too... There are times when I can really feel my editor's love for the characters, and I am filled with gratitude. If you are interested but do not read the Japanese magazine, please pick up an issue of *LaLa* to take a look. ♡ (Did I write about this before?)

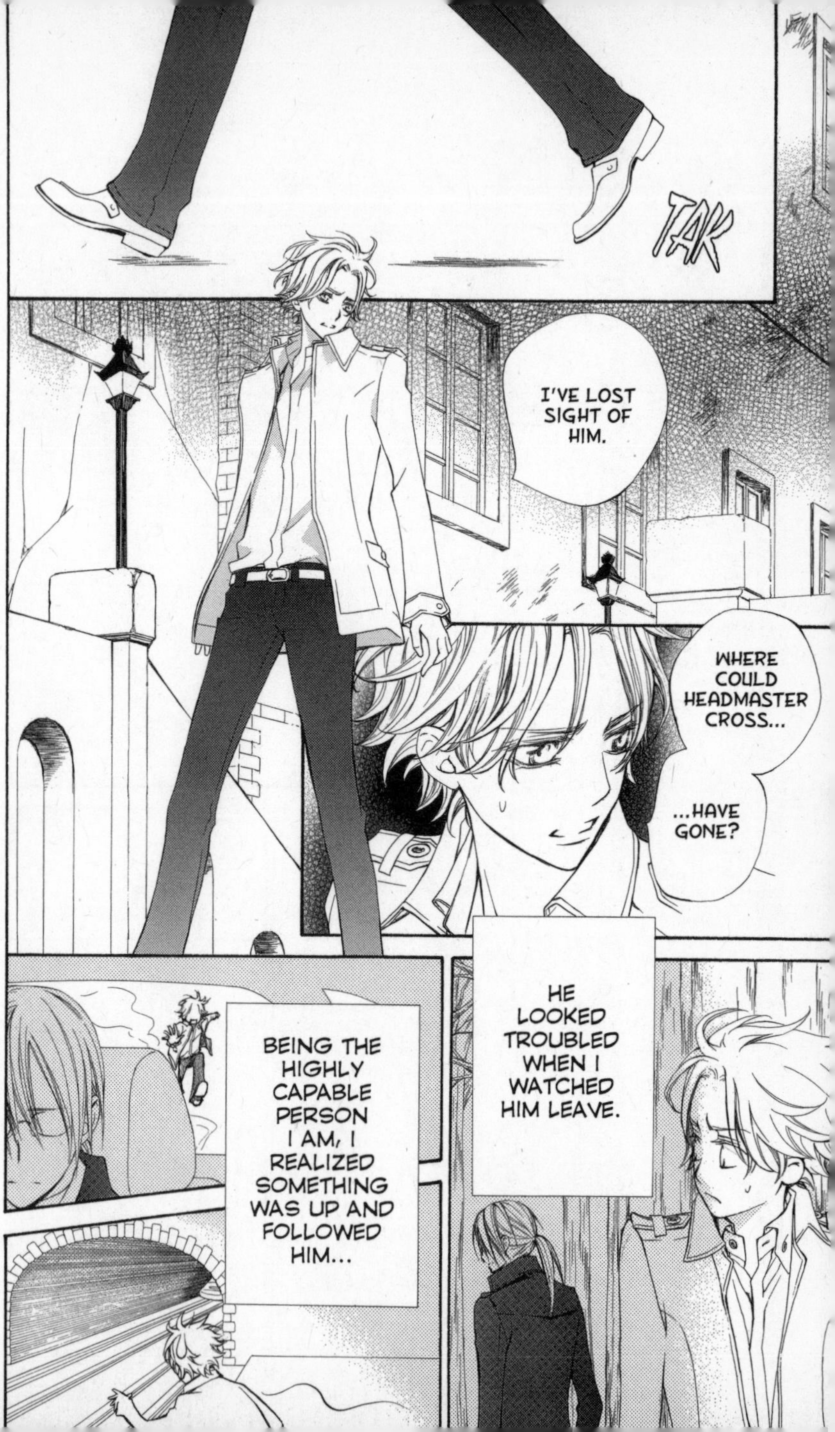
TAK
I'VE LOST SIGHT OF HIM.
WHERE COULD HEADMASTER CROSS...
...HAVE GONE?
HE LOOKED TROUBLED WHEN I WATCHED HIM LEAVE.
BEING THE HIGHLY CAPABLE PERSON I AM, I REALIZED SOMETHING WAS UP AND FOLLOWED HIM...

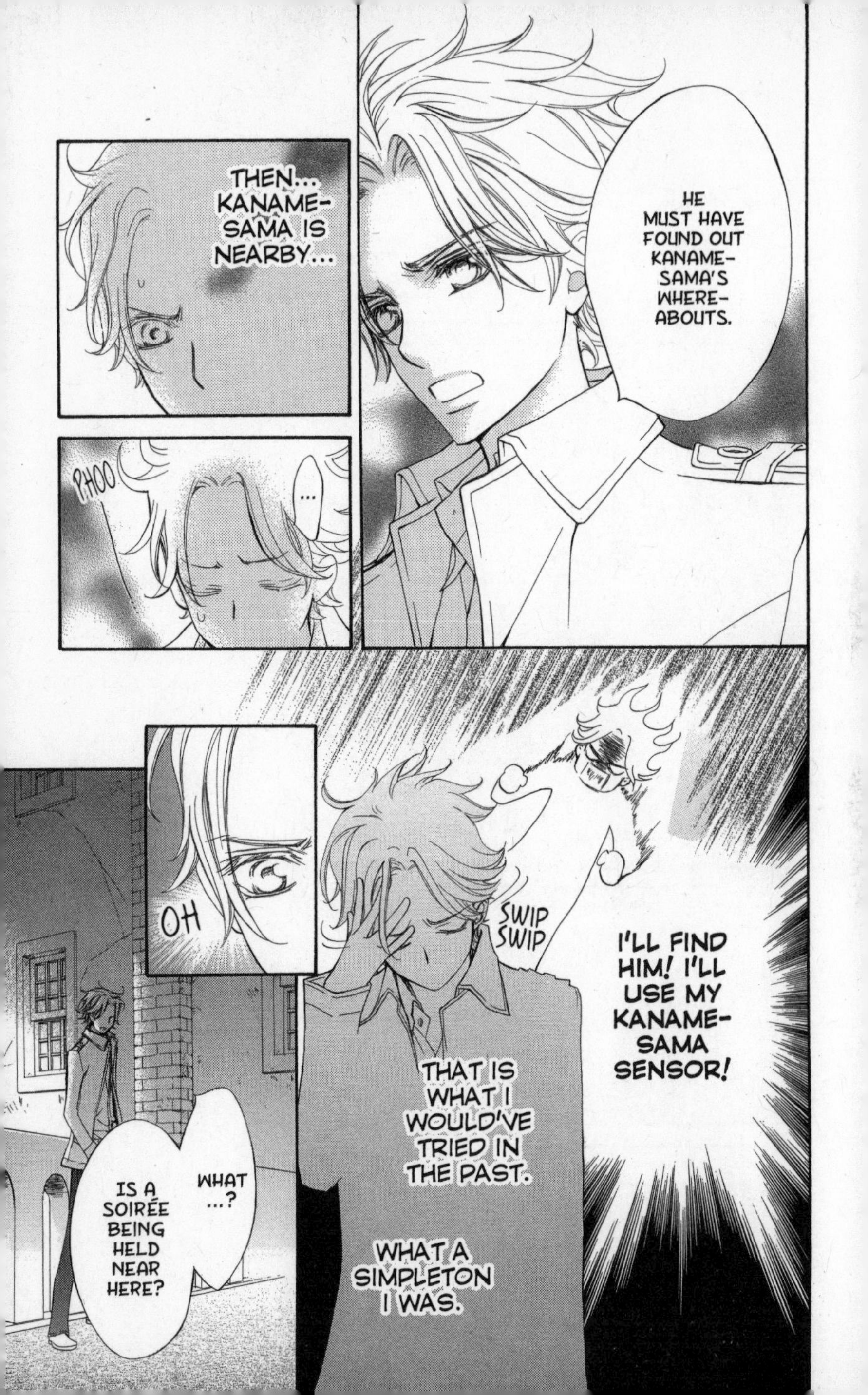
HE MUST HAVE FOUND OUT KANAME-SAMA'S WHEREABOUTS.
THEN... KANAME-SAMA IS NEARBY...
PHOO
...
I'LL FIND HIM! I'LL USE MY KANAME-SAMA SENSOR!
SWIP SWIP
OH
THAT IS WHAT I WOULD'VE TRIED IN THE PAST.
WHAT A SIMPLETON I WAS.
WHAT ...?
IS A SOIRÉE BEING HELD NEAR HERE?

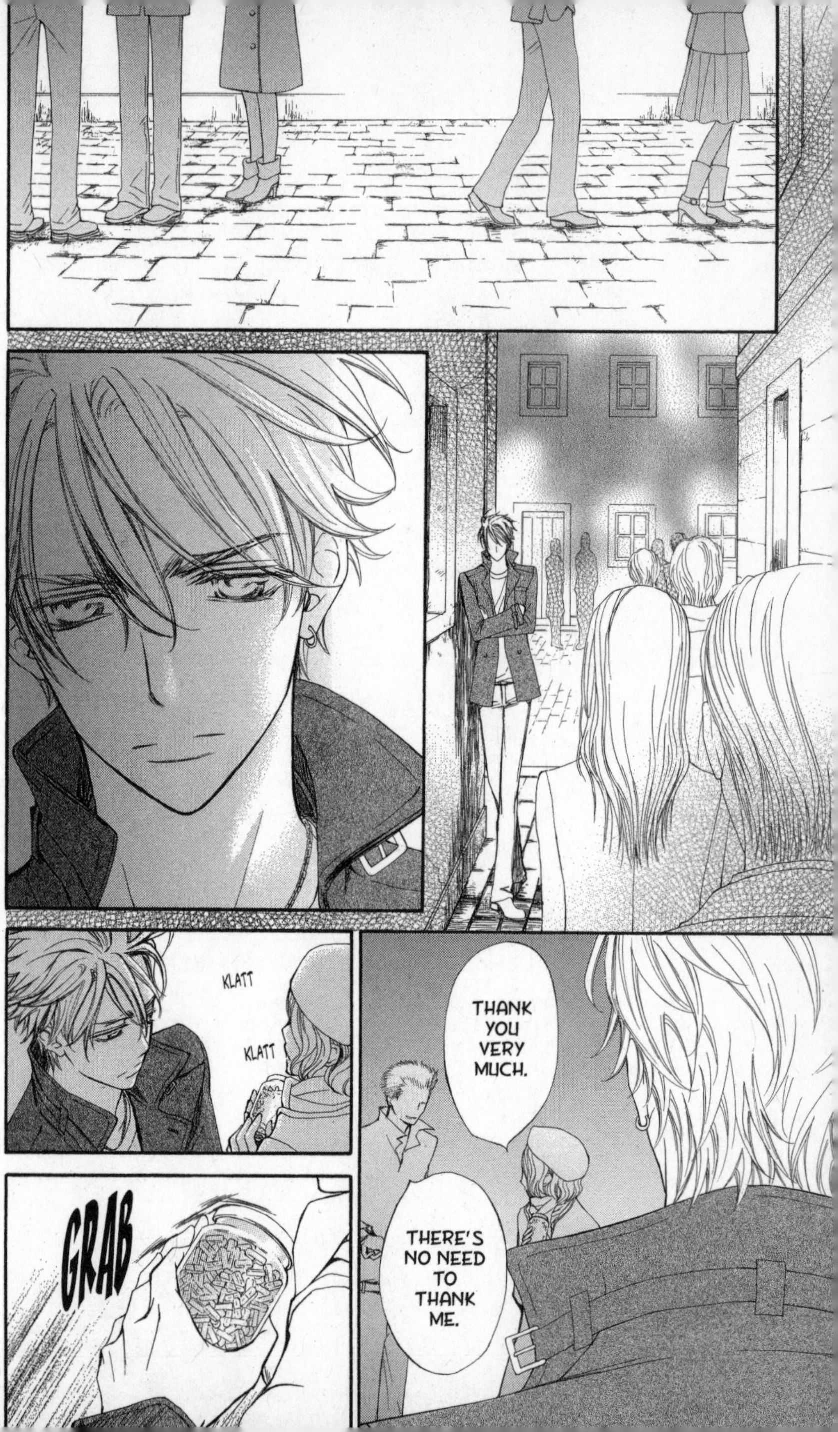
THANK YOU VERY MUCH.
THERE'S NO NEED TO THANK ME.
KLATT
KLATT
GRAB

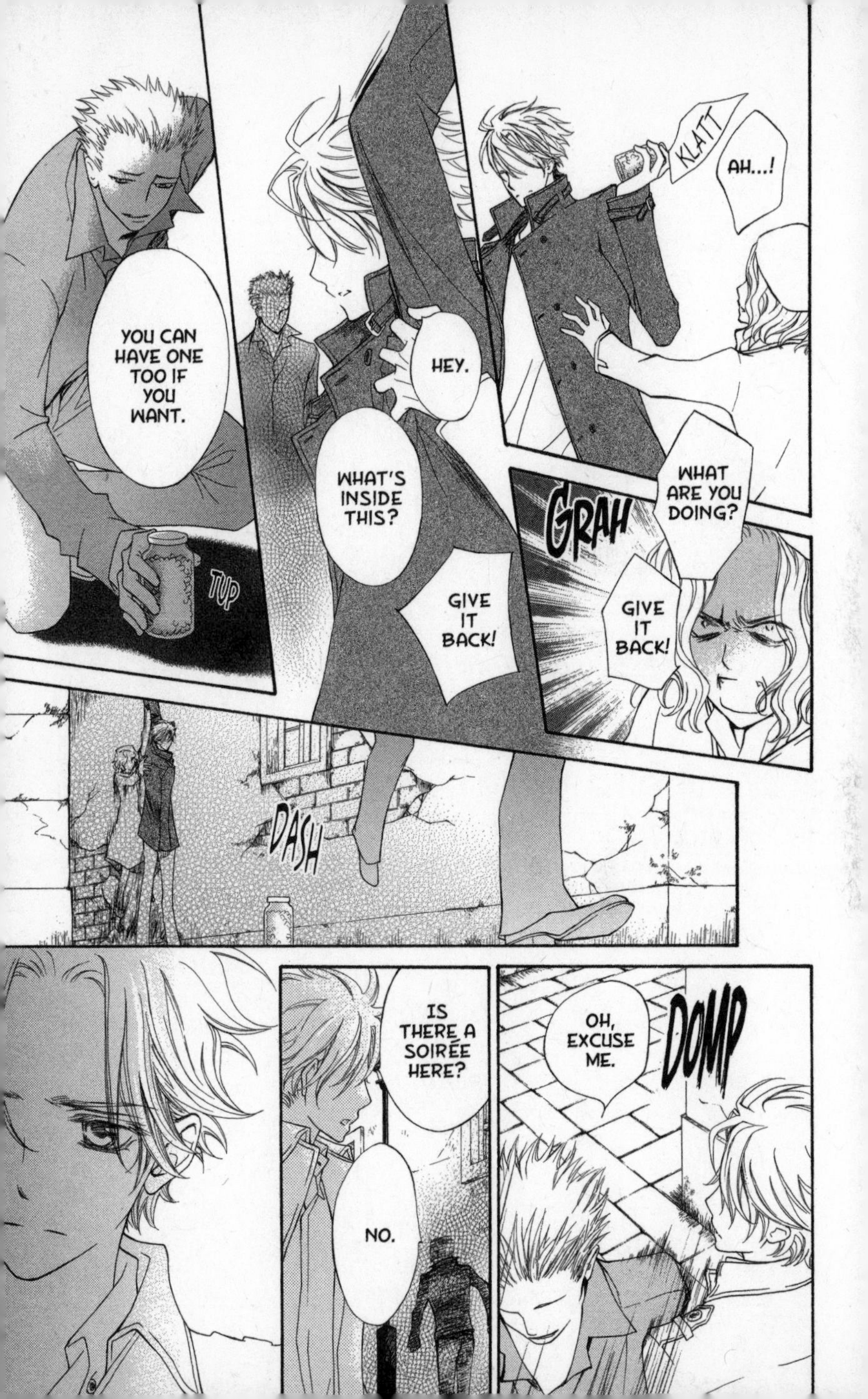
KLATT
AH...!
WHAT ARE YOU DOING?
GRAH
GIVE IT BACK!
HEY.
WHAT'S INSIDE THIS?
GIVE IT BACK!
YOU CAN HAVE ONE TOO IF YOU WANT.
TUP
DASH
DOMP
OH, EXCUSE ME.
IS THERE A SOIRÉE HERE?
NO.

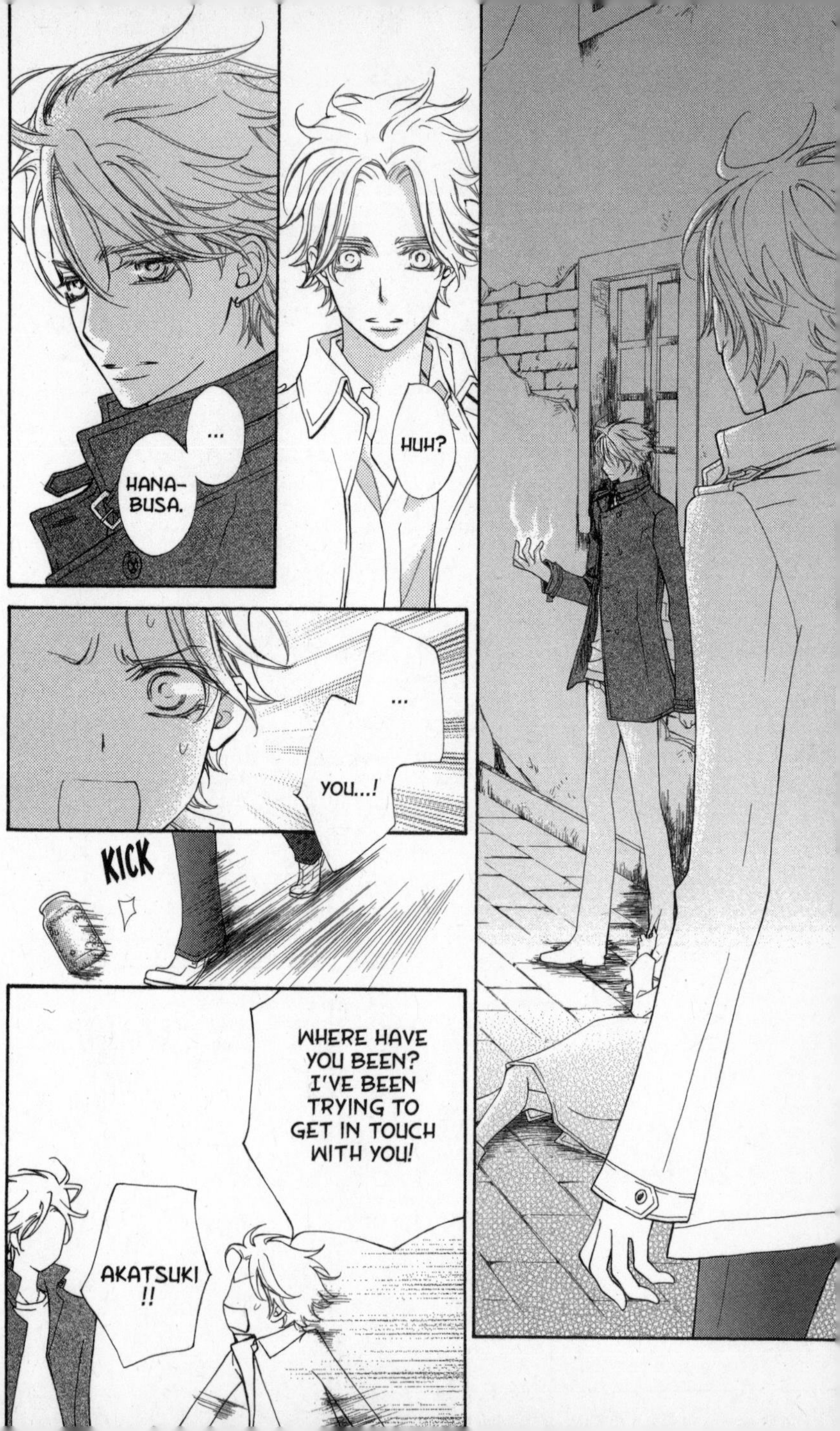
HUH?
...
HANA-BUSA.
...
YOU...!
KICK
WHERE HAVE YOU BEEN? I'VE BEEN TRYING TO GET IN TOUCH WITH YOU!
AKATSUKI!!

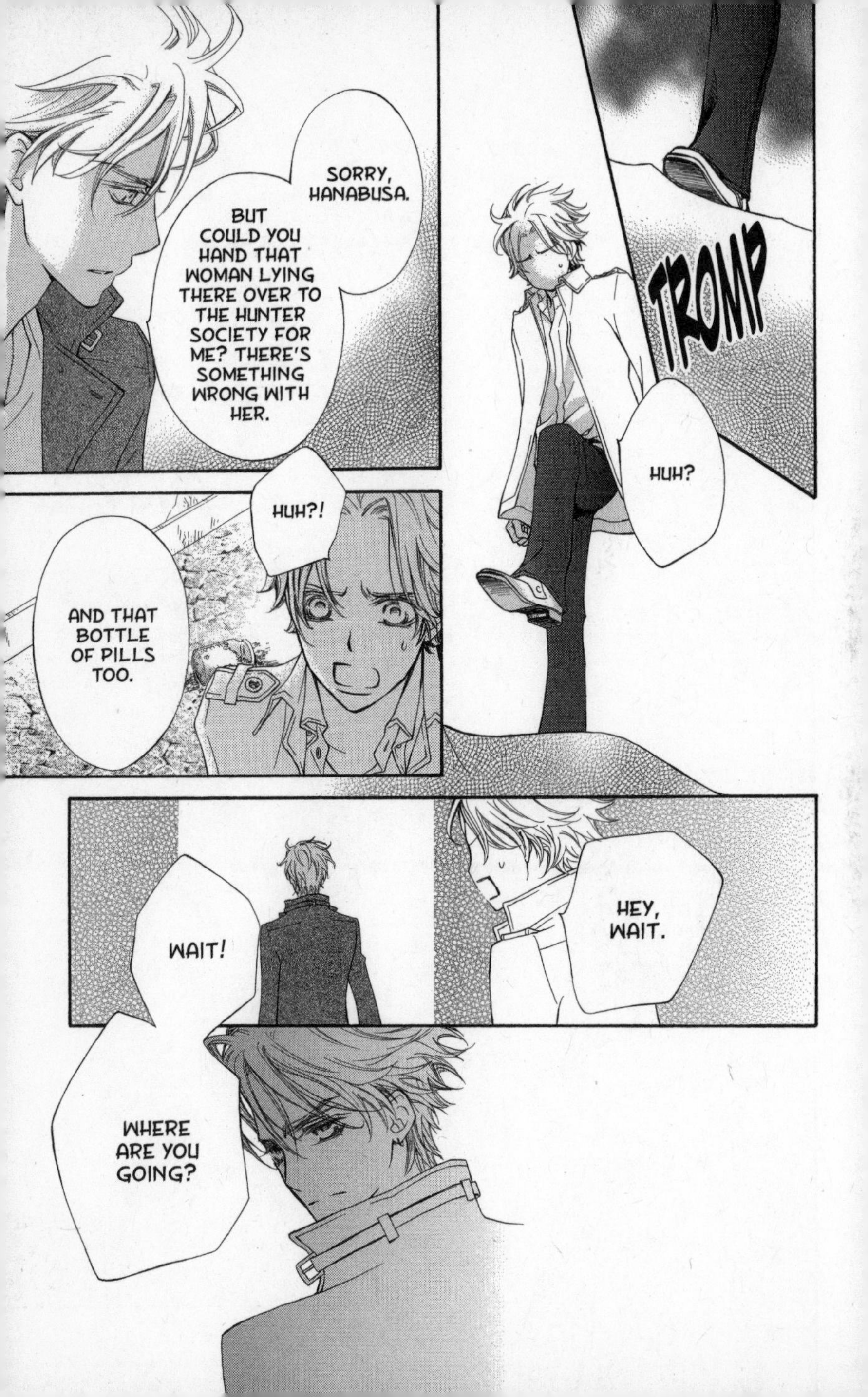
TROMP
HUH?
SORRY, HANABUSA.
BUT COULD YOU HAND THAT WOMAN LYING THERE OVER TO THE HUNTER SOCIETY FOR ME? THERE'S SOMETHING WRONG WITH HER.
HUH?!
AND THAT BOTTLE OF PILLS TOO.
HEY, WAIT.
WAIT!
WHERE ARE YOU GOING?

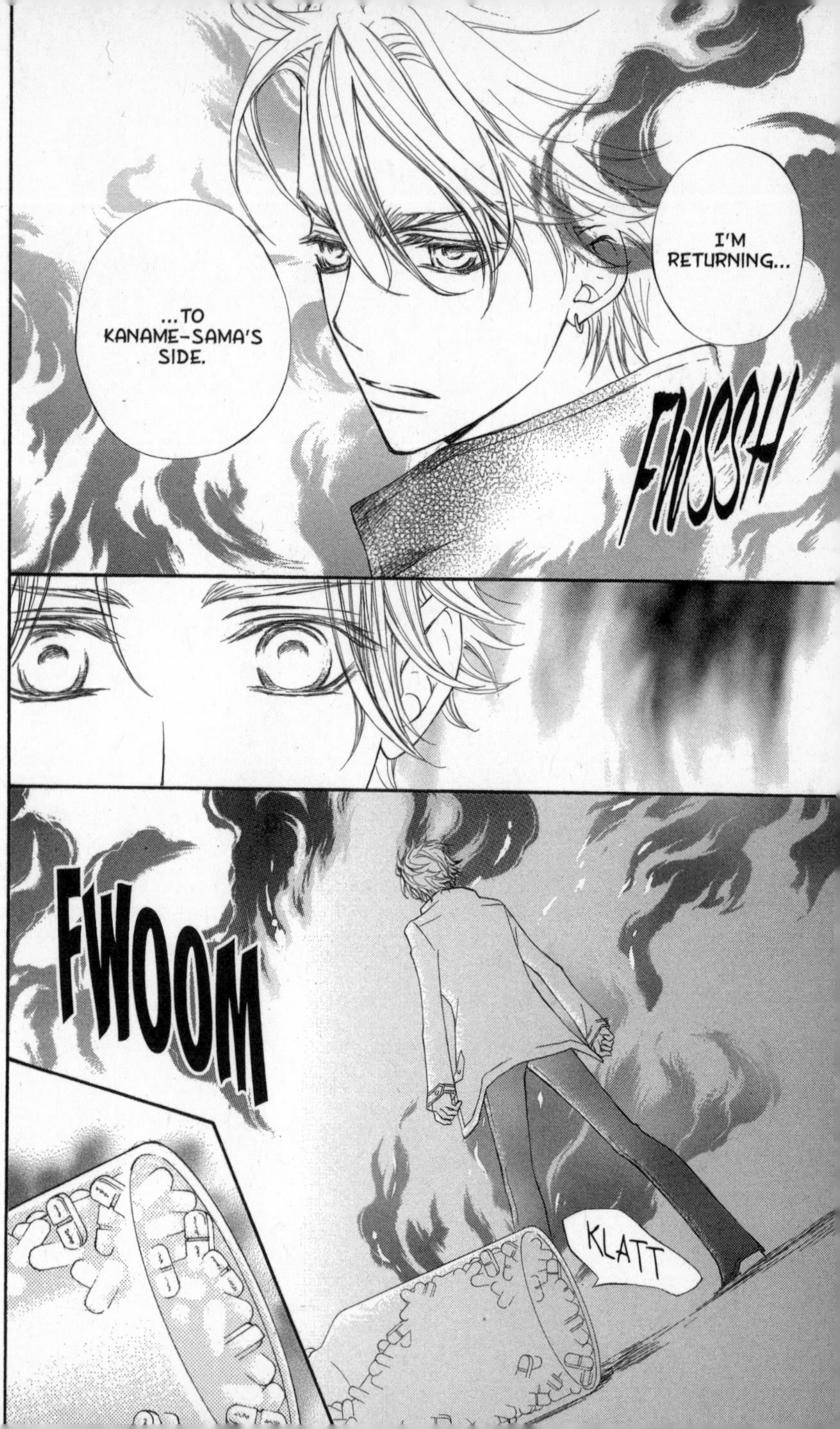
I'M RETURNING...
...TO KANAME-SAMA'S SIDE.
FWISH
FWOOM
KLATT

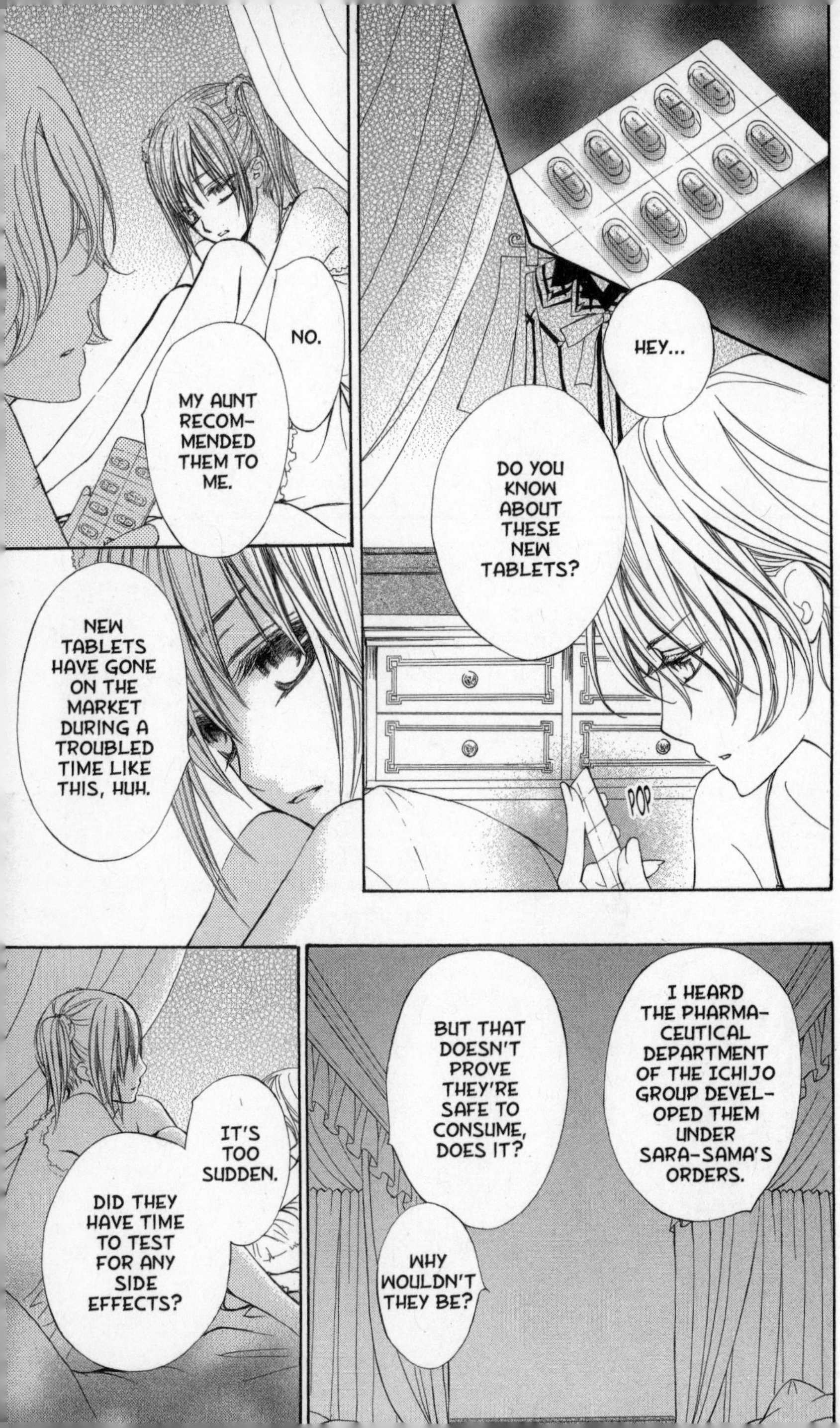
HEY...
DO YOU KNOW ABOUT THESE NEW TABLETS?
POP
NO.
MY AUNT RECOMMENDED THEM TO ME.
NEW TABLETS HAVE GONE ON THE MARKET DURING A TROUBLED TIME LIKE THIS, HUH.
I HEARD THE PHARMACEUTICAL DEPARTMENT OF THE ICHIJO GROUP DEVELOPED THEM UNDER SARA-SAMA'S ORDERS.
BUT THAT DOESN'T PROVE THEY'RE SAFE TO CONSUME, DOES IT?
WHY WOULDN'T THEY BE?
IT'S TOO SUDDEN.
DID THEY HAVE TIME TO TEST FOR ANY SIDE EFFECTS?

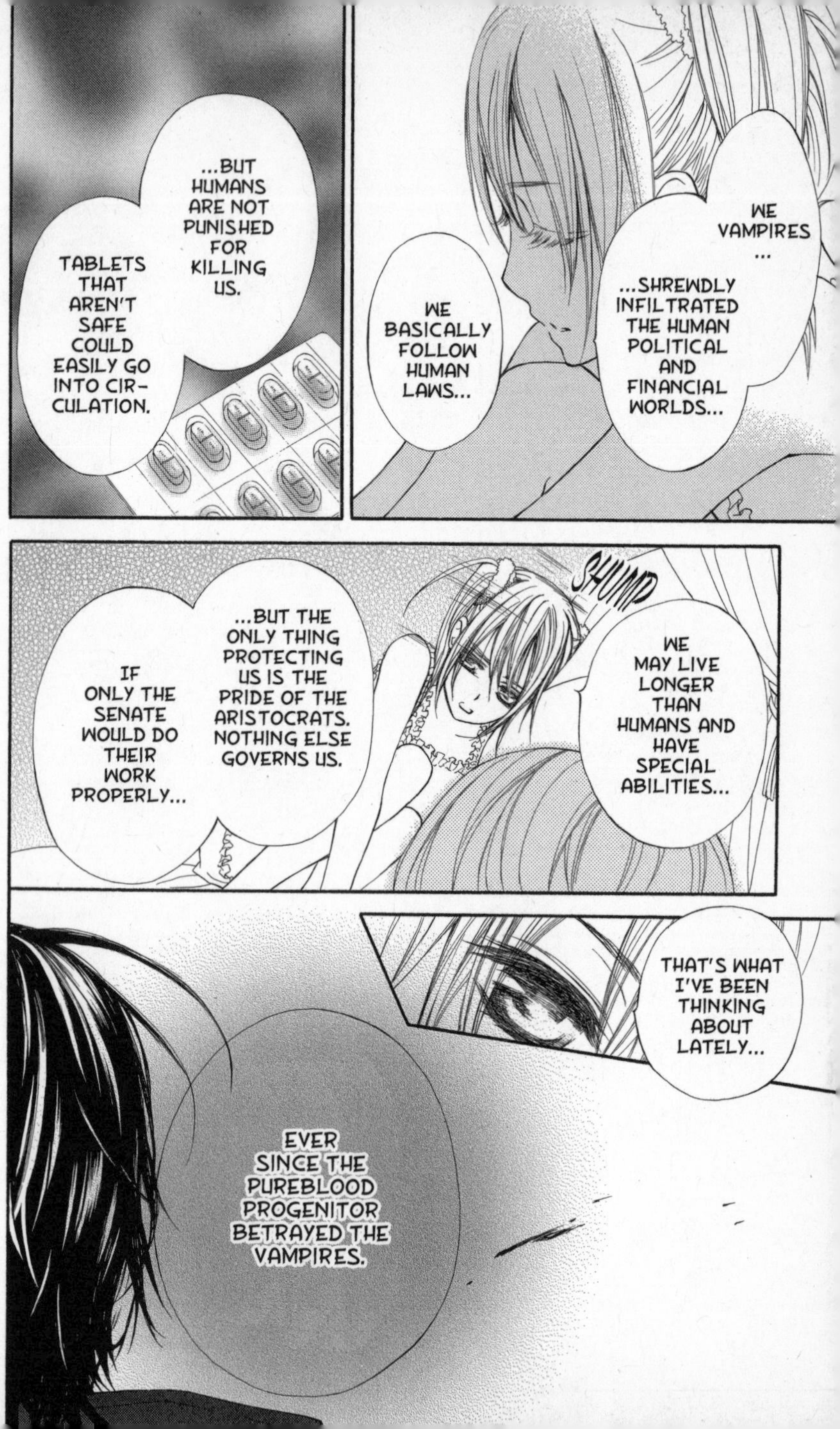
WE VAMPIRES...
...SHREWDLY INFILTRATED THE HUMAN POLITICAL AND FINANCIAL WORLDS...
WE BASICALLY FOLLOW HUMAN LAWS...
...BUT HUMANS ARE NOT PUNISHED FOR KILLING US.
TABLETS THAT AREN'T SAFE COULD EASILY GO INTO CIRCULATION.
SHUMP
WE MAY LIVE LONGER THAN HUMANS AND HAVE SPECIAL ABILITIES...
...BUT THE ONLY THING PROTECTING US IS THE PRIDE OF THE ARISTOCRATS. NOTHING ELSE GOVERNS US.
IF ONLY THE SENATE WOULD DO THEIR WORK PROPERLY...
THAT'S WHAT I'VE BEEN THINKING ABOUT LATELY...
EVER SINCE THE PUREBLOOD PROGENITOR BETRAYED THE VAMPIRES.

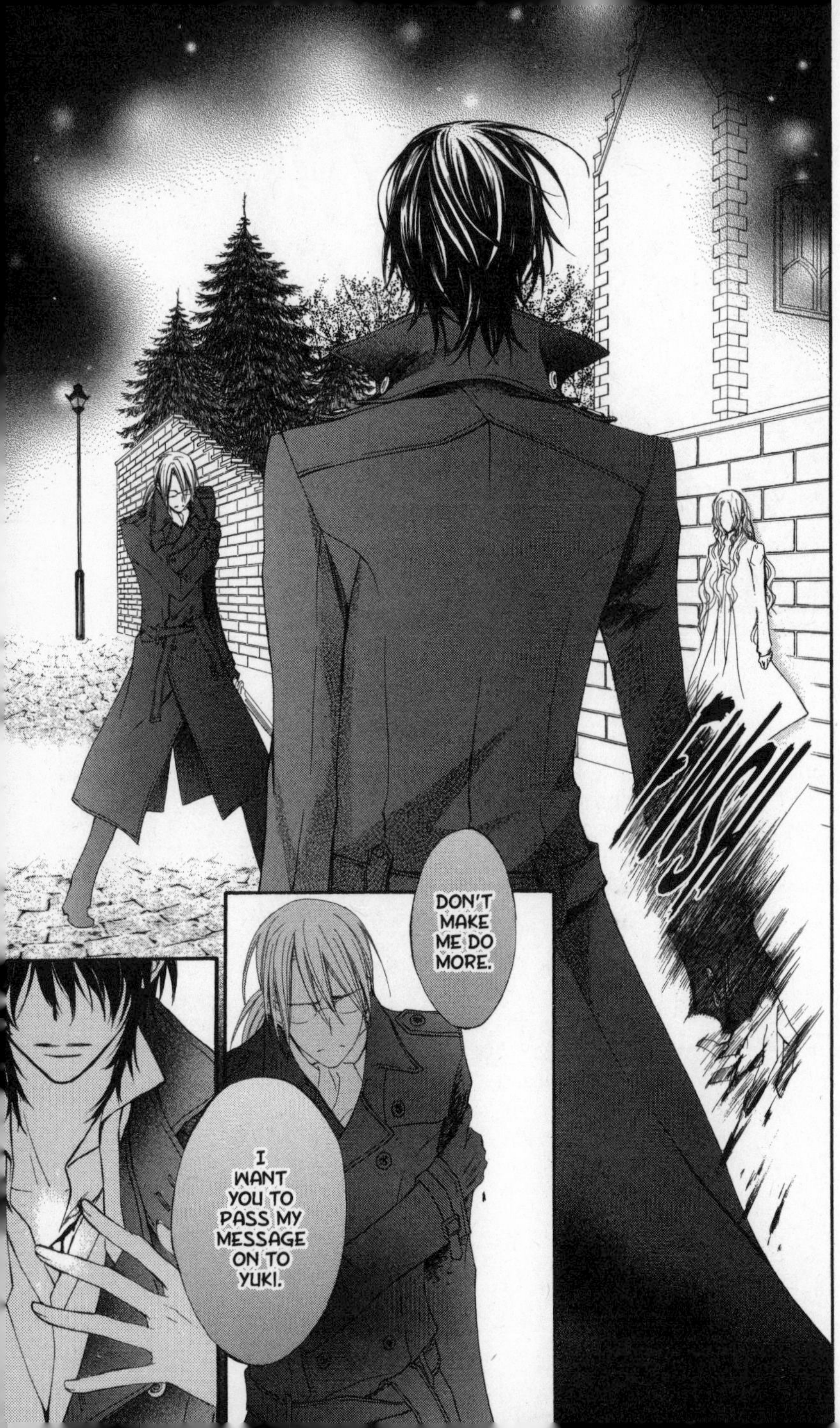
DON'T MAKE ME DO MORE.
I WANT YOU TO PASS MY MESSAGE ON TO YUKI.

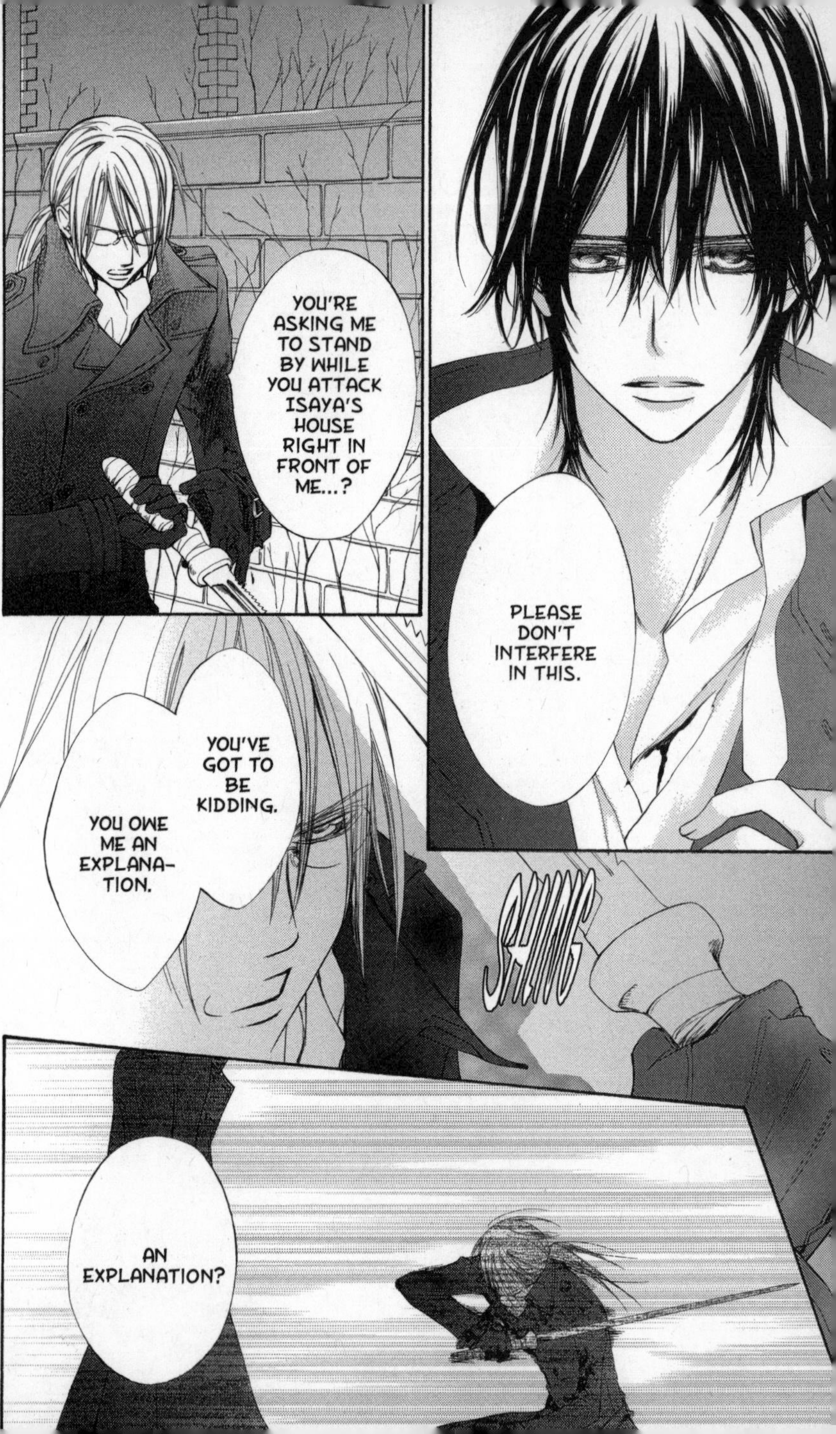
PLEASE DON'T INTERFERE IN THIS.
YOU'RE ASKING ME TO STAND BY WHILE YOU ATTACK ISAYA'S HOUSE RIGHT IN FRONT OF ME...?
YOU'VE GOT TO BE KIDDING.
YOU OWE ME AN EXPLANA-TION.
SHING
AN EXPLANATION?

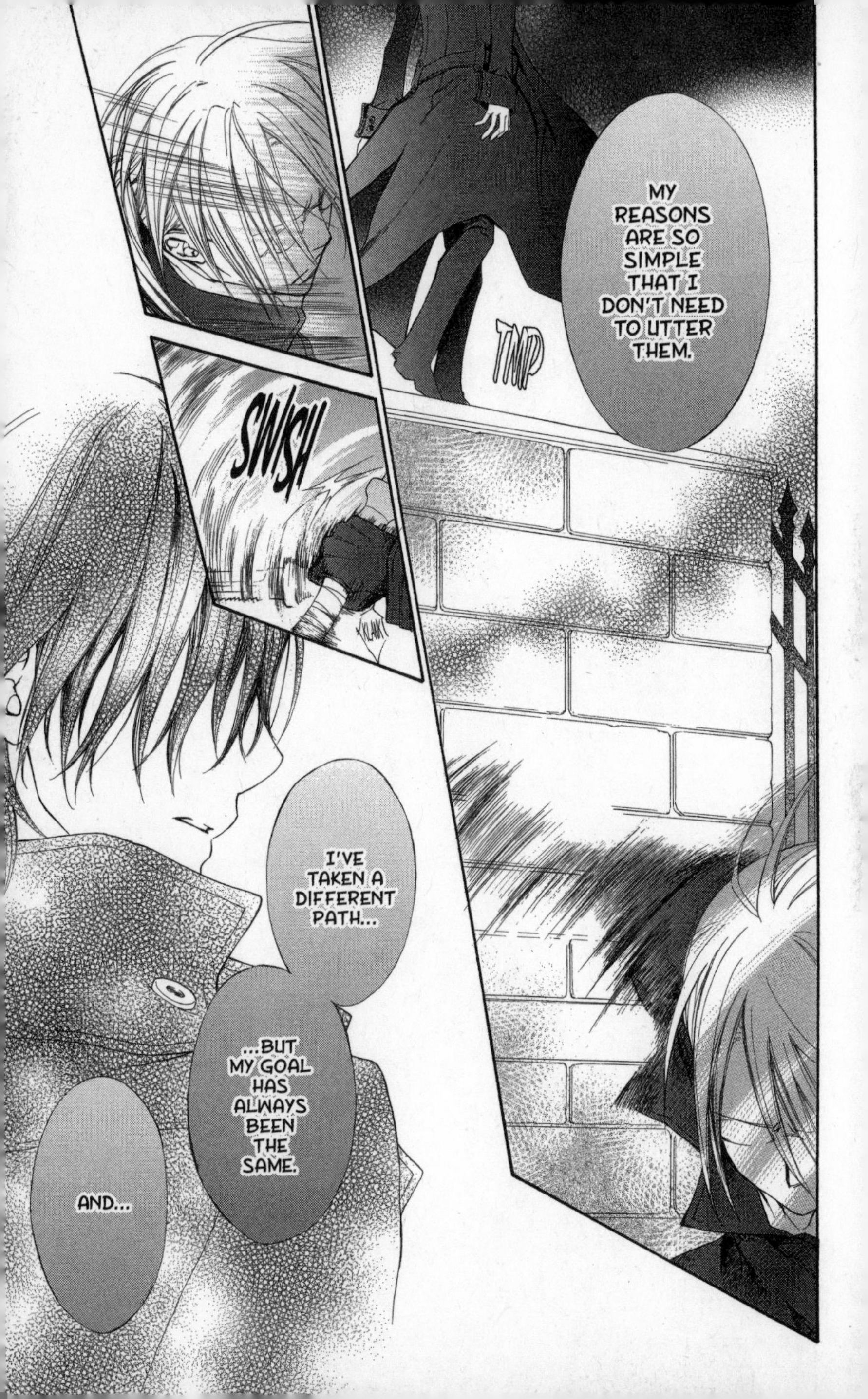
MY REASONS ARE SO SIMPLE THAT I DON'T NEED TO UTTER THEM.
TMP
SWISH
KLANK
I'VE TAKEN A DIFFERENT PATH...
...BUT MY GOAL HAS ALWAYS BEEN THE SAME.
AND...

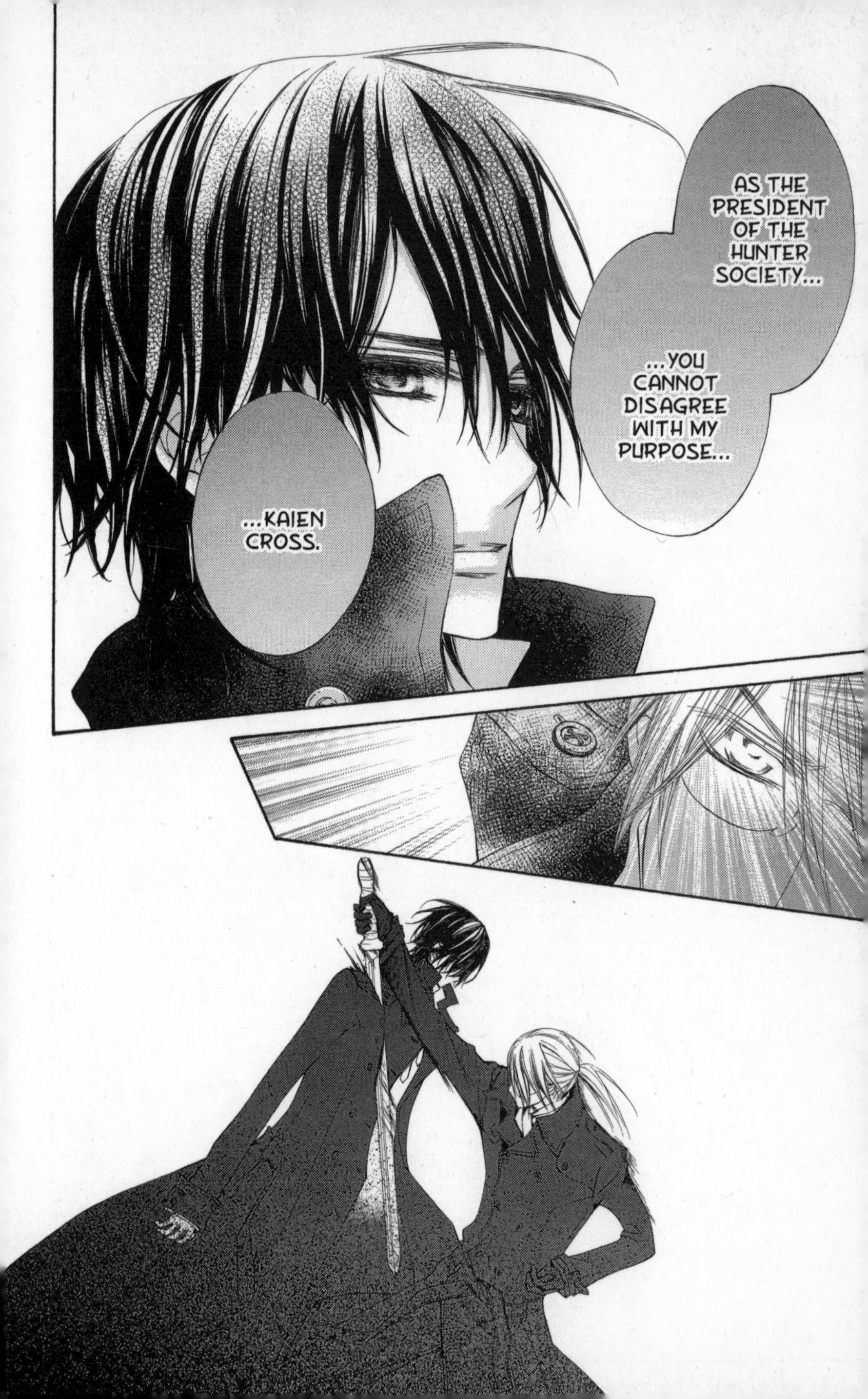
AS THE PRESIDENT OF THE HUNTER SOCIETY...
...YOU CANNOT DISAGREE WITH MY PURPOSE...
...KAIEN CROSS.

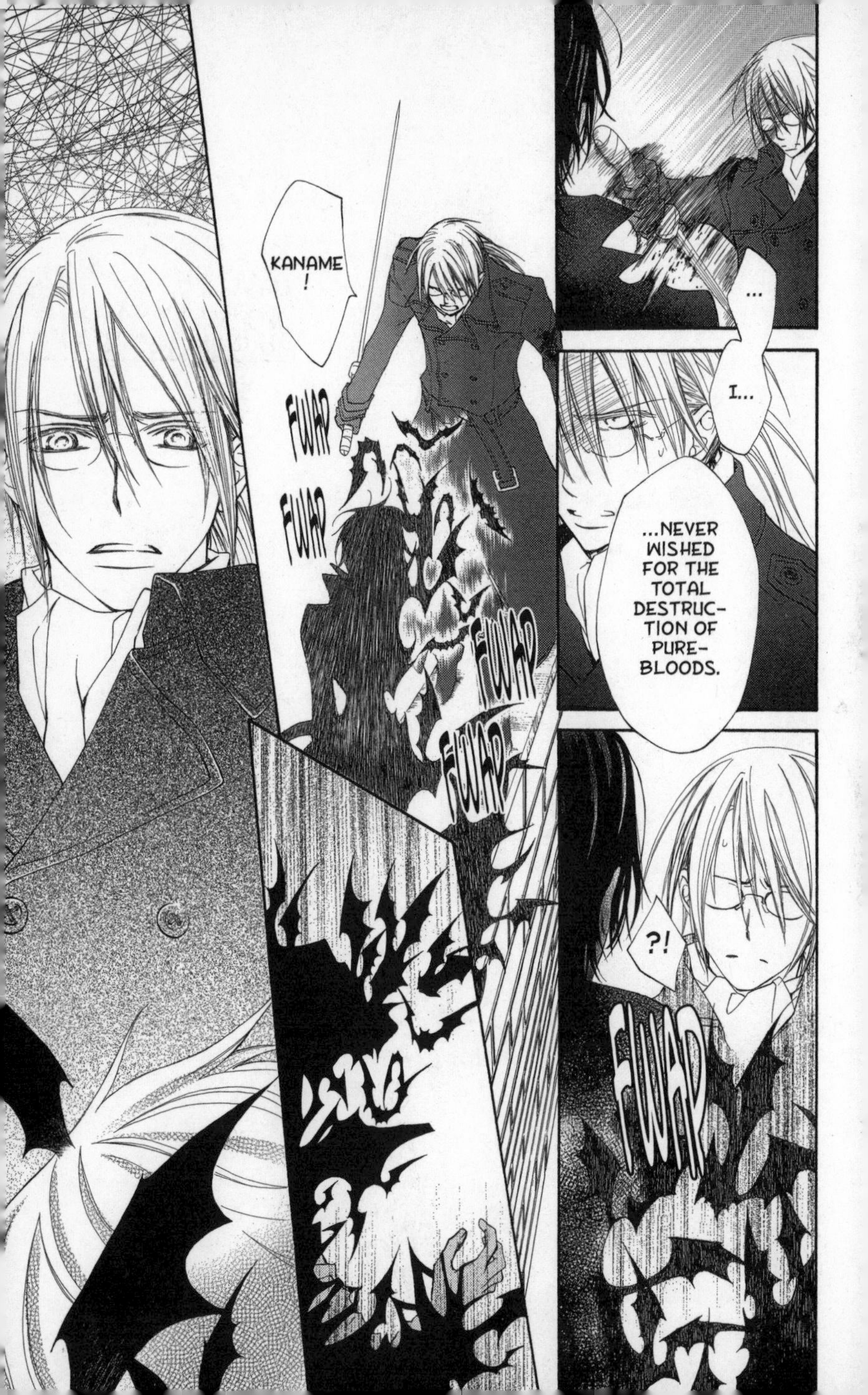
...
I...
...NEVER WISHED FOR THE TOTAL DESTRUCTION OF PURE-BLOODS.
?!
FWAP
KANAME!
FWAP
FWAP
FWAP
FWAP

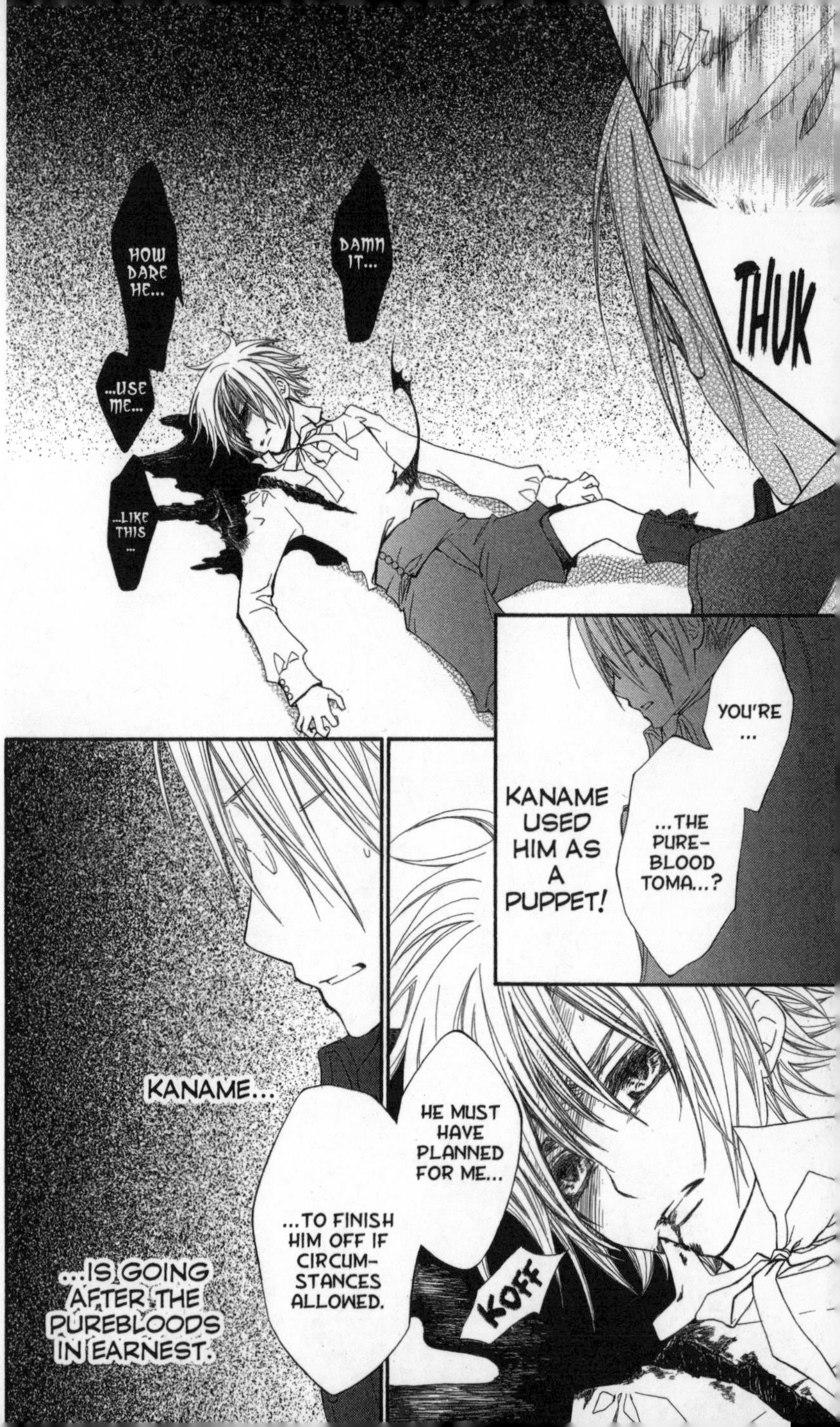
THUK
DAMN IT...
HOW DARE HE...
...USE ME...
...LIKE THIS...
YOU'RE...
...THE PURE-BLOOD TOMA...?
KANAME USED HIM AS A PUPPET!
HE MUST HAVE PLANNED FOR ME...
...TO FINISH HIM OFF IF CIRCUM-STANCES ALLOWED.
KOFF
KANAME...
...IS GOING AFTER THE PUREBLOODS IN EARNEST.

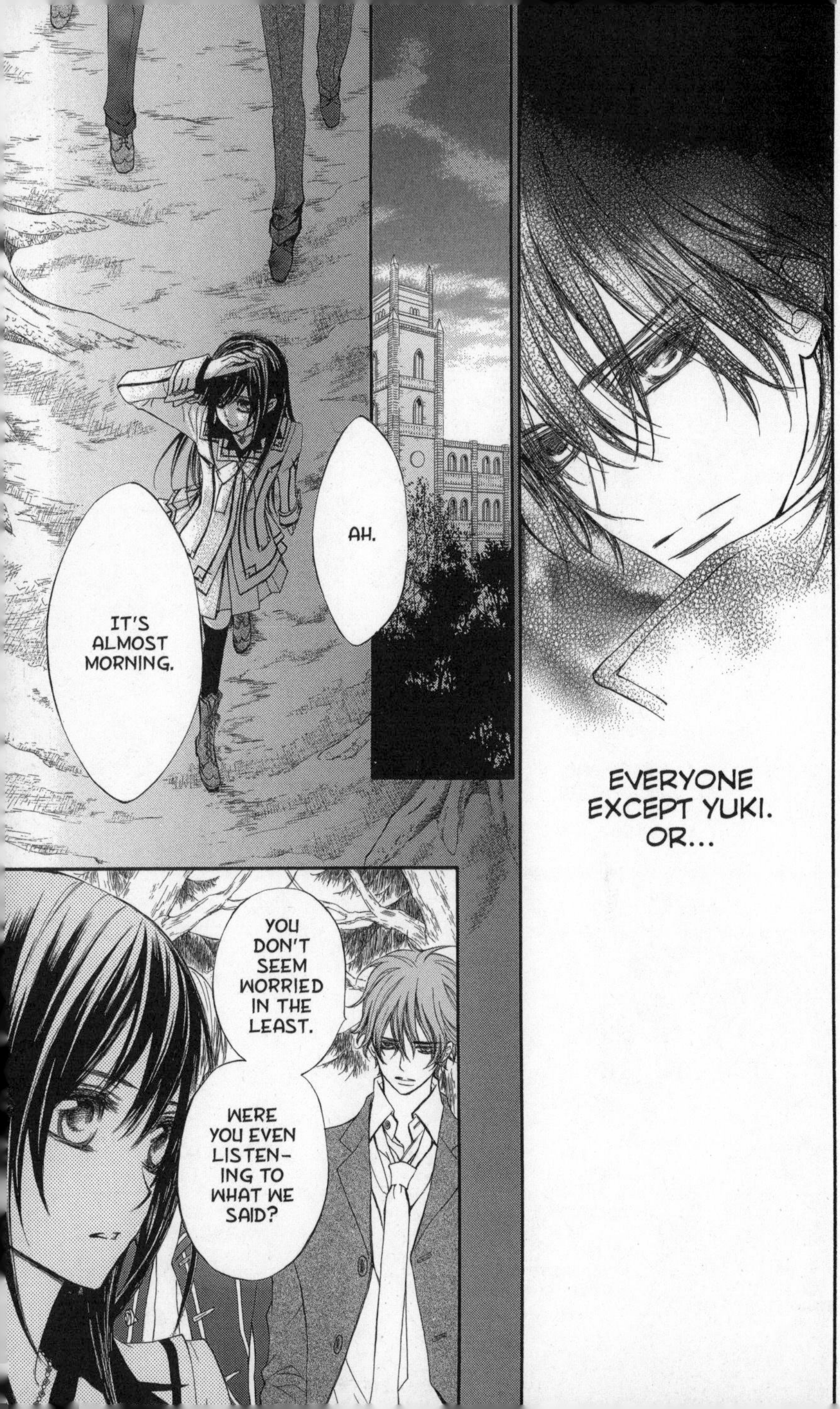
EVERYONE EXCEPT YUKI. OR...
AH.
IT'S ALMOST MORNING.
YOU DON'T SEEM WORRIED IN THE LEAST.
WERE YOU EVEN LISTENING TO WHAT WE SAID?

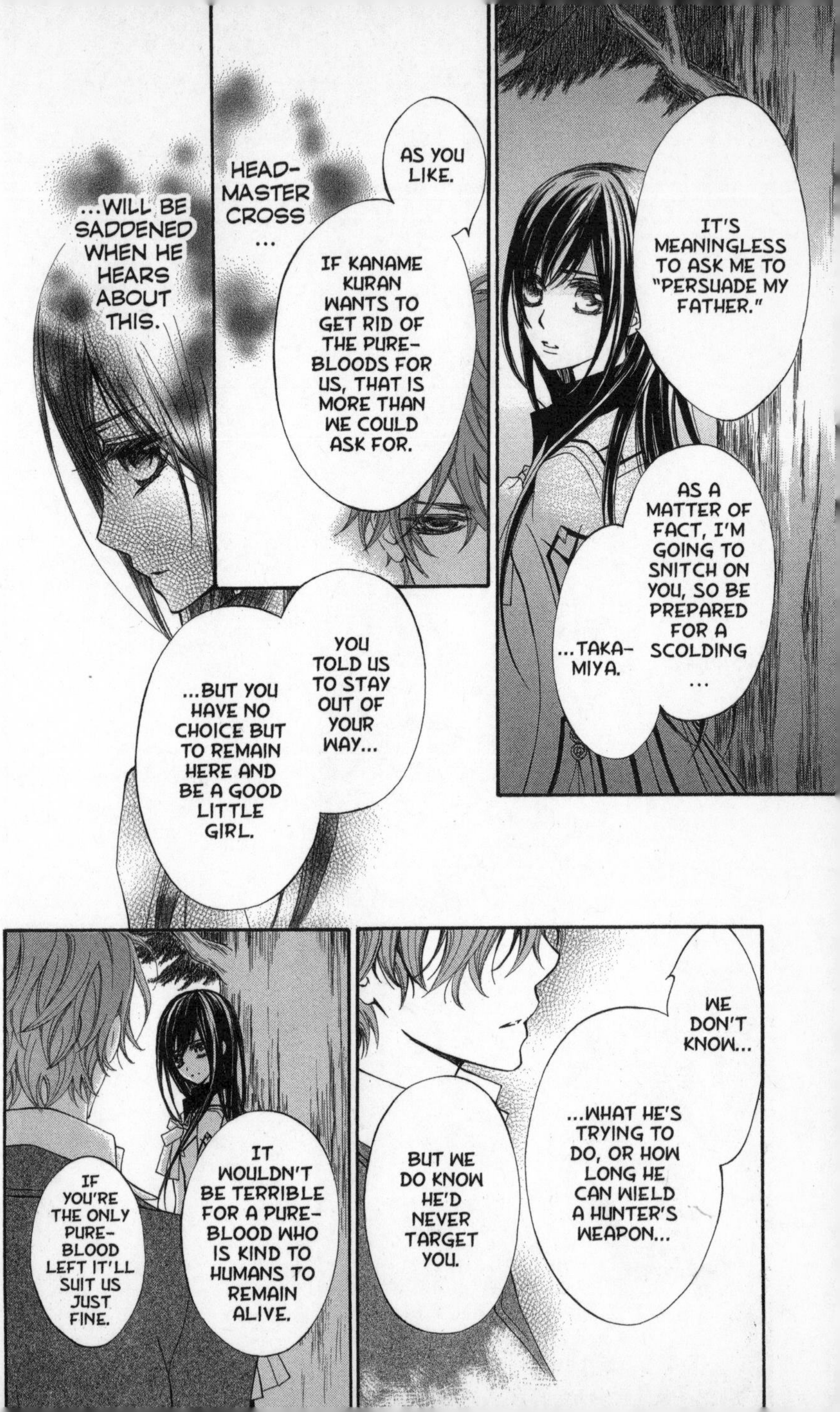
IT'S MEANINGLESS TO ASK ME TO "PERSUADE MY FATHER."
AS A MATTER OF FACT, I'M GOING TO SNITCH ON YOU, SO BE PREPARED FOR A SCOLDING…
…TAKAMIYA.
AS YOU LIKE.
IF KANAME KURAN WANTS TO GET RID OF THE PUREBLOODS FOR US, THAT IS MORE THAN WE COULD ASK FOR.
HEADMASTER CROSS…
…WILL BE SADDENED WHEN HE HEARS ABOUT THIS.
YOU TOLD US TO STAY OUT OF YOUR WAY…
…BUT YOU HAVE NO CHOICE BUT TO REMAIN HERE AND BE A GOOD LITTLE GIRL.
WE DON'T KNOW…
…WHAT HE'S TRYING TO DO, OR HOW LONG HE CAN WIELD A HUNTER'S WEAPON…
BUT WE DO KNOW HE'D NEVER TARGET YOU.
IT WOULDN'T BE TERRIBLE FOR A PURE-BLOOD WHO IS KIND TO HUMANS TO REMAIN ALIVE.
IF YOU'RE THE ONLY PUREBLOOD LEFT IT'LL SUIT US JUST FINE.

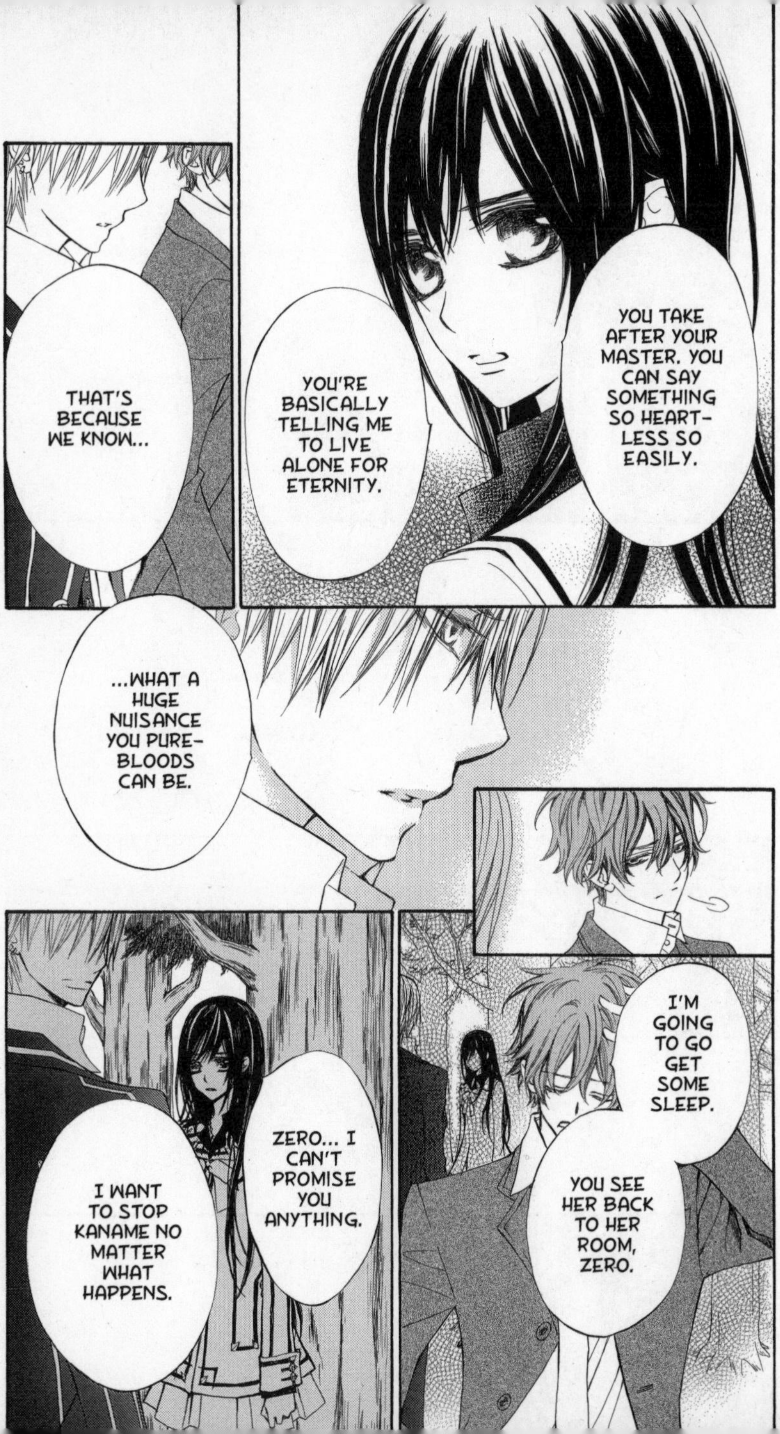
YOU TAKE AFTER YOUR MASTER. YOU CAN SAY SOMETHING SO HEART-LESS SO EASILY.
YOU'RE BASICALLY TELLING ME TO LIVE ALONE FOR ETERNITY.
THAT'S BECAUSE WE KNOW...
...WHAT A HUGE NUISANCE YOU PURE-BLOODS CAN BE.
I'M GOING TO GO GET SOME SLEEP.
YOU SEE HER BACK TO HER ROOM, ZERO.
ZERO... I CAN'T PROMISE YOU ANYTHING.
I WANT TO STOP KANAME NO MATTER WHAT HAPPENS.

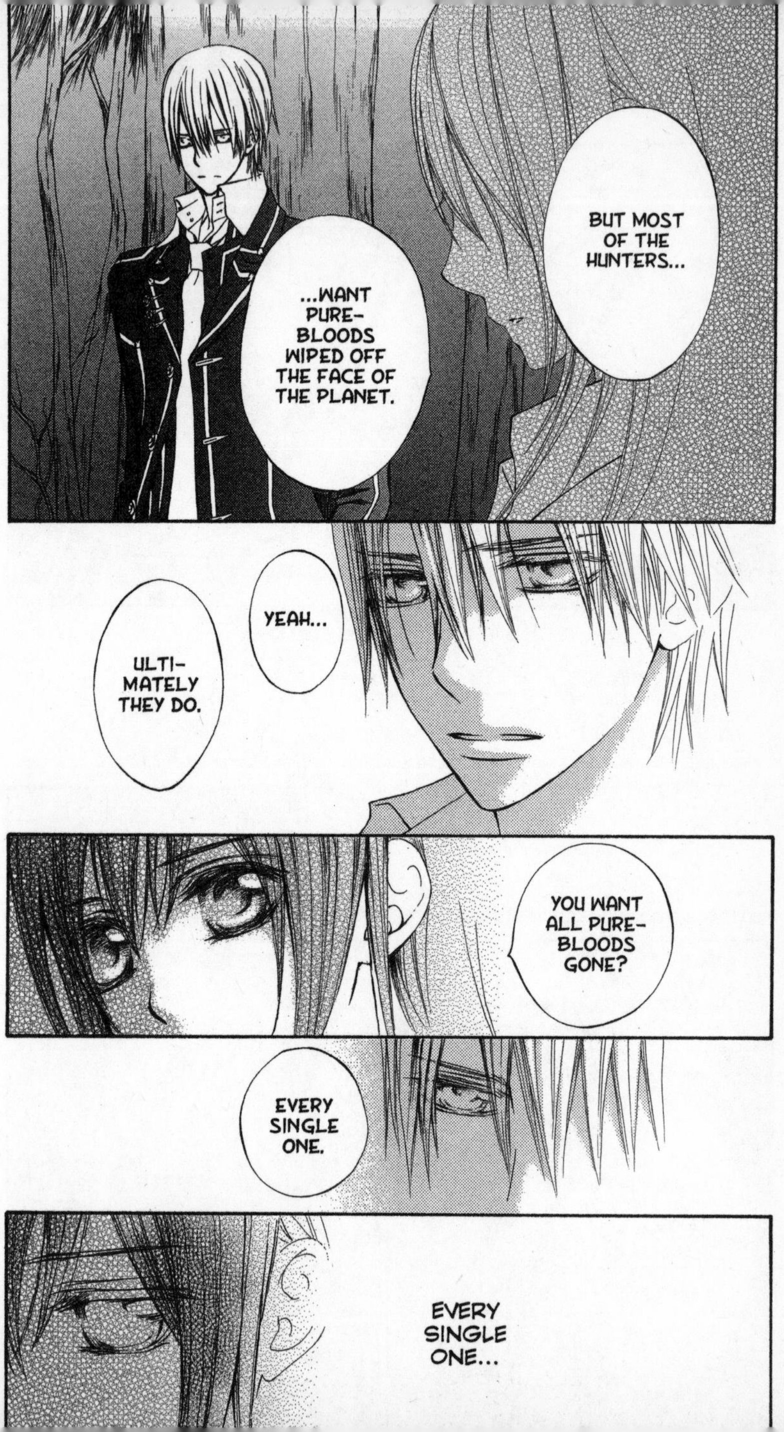
BUT MOST OF THE HUNTERS...
...WANT PURE-BLOODS WIPED OFF THE FACE OF THE PLANET.
YEAH...
ULTI-MATELY THEY DO.
YOU WANT ALL PURE-BLOODS GONE?
EVERY SINGLE ONE.
EVERY SINGLE ONE...

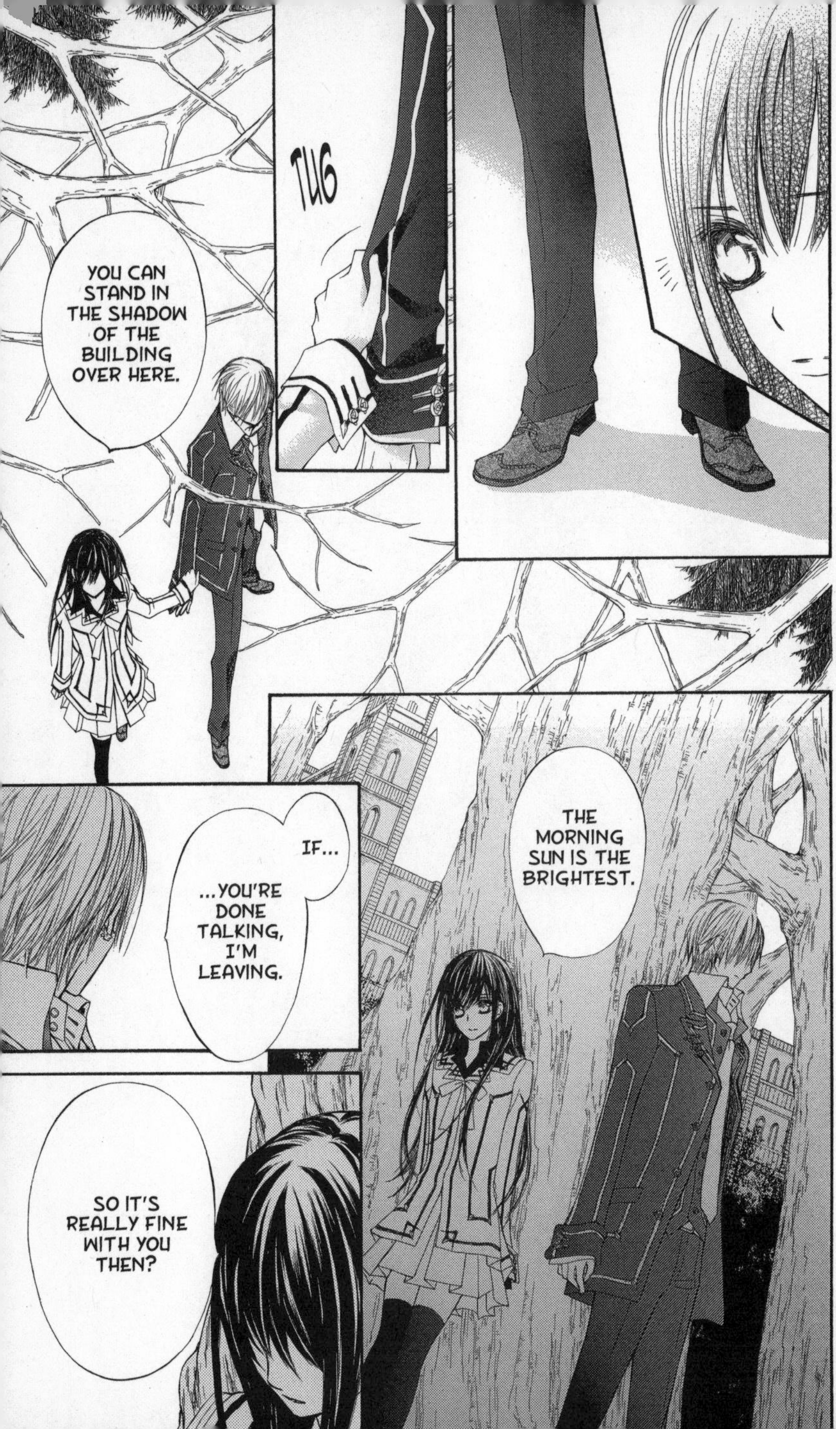
TUG
YOU CAN STAND IN THE SHADOW OF THE BUILDING OVER HERE.
THE MORNING SUN IS THE BRIGHTEST.
IF...
...YOU'RE DONE TALKING, I'M LEAVING.
SO IT'S REALLY FINE WITH YOU THEN?

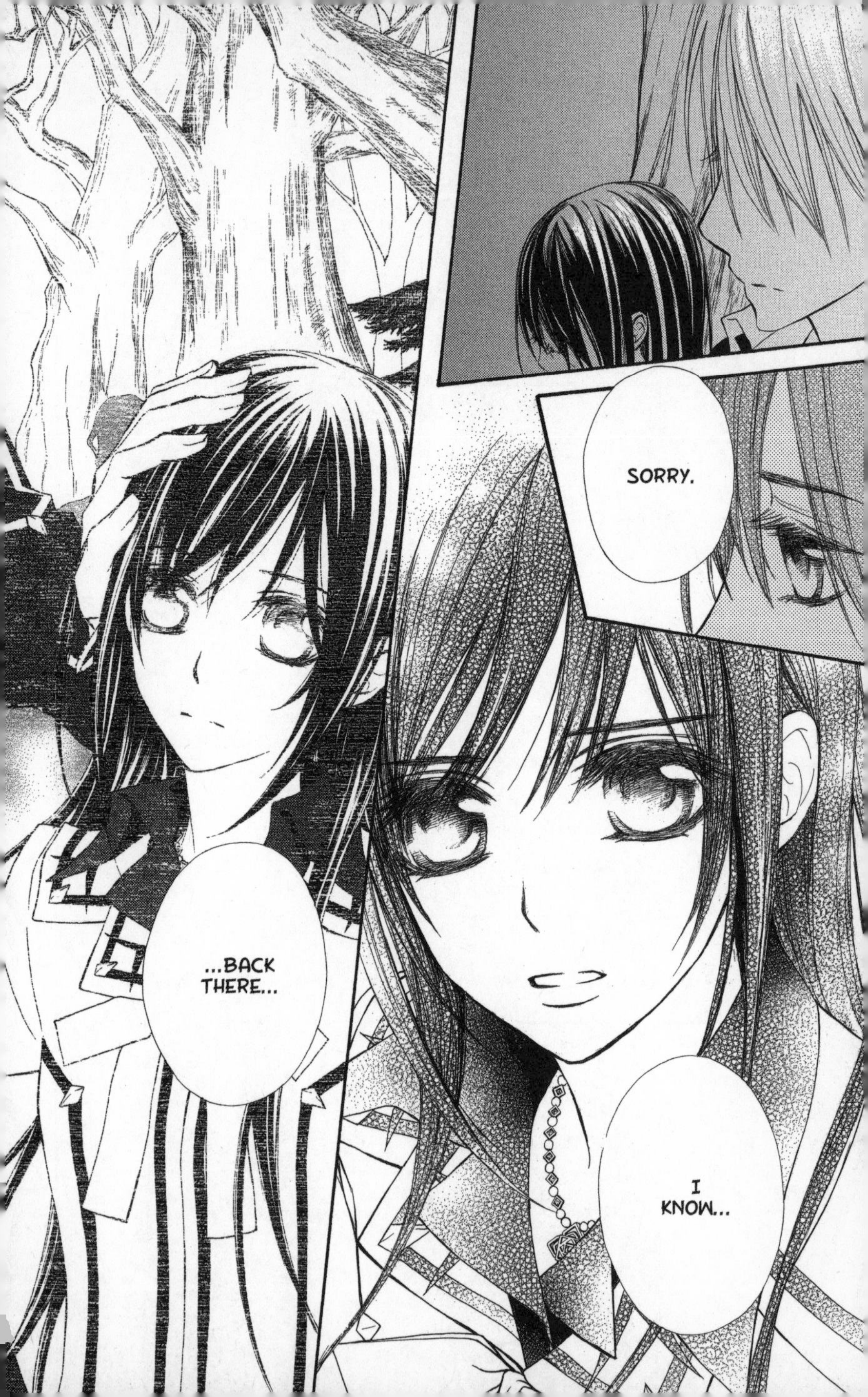
SORRY.
...BACK THERE...
I KNOW...

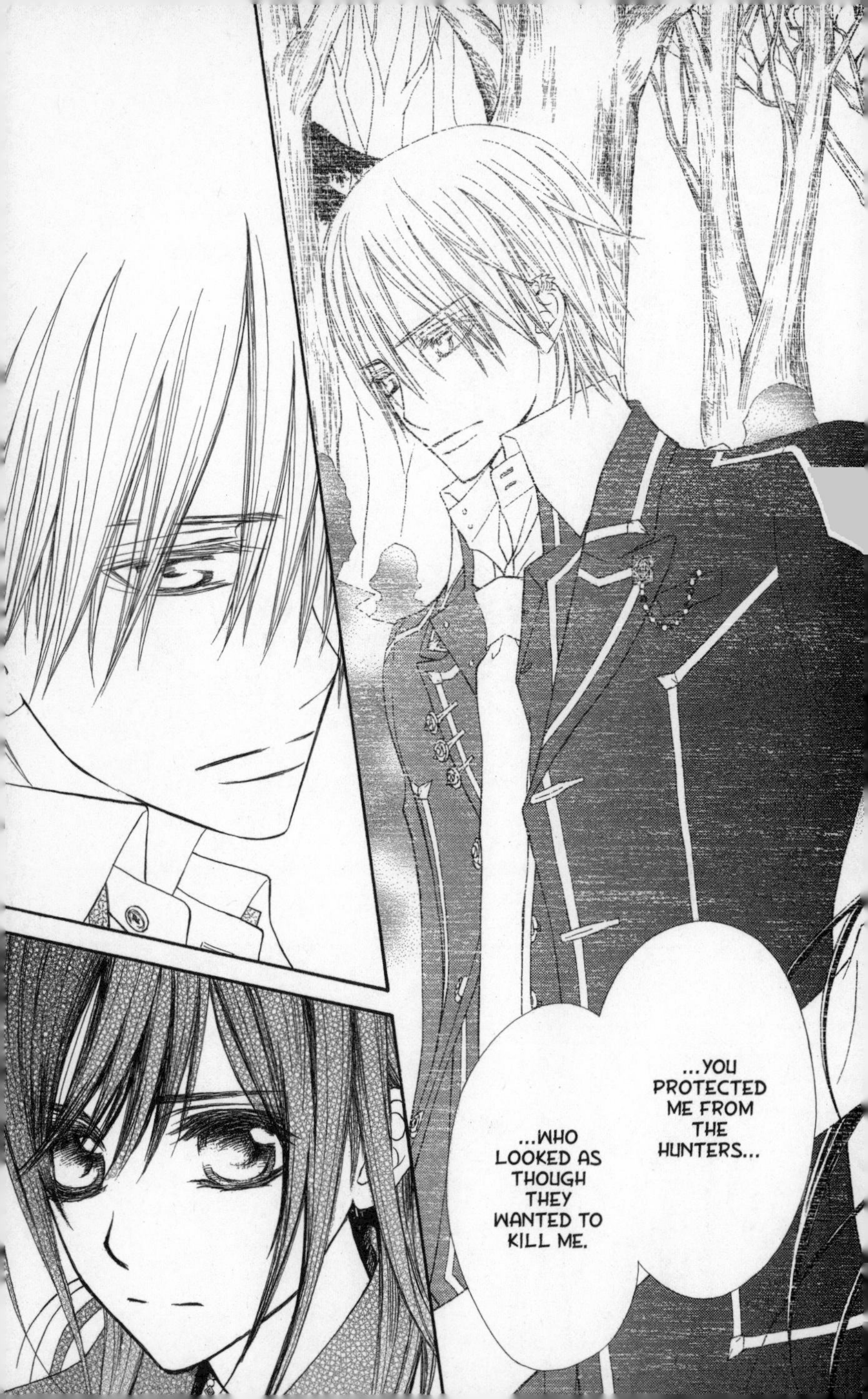
...YOU PROTECTED ME FROM THE HUNTERS...
...WHO LOOKED AS THOUGH THEY WANTED TO KILL ME.

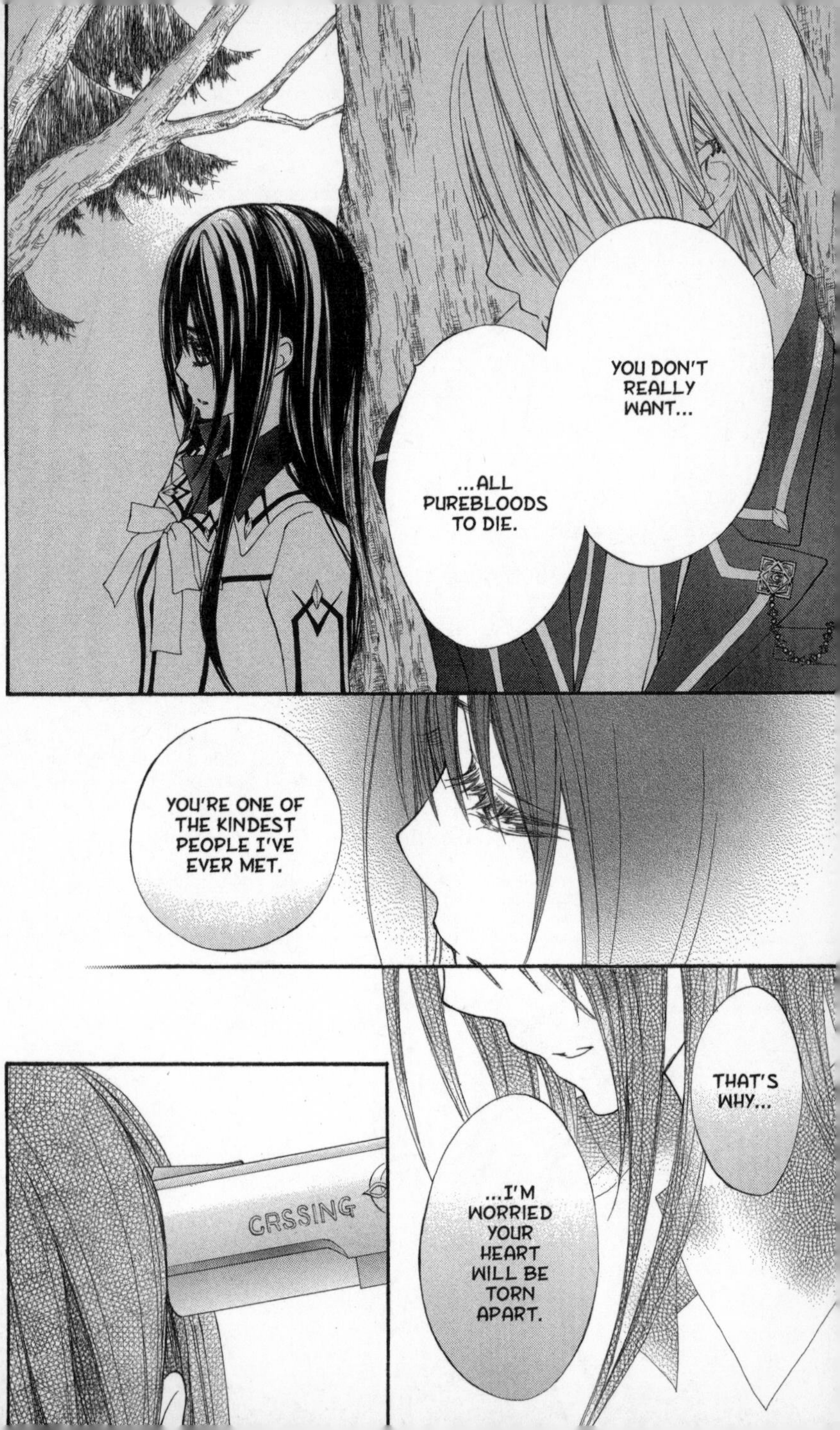
YOU DON'T REALLY WANT...
...ALL PUREBLOODS TO DIE.
YOU'RE ONE OF THE KINDEST PEOPLE I'VE EVER MET.
THAT'S WHY...
...I'M WORRIED YOUR HEART WILL BE TORN APART.
CRSSING

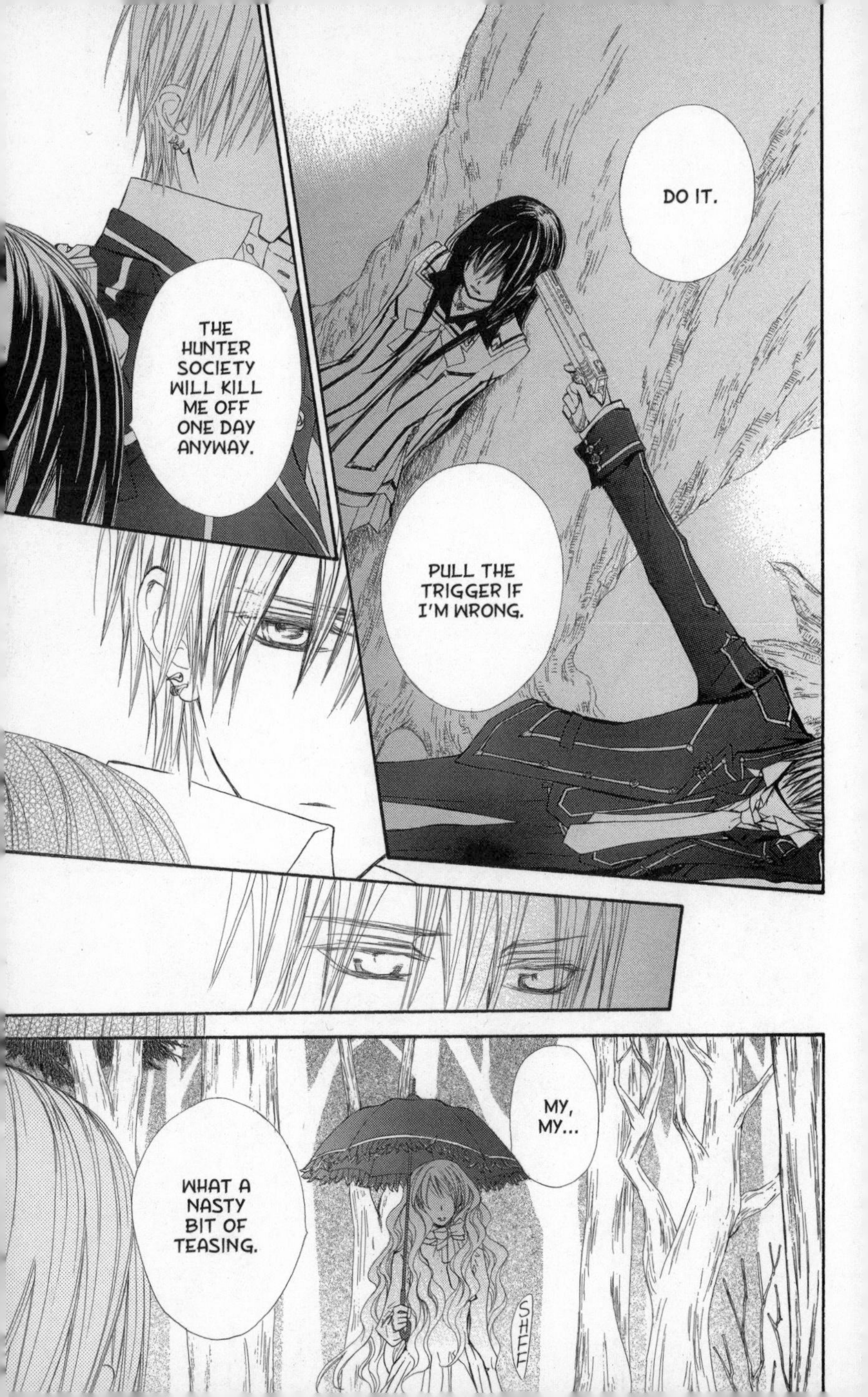
DO IT.
PULL THE TRIGGER IF I'M WRONG.
THE HUNTER SOCIETY WILL KILL ME OFF ONE DAY ANYWAY.
MY, MY...
WHAT A NASTY BIT OF TEASING.
SHFF

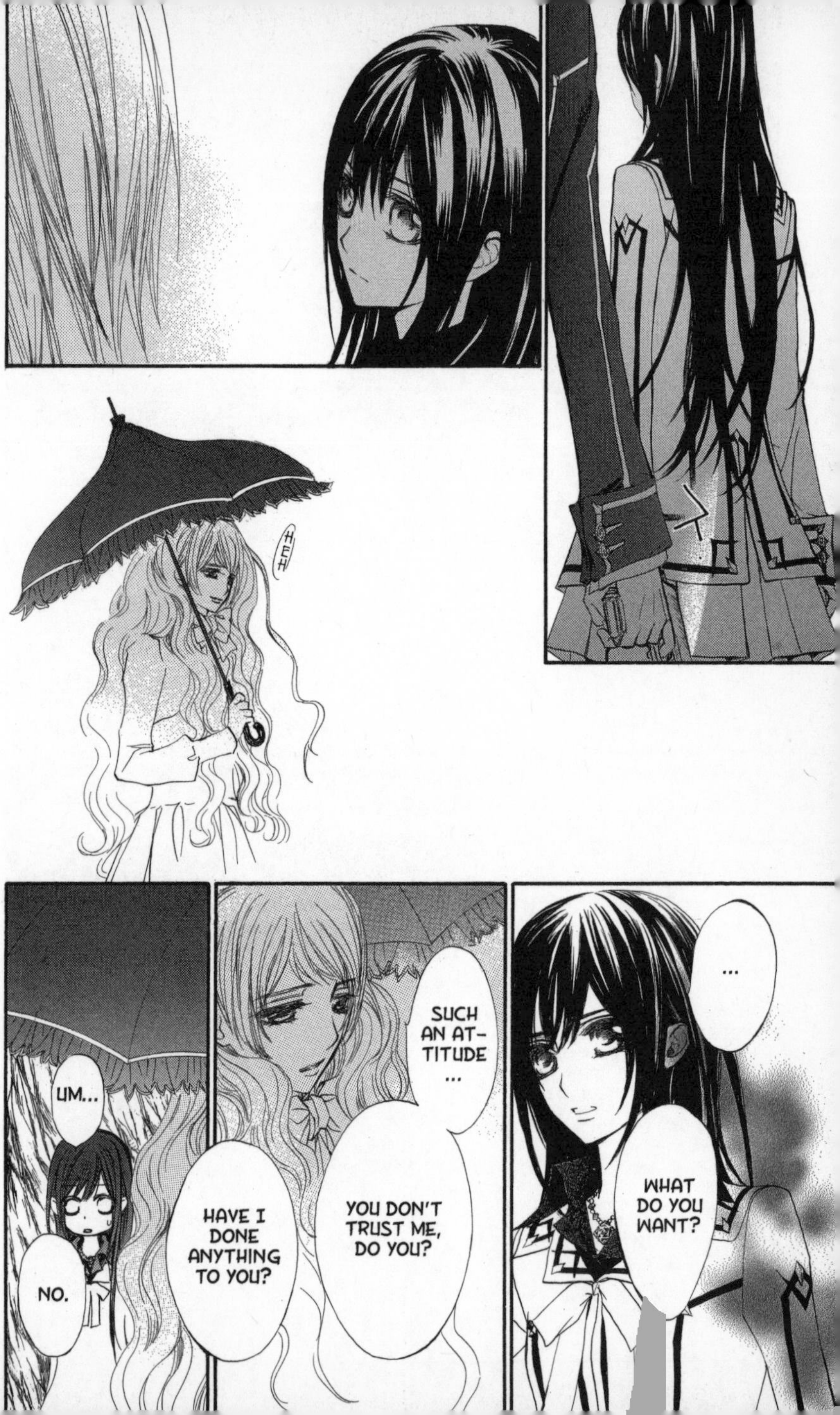
HEH
...
WHAT DO YOU WANT?
SUCH AN AT-TITUDE ...
YOU DON'T TRUST ME, DO YOU?
HAVE I DONE ANYTHING TO YOU?
UM...
NO.

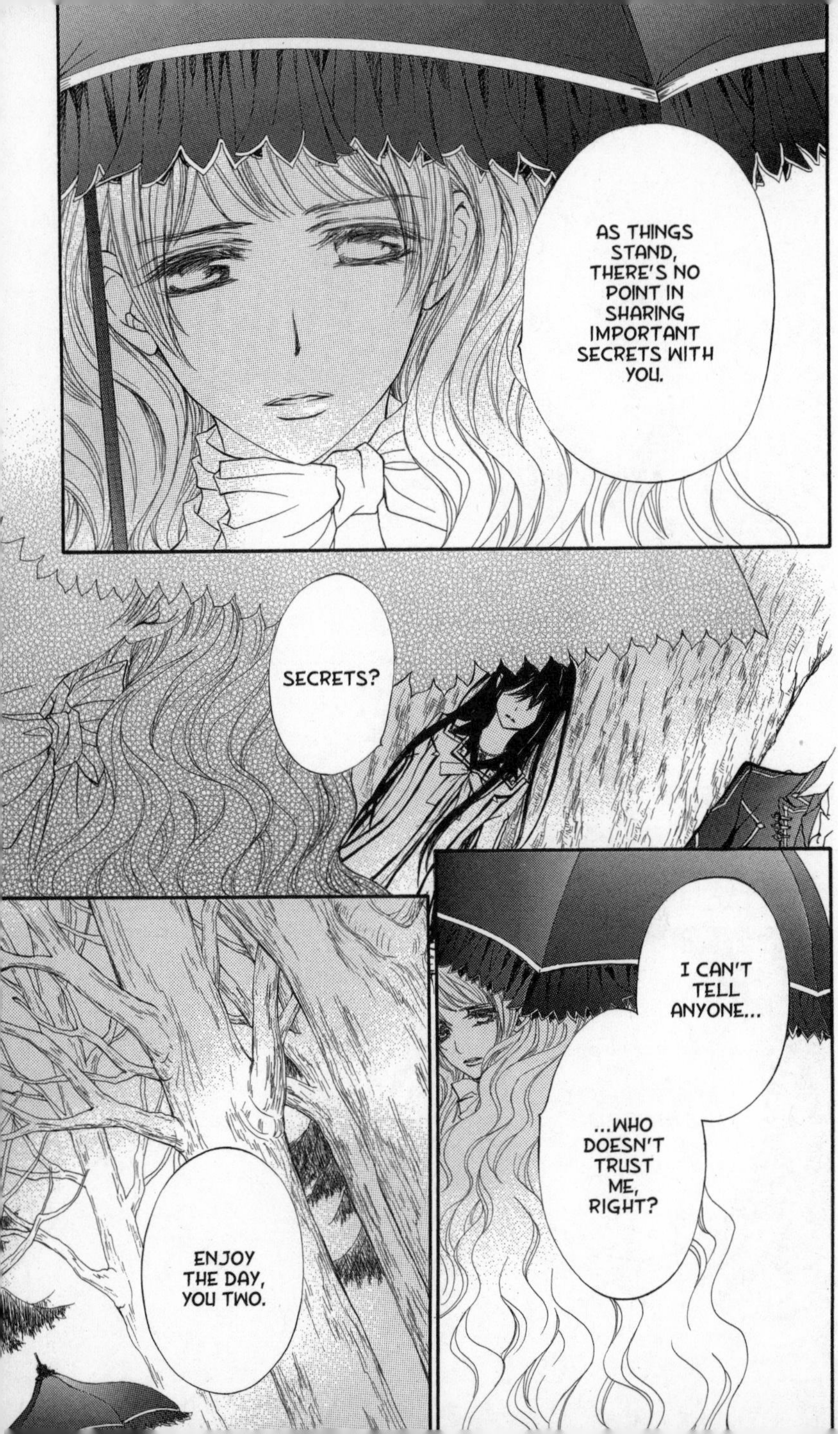
AS THINGS STAND, THERE'S NO POINT IN SHARING IMPORTANT SECRETS WITH YOU.
SECRETS?
I CAN'T TELL ANYONE...
...WHO DOESN'T TRUST ME, RIGHT?
ENJOY THE DAY, YOU TWO.

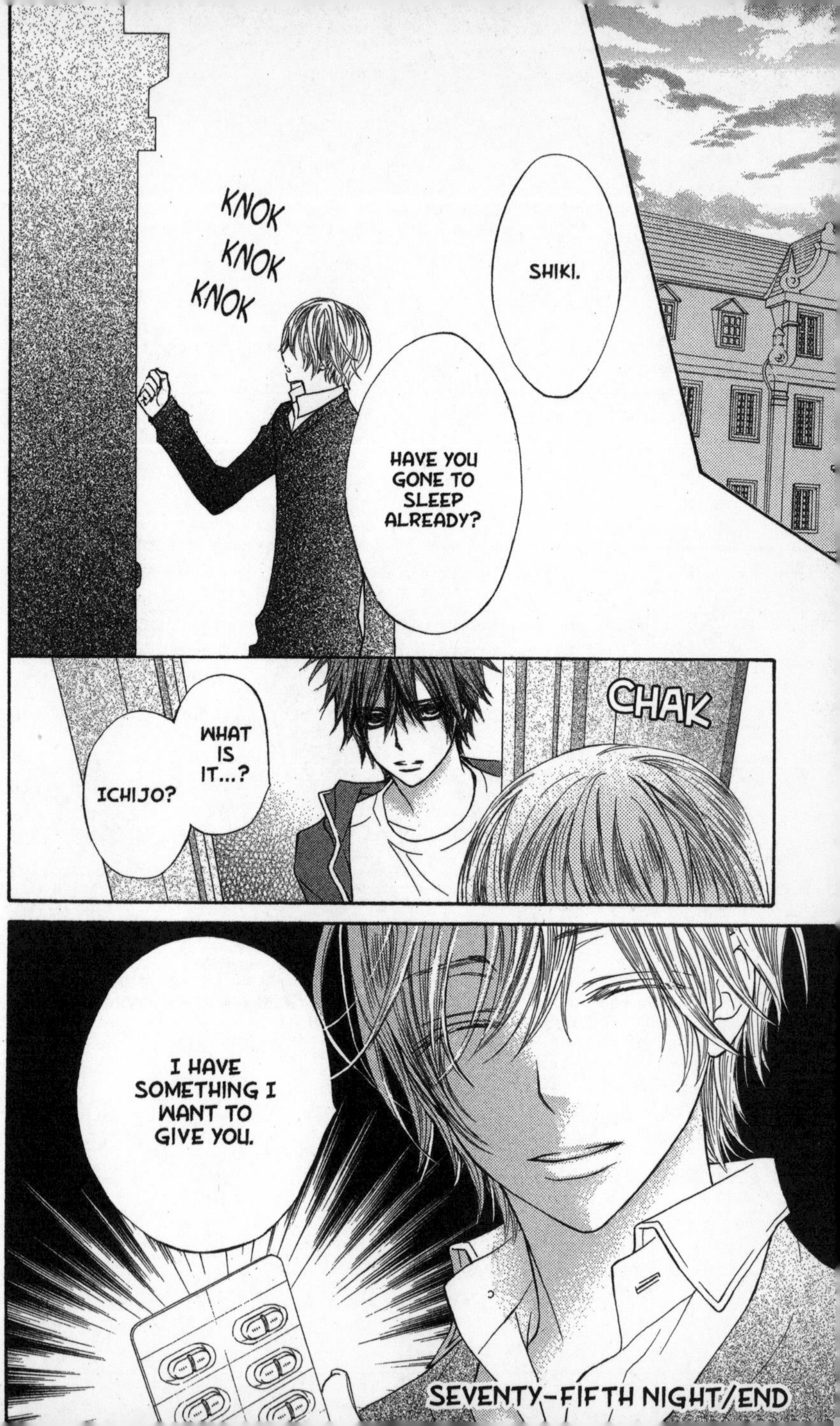
SHIKI.
HAVE YOU GONE TO SLEEP ALREADY?
KNOK KNOK KNOK
CHAK
WHAT IS IT...? ICHIJO?
I HAVE SOMETHING I WANT TO GIVE YOU.
SEVENTY-FIFTH NIGHT/END

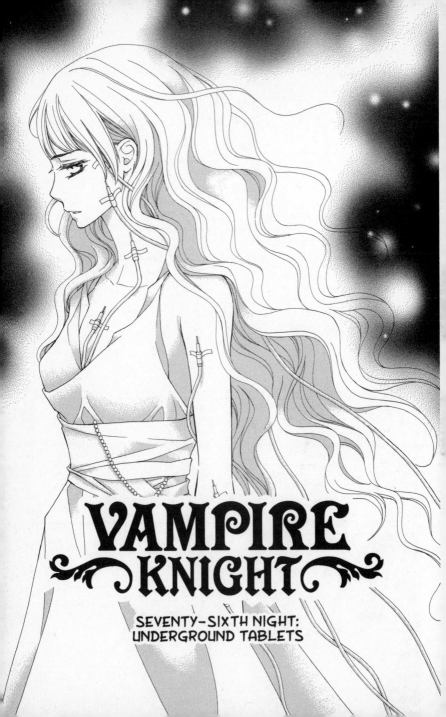

VAMPIRE KNIGHT

SEVENTY-SIXTH NIGHT: UNDERGROUND TABLETS

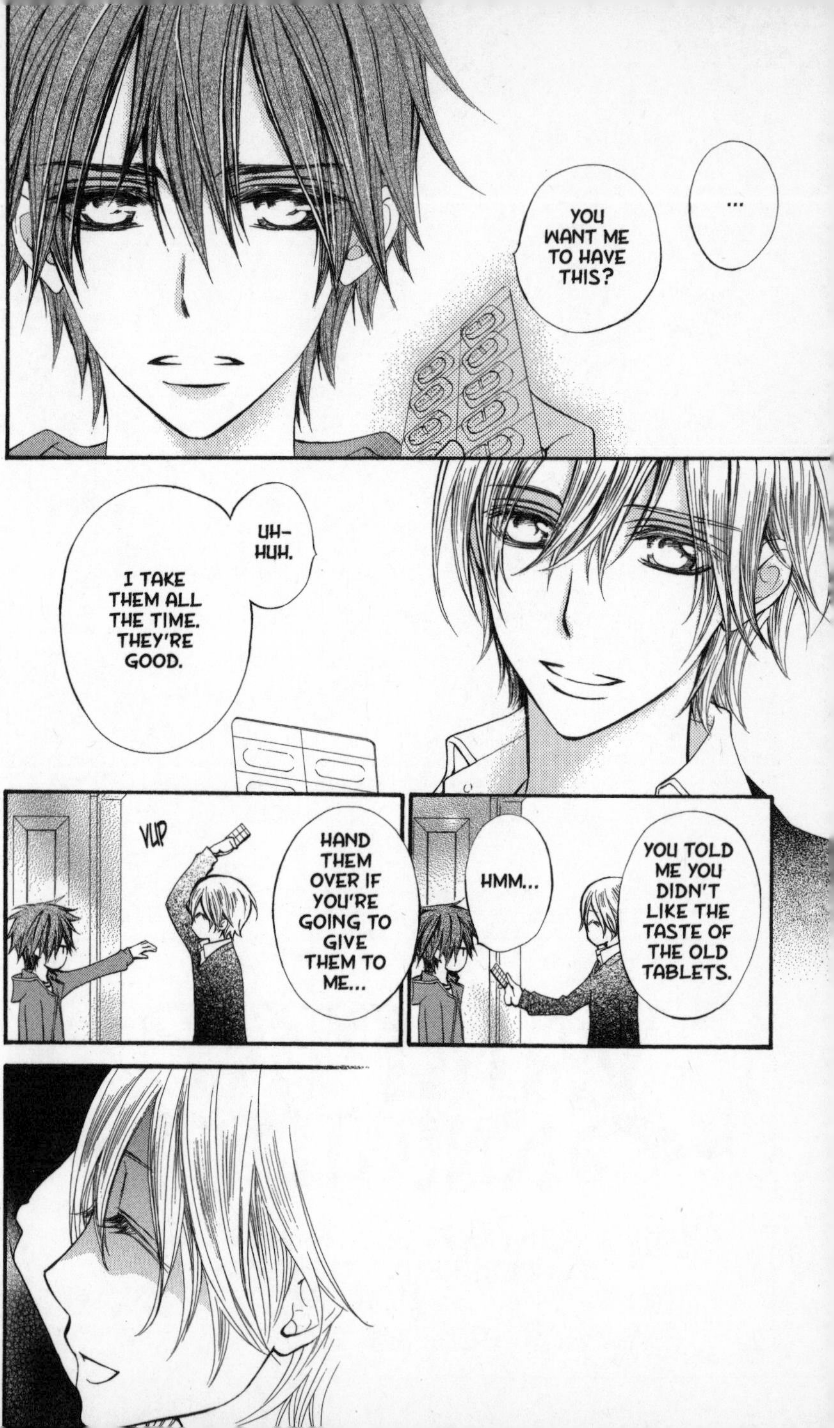
...
YOU WANT ME TO HAVE THIS?
UH-HUH.
I TAKE THEM ALL THE TIME. THEY'RE GOOD.
YOU TOLD ME YOU DIDN'T LIKE THE TASTE OF THE OLD TABLETS.
HMM...
HAND THEM OVER IF YOU'RE GOING TO GIVE THEM TO ME...
VUP

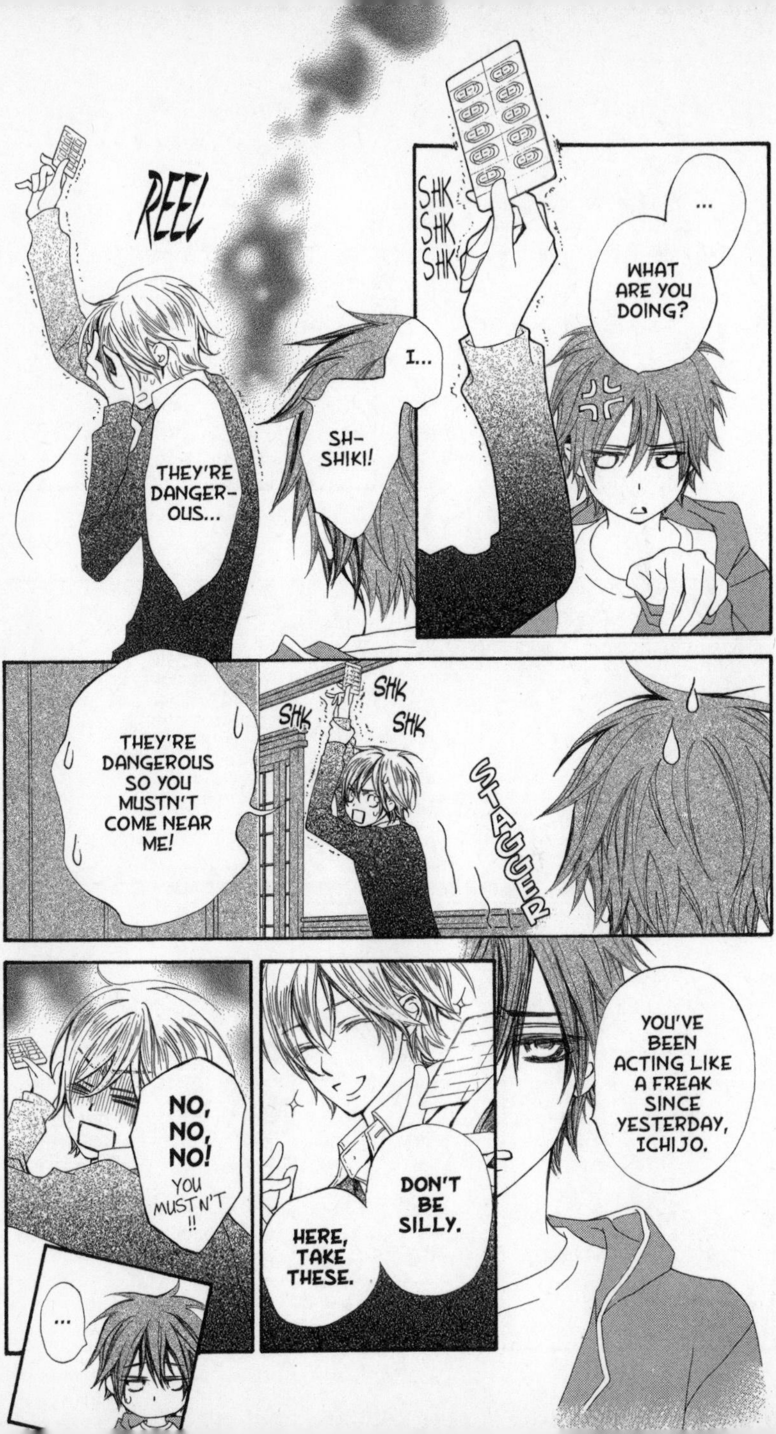
SHK SHK SHK
...
WHAT ARE YOU DOING?
I...
SH-SHIKI!
REEL
THEY'RE DANGEROUS...
STAGGER
SHK SHK SHK
THEY'RE DANGEROUS SO YOU MUSTN'T COME NEAR ME!
YOU'VE BEEN ACTING LIKE A FREAK SINCE YESTERDAY, ICHIJO.
DON'T BE SILLY.
HERE, TAKE THESE.
NO, NO, NO!
YOU MUSTN'T !!
...

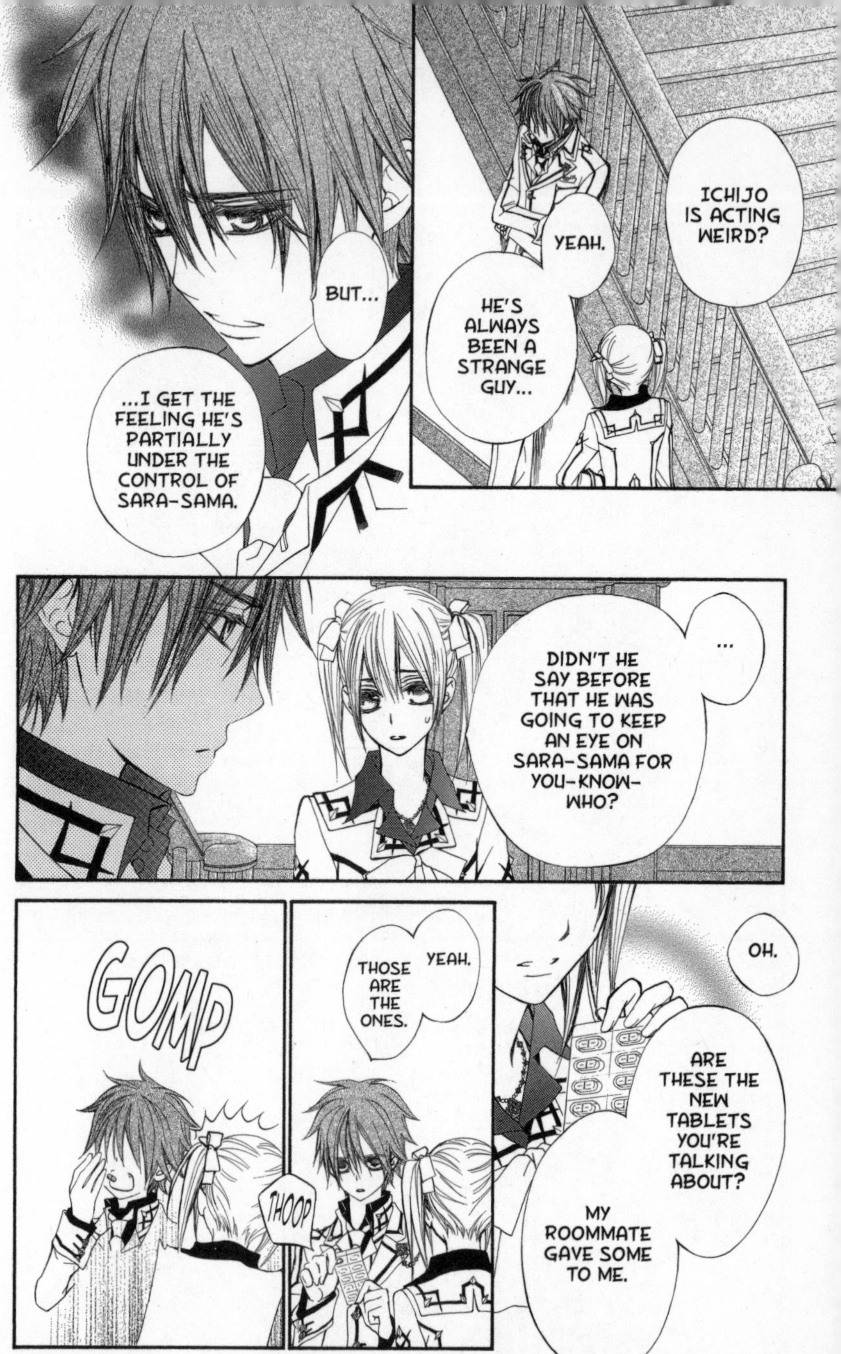
ICHIJO IS ACTING WEIRD?
YEAH.
HE'S ALWAYS BEEN A STRANGE GUY...
BUT...
...I GET THE FEELING HE'S PARTIALLY UNDER THE CONTROL OF SARA-SAMA.
...
DIDN'T HE SAY BEFORE THAT HE WAS GOING TO KEEP AN EYE ON SARA-SAMA FOR YOU-KNOW-WHO?
OH.
ARE THESE THE NEW TABLETS YOU'RE TALKING ABOUT?
MY ROOMMATE GAVE SOME TO ME.
YEAH.
THOSE ARE THE ONES.
THOOP
GOMP

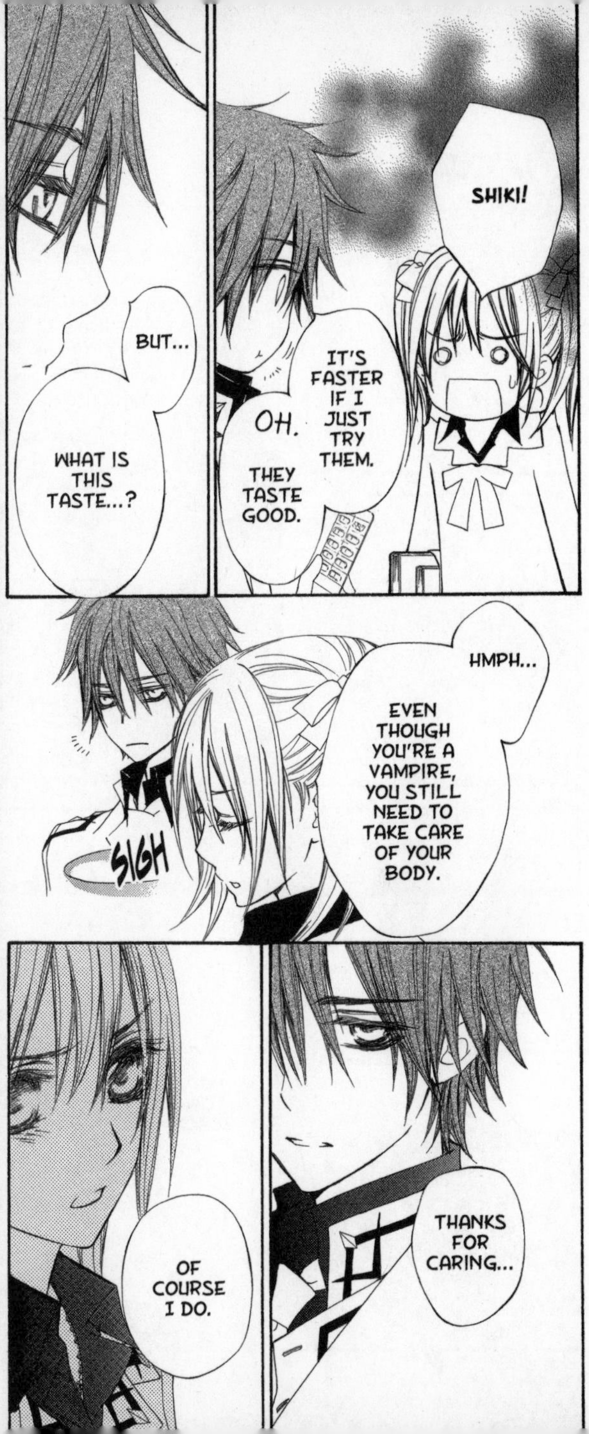
SHIKI!
IT'S FASTER IF I JUST TRY THEM.
OH.
THEY TASTE GOOD.
BUT...
WHAT IS THIS TASTE...?
HMPH...
EVEN THOUGH YOU'RE A VAMPIRE, YOU STILL NEED TO TAKE CARE OF YOUR BODY.
SIGH
THANKS FOR CARING...
OF COURSE I DO.

III

Did you notice? This cover illustration and the chapter title page illustration for the April 2010 issue of *LaLa*? (It was originally one of the choices for this cover...) I changed the color of the main outline. I used an ink that is a mixture of my two usual colors with water. I wish there were more variety to my color illustrations... ✿

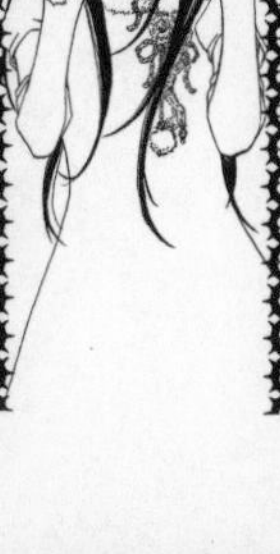

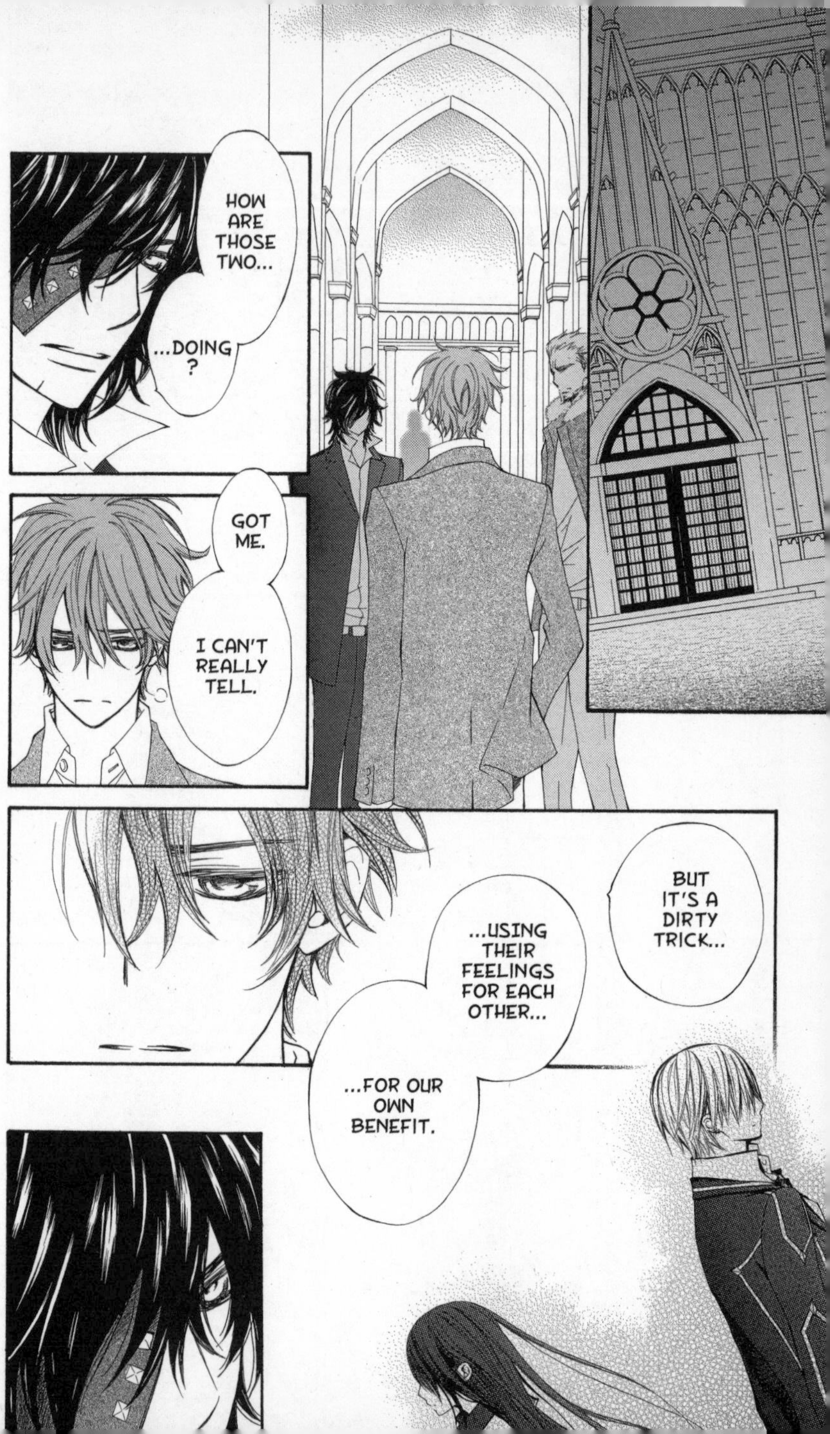
HOW ARE THOSE TWO...
...DOING?
GOT ME.
I CAN'T REALLY TELL.
BUT IT'S A DIRTY TRICK...
...USING THEIR FEELINGS FOR EACH OTHER...
...FOR OUR OWN BENEFIT.

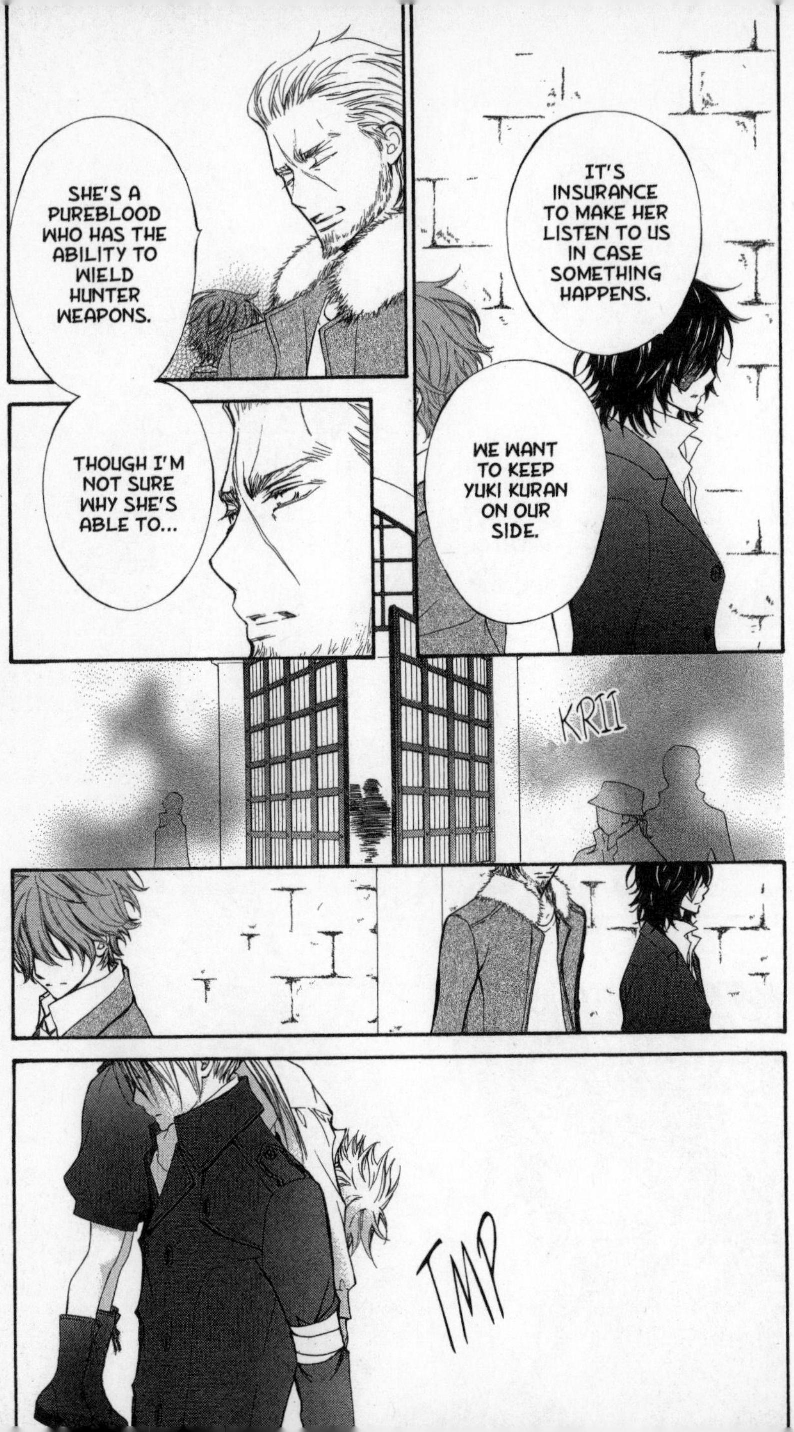
IT'S INSURANCE TO MAKE HER LISTEN TO US IN CASE SOMETHING HAPPENS.
WE WANT TO KEEP YUKI KURAN ON OUR SIDE.
SHE'S A PUREBLOOD WHO HAS THE ABILITY TO WIELD HUNTER WEAPONS.
THOUGH I'M NOT SURE WHY SHE'S ABLE TO...
KRII
TMP

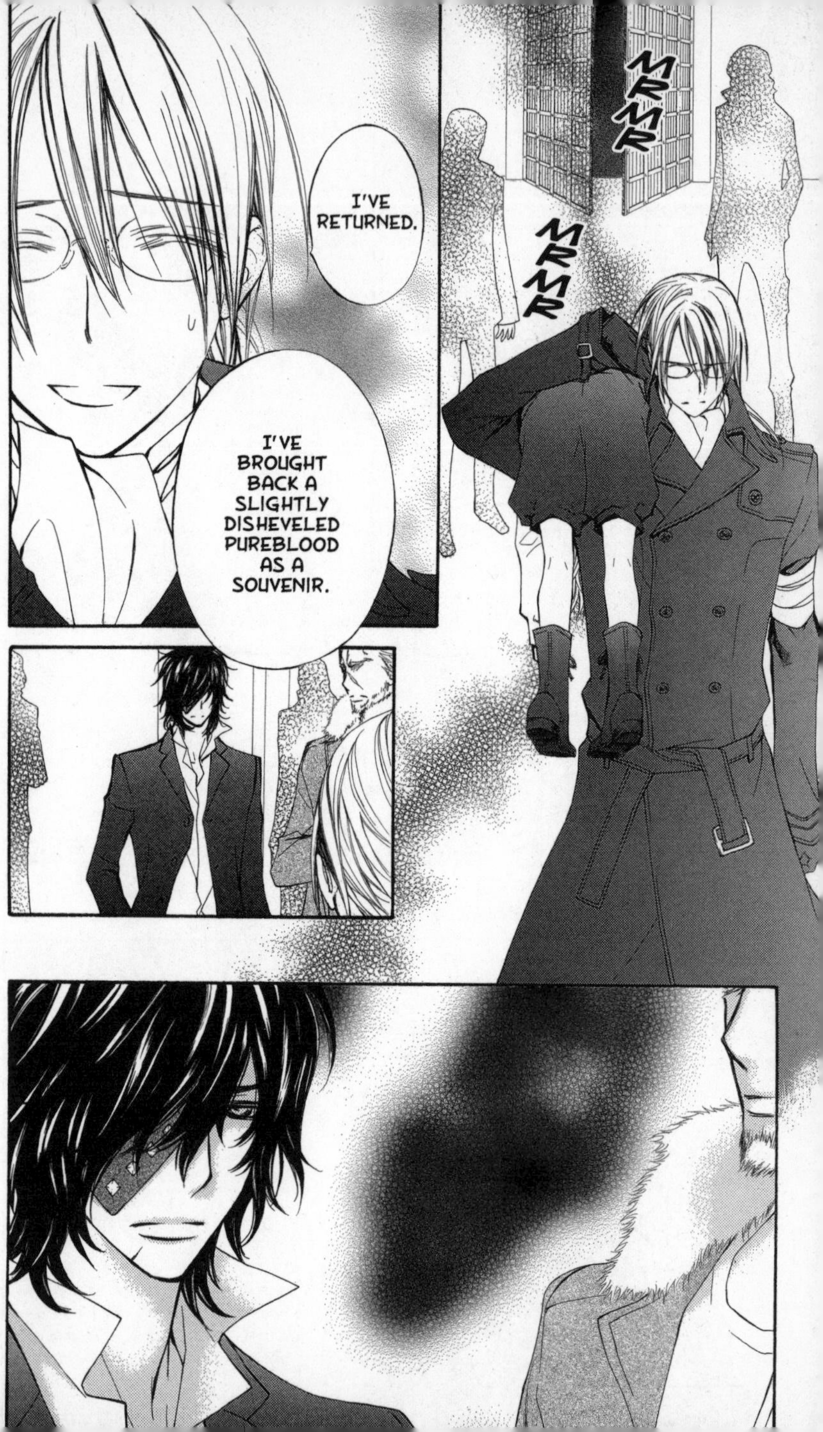
MRMR
MRMR
I'VE RETURNED.
I'VE BROUGHT BACK A SLIGHTLY DISHEVELED PUREBLOOD AS A SOUVENIR.

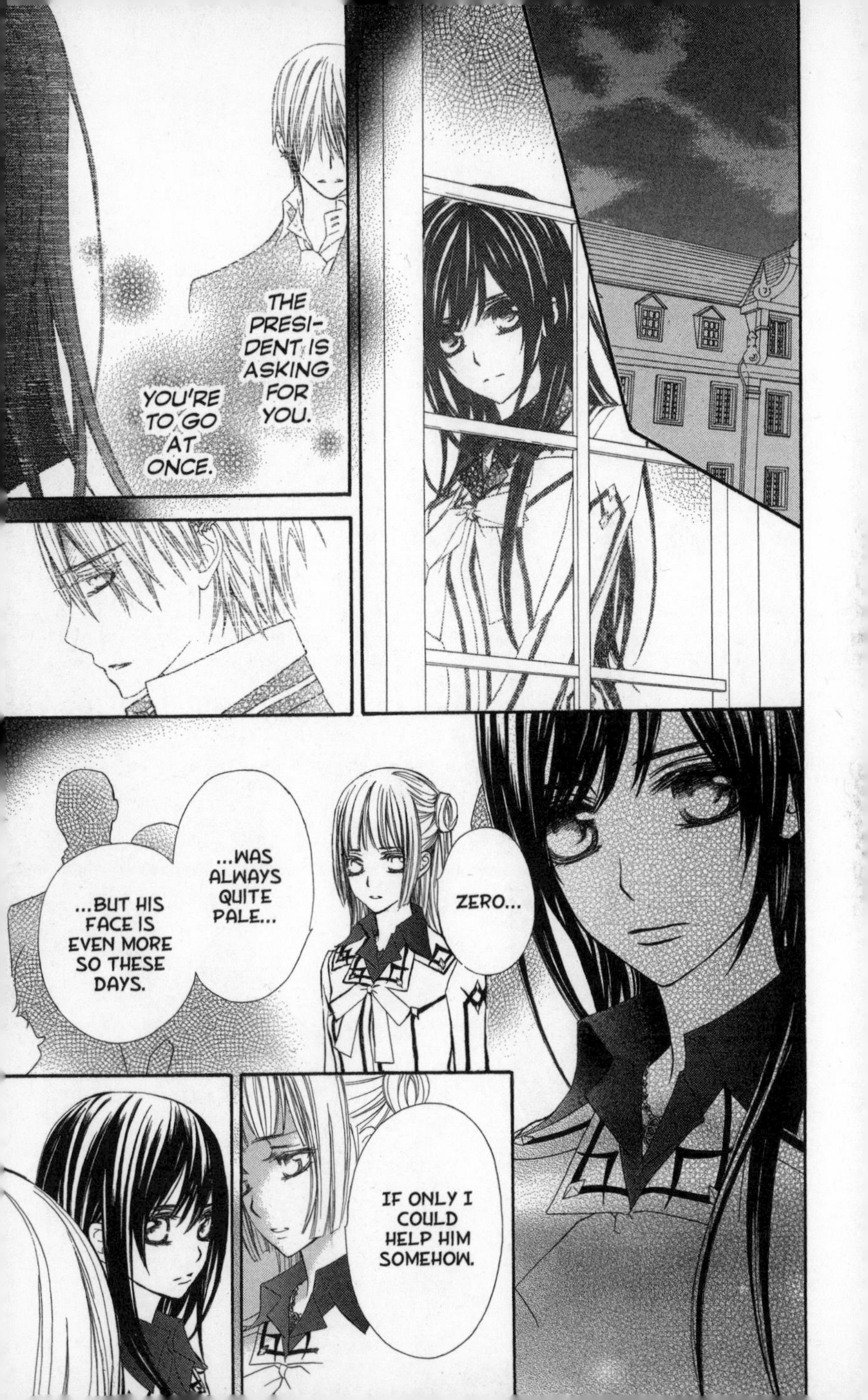
THE PRESIDENT IS ASKING FOR YOU.
YOU'RE TO GO AT ONCE.
ZERO...
...WAS ALWAYS QUITE PALE...
...BUT HIS FACE IS EVEN MORE SO THESE DAYS.
IF ONLY I COULD HELP HIM SOMEHOW.

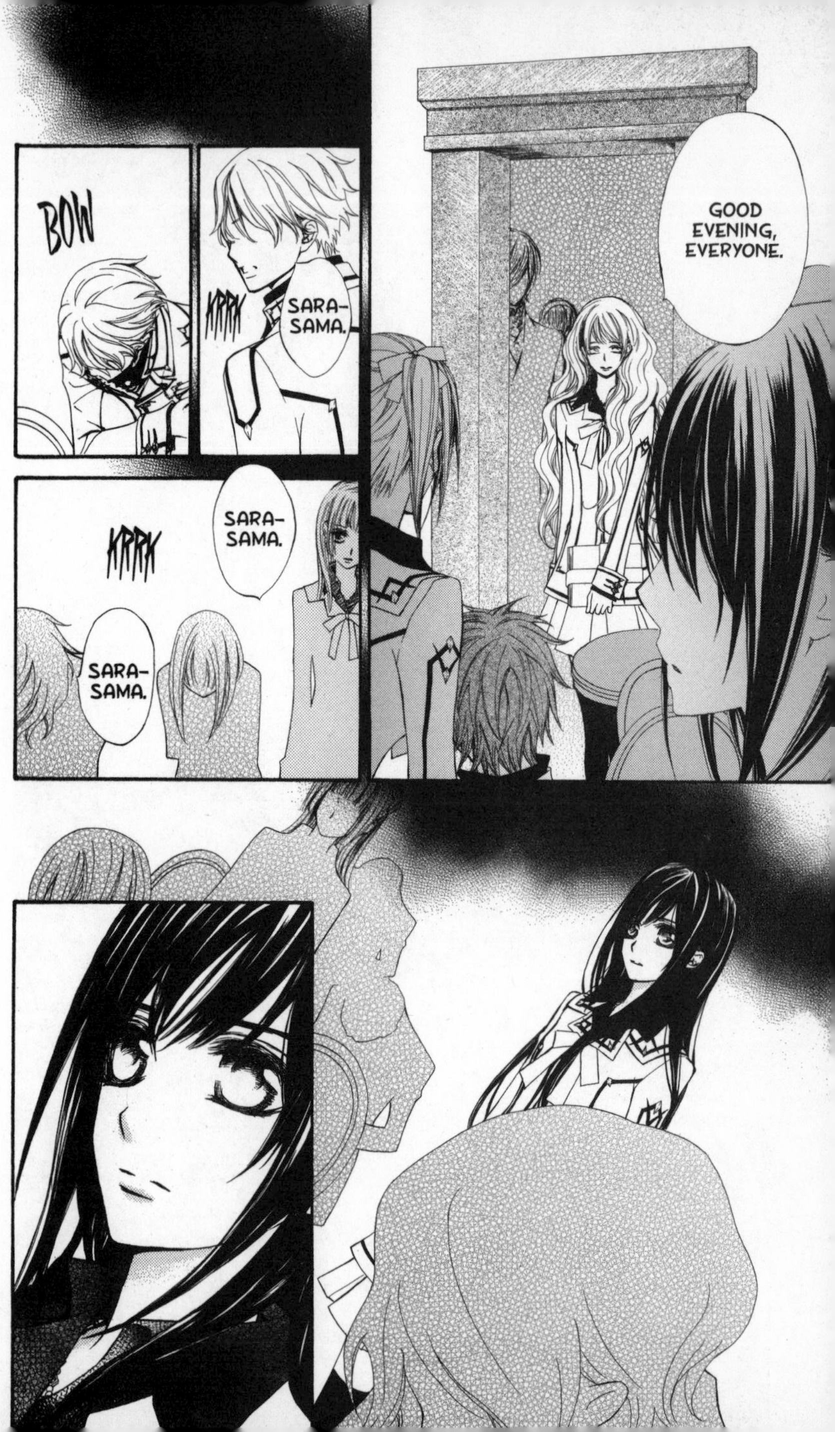
GOOD EVENING, EVERYONE.
KRRK
SARA-SAMA.
BOW
SARA-SAMA.
KRRK
SARA-SAMA.

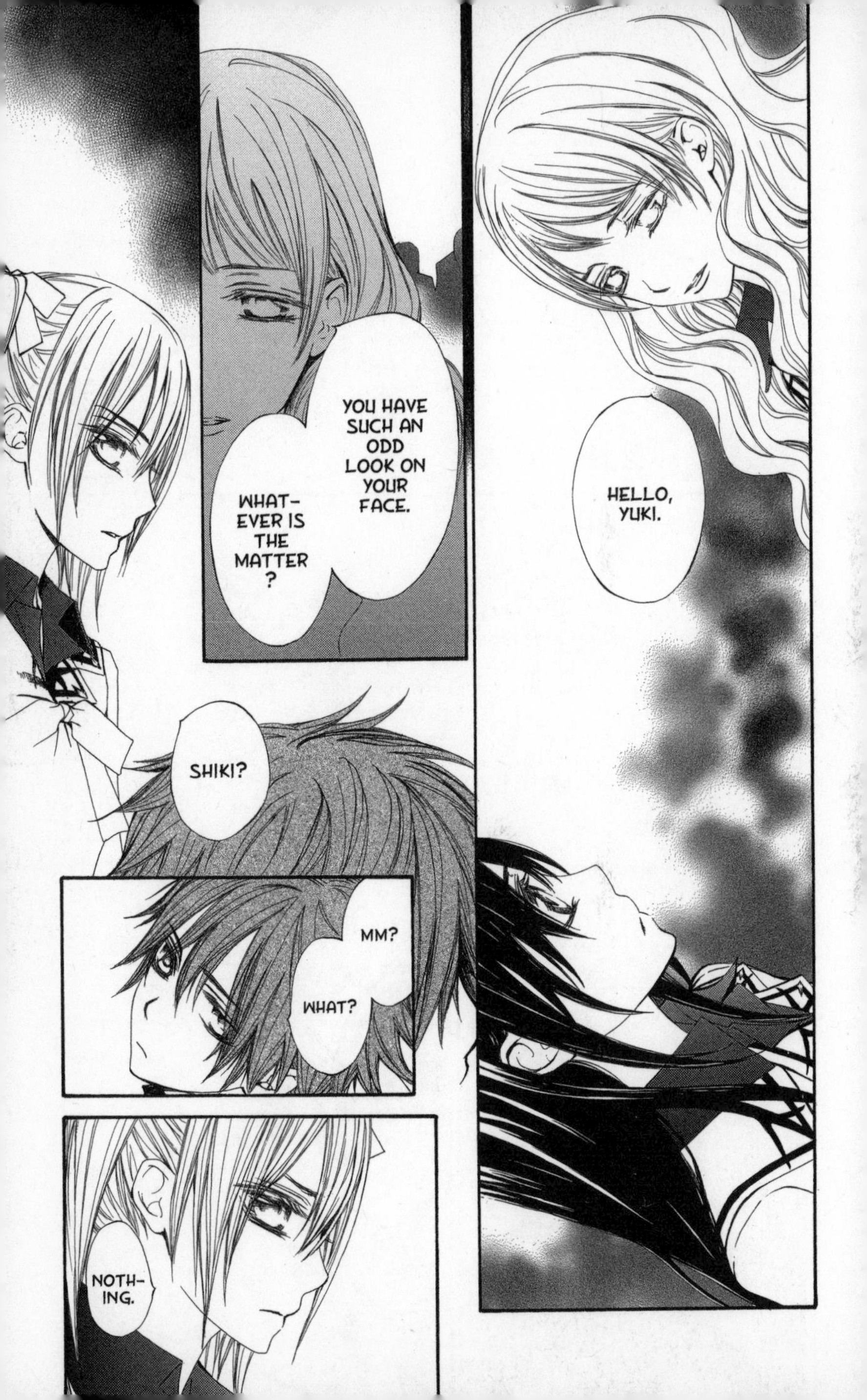
HELLO, YUKI.
YOU HAVE SUCH AN ODD LOOK ON YOUR FACE.
WHAT-EVER IS THE MATTER?
SHIKI?
MM?
WHAT?
NOTH-ING.

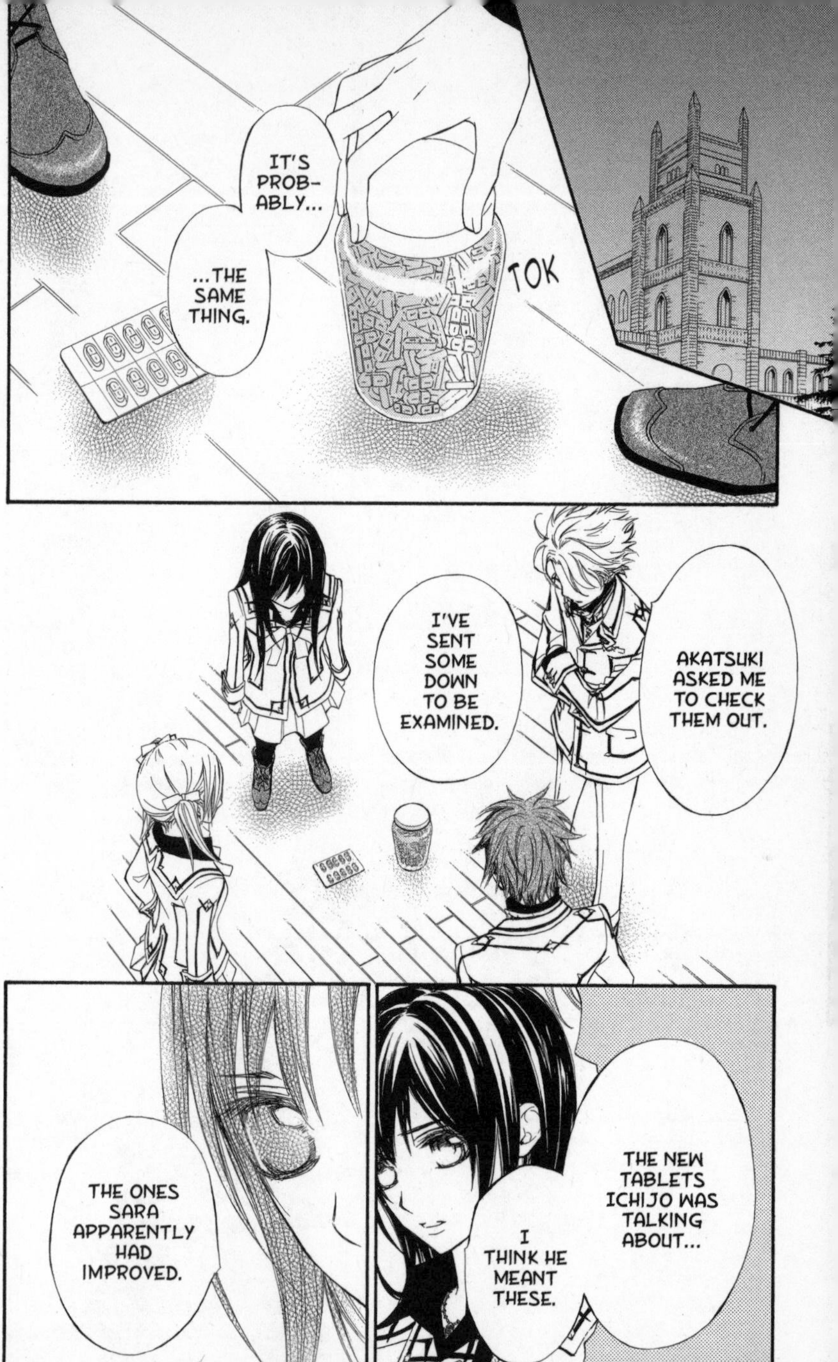
IT'S PROBABLY...
...THE SAME THING.
TOK
AKATSUKI ASKED ME TO CHECK THEM OUT.
I'VE SENT SOME DOWN TO BE EXAMINED.
THE NEW TABLETS ICHIJO WAS TALKING ABOUT...
I THINK HE MEANT THESE.
THE ONES SARA APPARENTLY HAD IMPROVED.

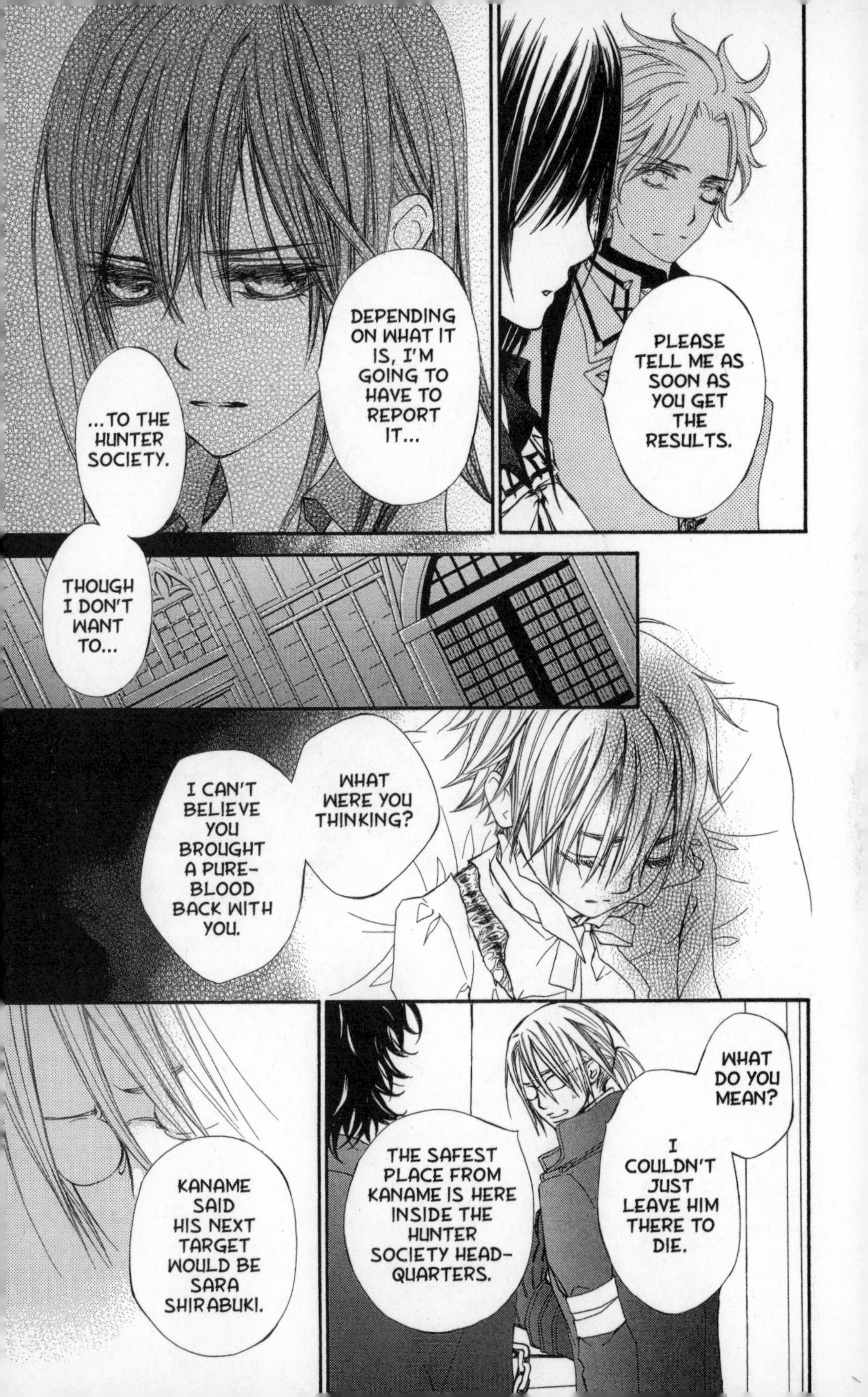
PLEASE TELL ME AS SOON AS YOU GET THE RESULTS.
DEPENDING ON WHAT IT IS, I'M GOING TO HAVE TO REPORT IT...
...TO THE HUNTER SOCIETY.
THOUGH I DON'T WANT TO...
WHAT WERE YOU THINKING?
I CAN'T BELIEVE YOU BROUGHT A PURE-BLOOD BACK WITH YOU.
WHAT DO YOU MEAN?
I COULDN'T JUST LEAVE HIM THERE TO DIE.
THE SAFEST PLACE FROM KANAME IS HERE INSIDE THE HUNTER SOCIETY HEAD-QUARTERS.
KANAME SAID HIS NEXT TARGET WOULD BE SARA SHIRABUKI.

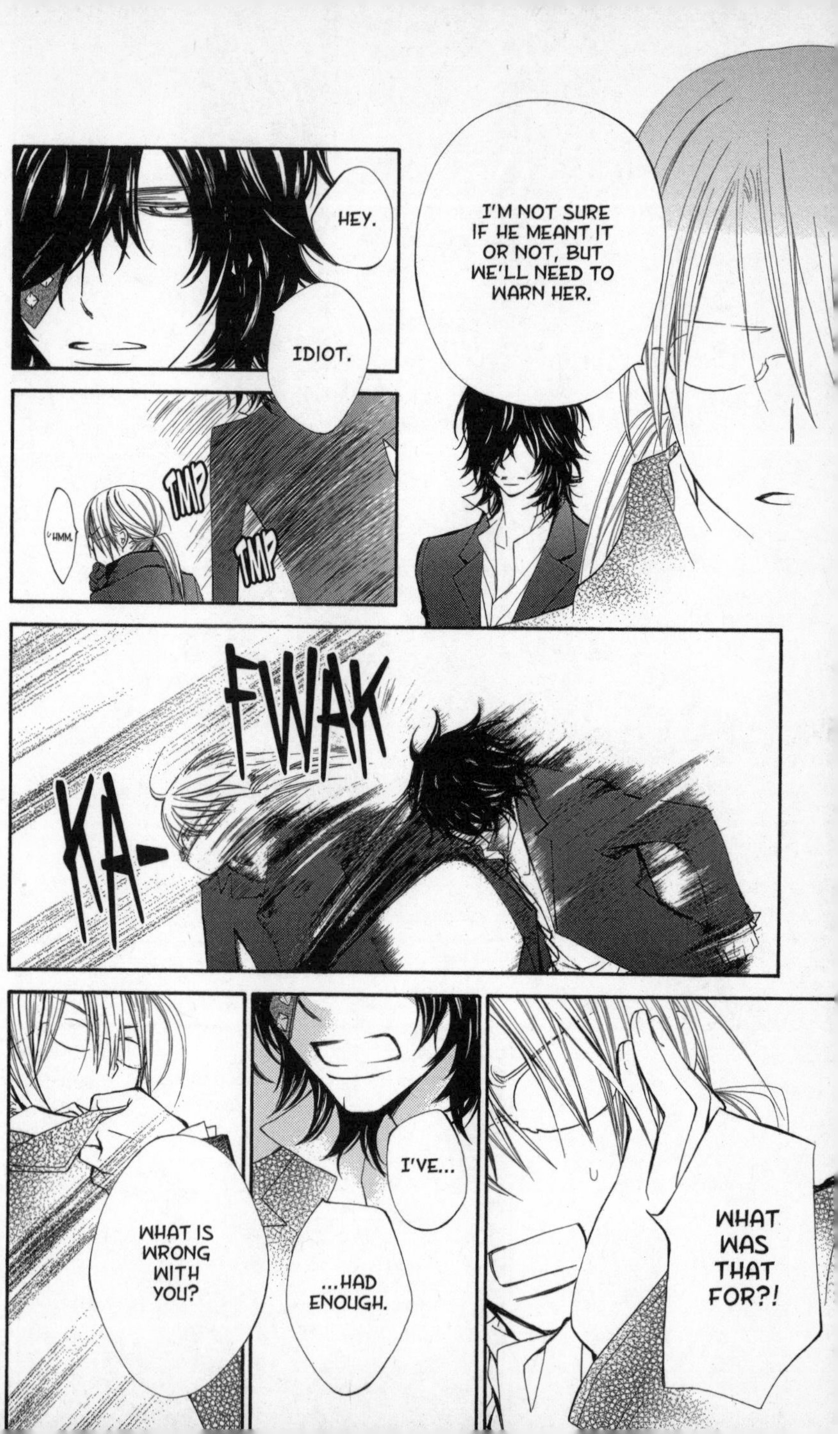
I'M NOT SURE IF HE MEANT IT OR NOT, BUT WE'LL NEED TO WARN HER.
HEY.
IDIOT.
TMP
TMP
HMM.
KA-
FWAK
WHAT WAS THAT FOR?!
I'VE...
...HAD ENOUGH.
WHAT IS WRONG WITH YOU?

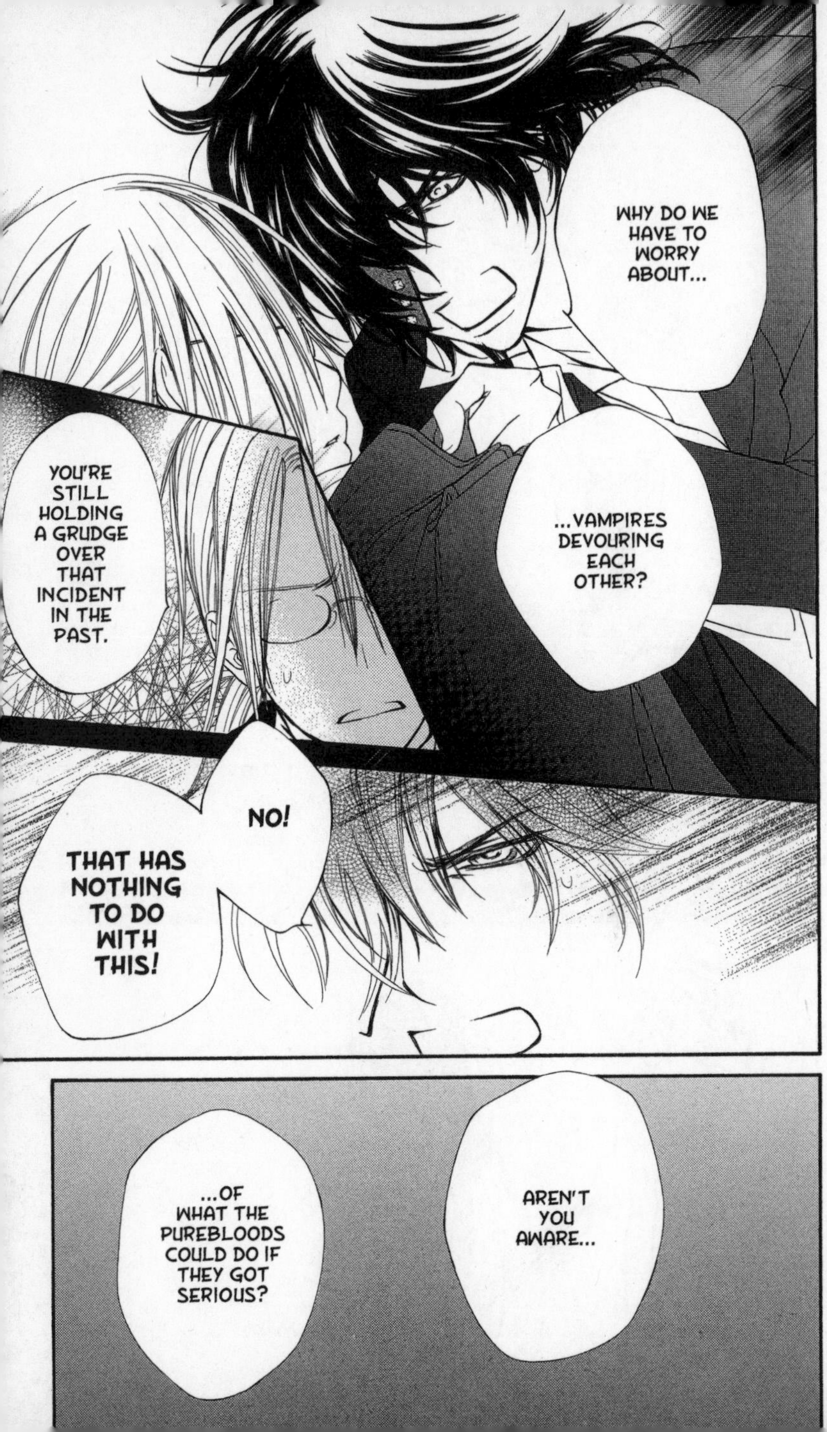
WHY DO WE HAVE TO WORRY ABOUT...
...VAMPIRES DEVOURING EACH OTHER?
YOU'RE STILL HOLDING A GRUDGE OVER THAT INCIDENT IN THE PAST.
NO!
THAT HAS NOTHING TO DO WITH THIS!
AREN'T YOU AWARE...
...OF WHAT THE PUREBLOODS COULD DO IF THEY GOT SERIOUS?

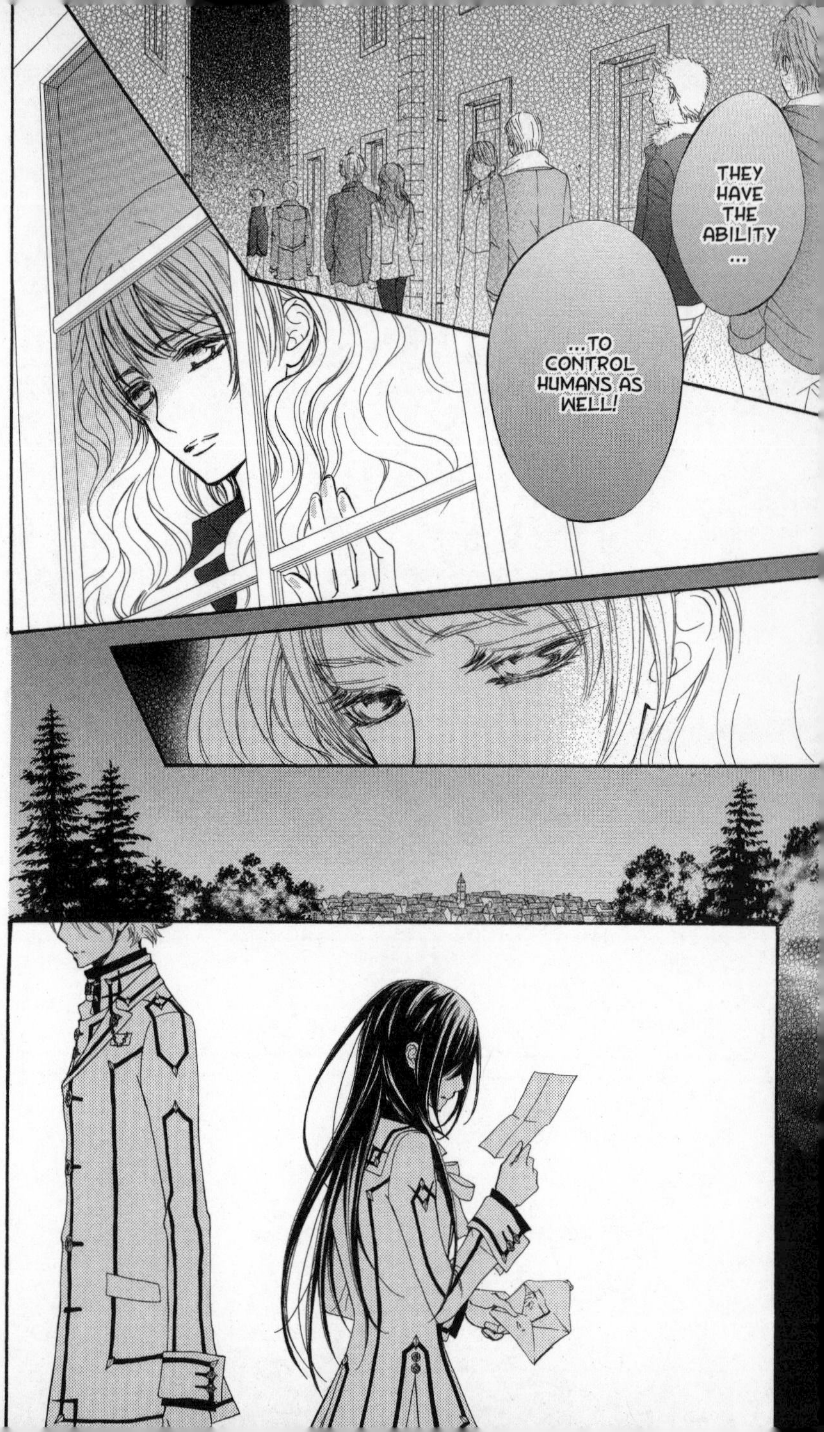
THEY HAVE THE ABILITY ...
...TO CONTROL HUMANS AS WELL!

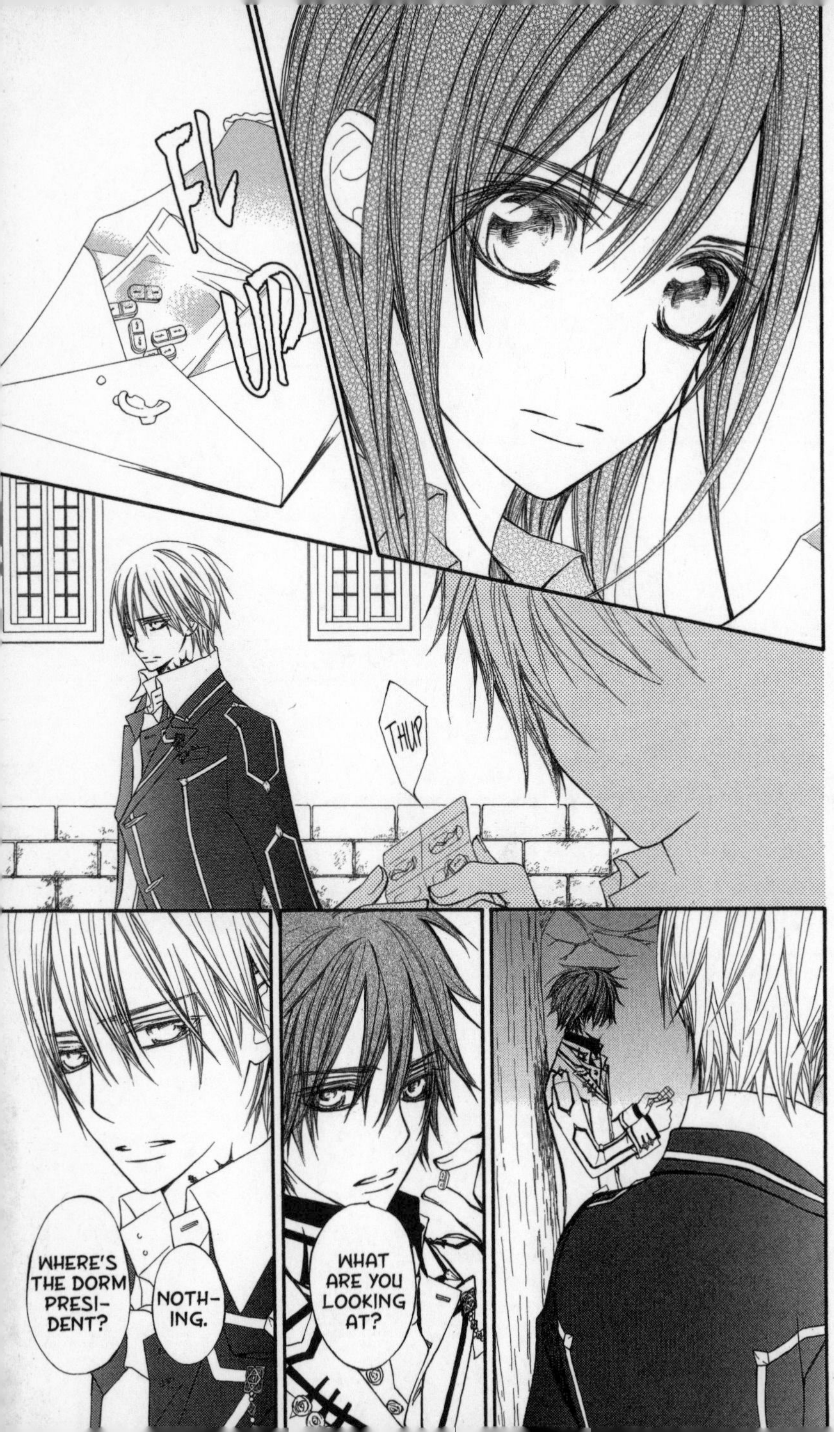
FL UP
THUP
WHAT ARE YOU LOOKING AT?
NOTH- ING.
WHERE'S THE DORM PRESI- DENT?

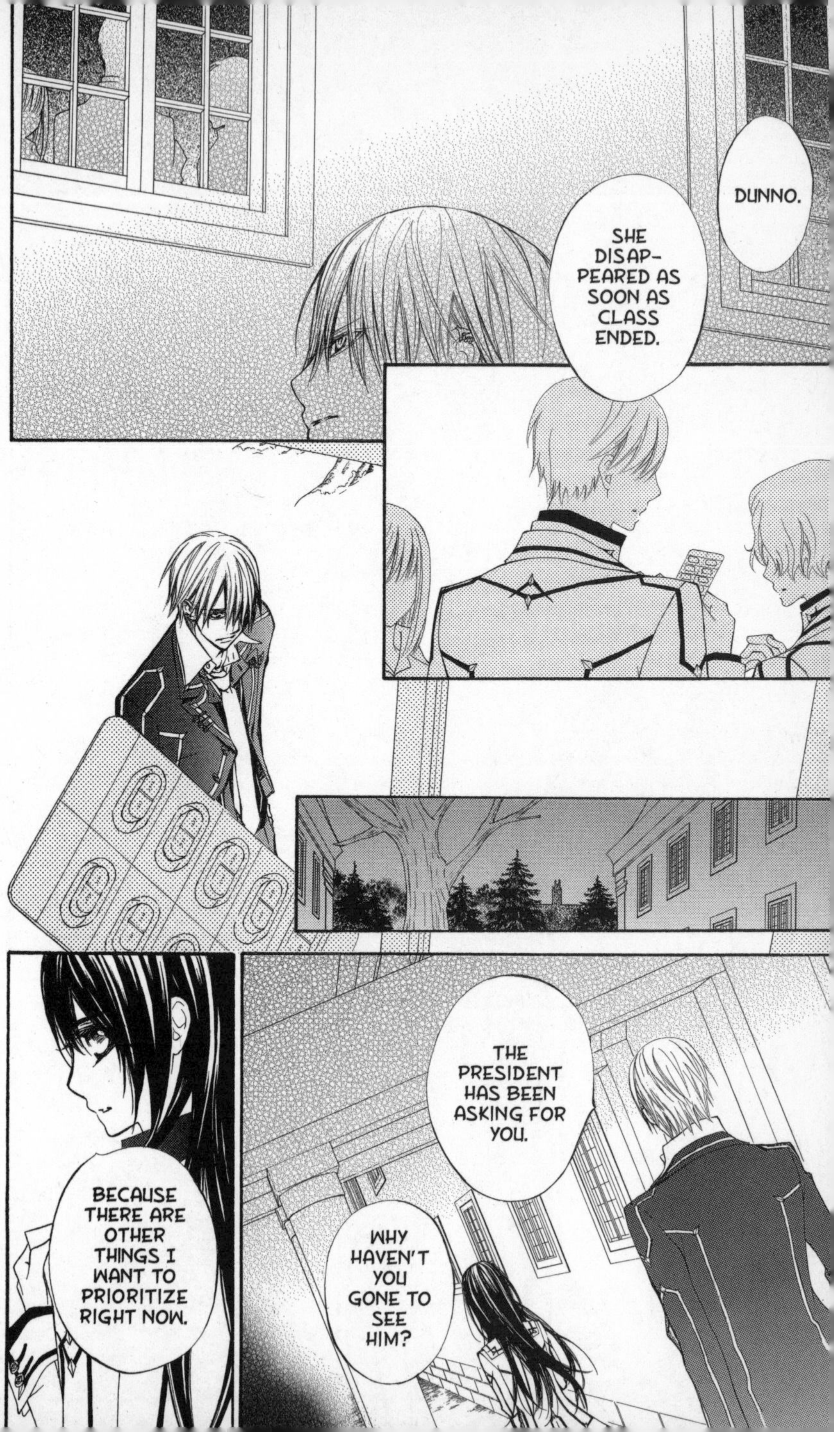
DUNNO.
SHE DISAP-PEARED AS SOON AS CLASS ENDED.
THE PRESIDENT HAS BEEN ASKING FOR YOU.
WHY HAVEN'T YOU GONE TO SEE HIM?
BECAUSE THERE ARE OTHER THINGS I WANT TO PRIORITIZE RIGHT NOW.

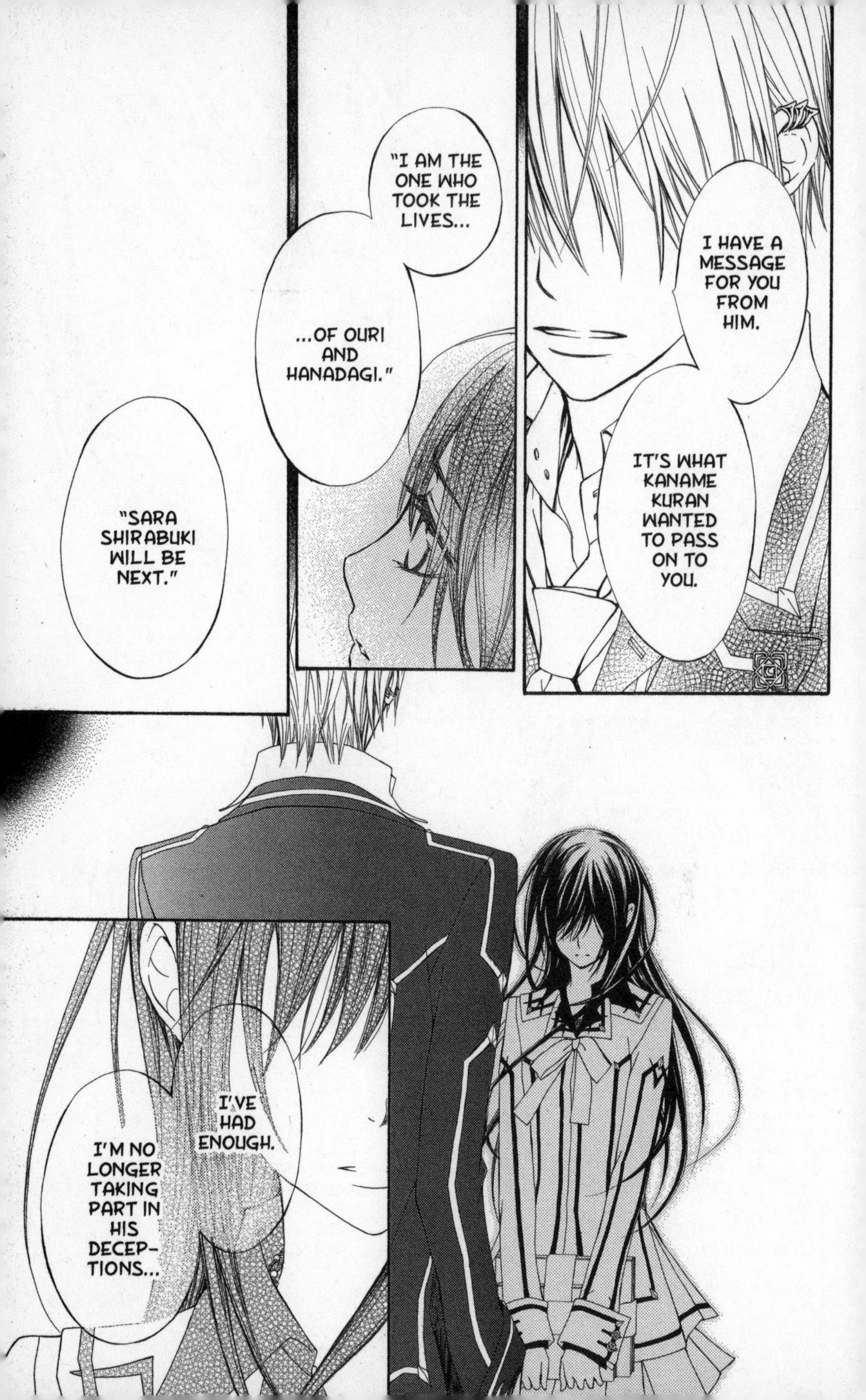
I HAVE A MESSAGE FOR YOU FROM HIM.
IT'S WHAT KANAME KURAN WANTED TO PASS ON TO YOU.
"I AM THE ONE WHO TOOK THE LIVES...
...OF OURI AND HANADAGI."
"SARA SHIRABUKI WILL BE NEXT."
I'VE HAD ENOUGH.
I'M NO LONGER TAKING PART IN HIS DECEP-TIONS...

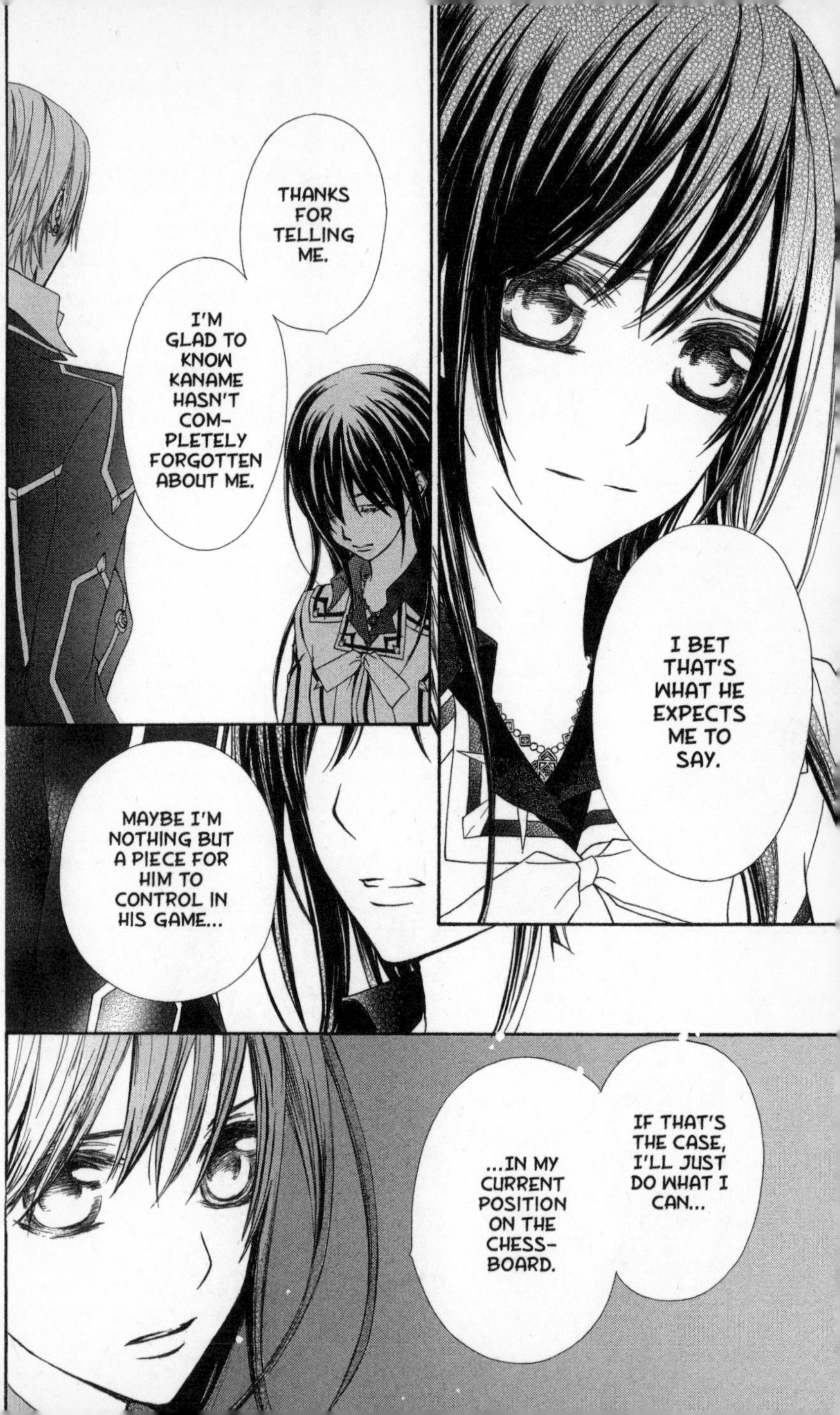

I BET THAT'S WHAT HE EXPECTS ME TO SAY.
THANKS FOR TELLING ME.
I'M GLAD TO KNOW KANAME HASN'T COM-PLETELY FORGOTTEN ABOUT ME.
MAYBE I'M NOTHING BUT A PIECE FOR HIM TO CONTROL IN HIS GAME...
IF THAT'S THE CASE, I'LL JUST DO WHAT I CAN...
...IN MY CURRENT POSITION ON THE CHESS-BOARD.

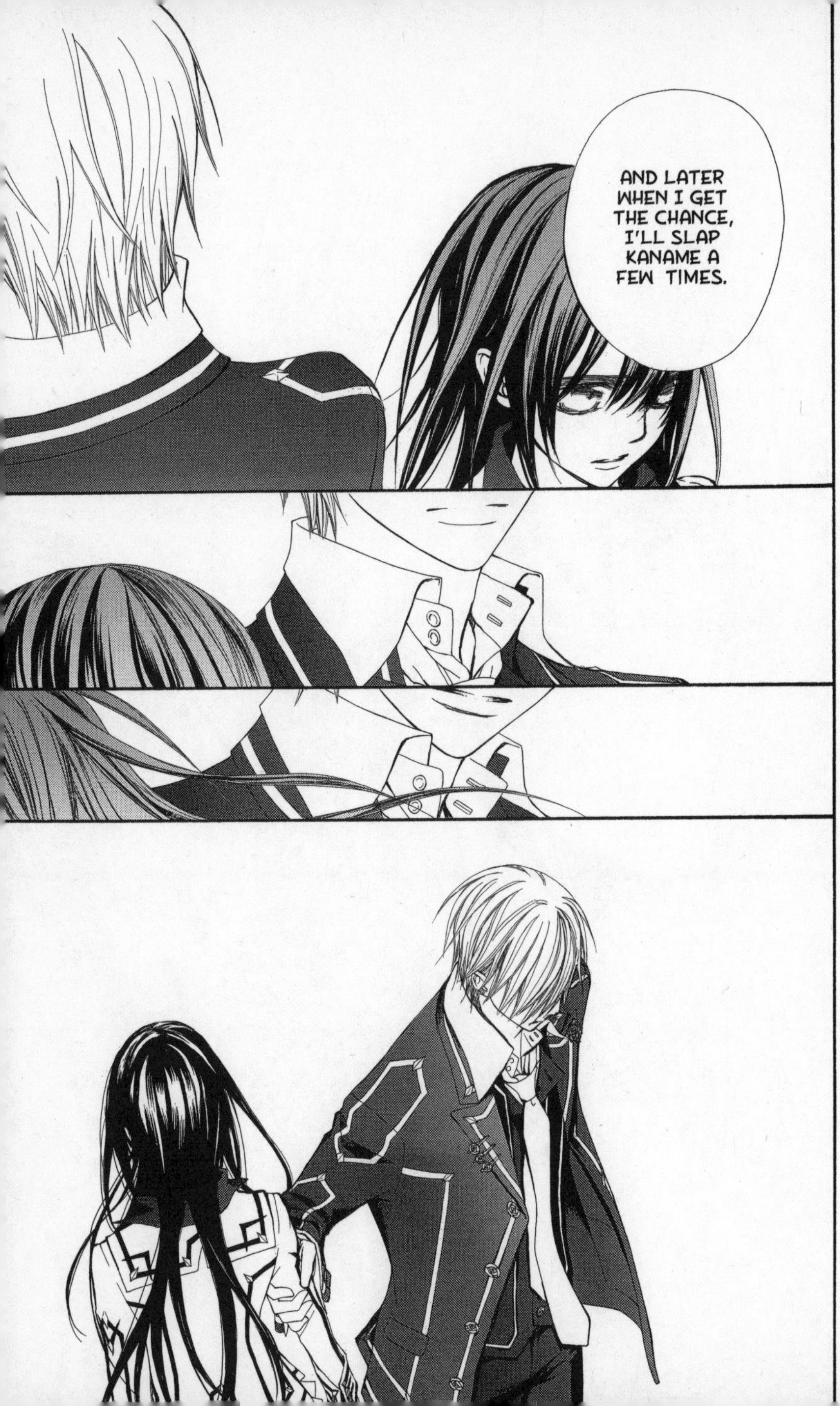
AND LATER WHEN I GET THE CHANCE, I'LL SLAP KANAME A FEW TIMES.

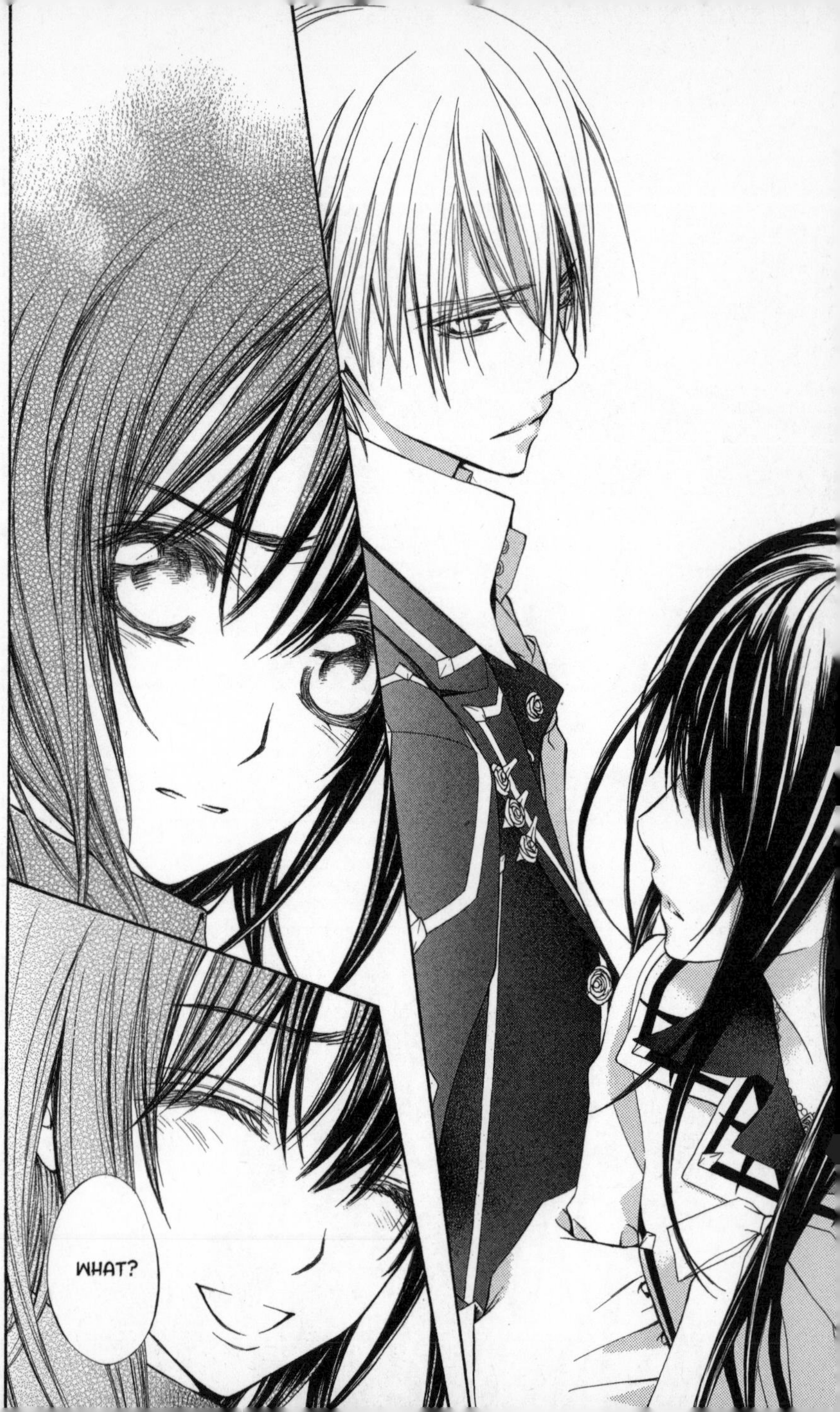
WHAT?

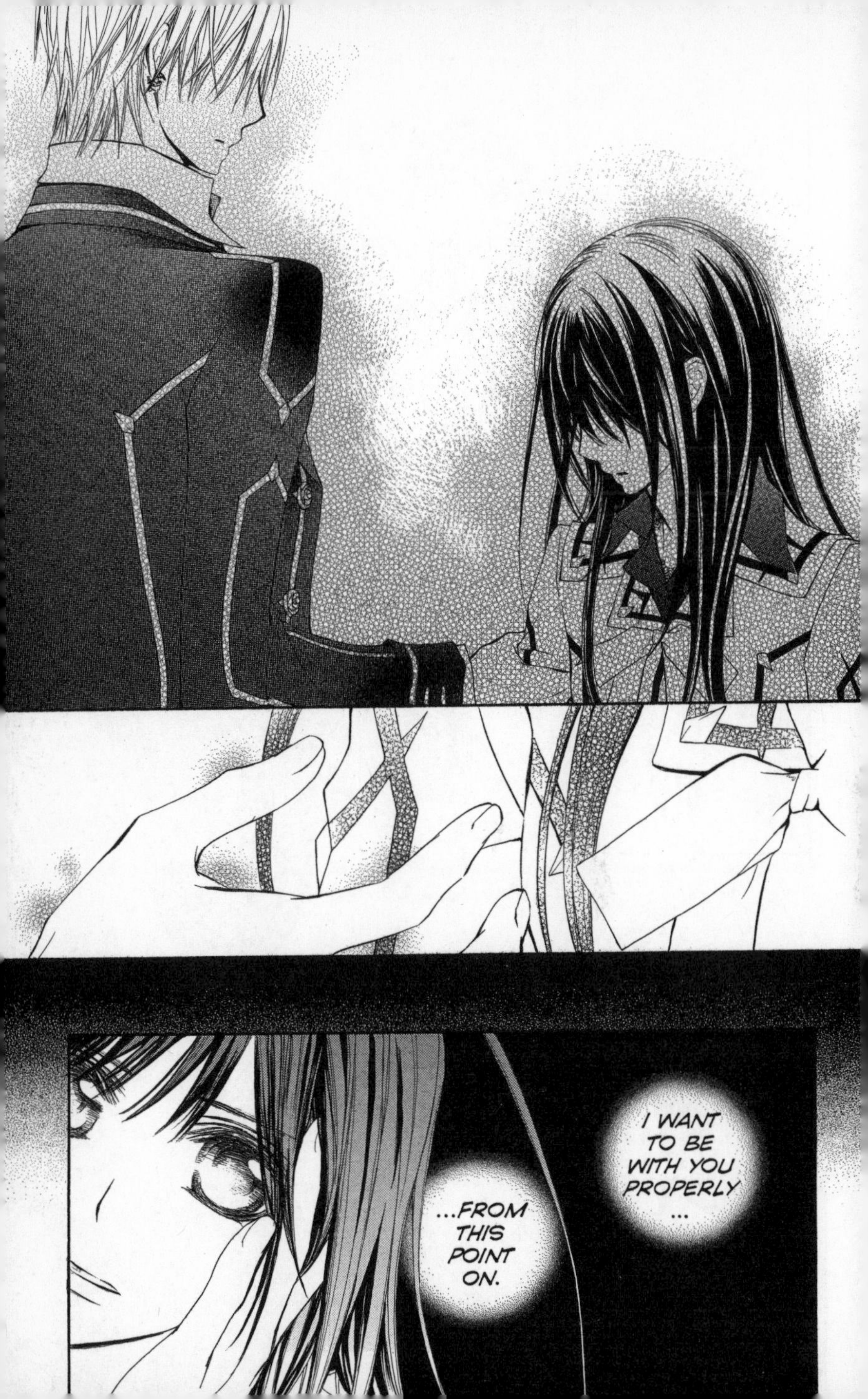
I WANT TO BE WITH YOU PROPERLY ...
...FROM THIS POINT ON.

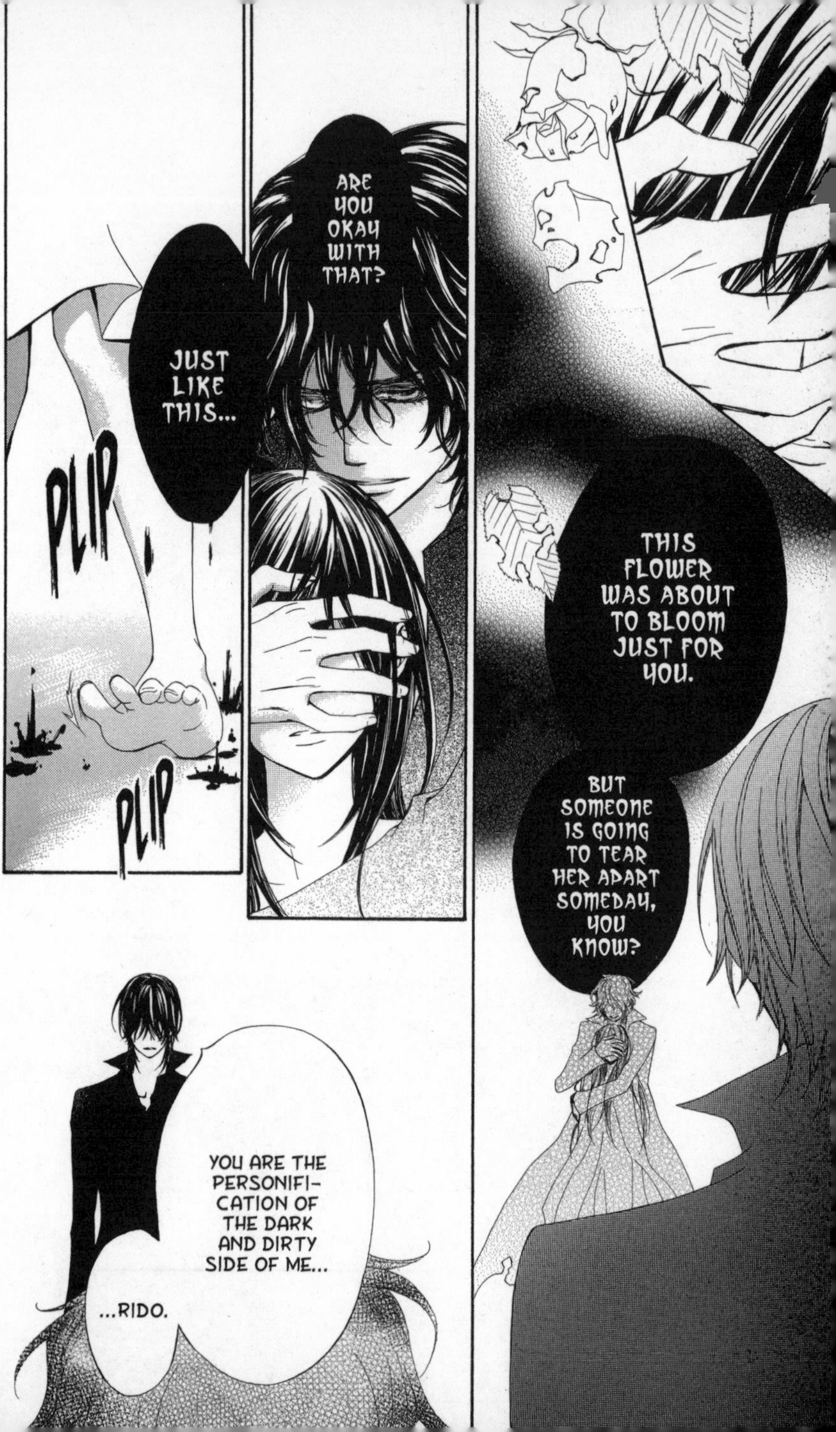
THIS FLOWER WAS ABOUT TO BLOOM JUST FOR YOU.
BUT SOMEONE IS GOING TO TEAR HER APART SOMEDAY, YOU KNOW?
ARE YOU OKAY WITH THAT?
JUST LIKE THIS...
PLIP
PLIP
YOU ARE THE PERSONIFICATION OF THE DARK AND DIRTY SIDE OF ME...
...RIDO.

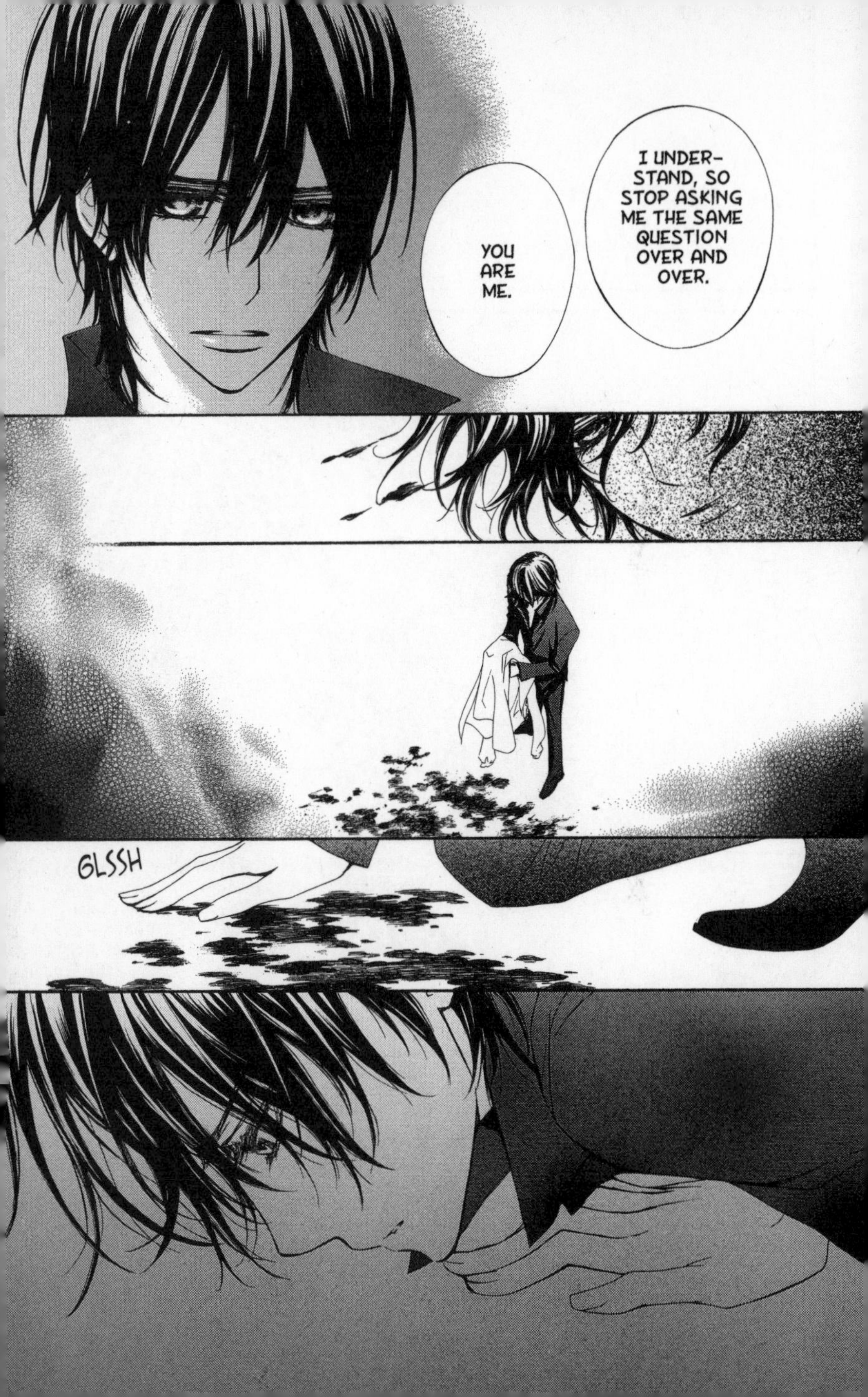
I UNDER-STAND, SO STOP ASKING ME THE SAME QUESTION OVER AND OVER.
YOU ARE ME.
GLSSH

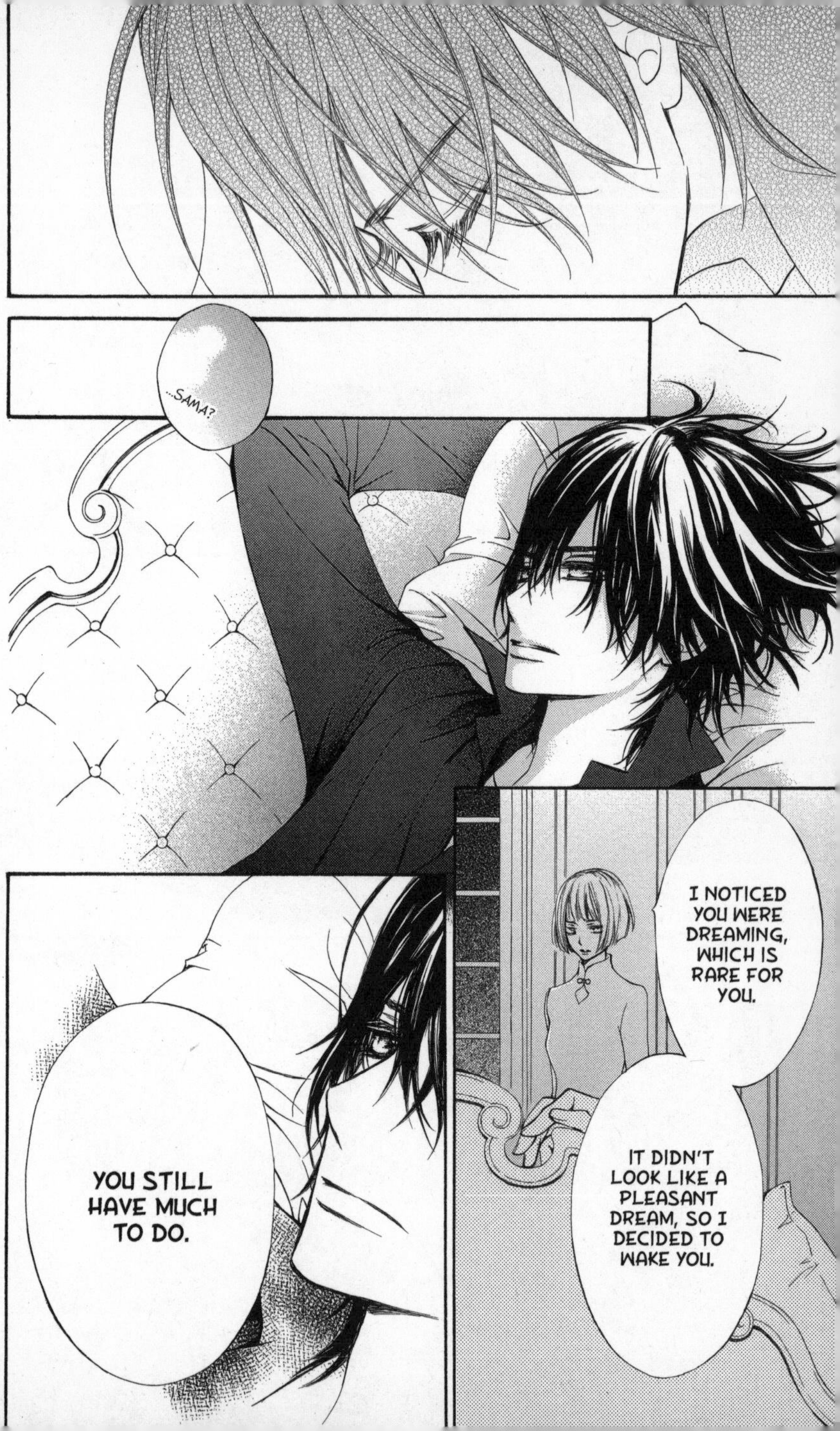
...SAMA?
I NOTICED YOU WERE DREAMING, WHICH IS RARE FOR YOU.
IT DIDN'T LOOK LIKE A PLEASANT DREAM, SO I DECIDED TO WAKE YOU.
YOU STILL HAVE MUCH TO DO.

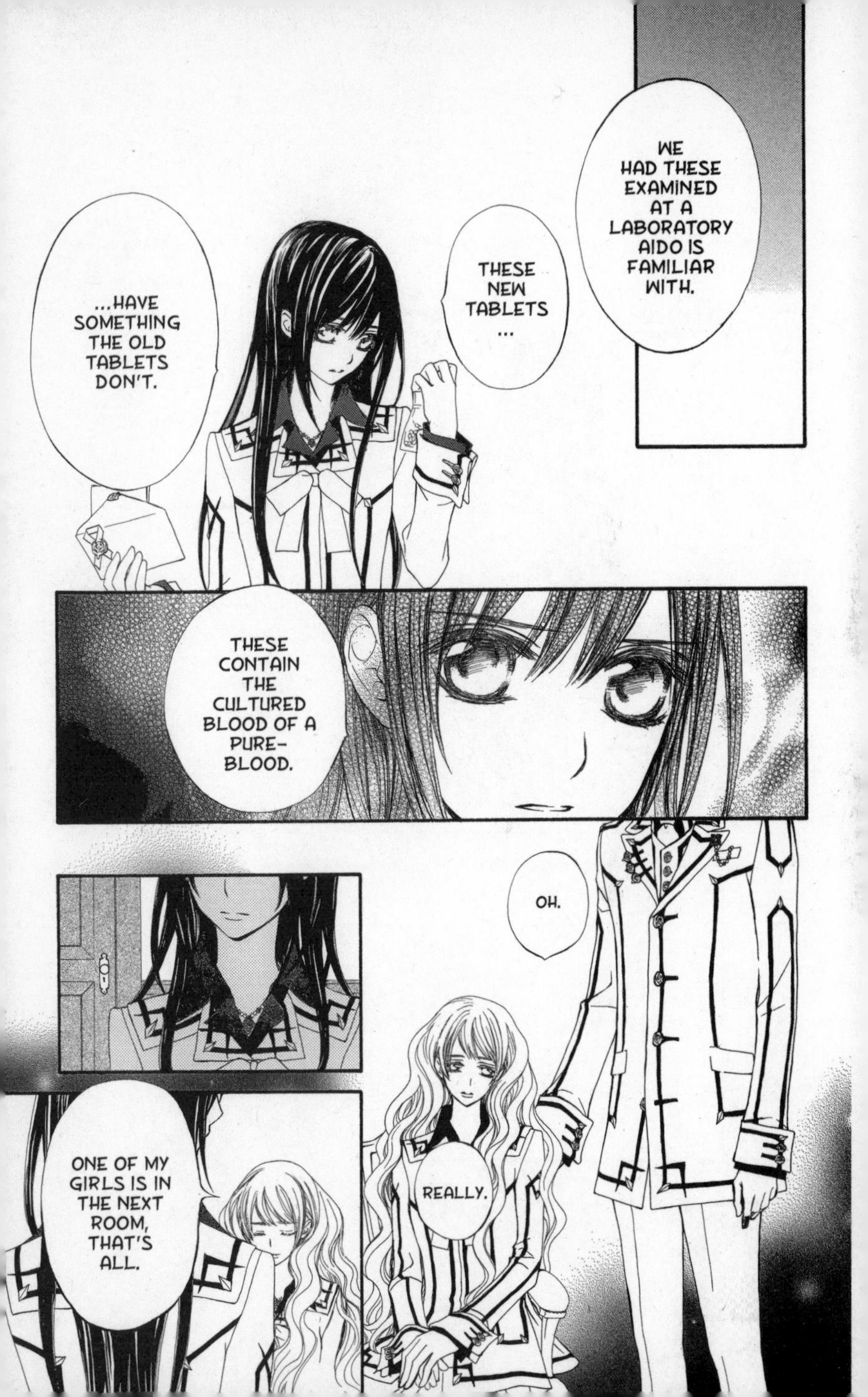
WE HAD THESE EXAMINED AT A LABORATORY AIDO IS FAMILIAR WITH.
THESE NEW TABLETS ...
...HAVE SOMETHING THE OLD TABLETS DON'T.
THESE CONTAIN THE CULTURED BLOOD OF A PURE-BLOOD.
OH.
REALLY.
ONE OF MY GIRLS IS IN THE NEXT ROOM, THAT'S ALL.

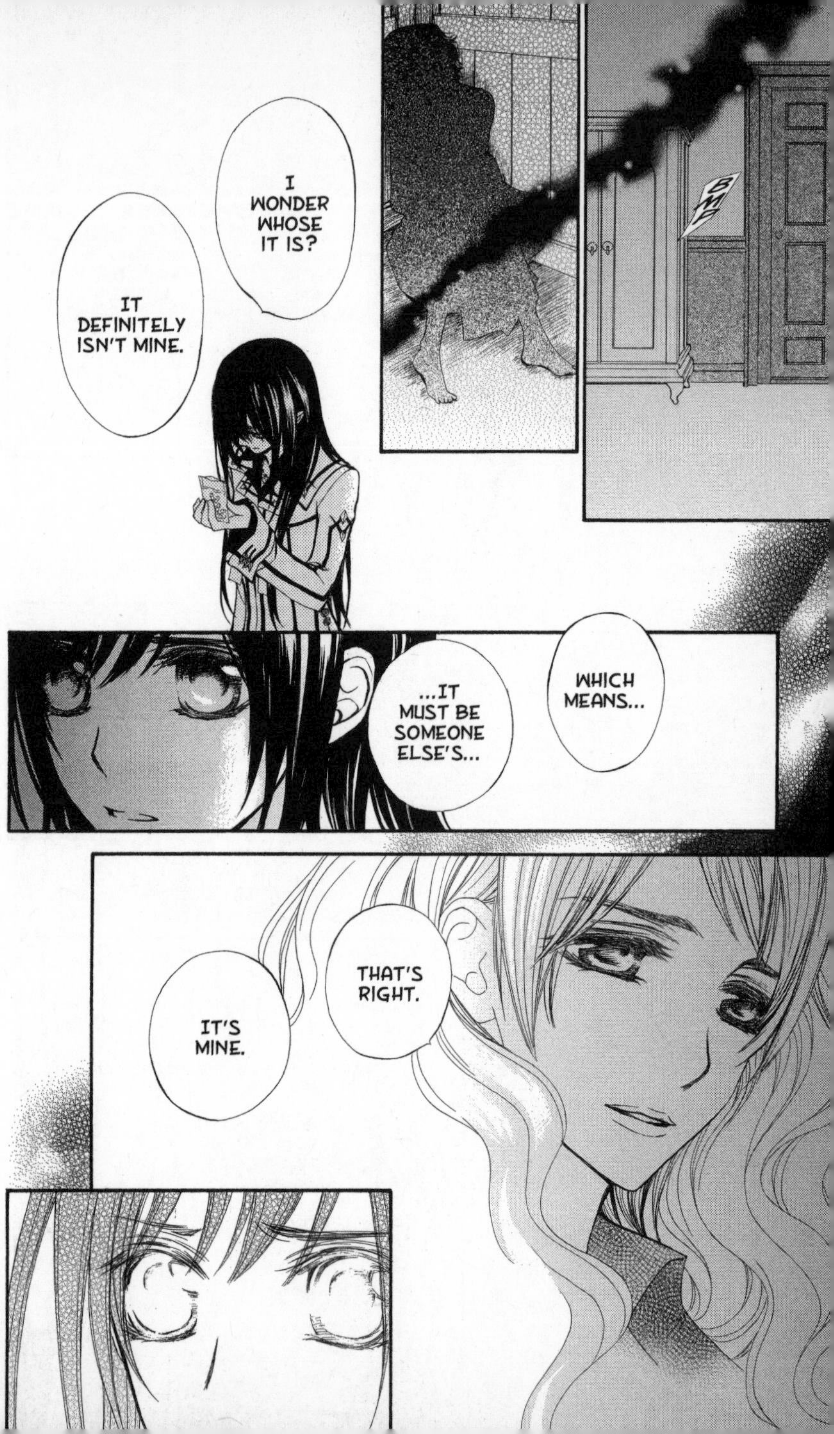
BMF
I WONDER WHOSE IT IS?
IT DEFINITELY ISN'T MINE.
WHICH MEANS...
...IT MUST BE SOMEONE ELSE'S...
THAT'S RIGHT.
IT'S MINE.

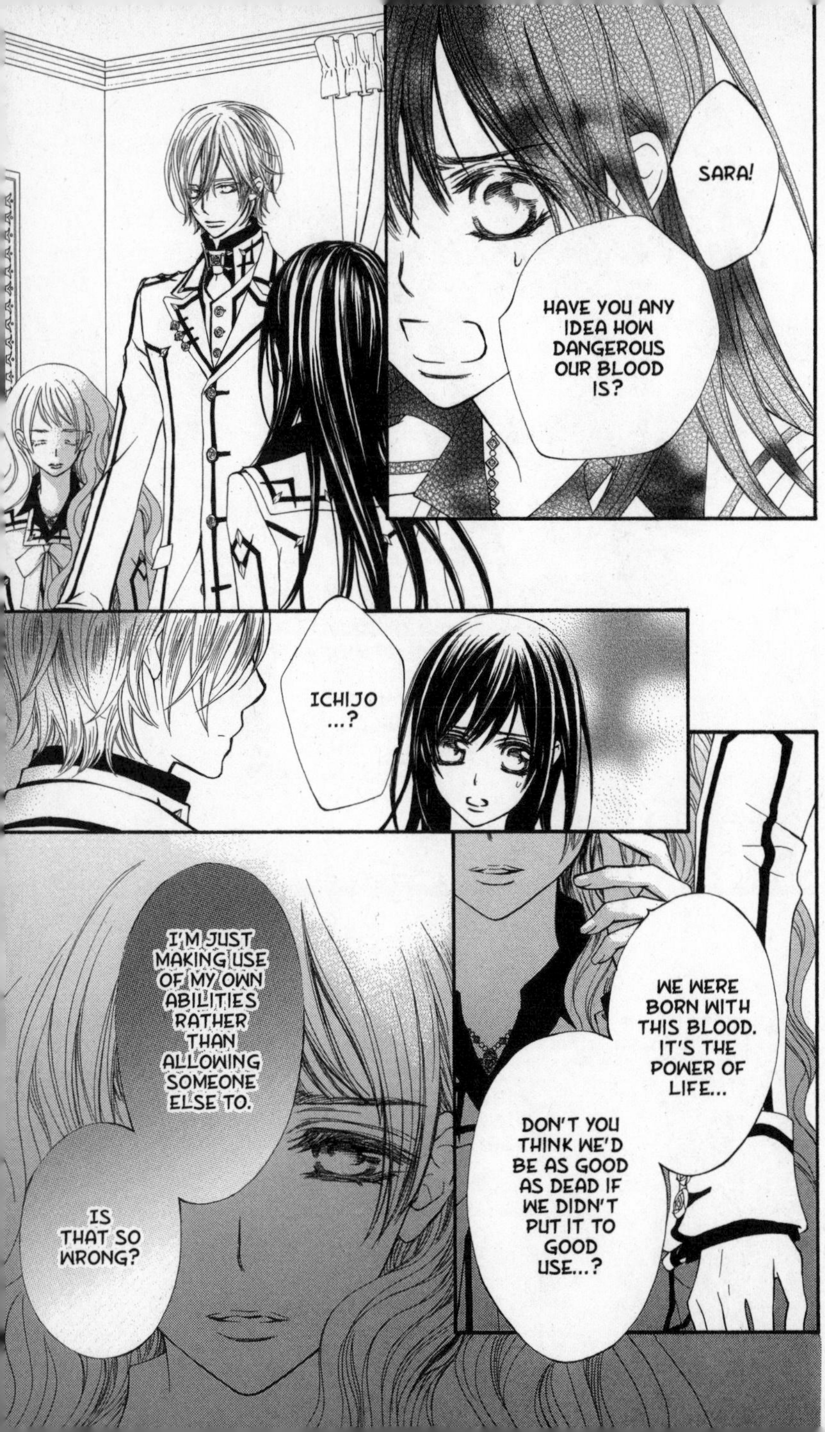
SARA!
HAVE YOU ANY IDEA HOW DANGEROUS OUR BLOOD IS?
ICHIJO ...?
WE WERE BORN WITH THIS BLOOD. IT'S THE POWER OF LIFE...
DON'T YOU THINK WE'D BE AS GOOD AS DEAD IF WE DIDN'T PUT IT TO GOOD USE...?
I'M JUST MAKING USE OF MY OWN ABILITIES RATHER THAN ALLOWING SOMEONE ELSE TO.
IS THAT SO WRONG?

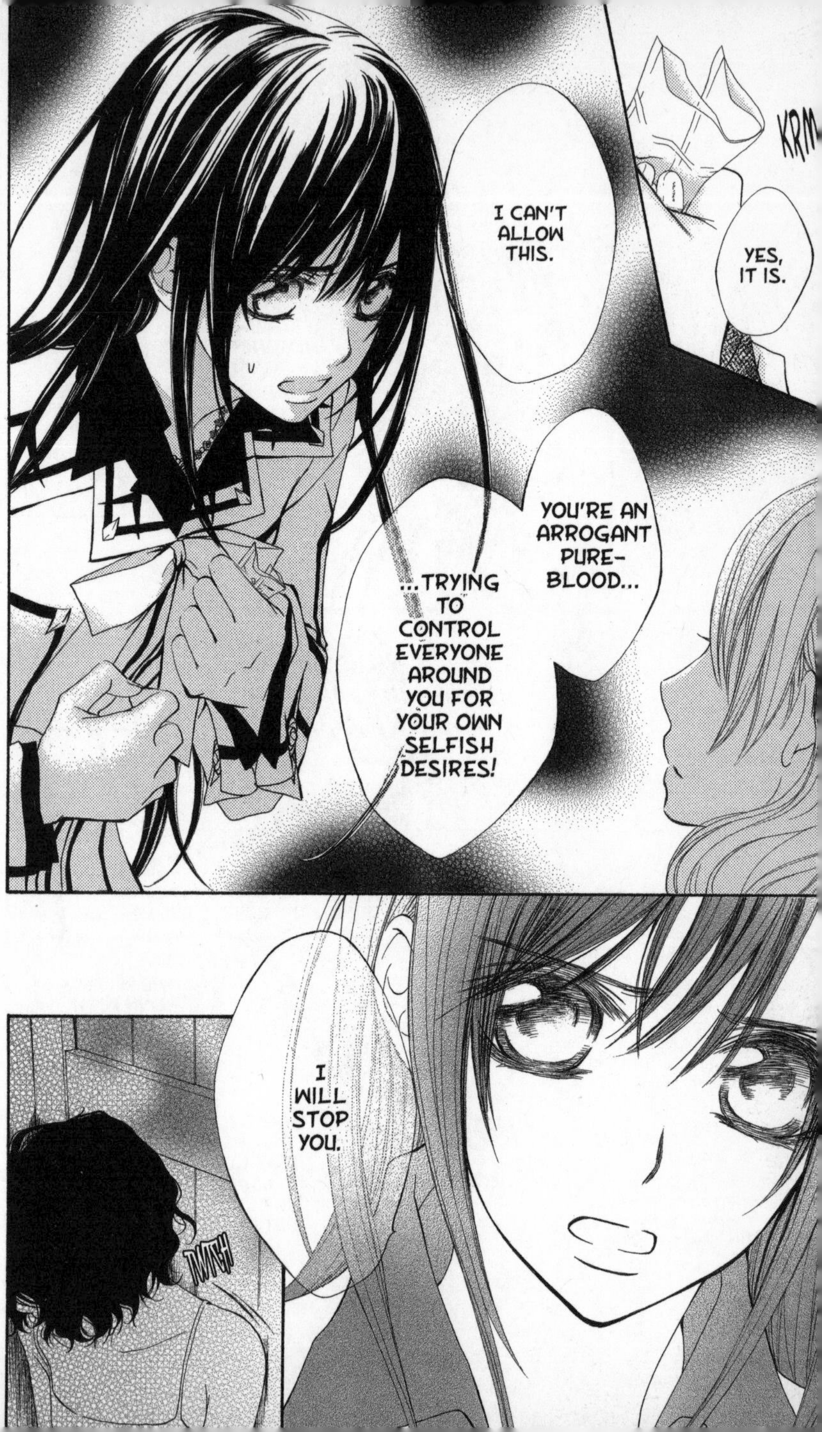
KRM
YES, IT IS.
I CAN'T ALLOW THIS.
YOU'RE AN ARROGANT PURE-BLOOD...
...TRYING TO CONTROL EVERYONE AROUND YOU FOR YOUR OWN SELFISH DESIRES!
I WILL STOP YOU.
TWITCH

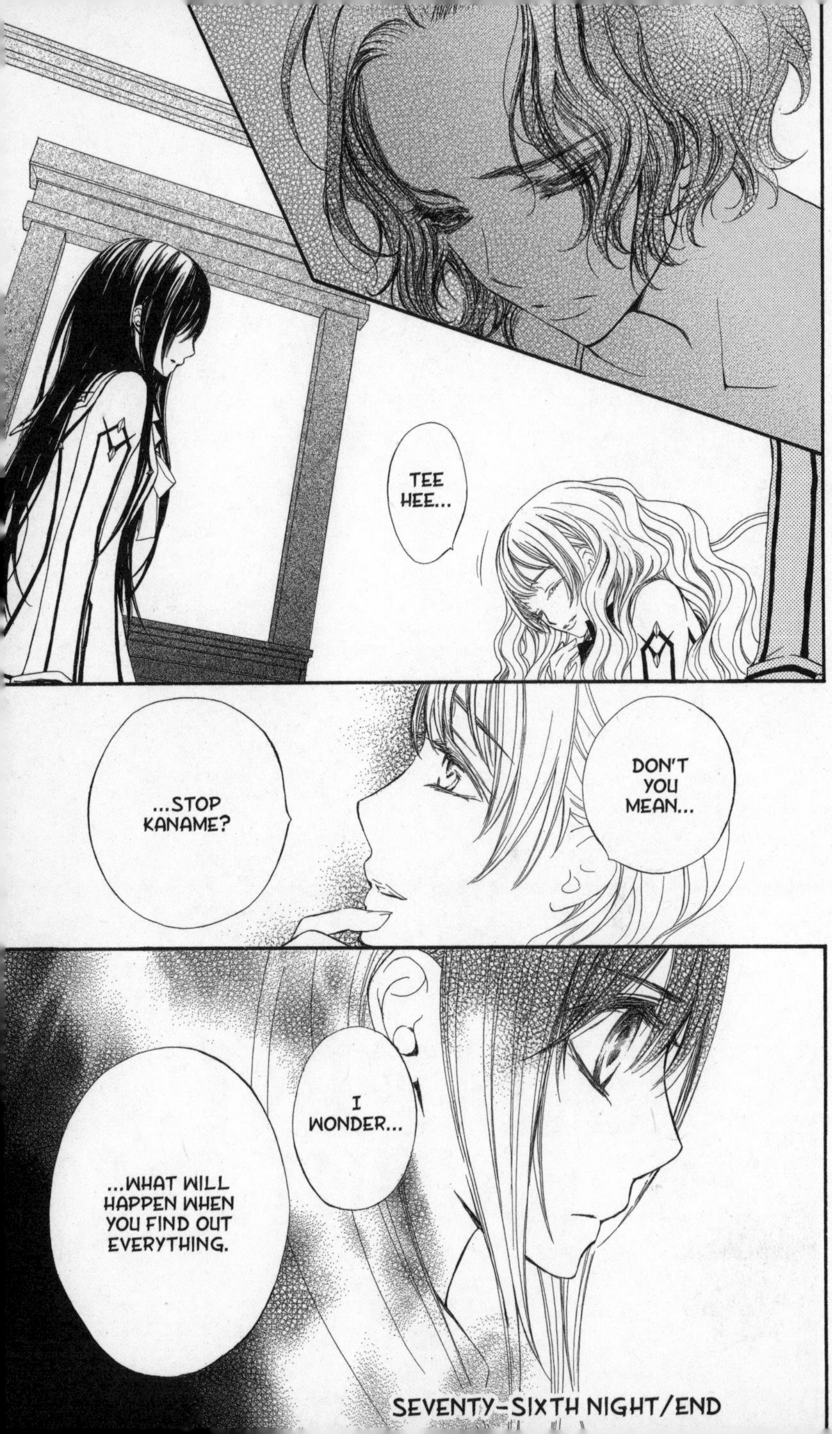
TEE HEE...
DON'T YOU MEAN...
...STOP KANAME?
I WONDER...
...WHAT WILL HAPPEN WHEN YOU FIND OUT EVERYTHING.
SEVENTY-SIXTH NIGHT/END

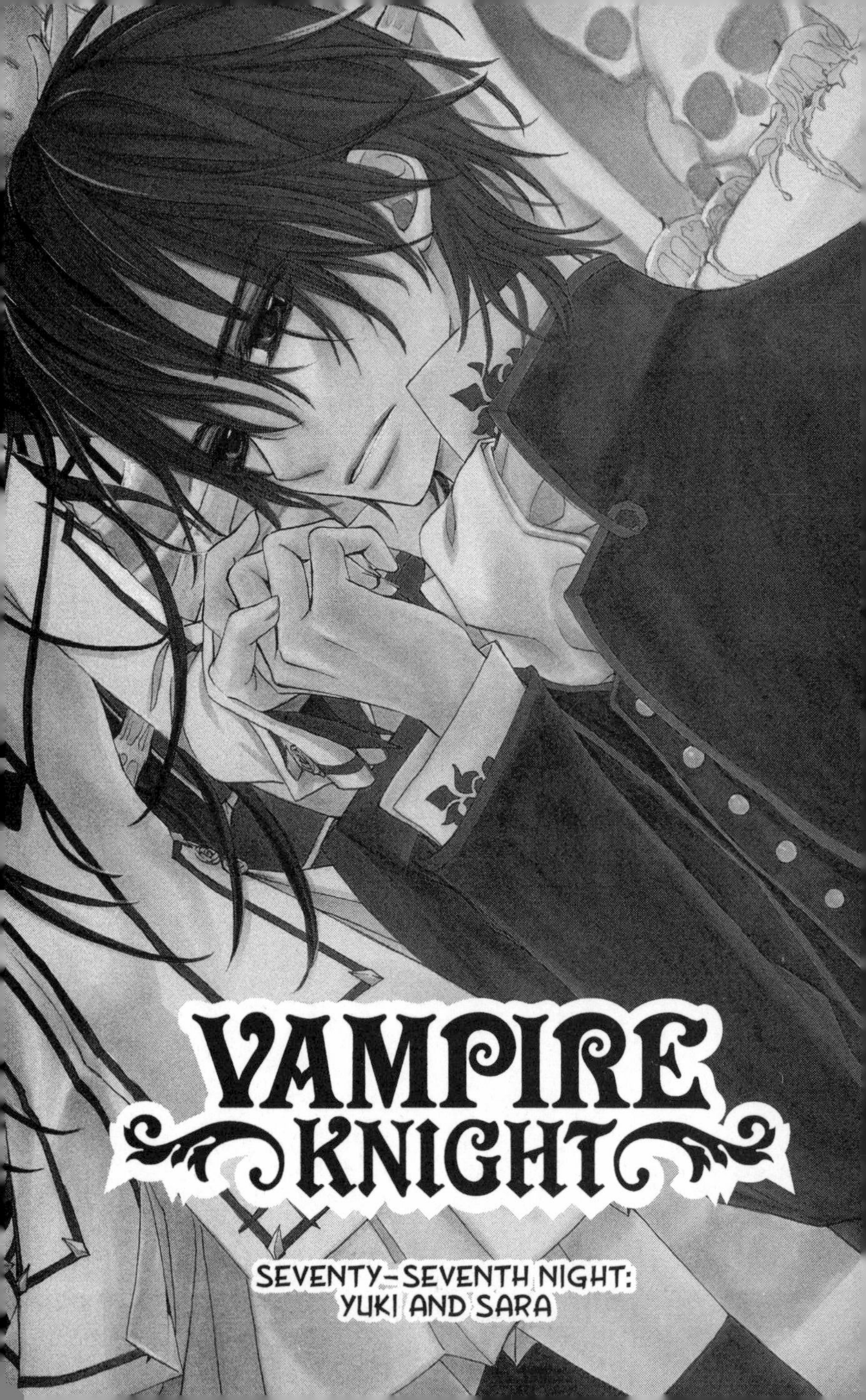
VAMPIRE
KNIGHT
SEVENTY-SEVENTH NIGHT:
YUKI AND SARA

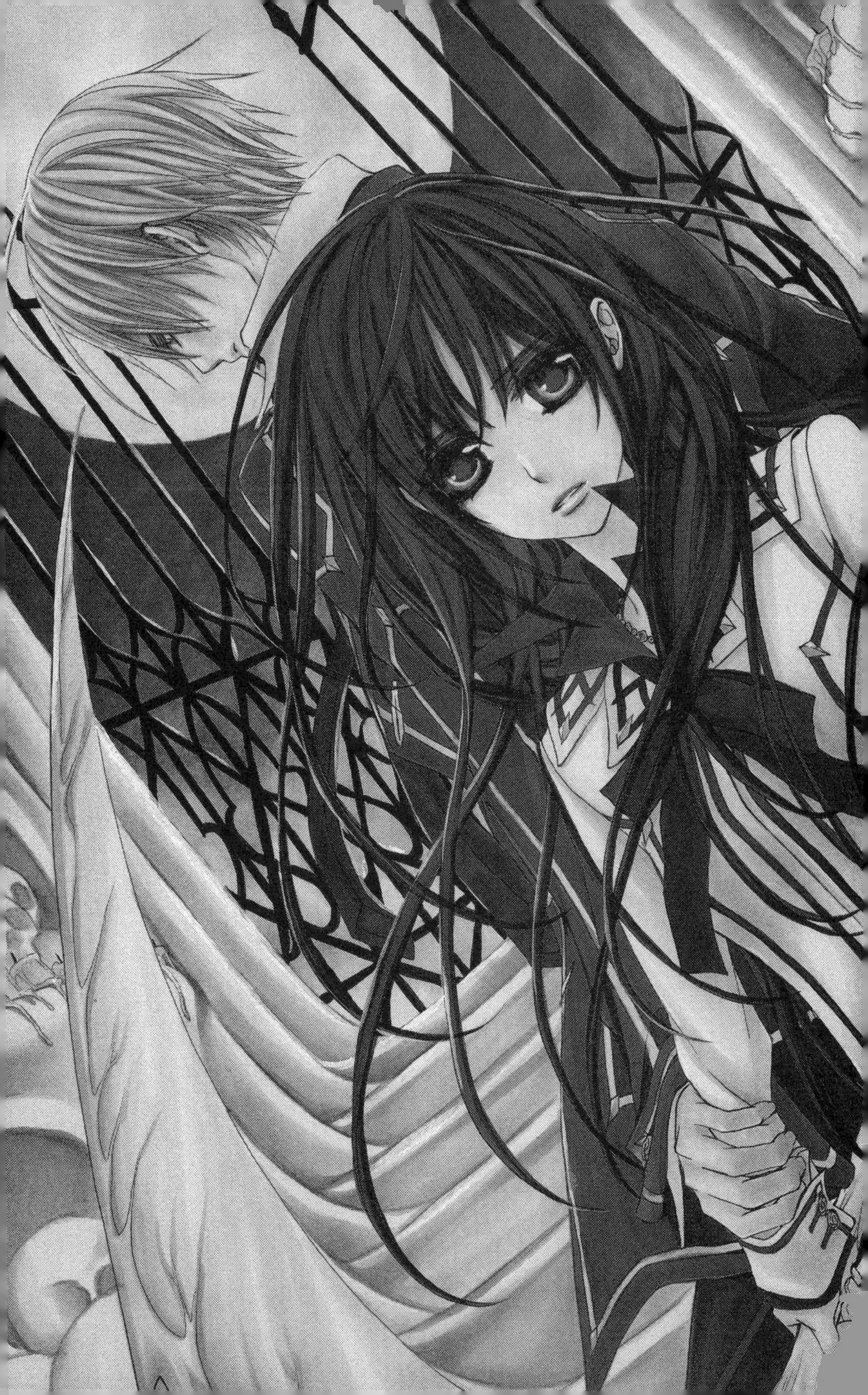

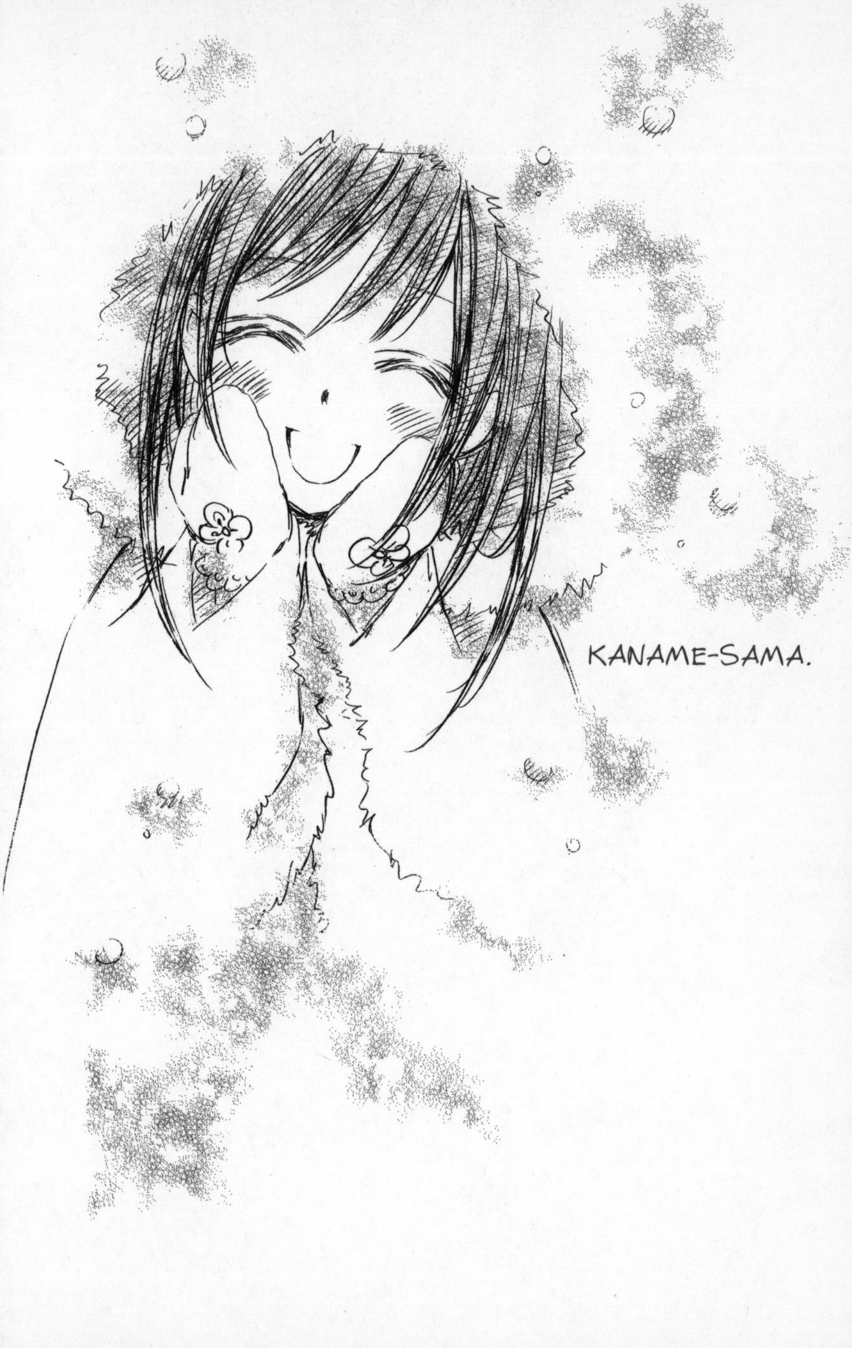
KANAME-SAMA.

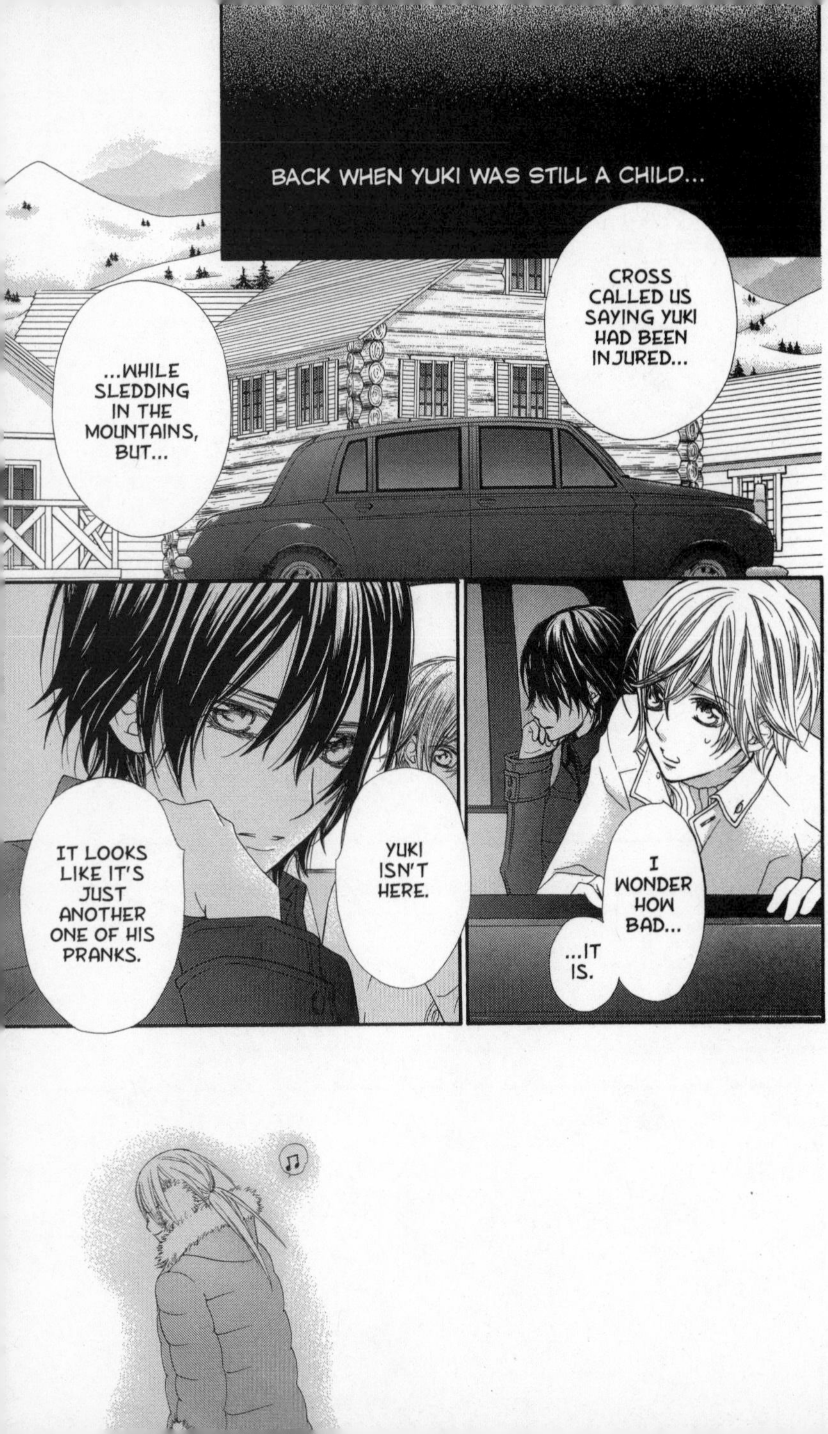
BACK WHEN YUKI WAS STILL A CHILD...
CROSS CALLED US SAYING YUKI HAD BEEN INJURED...
...WHILE SLEDDING IN THE MOUNTAINS, BUT...
I WONDER HOW BAD...
...IT IS.
YUKI ISN'T HERE.
IT LOOKS LIKE IT'S JUST ANOTHER ONE OF HIS PRANKS.
♫

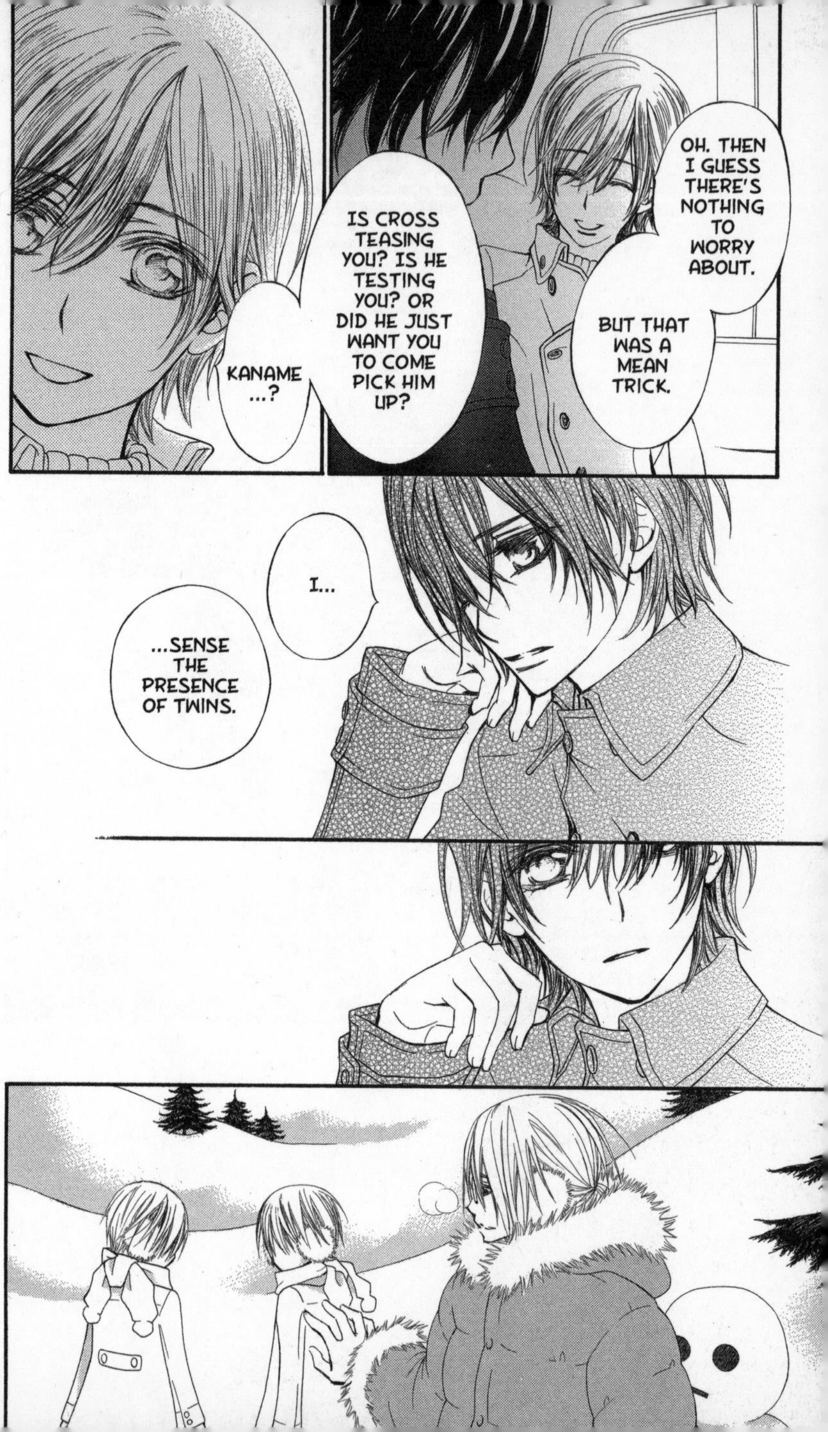
OH. THEN I GUESS THERE'S NOTHING TO WORRY ABOUT.
BUT THAT WAS A MEAN TRICK.
IS CROSS TEASING YOU? IS HE TESTING YOU? OR DID HE JUST WANT YOU TO COME PICK HIM UP?
KANAME ...?
I...
...SENSE THE PRESENCE OF TWINS.

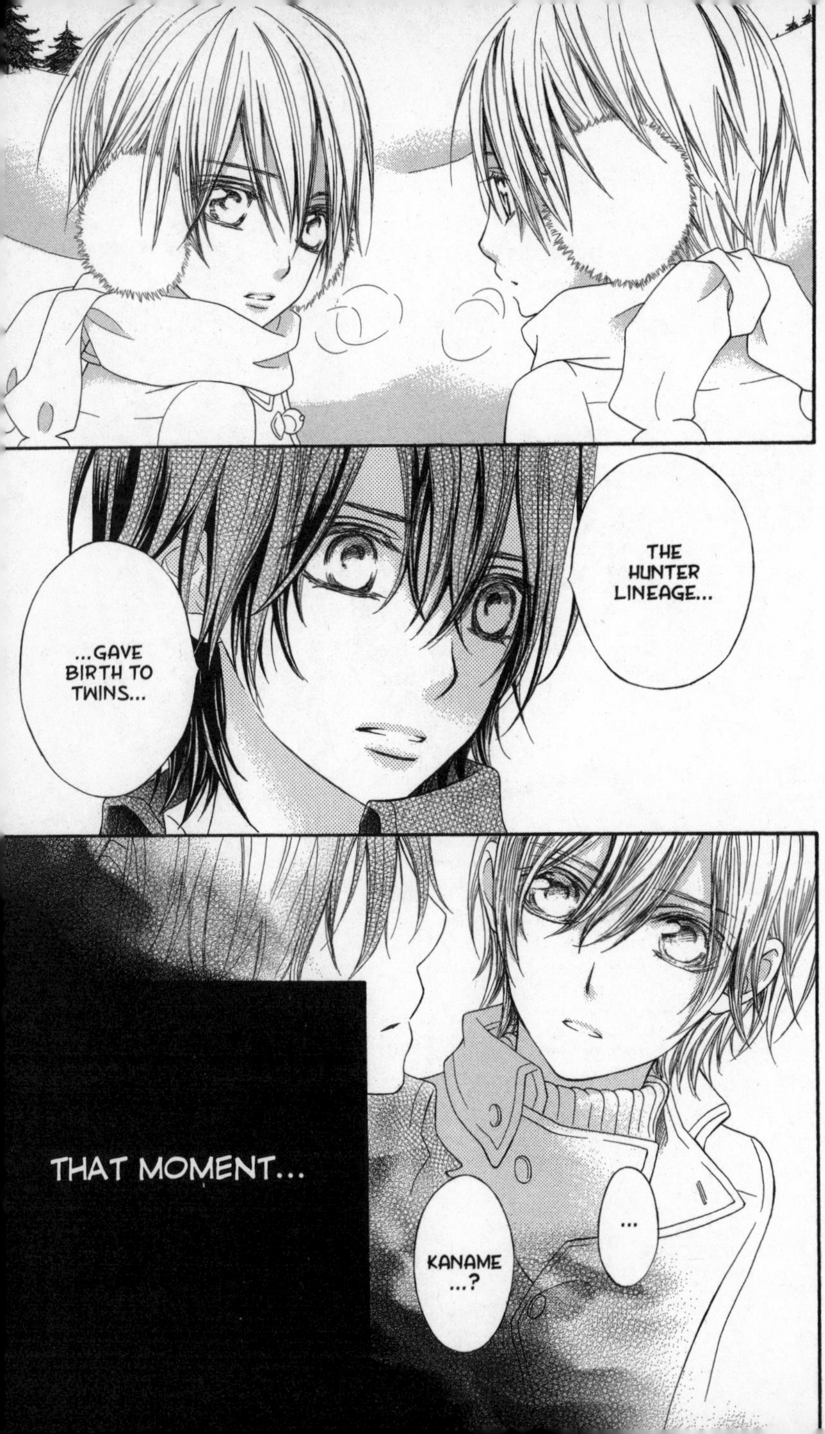
THE HUNTER LINEAGE...
...GAVE BIRTH TO TWINS...
...
KANAME ...?
THAT MOMENT...

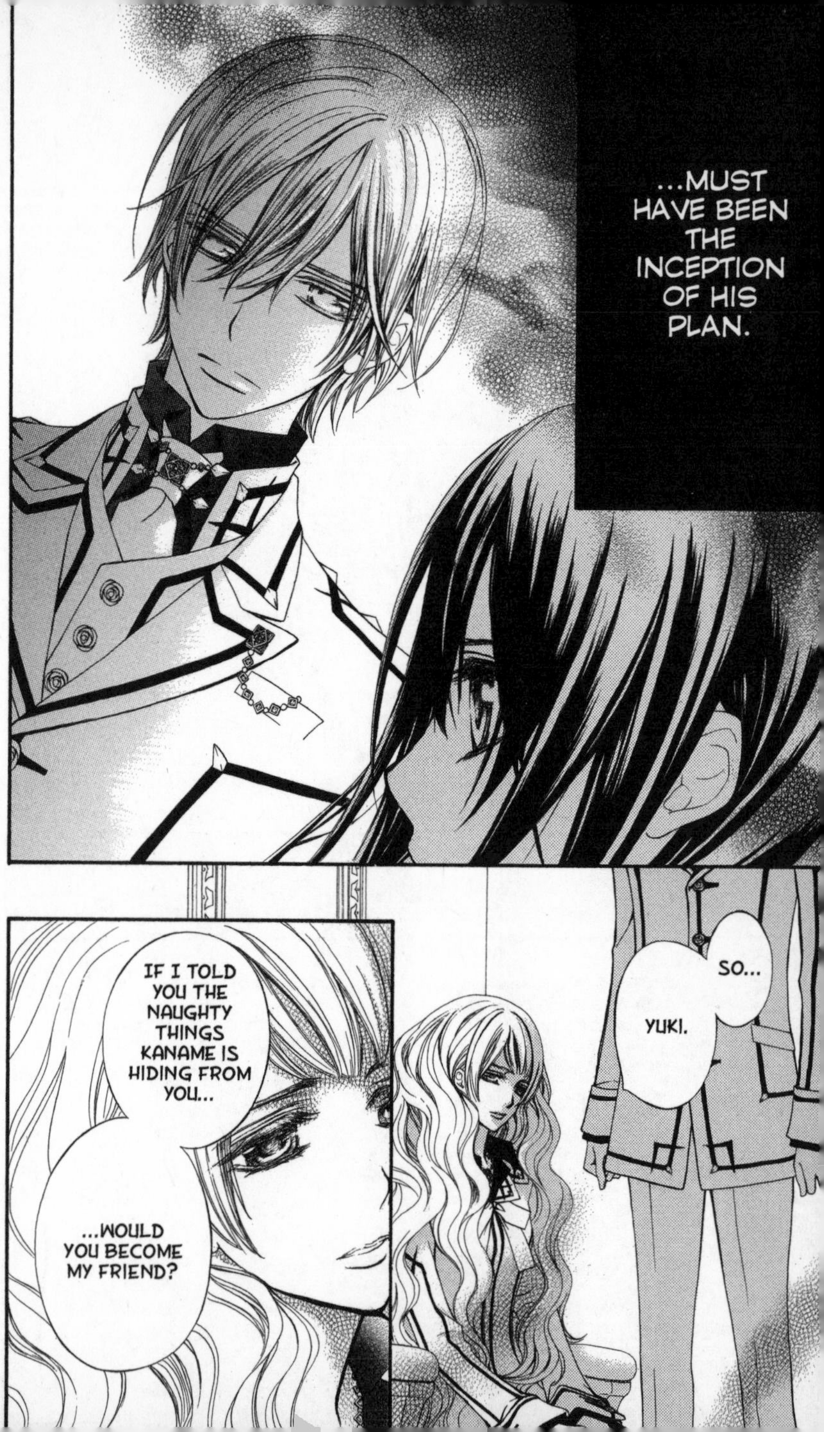
...MUST HAVE BEEN THE INCEPTION OF HIS PLAN.
SO...
YUKI.
IF I TOLD YOU THE NAUGHTY THINGS KANAME IS HIDING FROM YOU...
...WOULD YOU BECOME MY FRIEND?

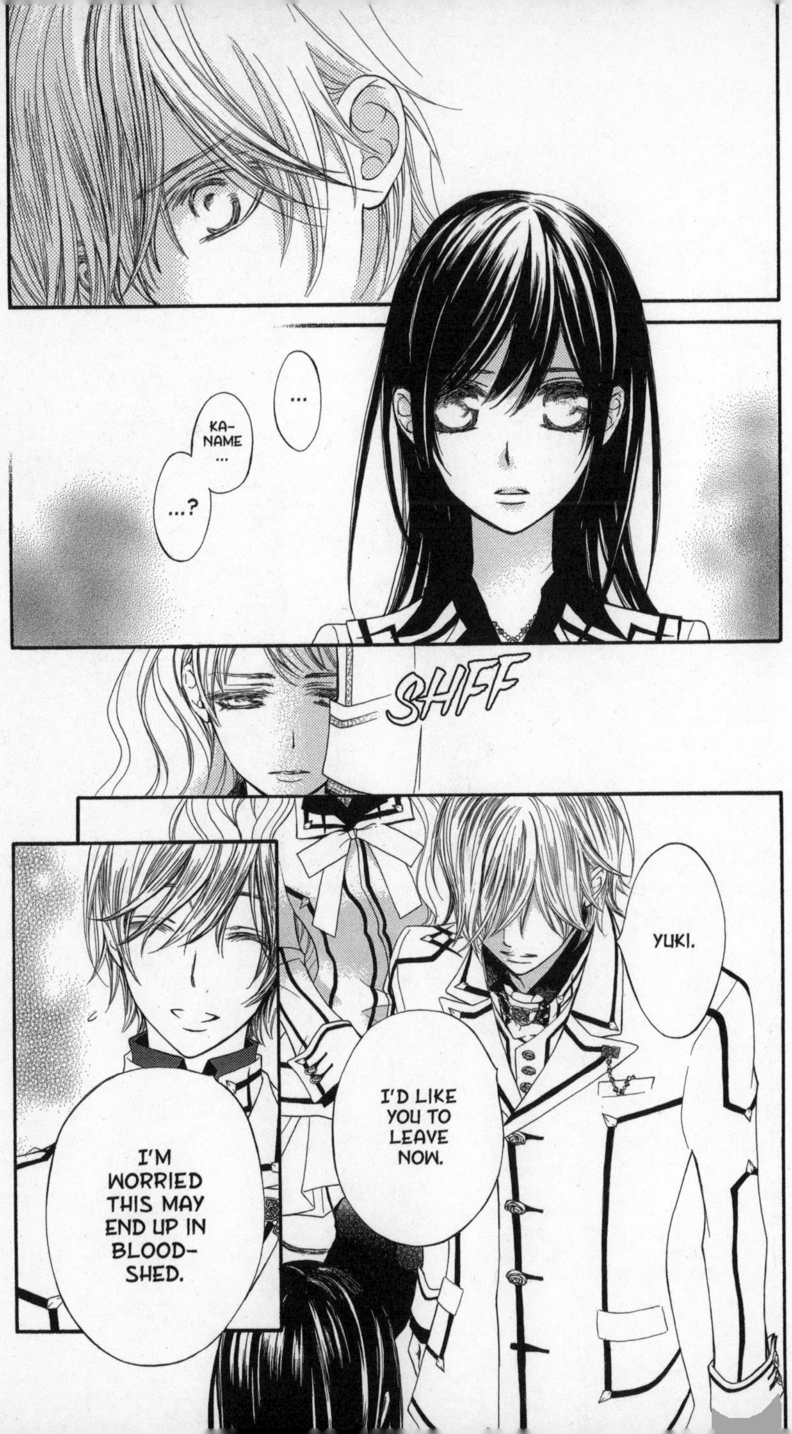
...
KA-NAME ...
...?
SHFF
YUKI.
I'D LIKE YOU TO LEAVE NOW.
I'M WORRIED THIS MAY END UP IN BLOOD-SHED.

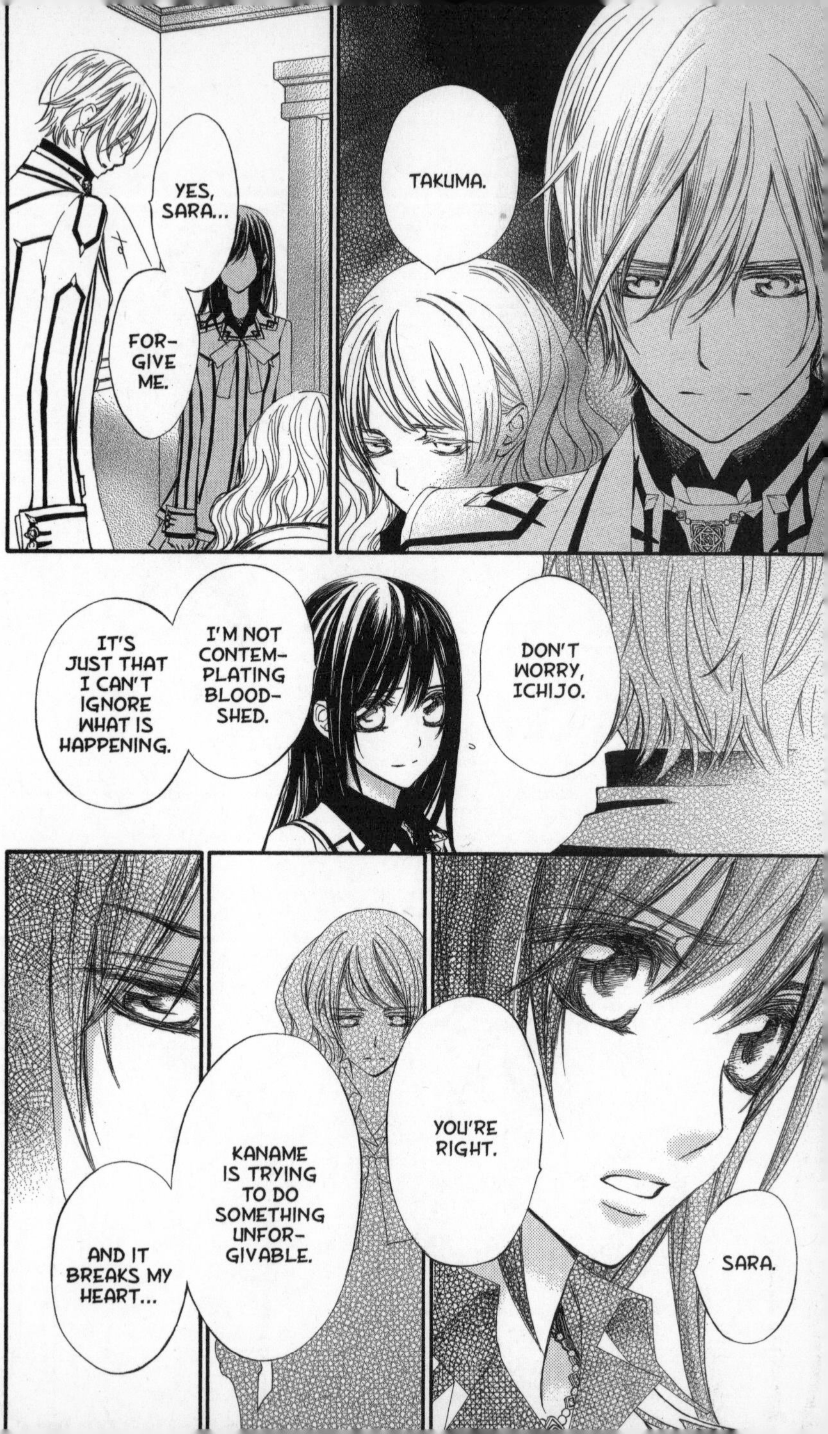
TAKUMA.
YES, SARA...
FOR-GIVE ME.
DON'T WORRY, ICHIJO.
I'M NOT CONTEM-PLATING BLOOD-SHED.
IT'S JUST THAT I CAN'T IGNORE WHAT IS HAPPENING.
SARA.
YOU'RE RIGHT.
KANAME IS TRYING TO DO SOMETHING UNFORGIVABLE.
AND IT BREAKS MY HEART...

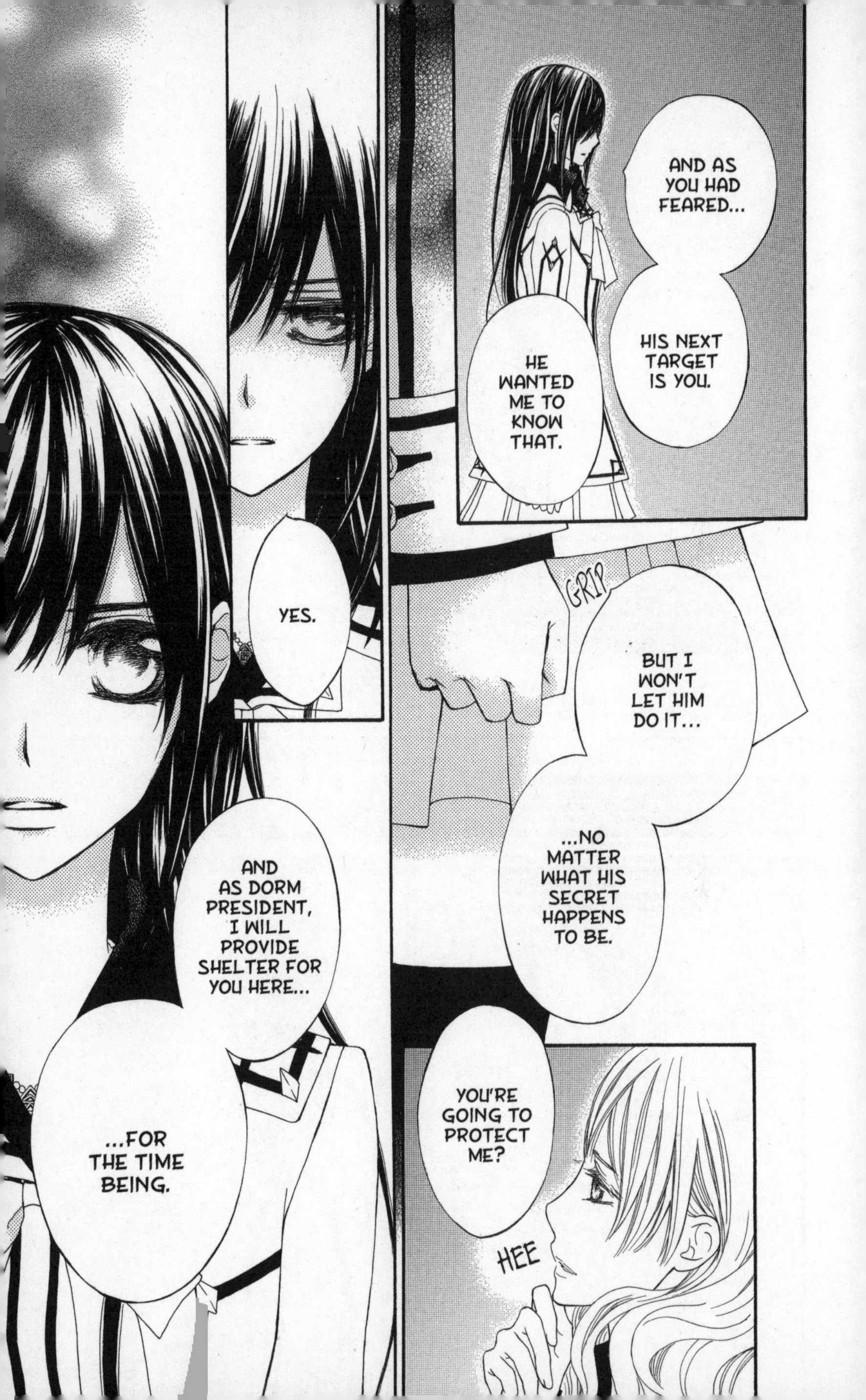
AND AS YOU HAD FEARED...
HIS NEXT TARGET IS YOU.
HE WANTED ME TO KNOW THAT.
YES.
GRIP
BUT I WON'T LET HIM DO IT...
...NO MATTER WHAT HIS SECRET HAPPENS TO BE.
YOU'RE GOING TO PROTECT ME?
HEE
AND AS DORM PRESIDENT, I WILL PROVIDE SHELTER FOR YOU HERE...
...FOR THE TIME BEING.

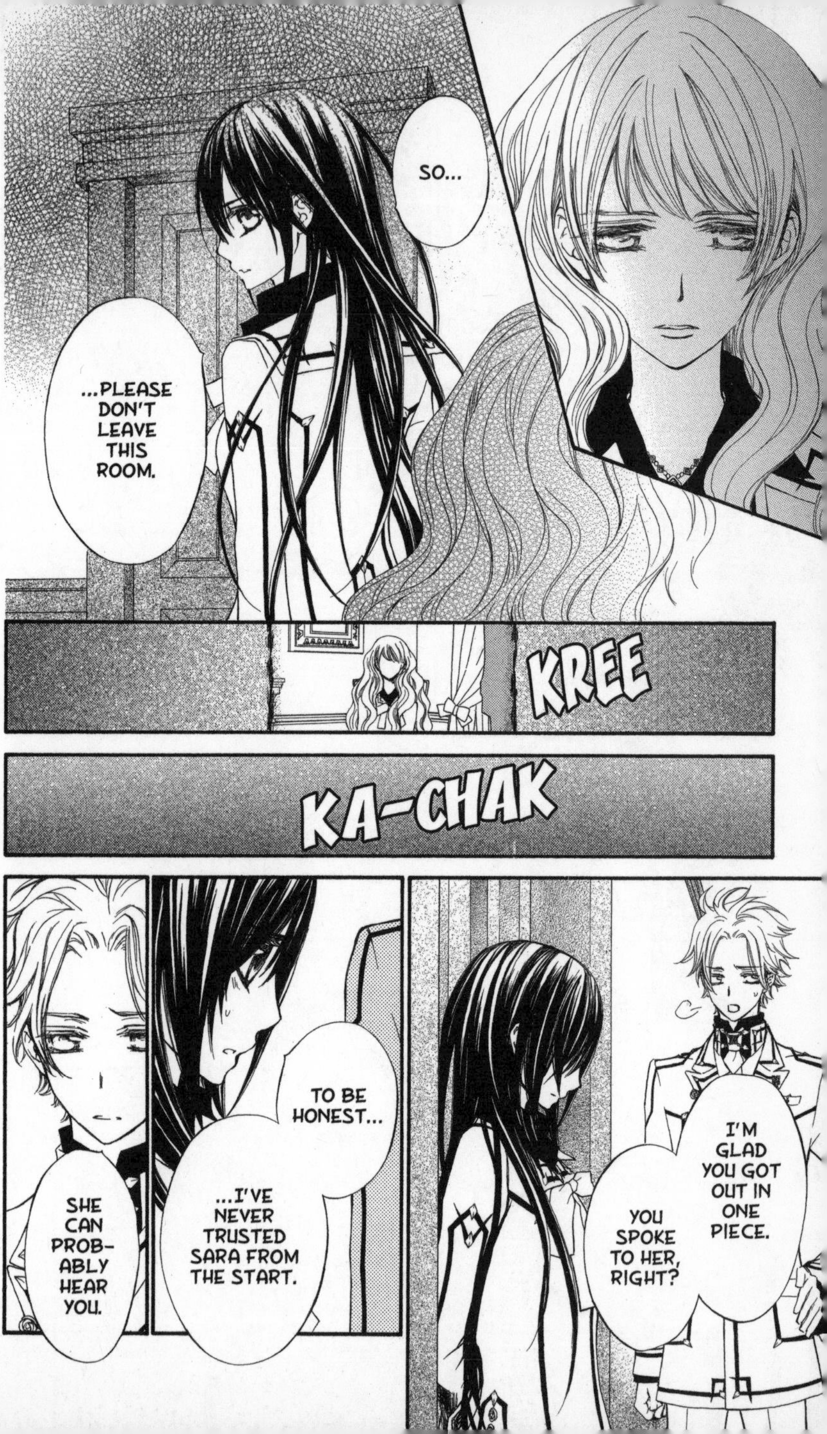
SO...
...PLEASE DON'T LEAVE THIS ROOM.
KREE
KA-CHAK
I'M GLAD YOU GOT OUT IN ONE PIECE.
YOU SPOKE TO HER, RIGHT?
TO BE HONEST...
...I'VE NEVER TRUSTED SARA FROM THE START.
SHE CAN PROB-ABLY HEAR YOU.

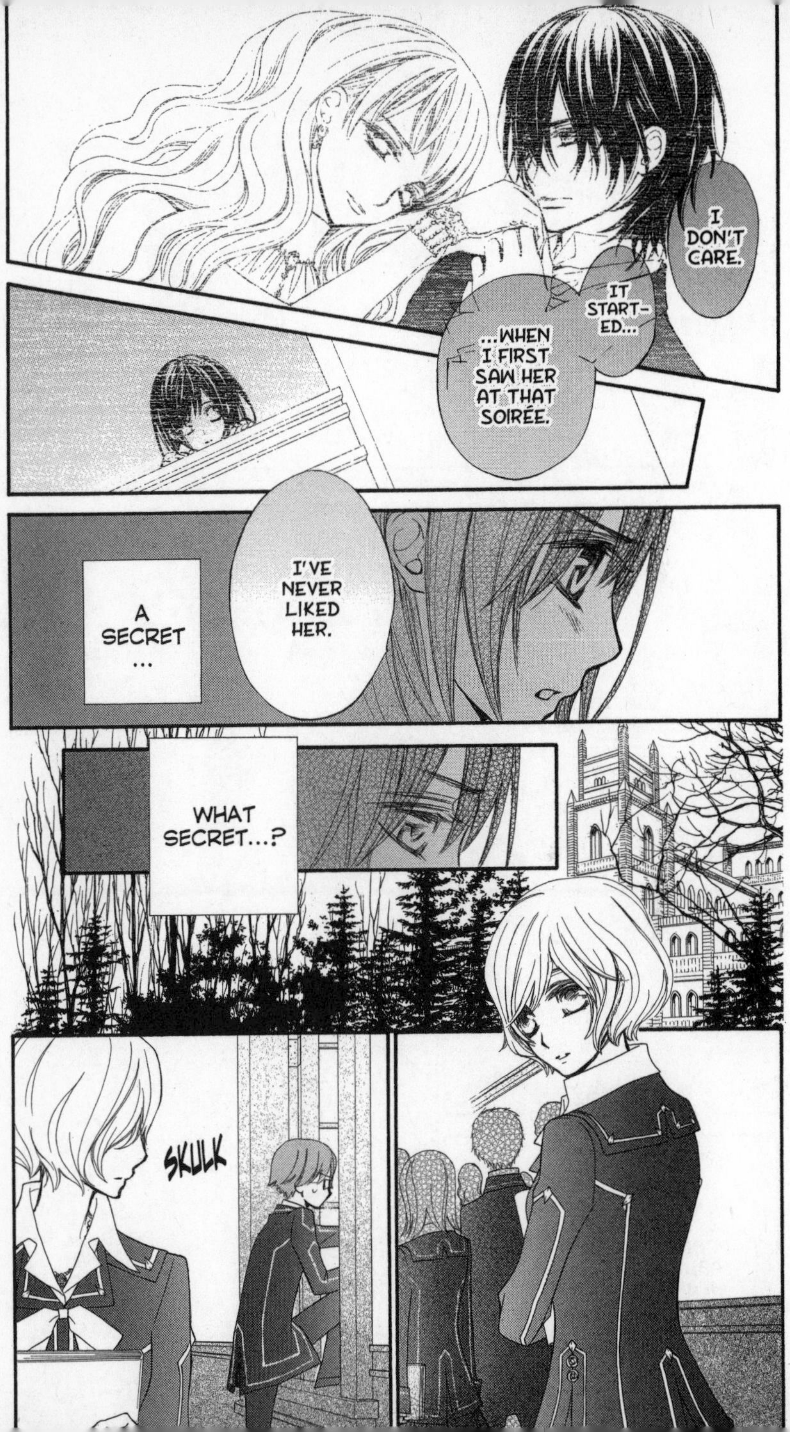
I DON'T CARE.
IT START-ED...
...WHEN I FIRST SAW HER AT THAT SOIRÉE.
I'VE NEVER LIKED HER.
A SECRET ...
WHAT SECRET...?
SKULK

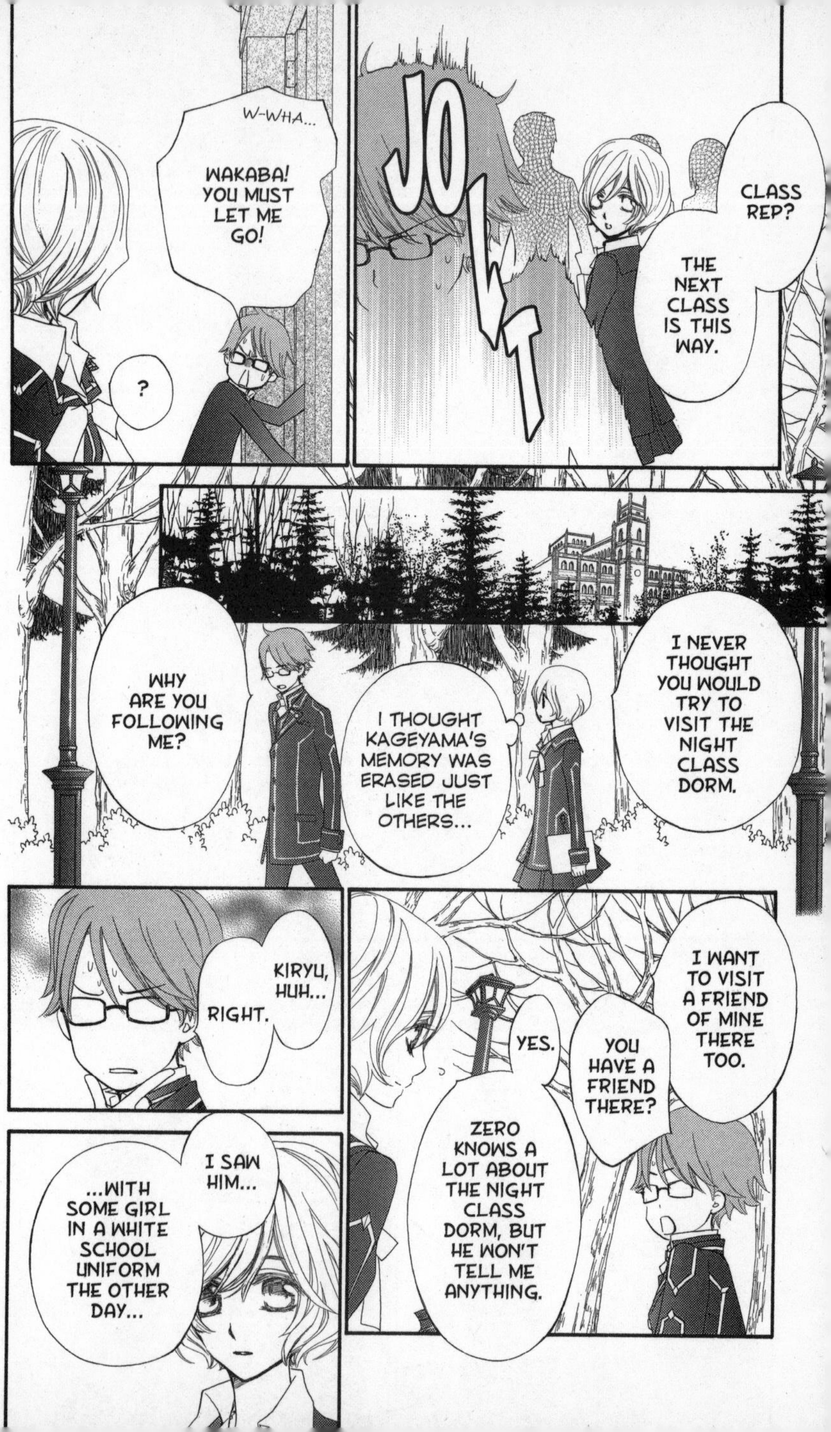
CLASS REP?
THE NEXT CLASS IS THIS WAY.
JOLT
W-WHA...
WAKABA! YOU MUST LET ME GO!
?
I NEVER THOUGHT YOU WOULD TRY TO VISIT THE NIGHT CLASS DORM.
I THOUGHT KAGEYAMA'S MEMORY WAS ERASED JUST LIKE THE OTHERS...
WHY ARE YOU FOLLOWING ME?
I WANT TO VISIT A FRIEND OF MINE THERE TOO.
YOU HAVE A FRIEND THERE?
YES.
ZERO KNOWS A LOT ABOUT THE NIGHT CLASS DORM, BUT HE WON'T TELL ME ANYTHING.
KIRYU, HUH...
RIGHT.
I SAW HIM...
...WITH SOME GIRL IN A WHITE SCHOOL UNIFORM THE OTHER DAY...

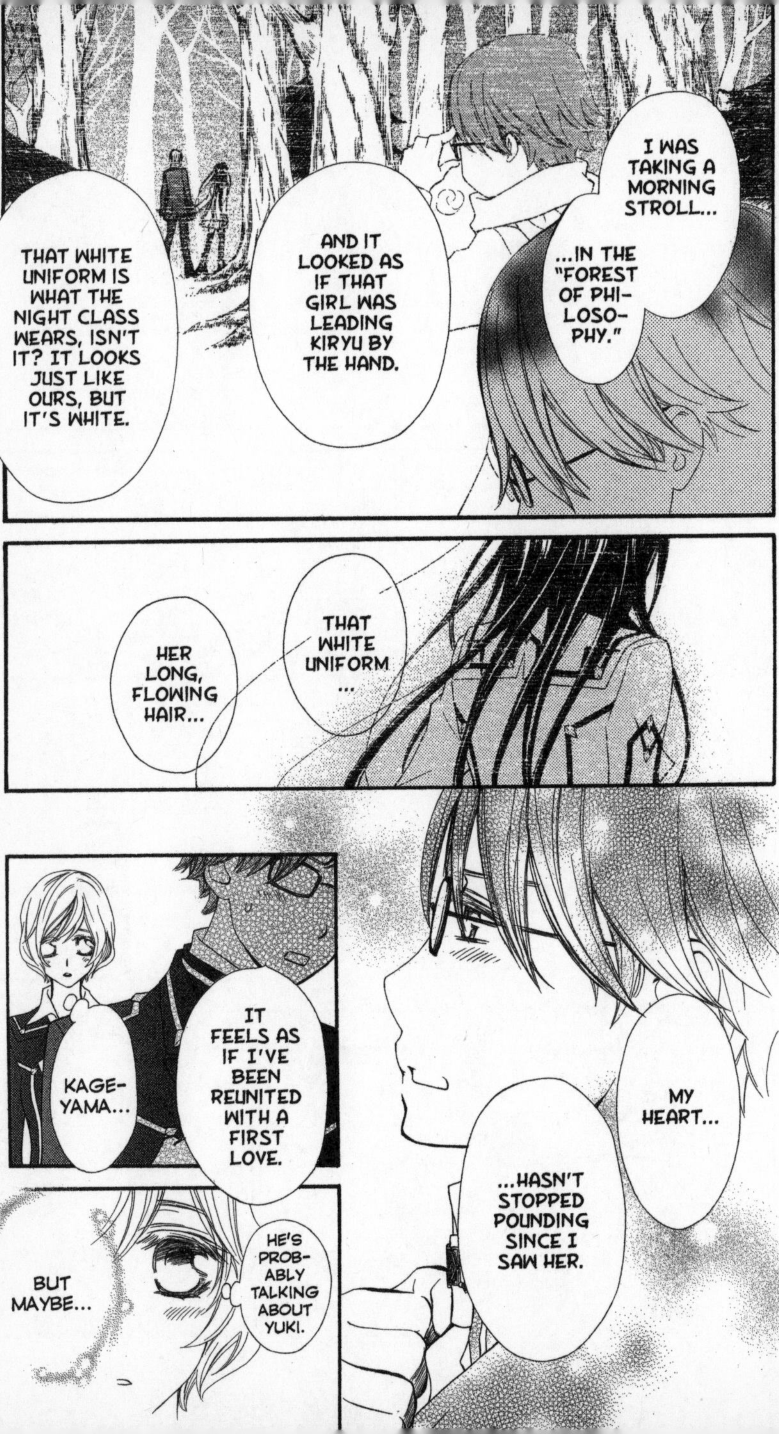
I WAS TAKING A MORNING STROLL...
...IN THE "FOREST OF PHILOSOPHY."
AND IT LOOKED AS IF THAT GIRL WAS LEADING KIRYU BY THE HAND.
THAT WHITE UNIFORM IS WHAT THE NIGHT CLASS WEARS, ISN'T IT? IT LOOKS JUST LIKE OURS, BUT IT'S WHITE.
THAT WHITE UNIFORM...
HER LONG, FLOWING HAIR...
MY HEART...
...HASN'T STOPPED POUNDING SINCE I SAW HER.
IT FEELS AS IF I'VE BEEN REUNITED WITH A FIRST LOVE.
KAGE-YAMA...
HE'S PROBABLY TALKING ABOUT YUKI.
BUT MAYBE...

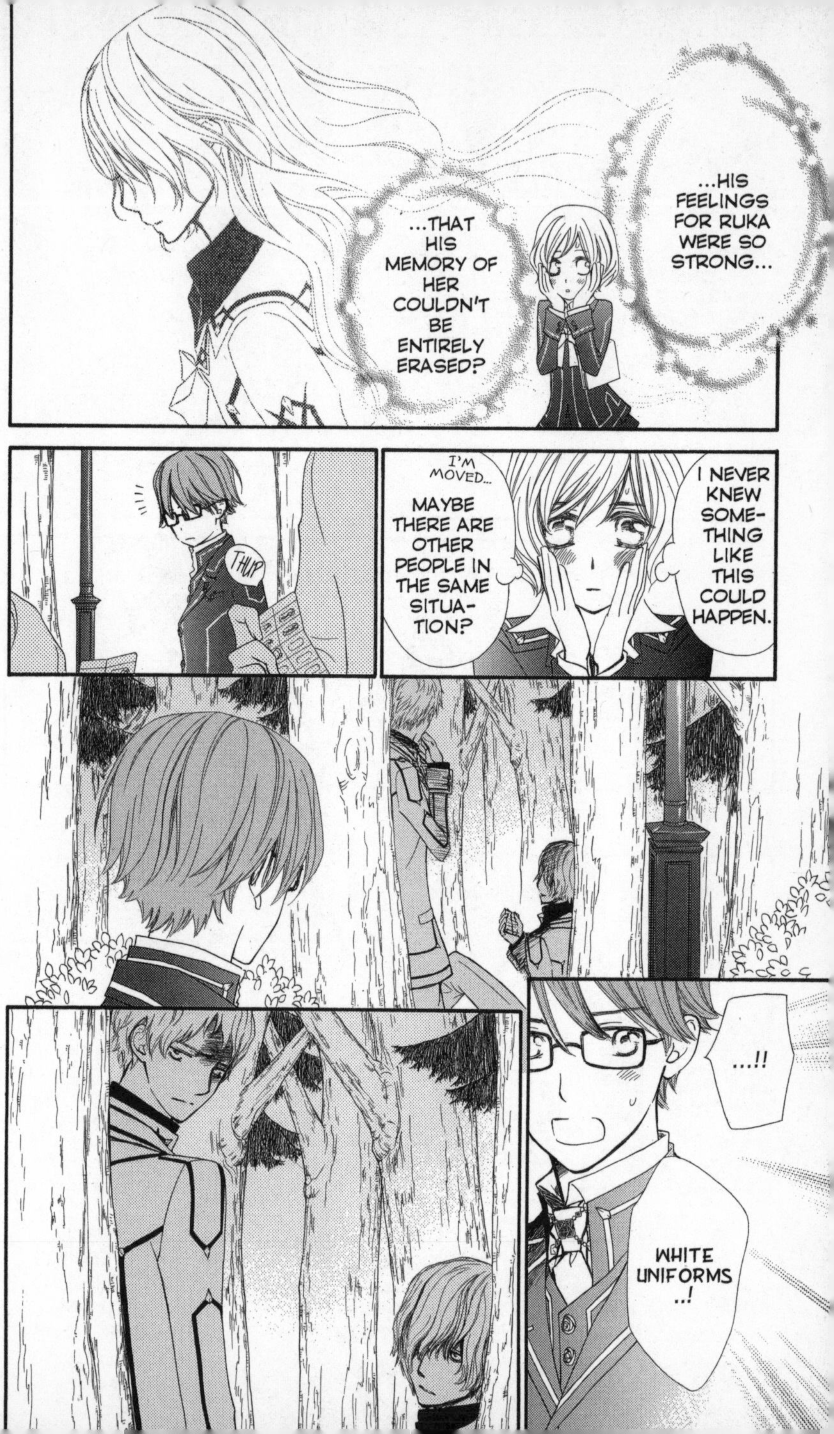
...HIS FEELINGS FOR RUKA WERE SO STRONG...
...THAT HIS MEMORY OF HER COULDN'T BE ENTIRELY ERASED?
I NEVER KNEW SOME-THING LIKE THIS COULD HAPPEN.
I'M MOVED...
MAYBE THERE ARE OTHER PEOPLE IN THE SAME SITUA-TION?
THUP
...!!
WHITE UNIFORMS ..!

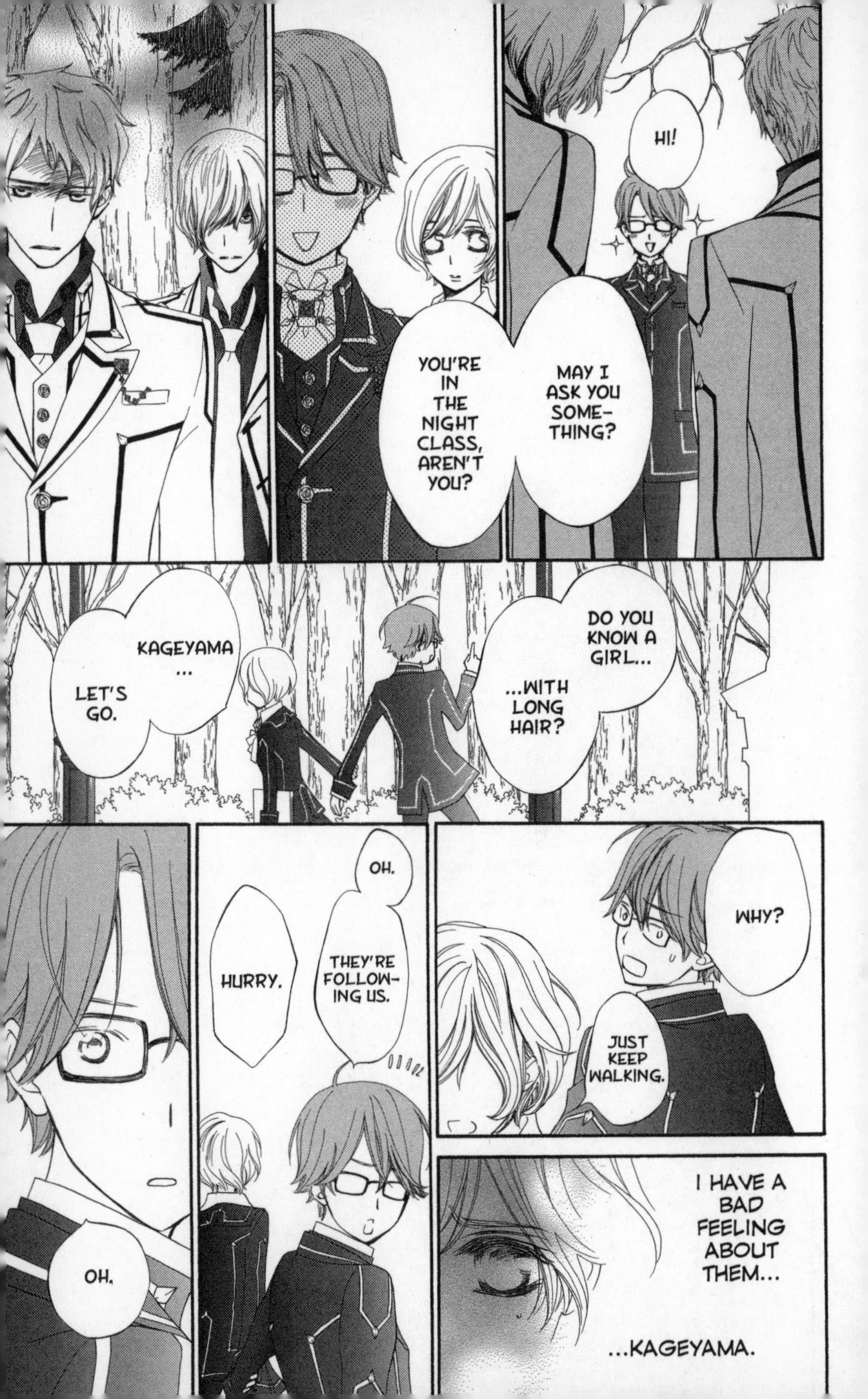
HI!
MAY I ASK YOU SOME-THING?
YOU'RE IN THE NIGHT CLASS, AREN'T YOU?
DO YOU KNOW A GIRL...
...WITH LONG HAIR?
KAGEYAMA...
LET'S GO.
WHY?
JUST KEEP WALKING.
I HAVE A BAD FEELING ABOUT THEM...
...KAGEYAMA.
OH.
THEY'RE FOLLOW-ING US.
HURRY.
OH.

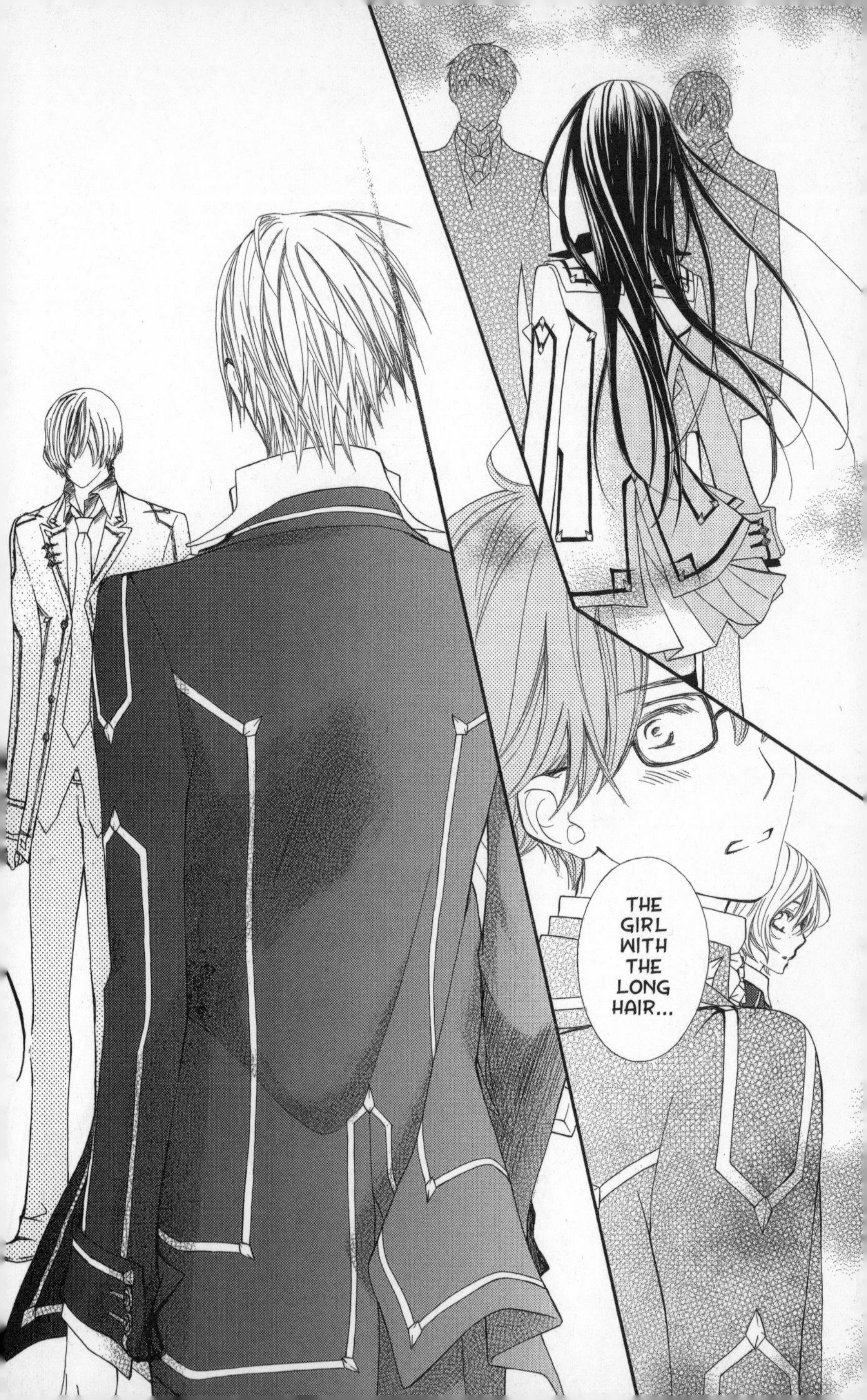
THE GIRL WITH THE LONG HAIR...

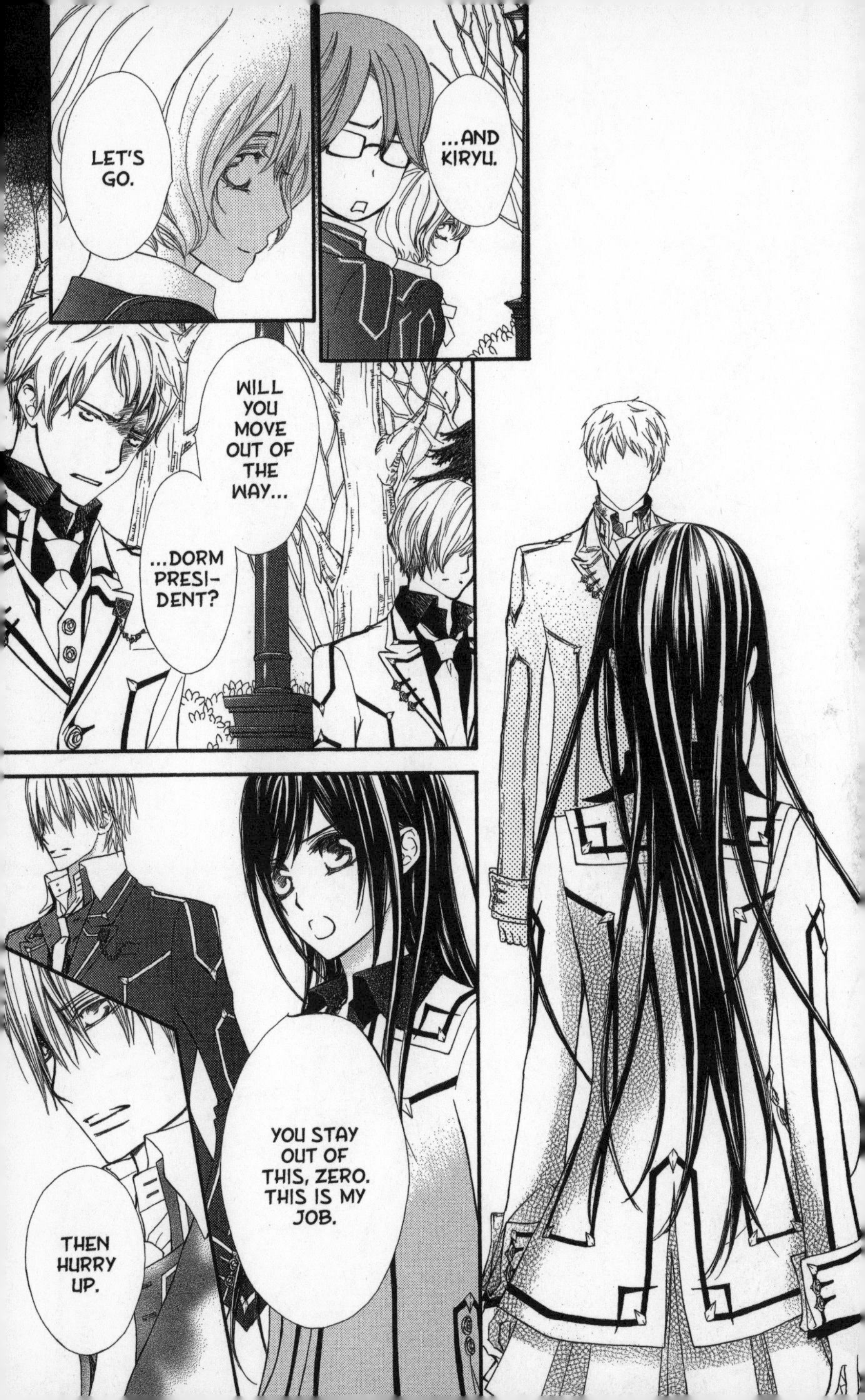
...AND KIRYU.
LET'S GO.
WILL YOU MOVE OUT OF THE WAY...
...DORM PRESI-DENT?
YOU STAY OUT OF THIS, ZERO. THIS IS MY JOB.
THEN HURRY UP.

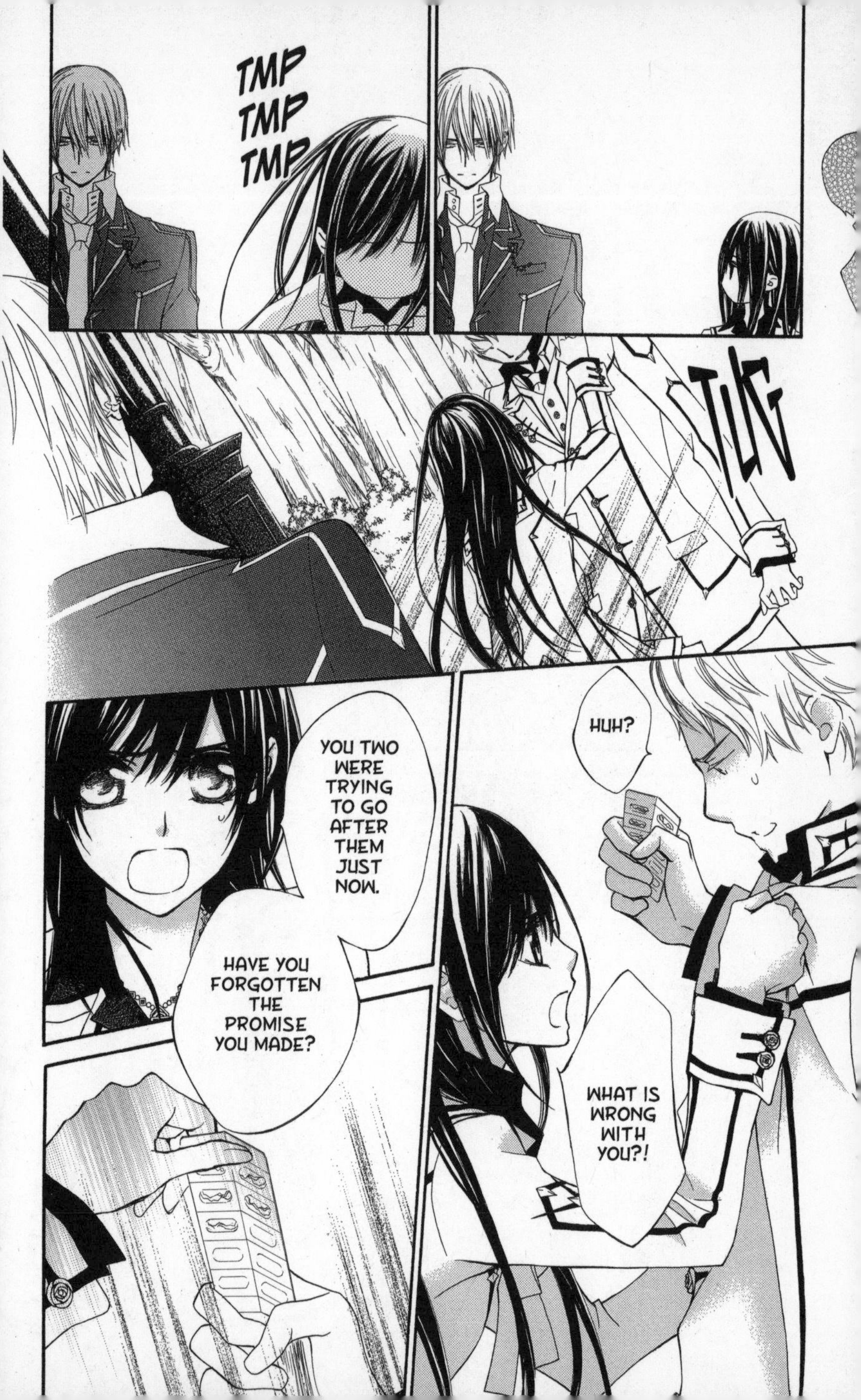
TMP TMP TMP
TUG
HUH?
WHAT IS WRONG WITH YOU?!
YOU TWO WERE TRYING TO GO AFTER THEM JUST NOW.
HAVE YOU FORGOTTEN THE PROMISE YOU MADE?

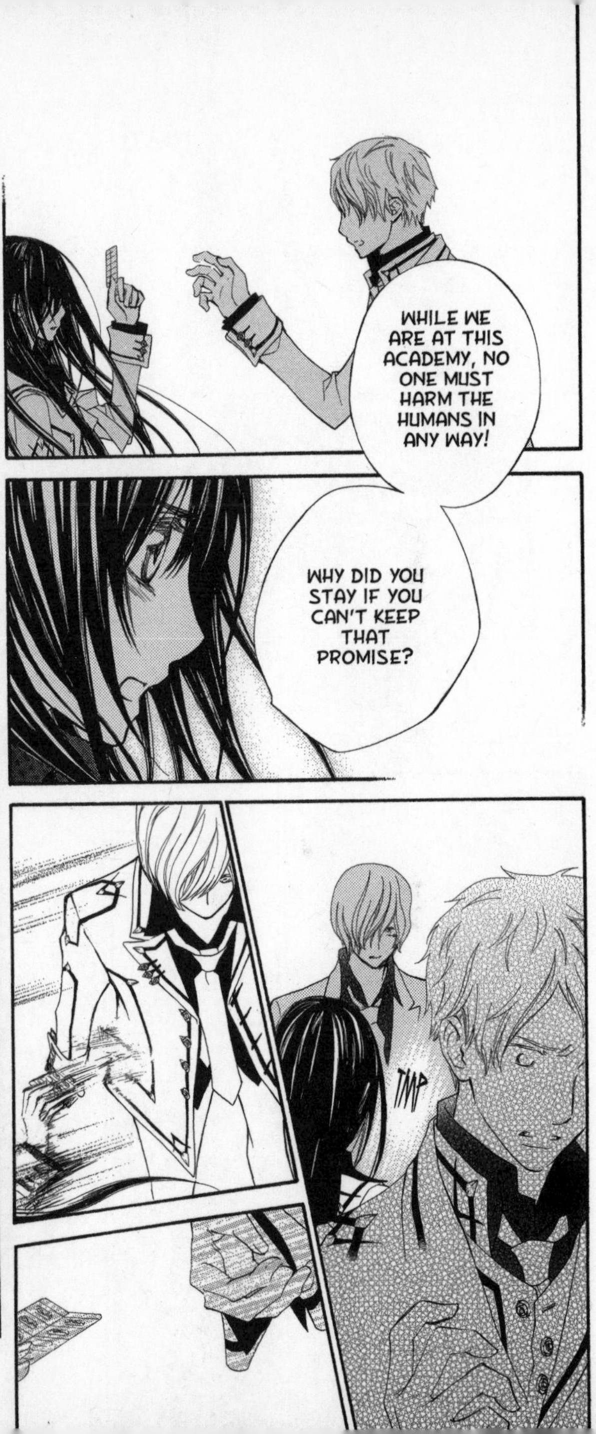
WHILE WE ARE AT THIS ACADEMY, NO ONE MUST HARM THE HUMANS IN ANY WAY!
WHY DID YOU STAY IF YOU CAN'T KEEP THAT PROMISE?
TMP

IV

Thank you very much for all your fan mail. ✿ The letters are a huge support to me. I will do my best to repay you with my manga!

But I am slightly worried because every now and then I receive letters with the wrong address on them, which takes some time to get to me... ? ✿

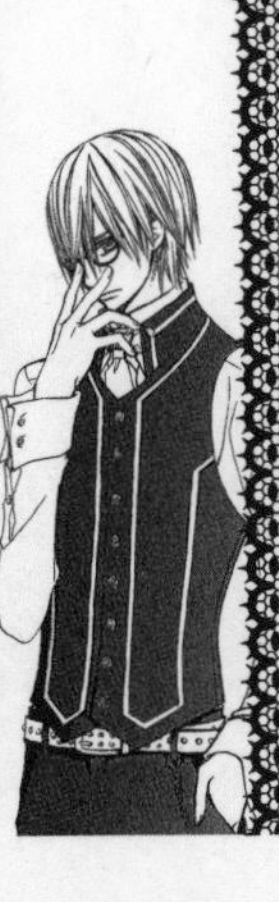

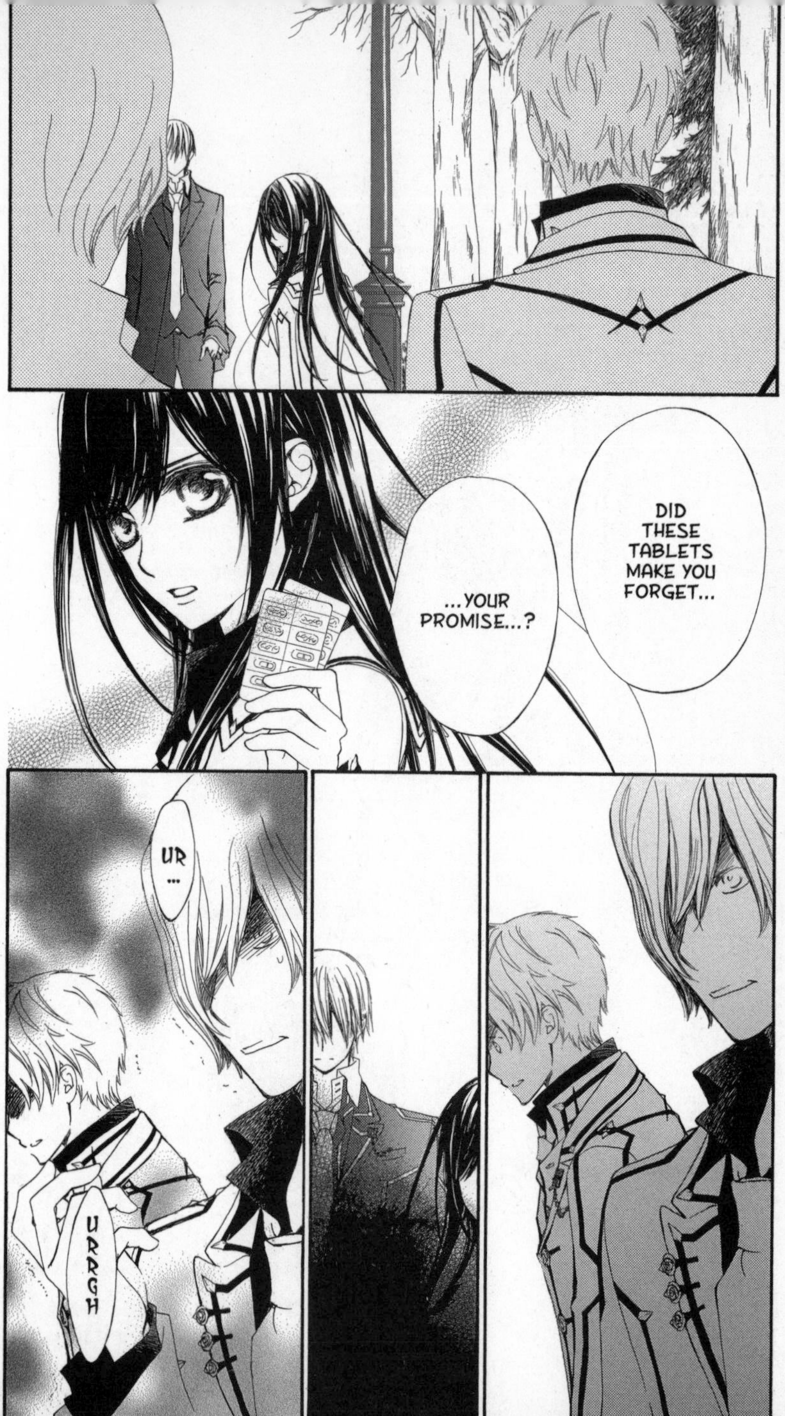
DID THESE TABLETS MAKE YOU FORGET...
...YOUR PROMISE...?
UR ...
URRGH

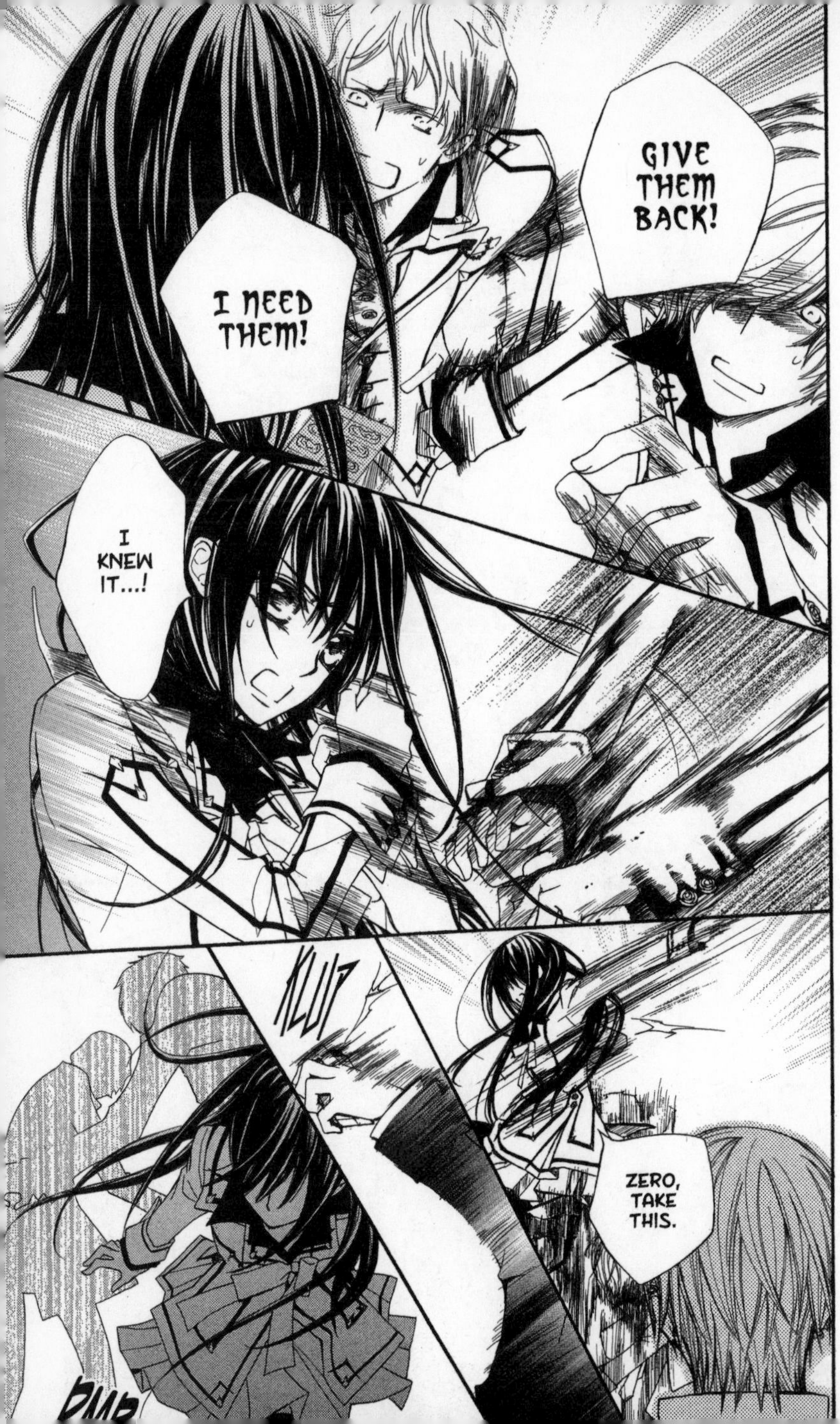
GIVE THEM BACK!
I NEED THEM!
I KNEW IT...!
ZERO, TAKE THIS.

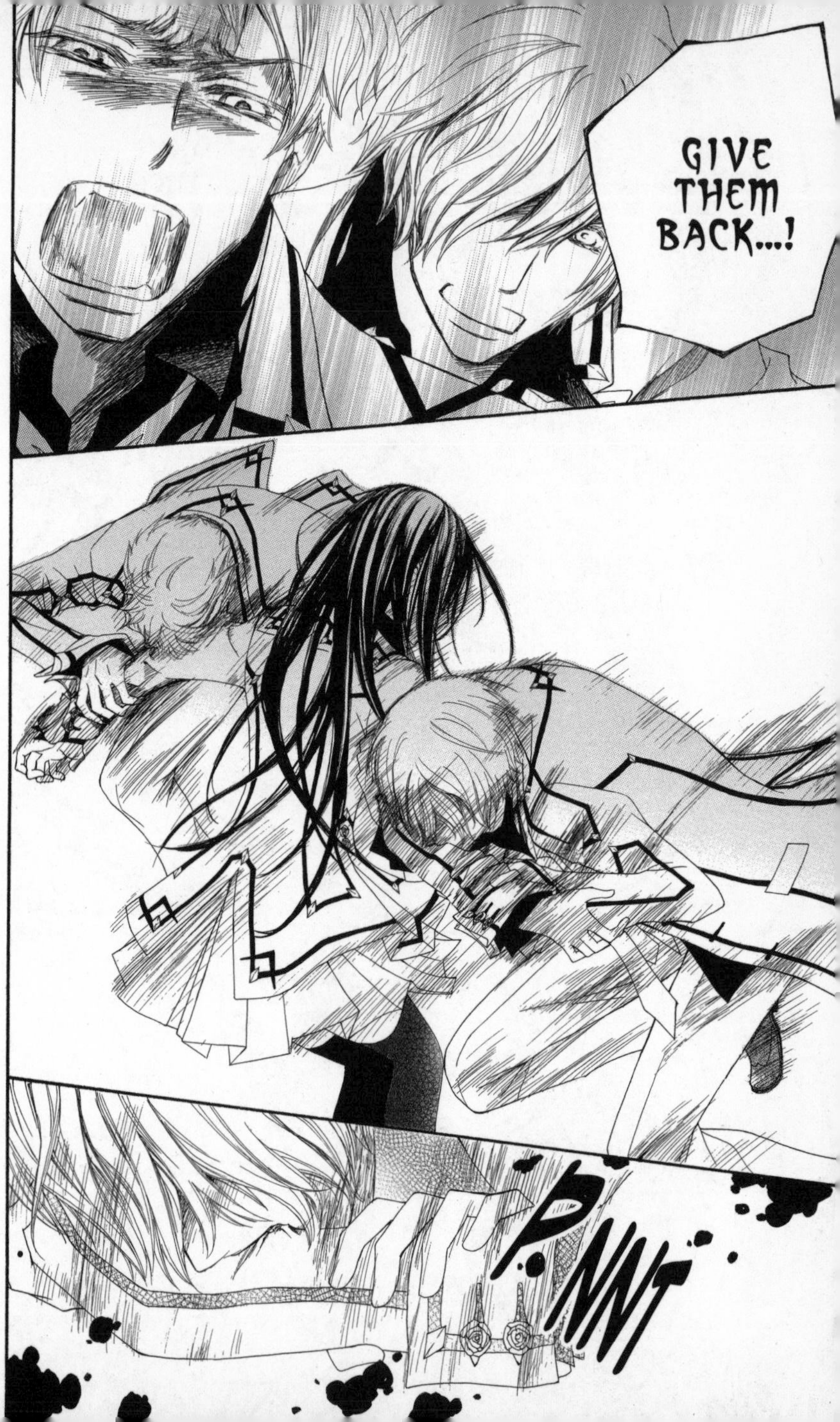
GIVE THEM BACK...!
PINNT

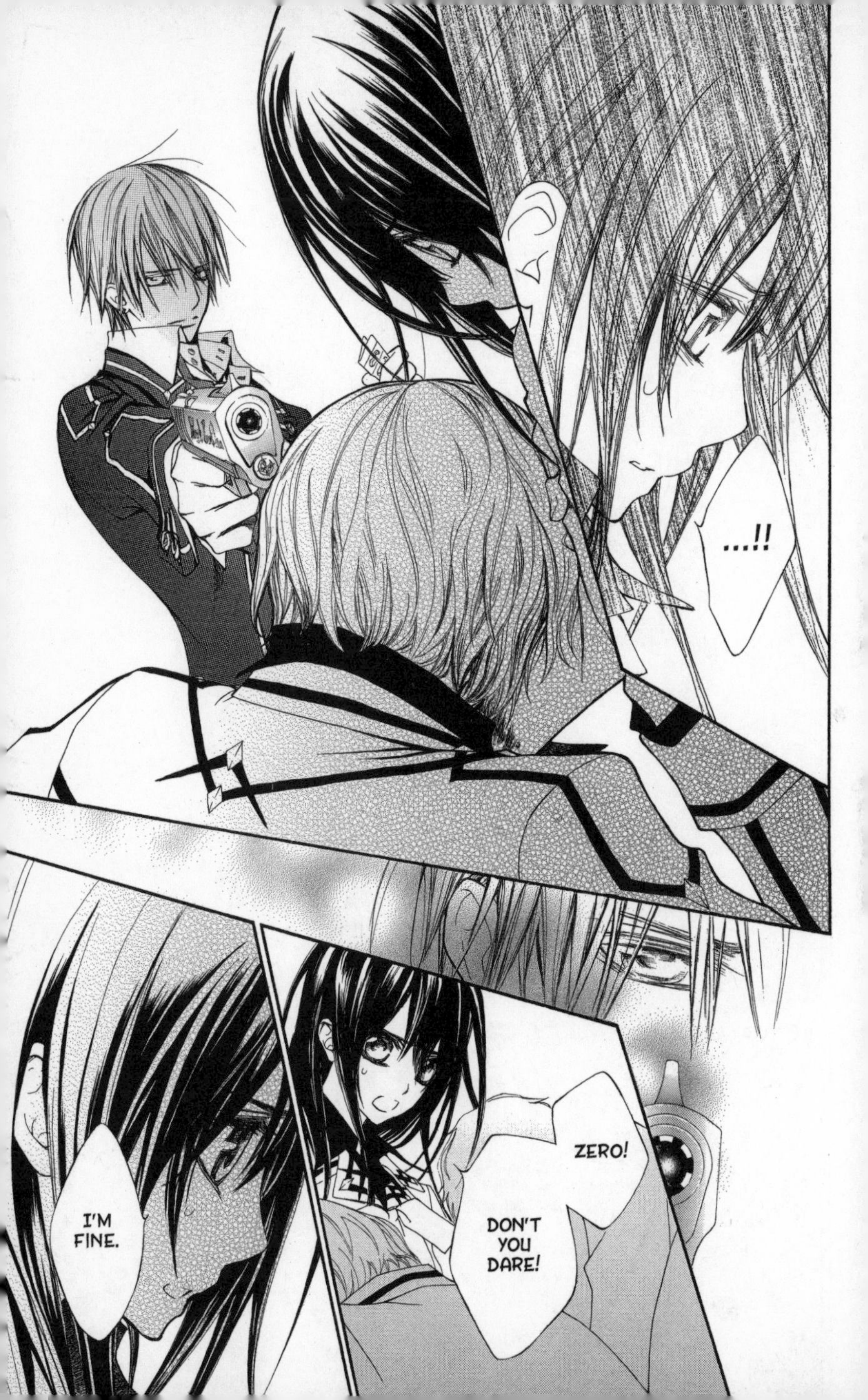
...!!
ZERO!
DON'T YOU DARE!
I'M FINE.

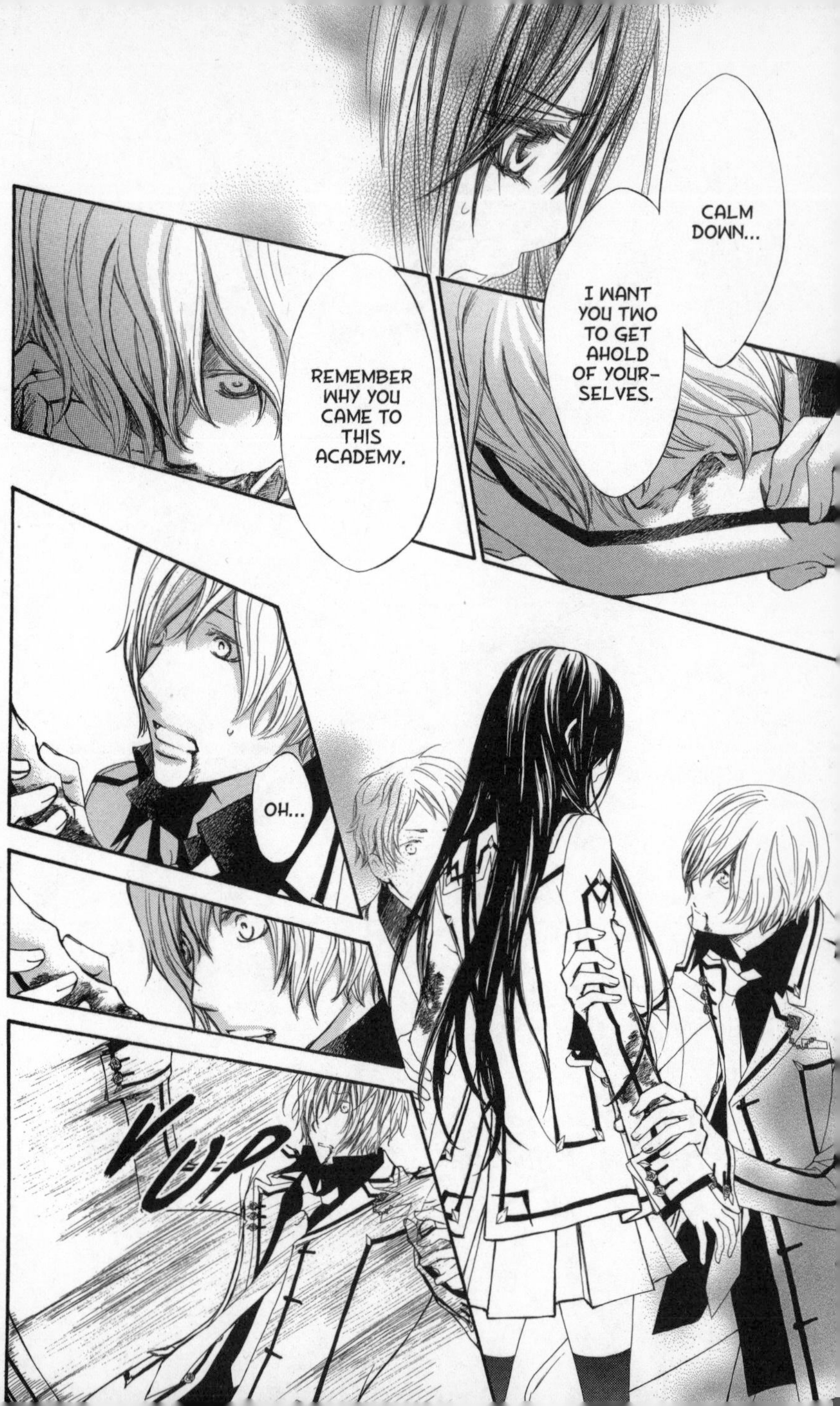
CALM DOWN...
I WANT YOU TWO TO GET AHOLD OF YOUR-SELVES.
REMEMBER WHY YOU CAME TO THIS ACADEMY.
OH...
VUP

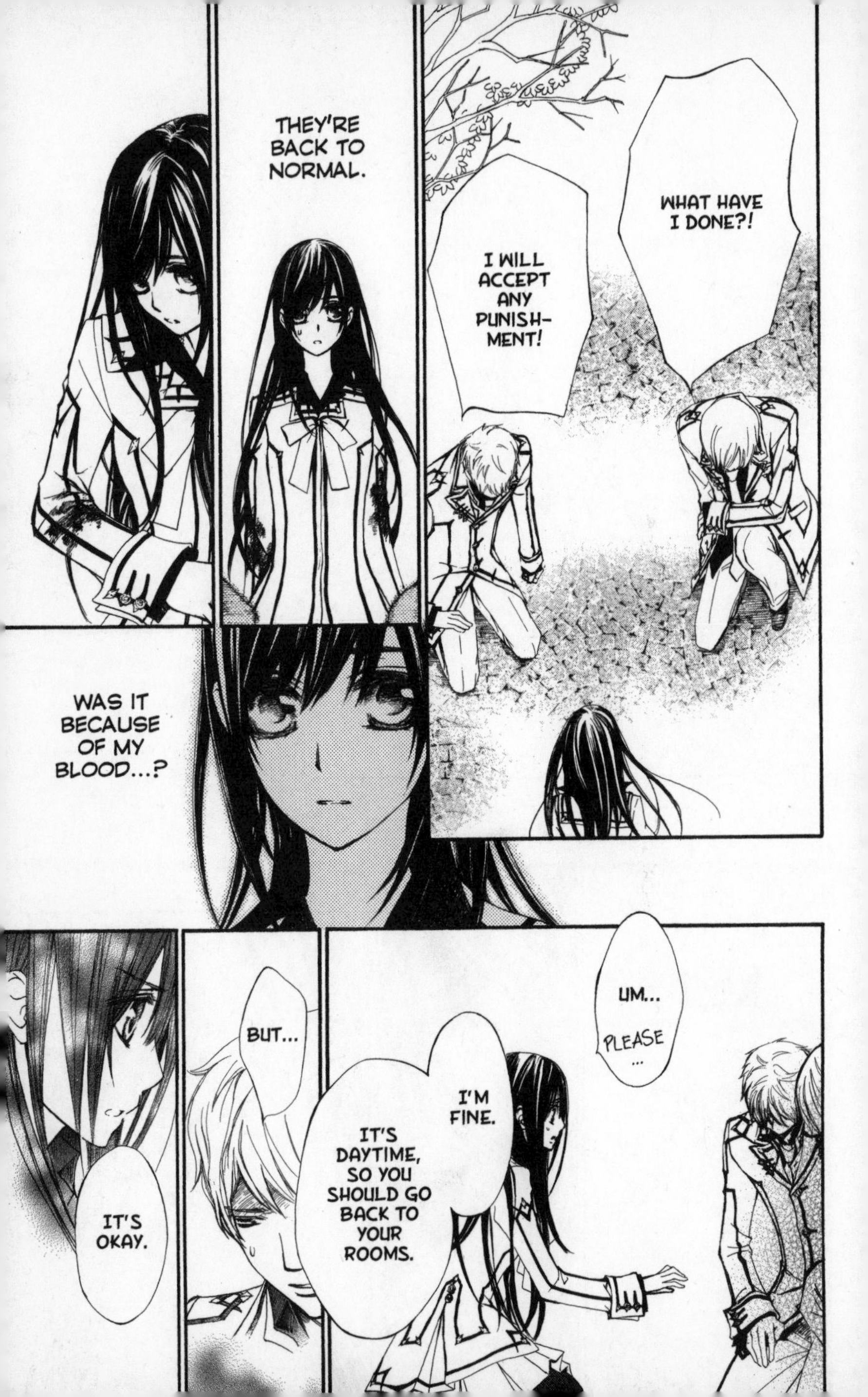
WHAT HAVE I DONE?!
I WILL ACCEPT ANY PUNISHMENT!
THEY'RE BACK TO NORMAL.
WAS IT BECAUSE OF MY BLOOD...?
UM... PLEASE ...
I'M FINE.
IT'S DAYTIME, SO YOU SHOULD GO BACK TO YOUR ROOMS.
BUT...
IT'S OKAY.

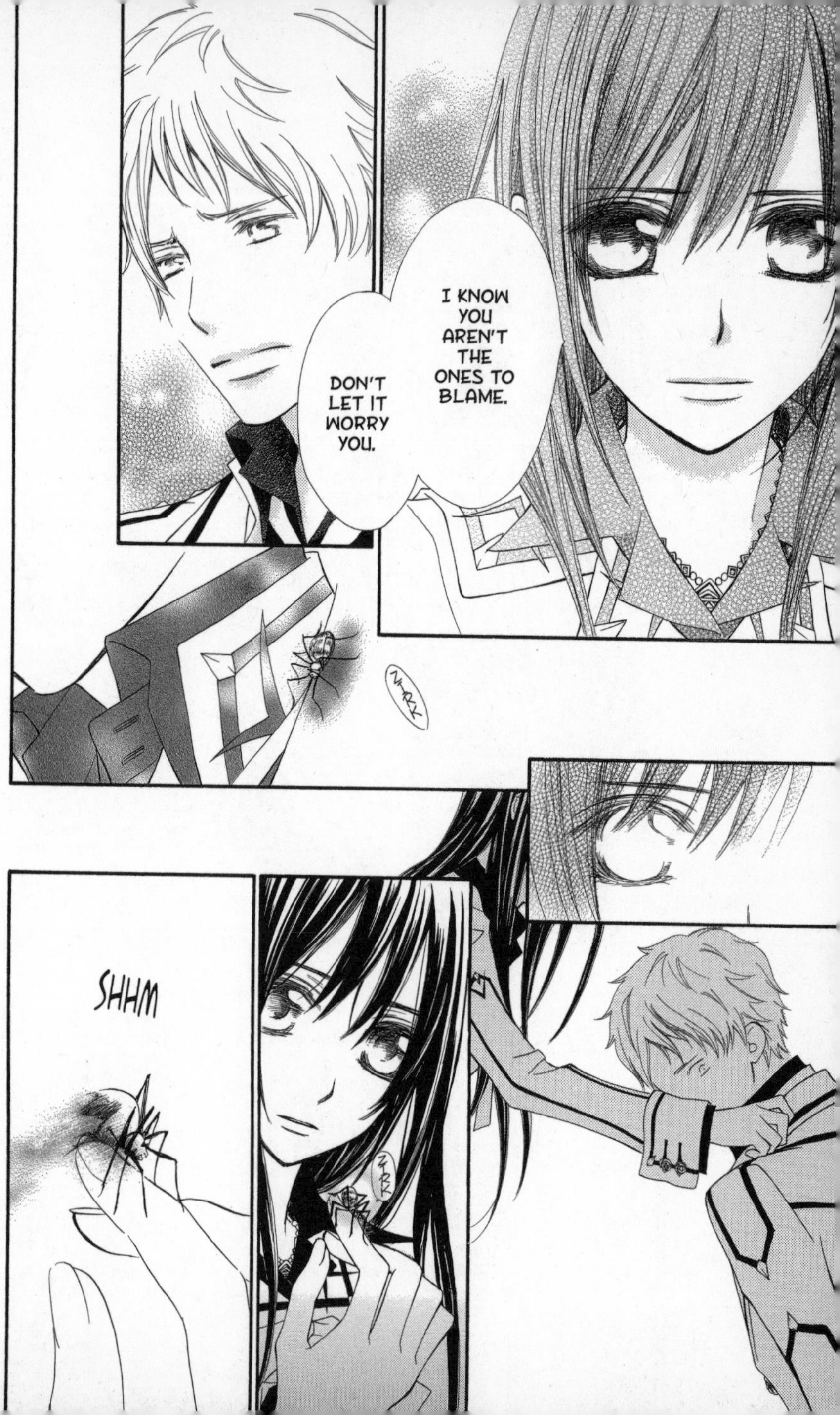
I KNOW YOU AREN'T THE ONES TO BLAME.
DON'T LET IT WORRY YOU.
ZIRRK
SHHM
ZIRRK

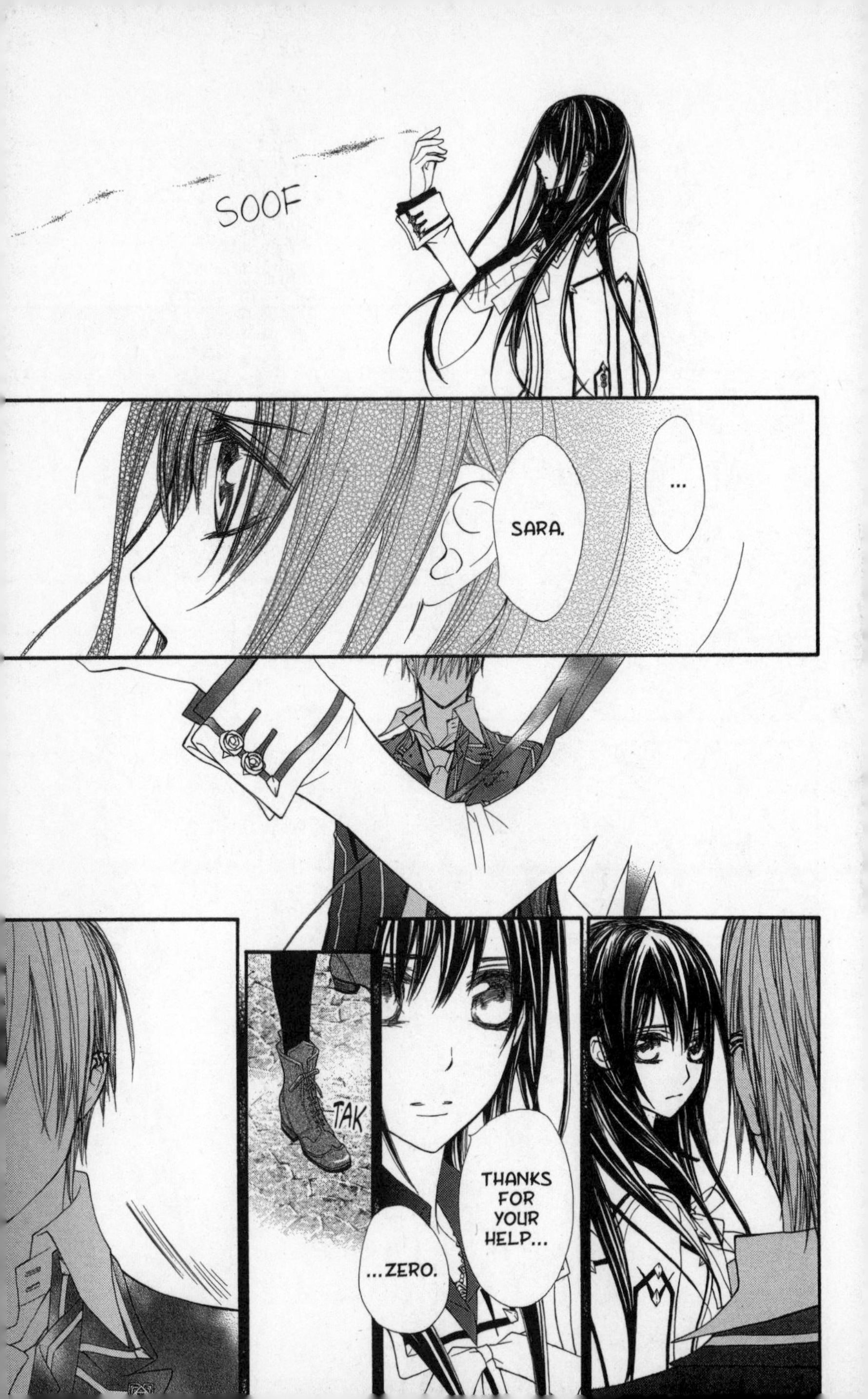
SOOF
...
SARA.
TAK
THANKS FOR YOUR HELP...
...ZERO.

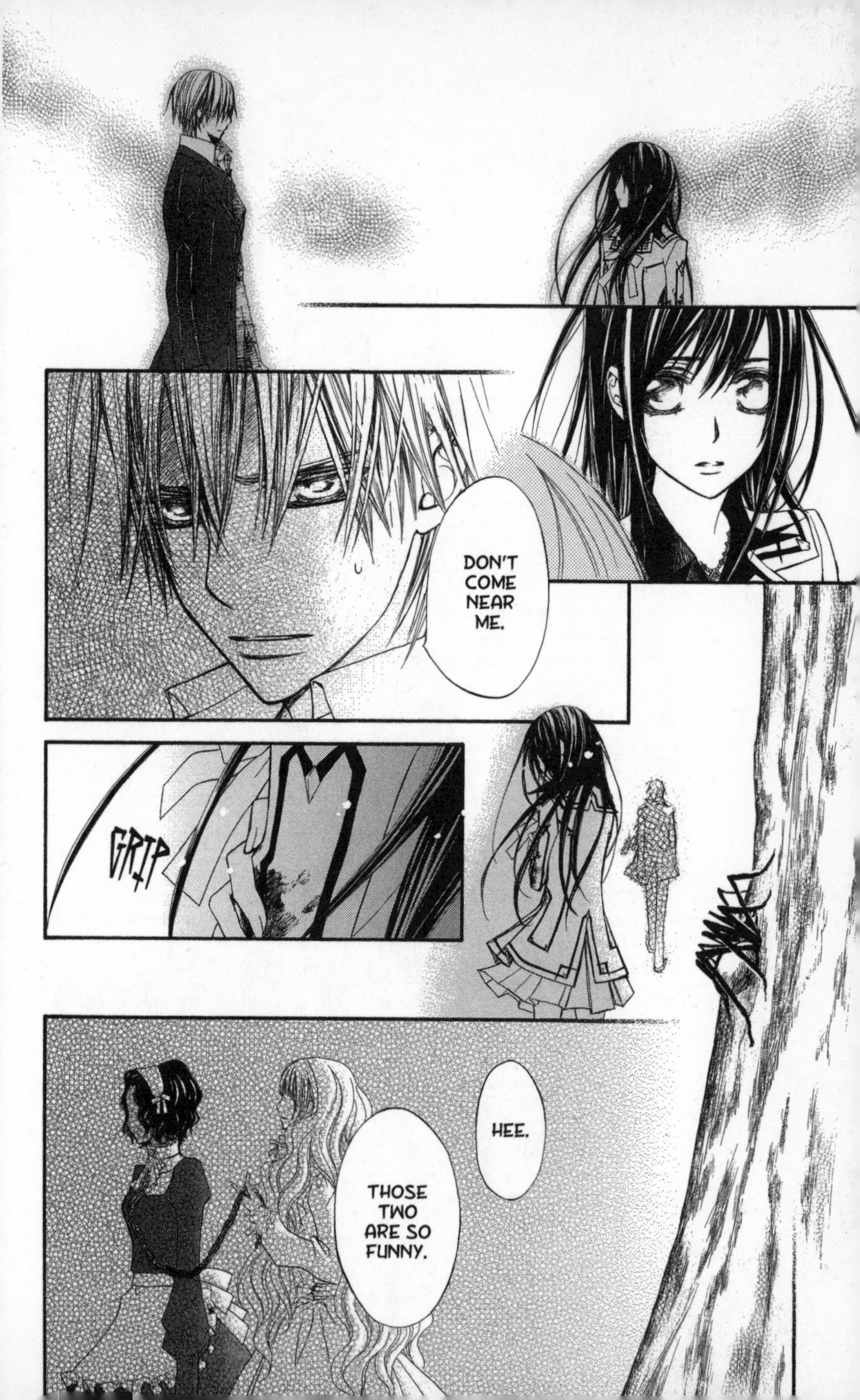
DON'T COME NEAR ME.
GRIP
HEE.
THOSE TWO ARE SO FUNNY.

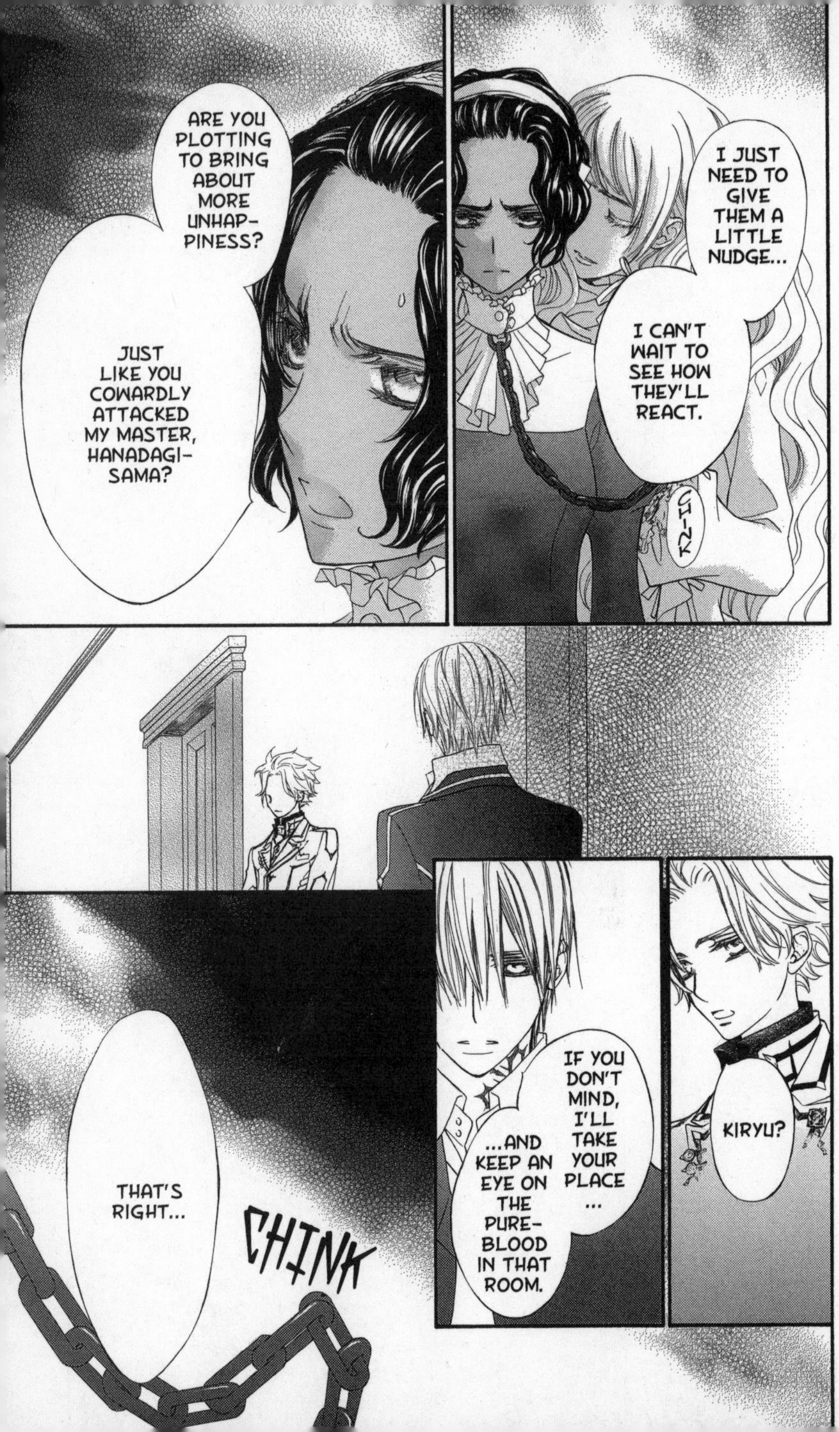
I JUST NEED TO GIVE THEM A LITTLE NUDGE...
I CAN'T WAIT TO SEE HOW THEY'LL REACT.
CHINK
ARE YOU PLOTTING TO BRING ABOUT MORE UNHAP-PINESS?
JUST LIKE YOU COWARDLY ATTACKED MY MASTER, HANADAGI-SAMA?
KIRYU?
IF YOU DON'T MIND, I'LL TAKE YOUR PLACE ...
...AND KEEP AN EYE ON THE PURE-BLOOD IN THAT ROOM.
THAT'S RIGHT...
CHINK

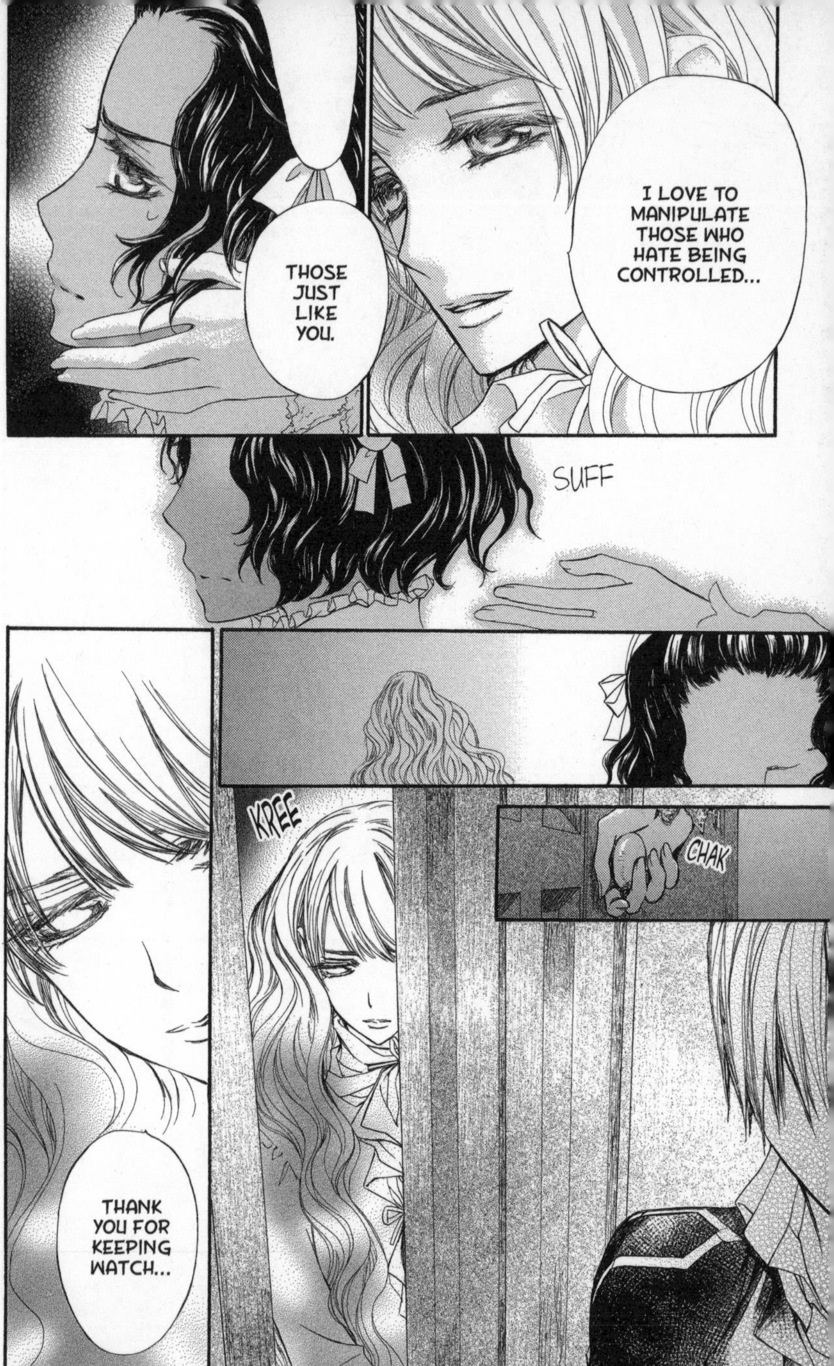
I LOVE TO MANIPULATE THOSE WHO HATE BEING CONTROLLED...
THOSE JUST LIKE YOU.
SUFF
CHAK
KREE
THANK YOU FOR KEEPING WATCH...

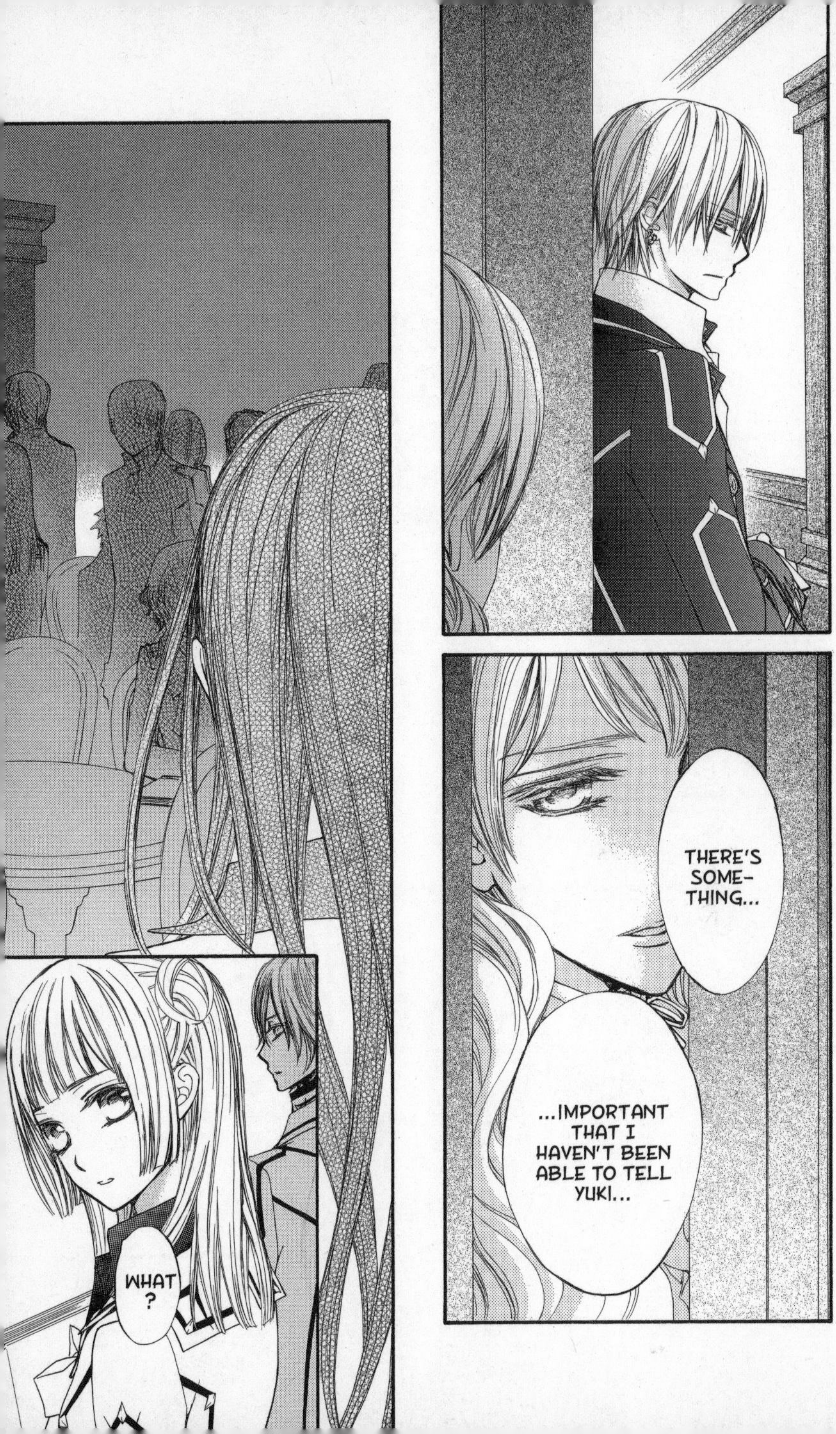
THERE'S SOME-THING...
...IMPORTANT THAT I HAVEN'T BEEN ABLE TO TELL YUKI...
WHAT?

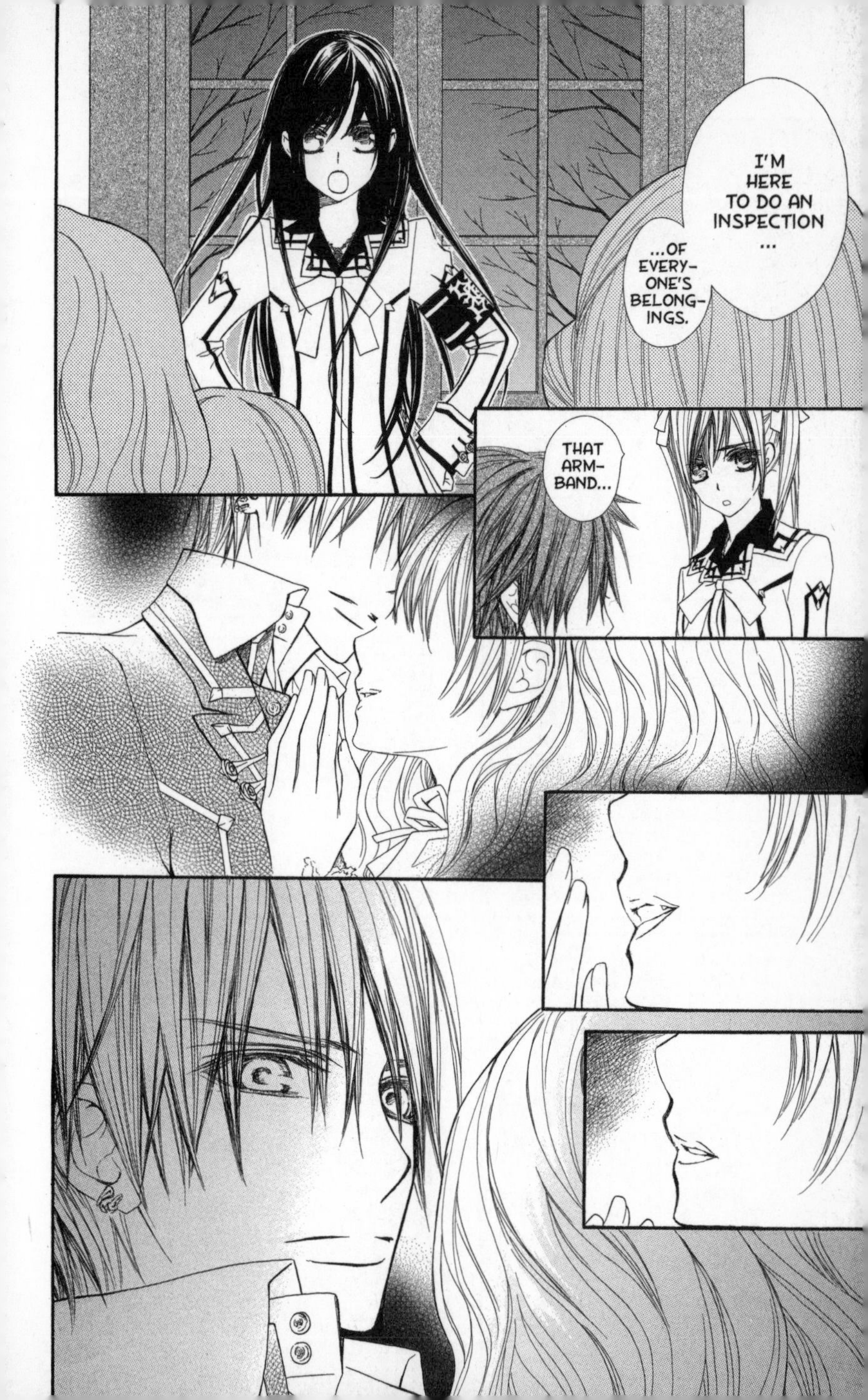
I'M HERE TO DO AN INSPECTION ...
...OF EVERY-ONE'S BELONG-INGS.
THAT ARM-BAND...

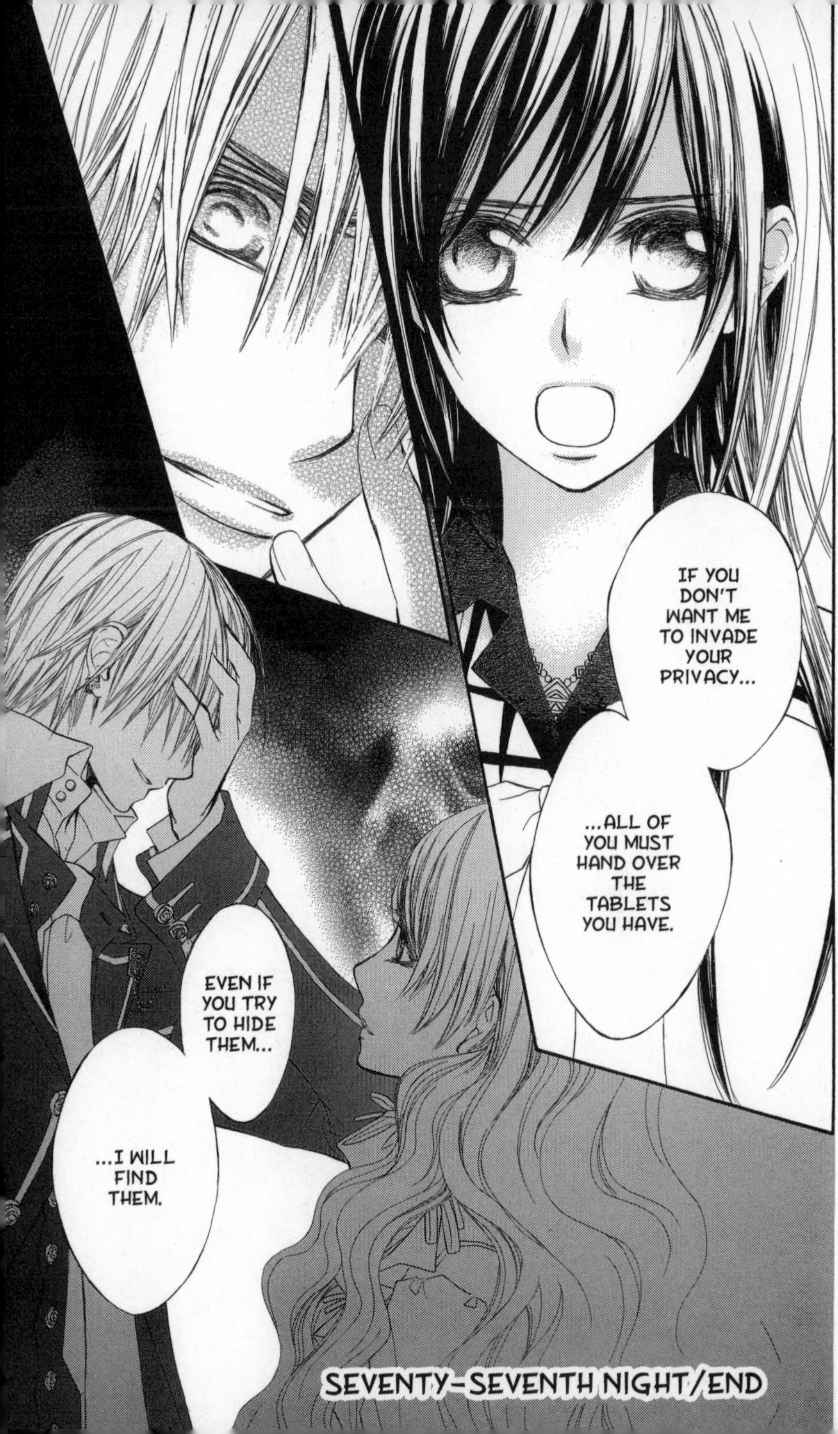
IF YOU DON'T WANT ME TO INVADE YOUR PRIVACY...
...ALL OF YOU MUST HAND OVER THE TABLETS YOU HAVE.
EVEN IF YOU TRY TO HIDE THEM...
...I WILL FIND THEM.
SEVENTY-SEVENTH NIGHT/END

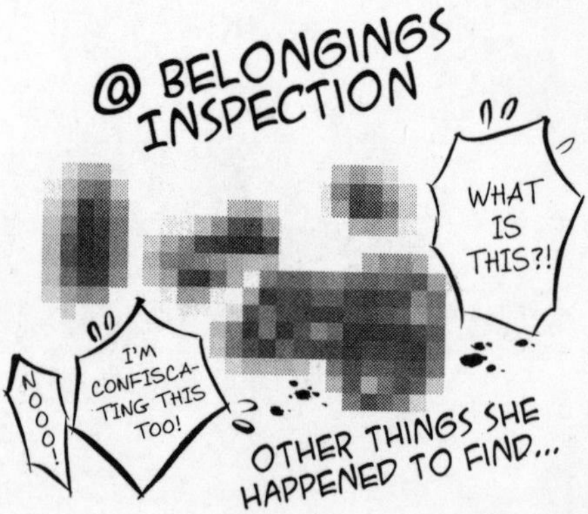
@ BELONGINGS INSPECTION
WHAT IS THIS?!
I'M CONFISCA-TING THIS TOO!
NOOO!
OTHER THINGS SHE HAPPENED TO FIND...

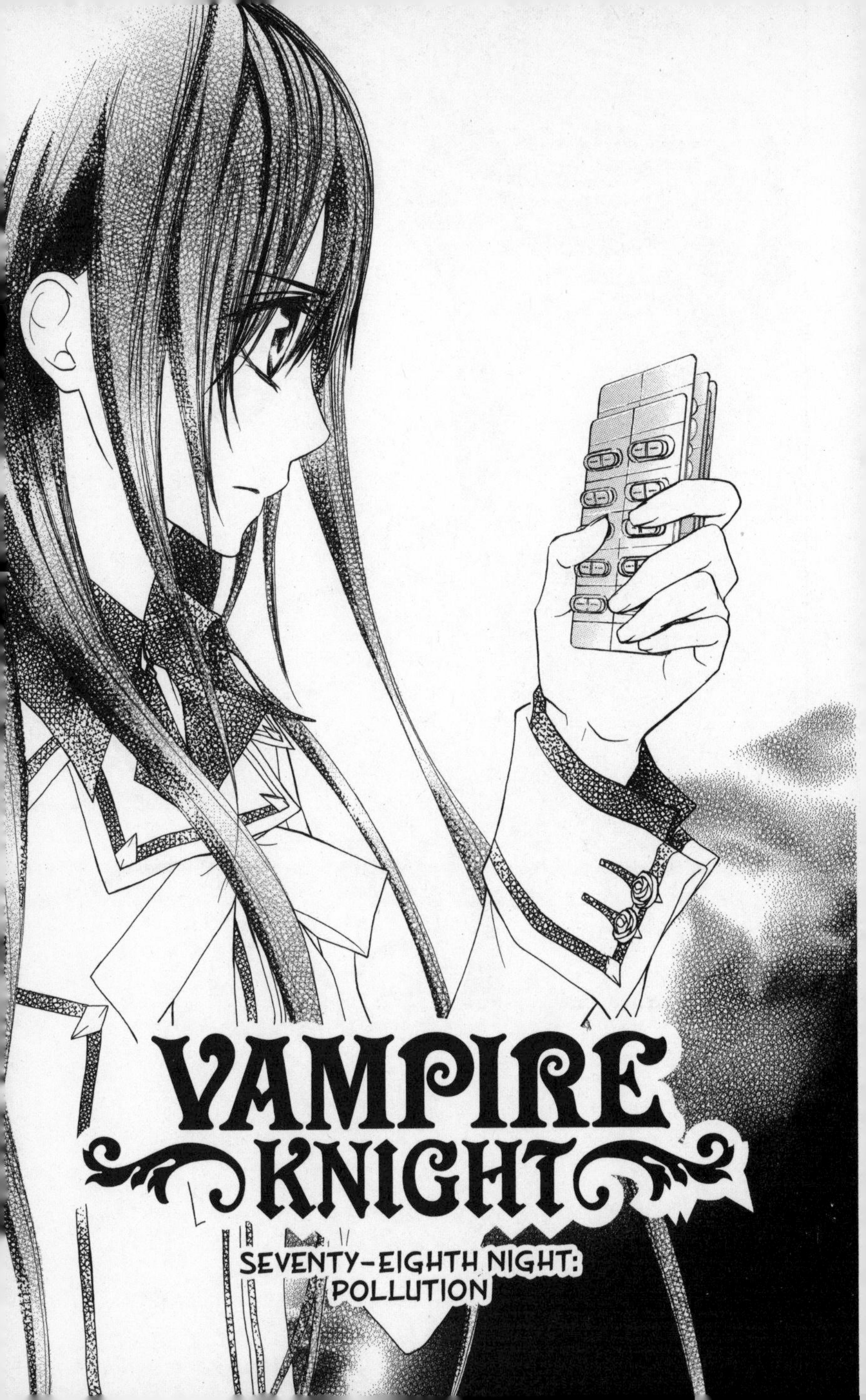
VAMPIRE KNIGHT
SEVENTY-EIGHTH NIGHT: POLLUTION

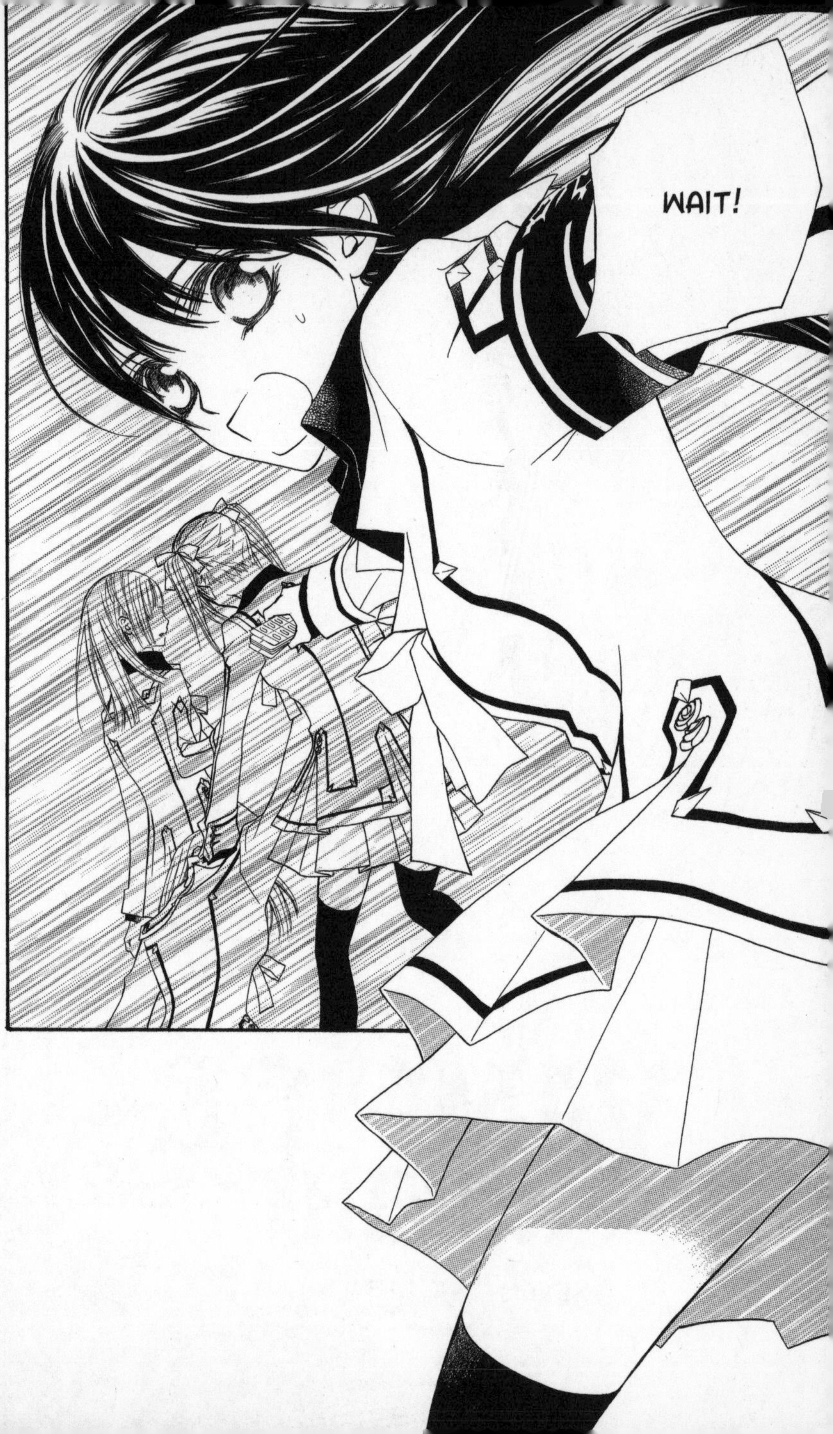
WAIT!

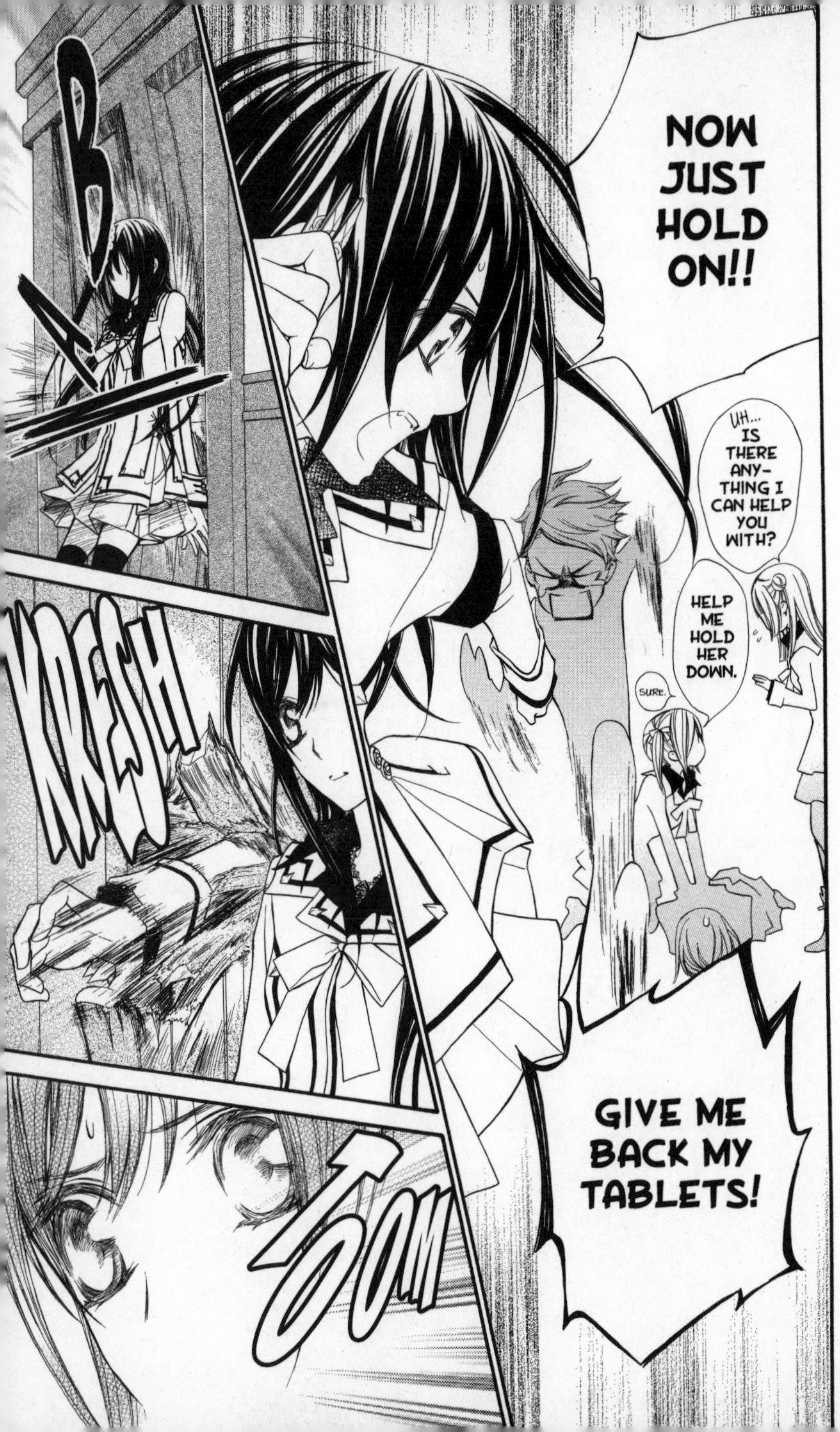
NOW JUST HOLD ON!!
UH... IS THERE ANY-THING I CAN HELP YOU WITH?
HELP ME HOLD HER DOWN.
SURE.
GIVE ME BACK MY TABLETS!
KRESH

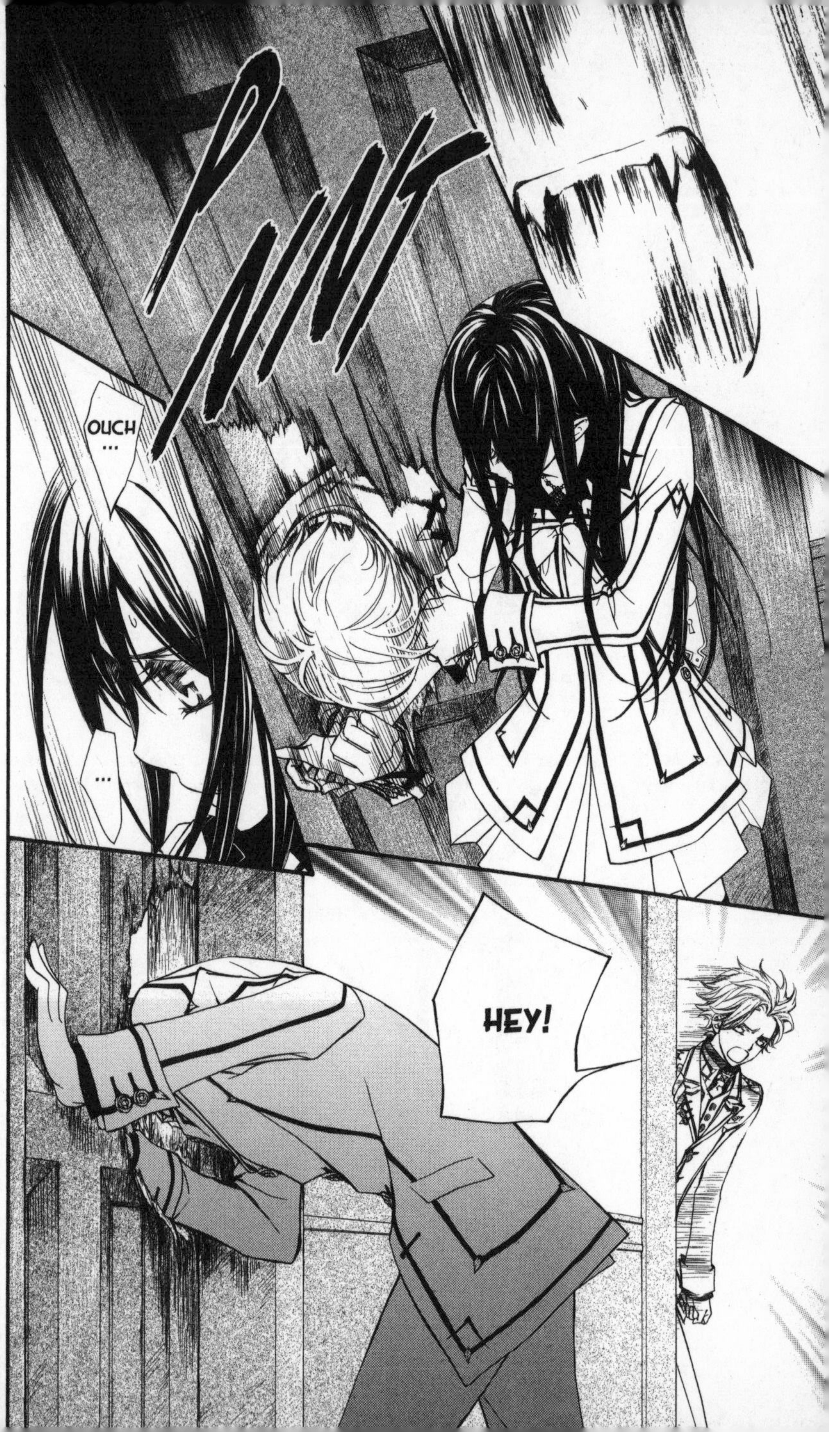
PUNK
OUCH ...
...
HEY!

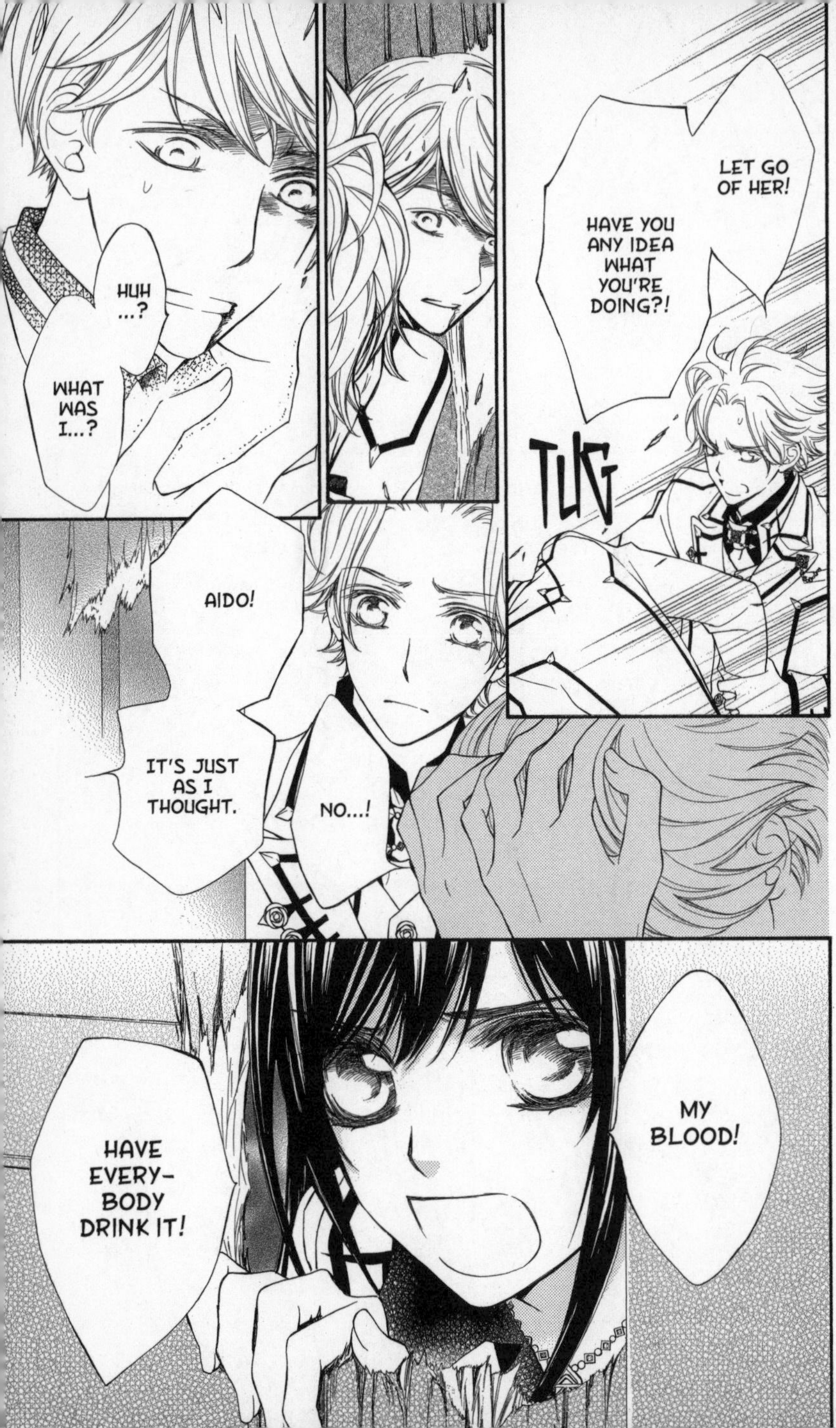
LET GO OF HER!
HAVE YOU ANY IDEA WHAT YOU'RE DOING?!
TUG
HUH ...?
WHAT WAS I...?
AIDO!
NO...!
IT'S JUST AS I THOUGHT.
MY BLOOD!
HAVE EVERY-BODY DRINK IT!

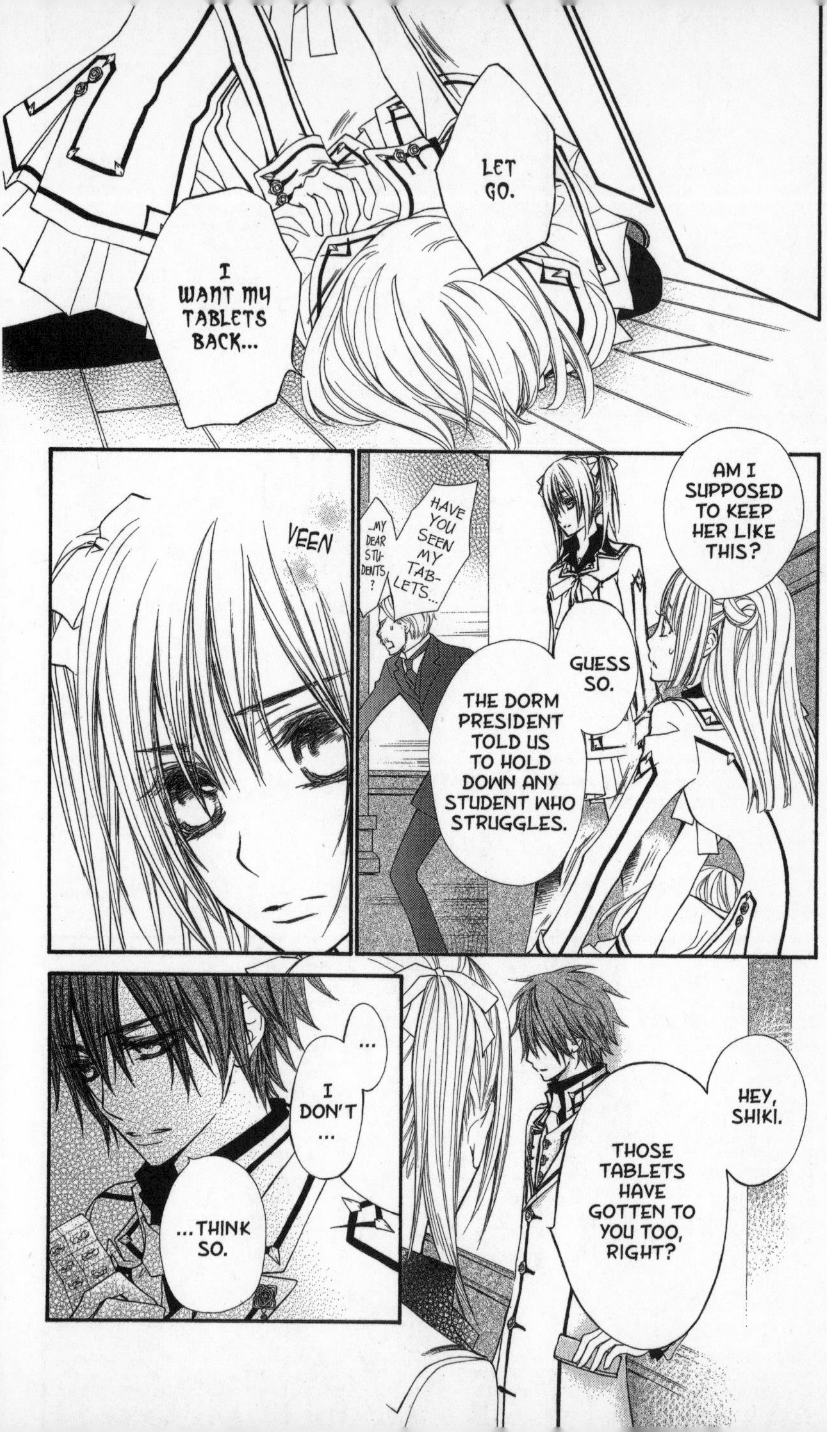
LET GO.
I WANT MY TABLETS BACK...
AM I SUPPOSED TO KEEP HER LIKE THIS?
HAVE YOU SEEN MY TAB-LETS...
...MY DEAR STU-DENTS?
GUESS SO.
THE DORM PRESIDENT TOLD US TO HOLD DOWN ANY STUDENT WHO STRUGGLES.
VEEN
HEY, SHIKI.
THOSE TABLETS HAVE GOTTEN TO YOU TOO, RIGHT?
...
I DON'T ...
...THINK SO.

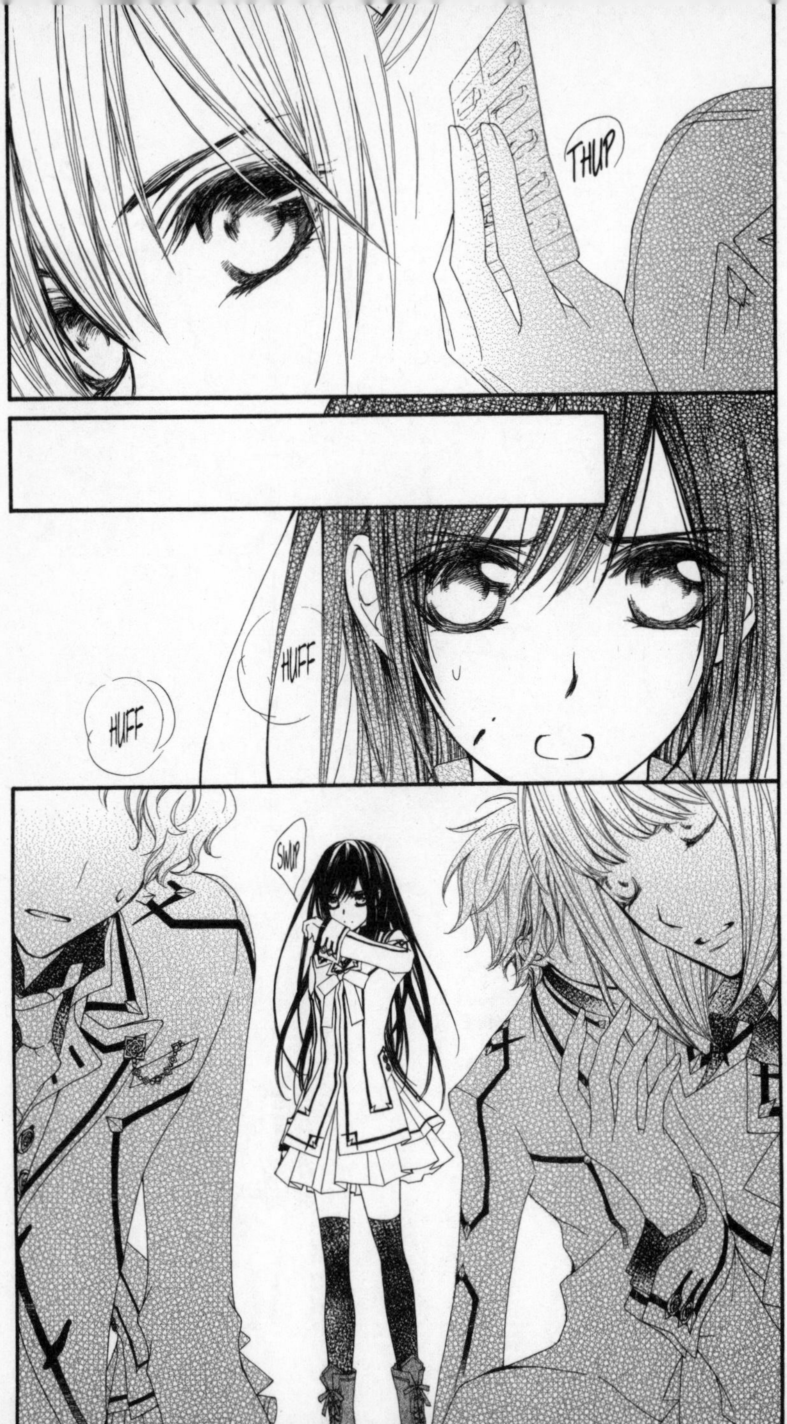
THUP
HUFF
HUFF
SWIP

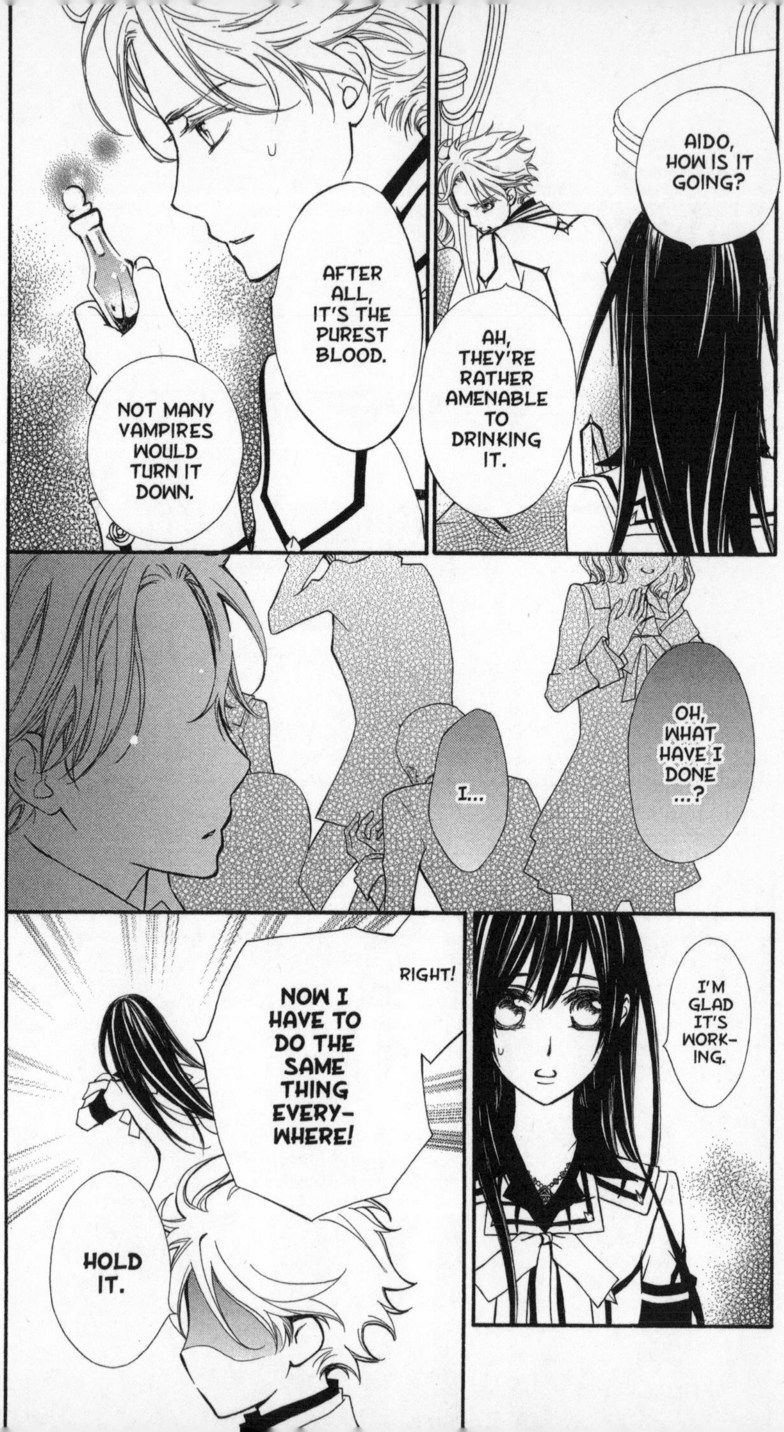
AIDO, HOW IS IT GOING?
AH, THEY'RE RATHER AMENABLE TO DRINKING IT.
AFTER ALL, IT'S THE PUREST BLOOD.
NOT MANY VAMPIRES WOULD TURN IT DOWN.
OH, WHAT HAVE I DONE ...?
I...
I'M GLAD IT'S WORKING.
RIGHT!
NOW I HAVE TO DO THE SAME THING EVERYWHERE!
HOLD IT.

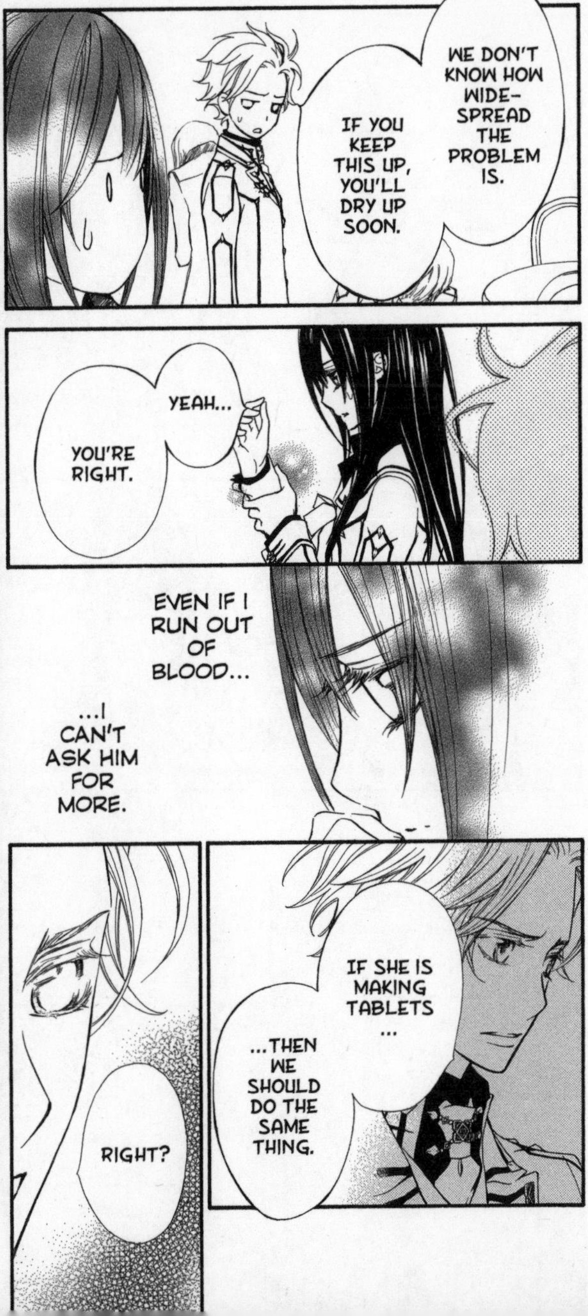
WE DON'T KNOW HOW WIDE-SPREAD THE PROBLEM IS.
IF YOU KEEP THIS UP, YOU'LL DRY UP SOON.
YEAH...
YOU'RE RIGHT.
EVEN IF I RUN OUT OF BLOOD...
...I CAN'T ASK HIM FOR MORE.
IF SHE IS MAKING TABLETS ...
...THEN WE SHOULD DO THE SAME THING.
RIGHT?

V

Lastly...

I would like to thank my assistants who help me with my monthly work.

O. Mio-sama
K. Midori-sama
I. Asami-sama
A. Ichiya-sama

My mother and father, my friends...

My editor and everyone else involved with this work.

And to all you readers who have purchased this series.

Thank you very much.

It is thanks to your support that I have been able to publish 16 volumes.

I hope you will support me in volume 17 as well.

樋野まつり
Matsuri Hino

2012. Towards the end of winter.

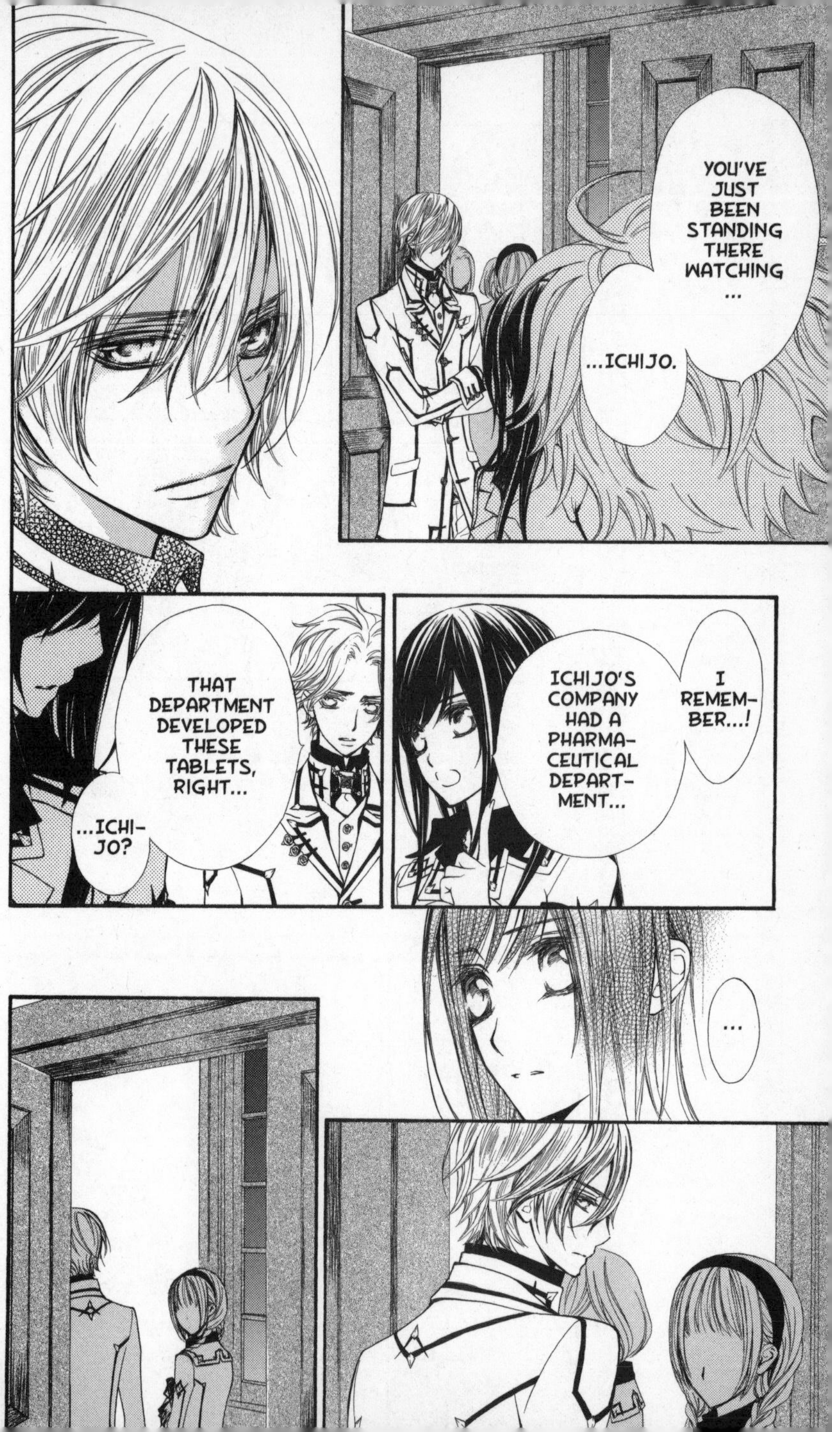
YOU'VE JUST BEEN STANDING THERE WATCHING ...
...ICHIJO.
I REMEMBER...!
ICHIJO'S COMPANY HAD A PHARMACEUTICAL DEPARTMENT...
THAT DEPARTMENT DEVELOPED THESE TABLETS, RIGHT...
...ICHIJO?
...

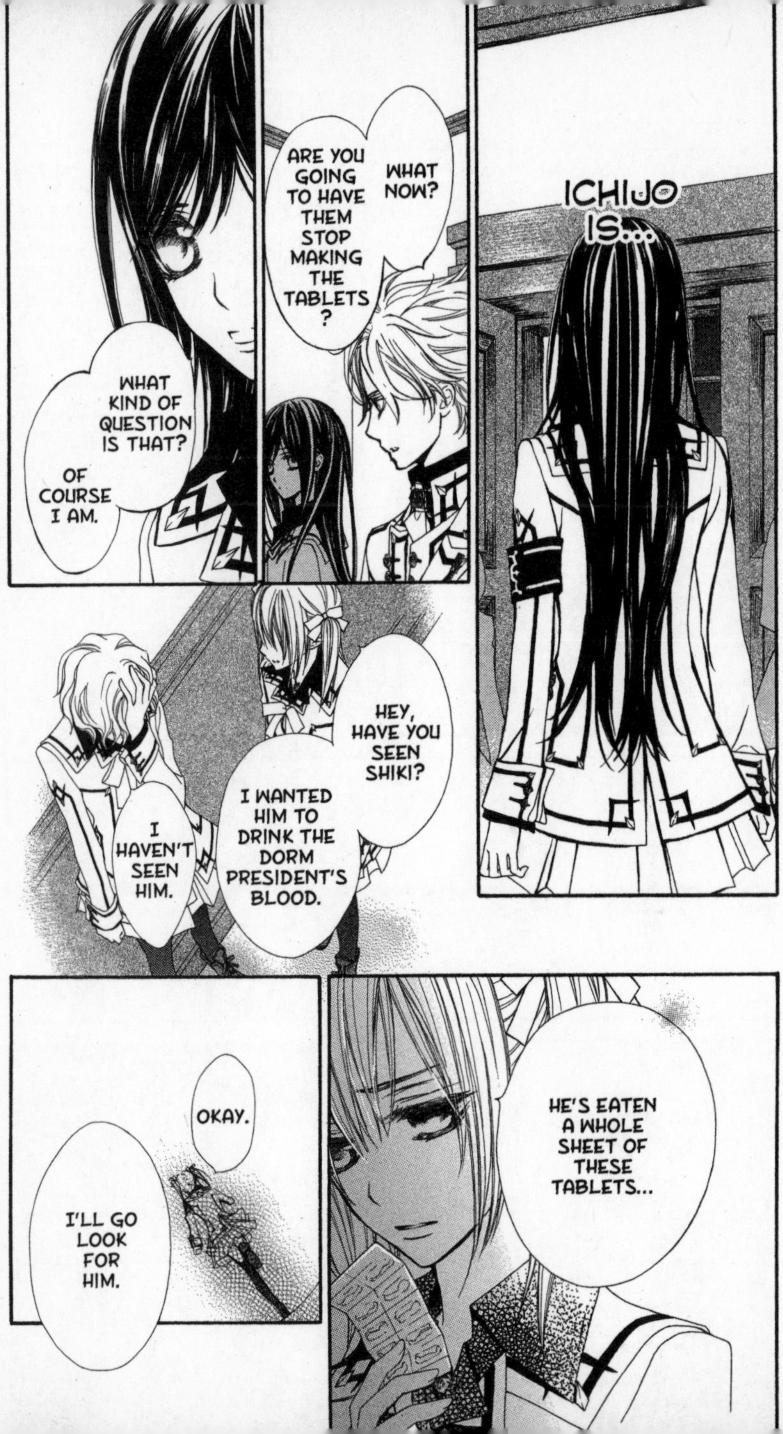

ICHIJO IS...
WHAT NOW?
ARE YOU GOING TO HAVE THEM STOP MAKING THE TABLETS?
WHAT KIND OF QUESTION IS THAT?
OF COURSE I AM.
HEY, HAVE YOU SEEN SHIKI?
I WANTED HIM TO DRINK THE DORM PRESIDENT'S BLOOD.
I HAVEN'T SEEN HIM.
HE'S EATEN A WHOLE SHEET OF THESE TABLETS...
OKAY.
I'LL GO LOOK FOR HIM.

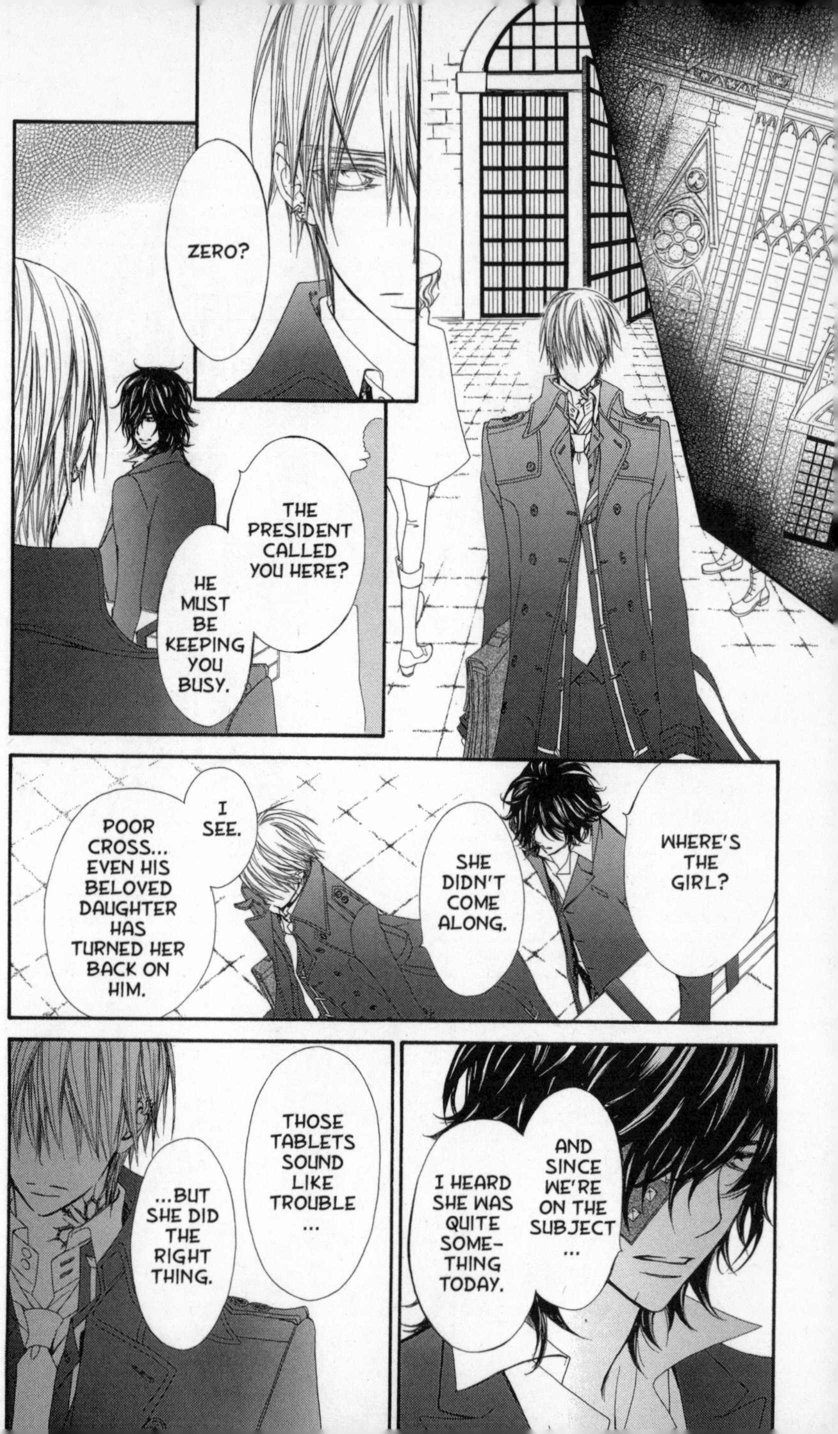
ZERO?
THE PRESIDENT CALLED YOU HERE?
HE MUST BE KEEPING YOU BUSY.
WHERE'S THE GIRL?
SHE DIDN'T COME ALONG.
I SEE.
POOR CROSS... EVEN HIS BELOVED DAUGHTER HAS TURNED HER BACK ON HIM.
AND SINCE WE'RE ON THE SUBJECT...
I HEARD SHE WAS QUITE SOME-THING TODAY.
THOSE TABLETS SOUND LIKE TROUBLE...
...BUT SHE DID THE RIGHT THING.

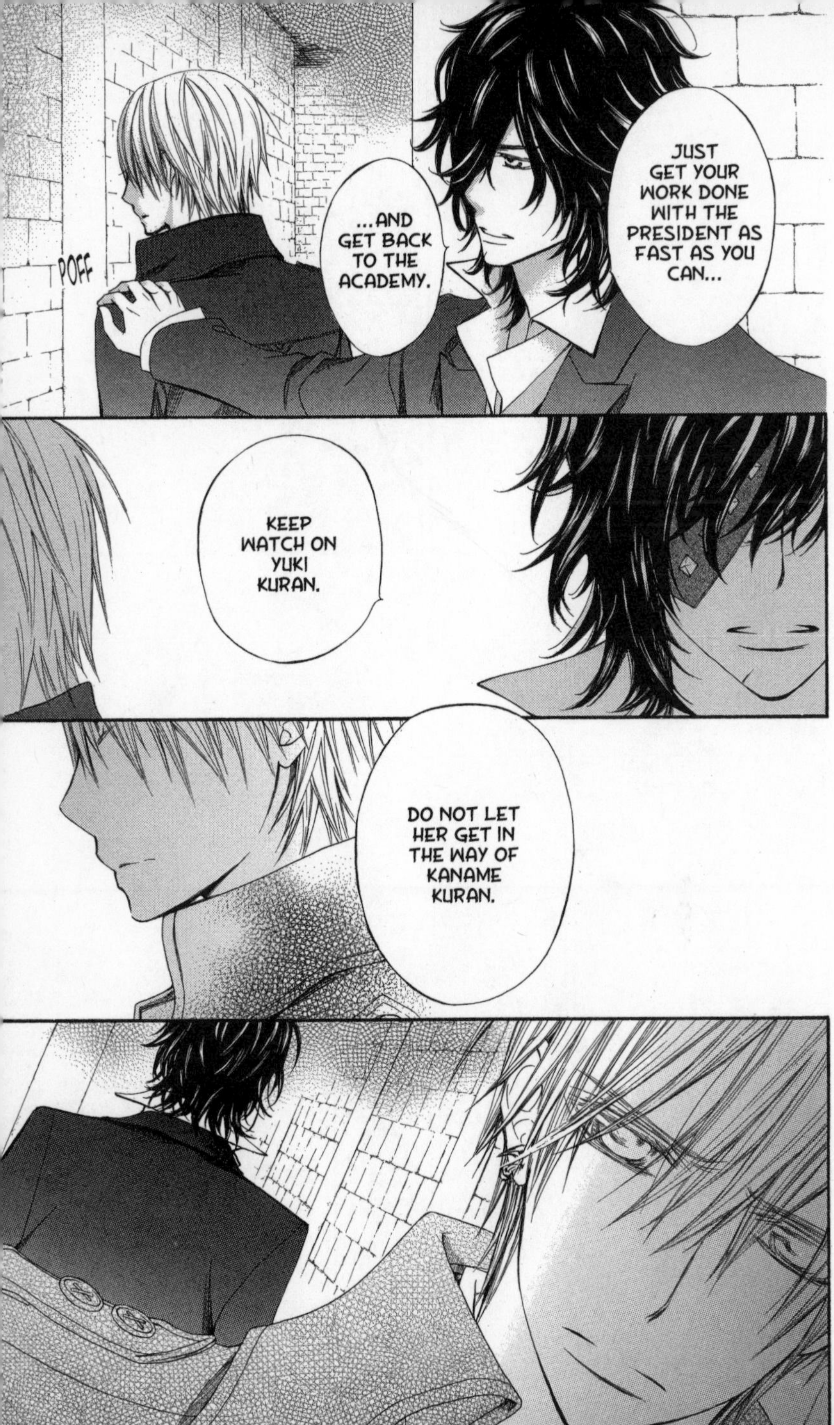
JUST GET YOUR WORK DONE WITH THE PRESIDENT AS FAST AS YOU CAN...
...AND GET BACK TO THE ACADEMY.
POFF
KEEP WATCH ON YUKI KURAN.
DO NOT LET HER GET IN THE WAY OF KANAME KURAN.

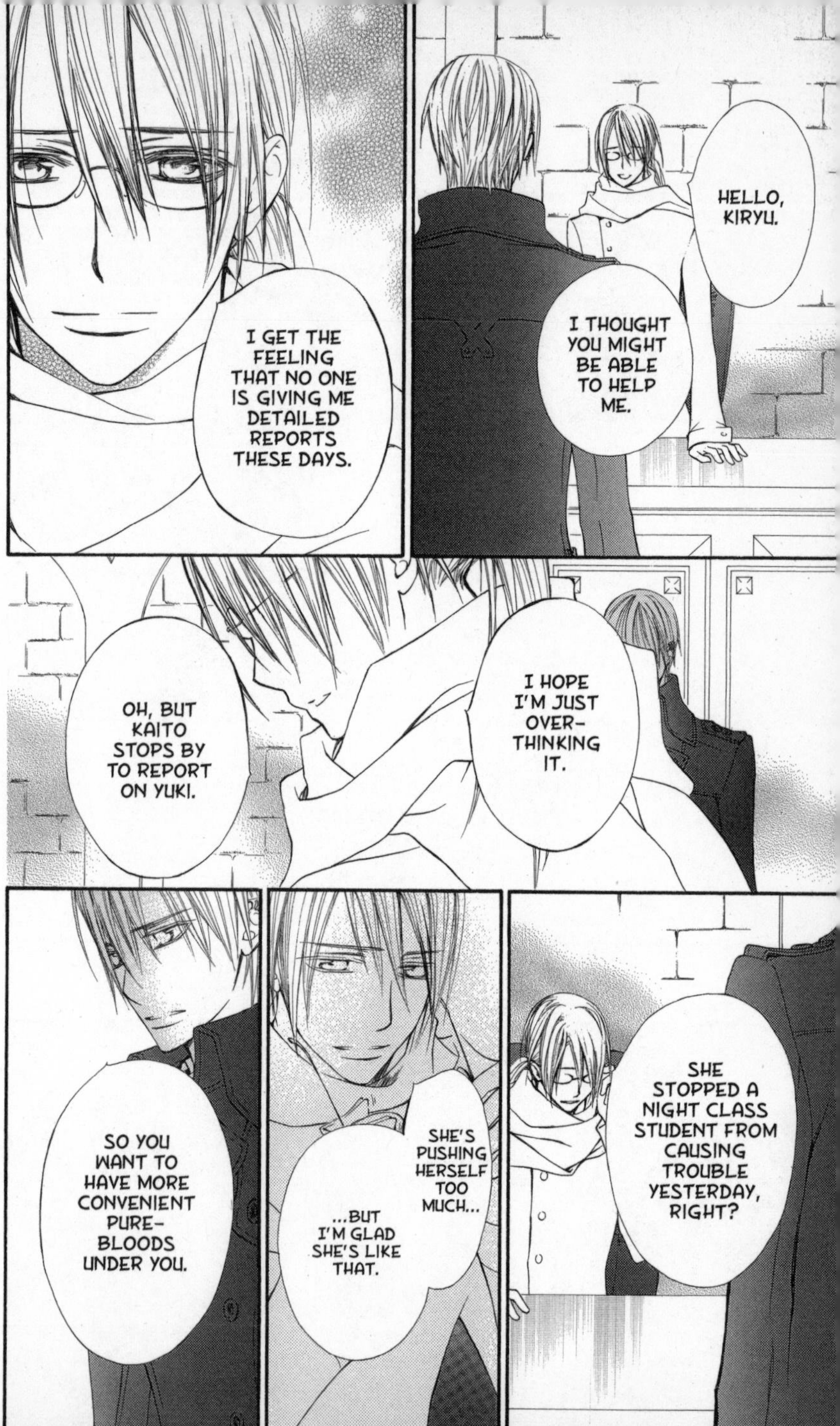
HELLO, KIRYU.
I THOUGHT YOU MIGHT BE ABLE TO HELP ME.
I GET THE FEELING THAT NO ONE IS GIVING ME DETAILED REPORTS THESE DAYS.
I HOPE I'M JUST OVER-THINKING IT.
OH, BUT KAITO STOPS BY TO REPORT ON YUKI.
SHE STOPPED A NIGHT CLASS STUDENT FROM CAUSING TROUBLE YESTERDAY, RIGHT?
SHE'S PUSHING HERSELF TOO MUCH...
...BUT I'M GLAD SHE'S LIKE THAT.
SO YOU WANT TO HAVE MORE CONVENIENT PURE-BLOODS UNDER YOU.

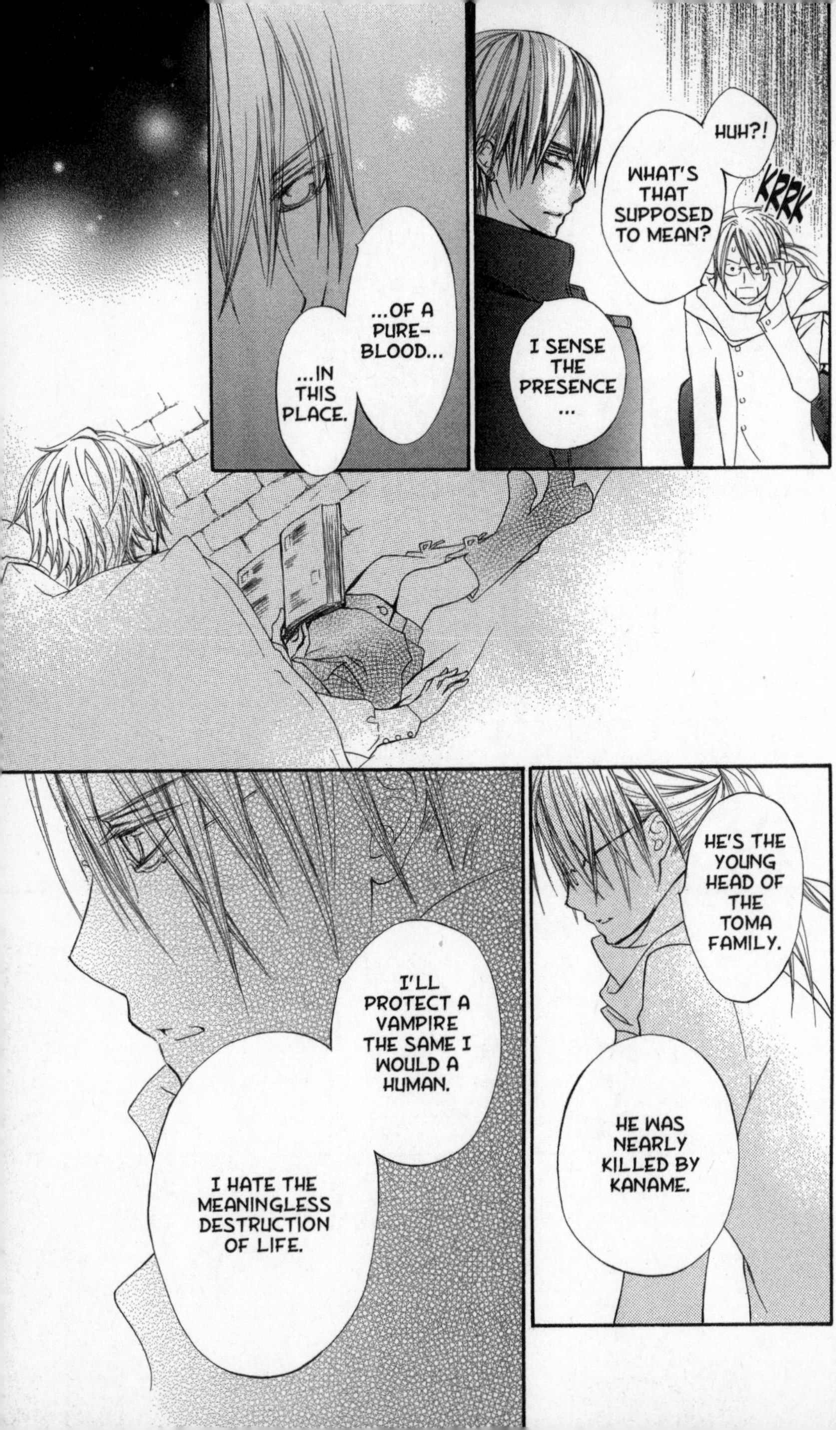
HUH?!
KRRK
WHAT'S THAT SUPPOSED TO MEAN?
I SENSE THE PRESENCE ...
...OF A PURE-BLOOD...
...IN THIS PLACE.
HE'S THE YOUNG HEAD OF THE TOMA FAMILY.
HE WAS NEARLY KILLED BY KANAME.
I'LL PROTECT A VAMPIRE THE SAME I WOULD A HUMAN.
I HATE THE MEANINGLESS DESTRUCTION OF LIFE.

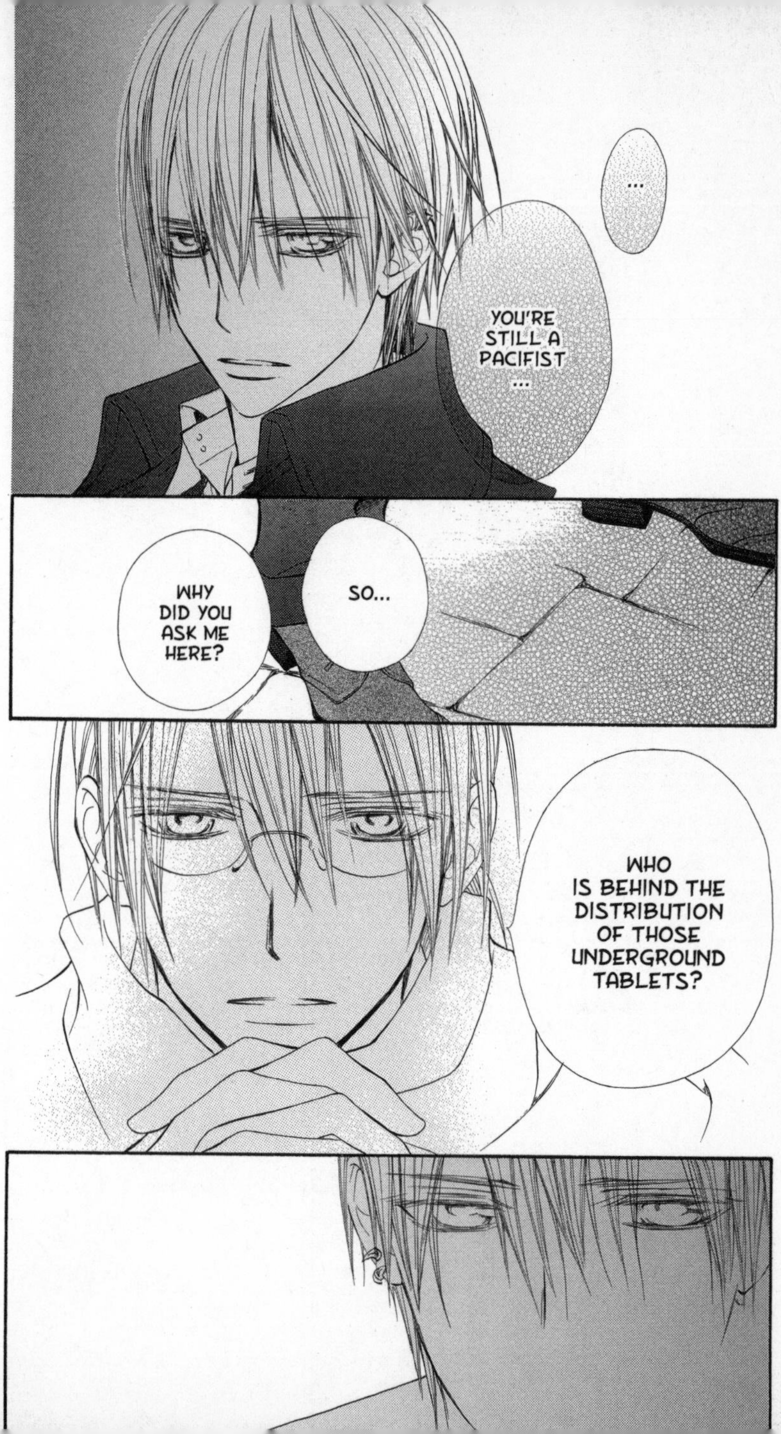
...
YOU'RE STILL A PACIFIST ...
SO...
WHY DID YOU ASK ME HERE?
WHO IS BEHIND THE DISTRIBUTION OF THOSE UNDERGROUND TABLETS?

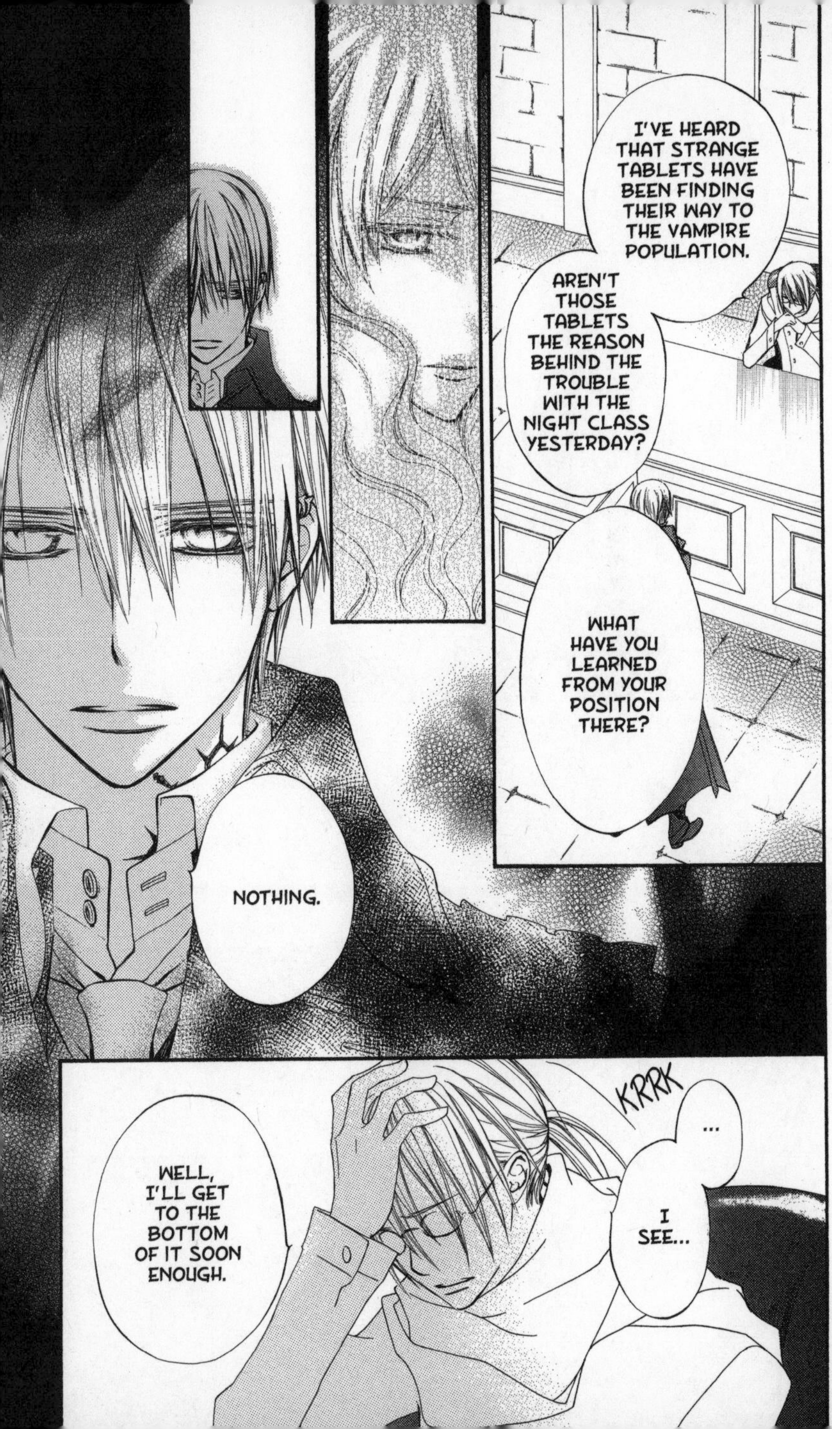
I'VE HEARD THAT STRANGE TABLETS HAVE BEEN FINDING THEIR WAY TO THE VAMPIRE POPULATION.
AREN'T THOSE TABLETS THE REASON BEHIND THE TROUBLE WITH THE NIGHT CLASS YESTERDAY?
WHAT HAVE YOU LEARNED FROM YOUR POSITION THERE?
NOTHING.
KRRK
...
I SEE...
WELL, I'LL GET TO THE BOTTOM OF IT SOON ENOUGH.

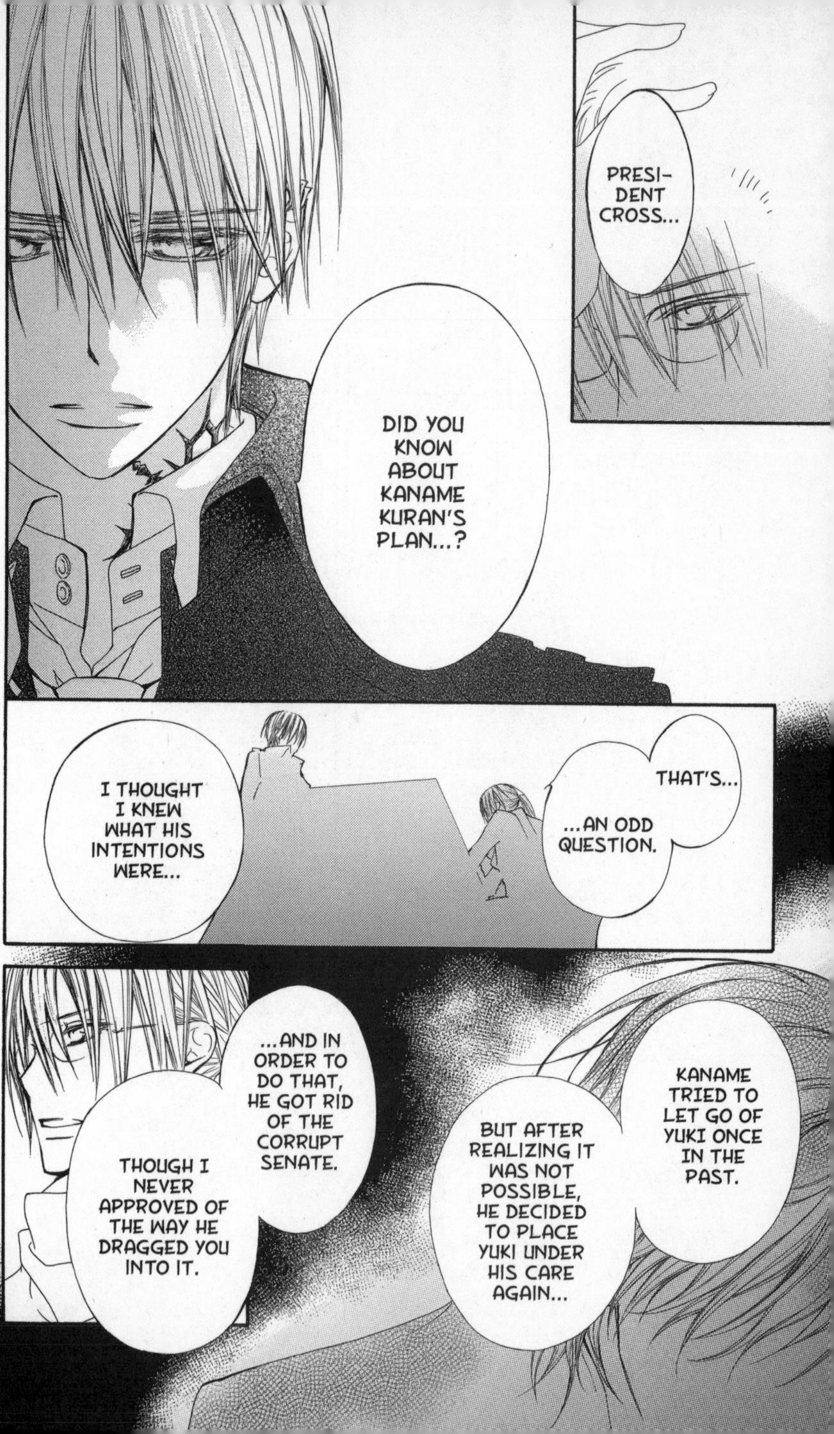
PRESI-DENT CROSS...
DID YOU KNOW ABOUT KANAME KURAN'S PLAN...?
THAT'S...
...AN ODD QUESTION.
I THOUGHT I KNEW WHAT HIS INTENTIONS WERE...
KANAME TRIED TO LET GO OF YUKI ONCE IN THE PAST.
BUT AFTER REALIZING IT WAS NOT POSSIBLE, HE DECIDED TO PLACE YUKI UNDER HIS CARE AGAIN...
...AND IN ORDER TO DO THAT, HE GOT RID OF THE CORRUPT SENATE.
THOUGH I NEVER APPROVED OF THE WAY HE DRAGGED YOU INTO IT.

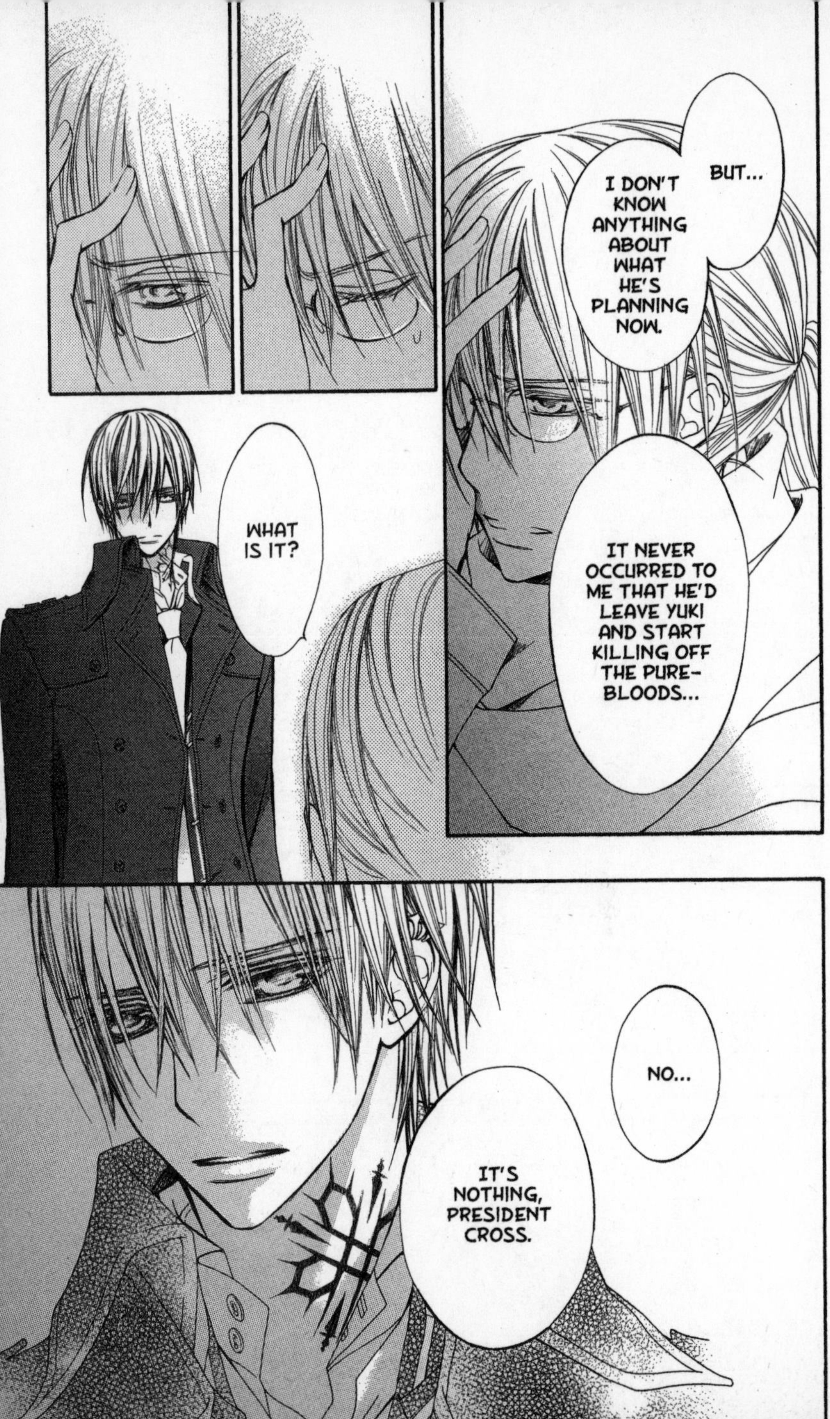
BUT...
I DON'T KNOW ANYTHING ABOUT WHAT HE'S PLANNING NOW.
IT NEVER OCCURRED TO ME THAT HE'D LEAVE YUKI AND START KILLING OFF THE PURE-BLOODS...
WHAT IS IT?
NO...
IT'S NOTHING, PRESIDENT CROSS.

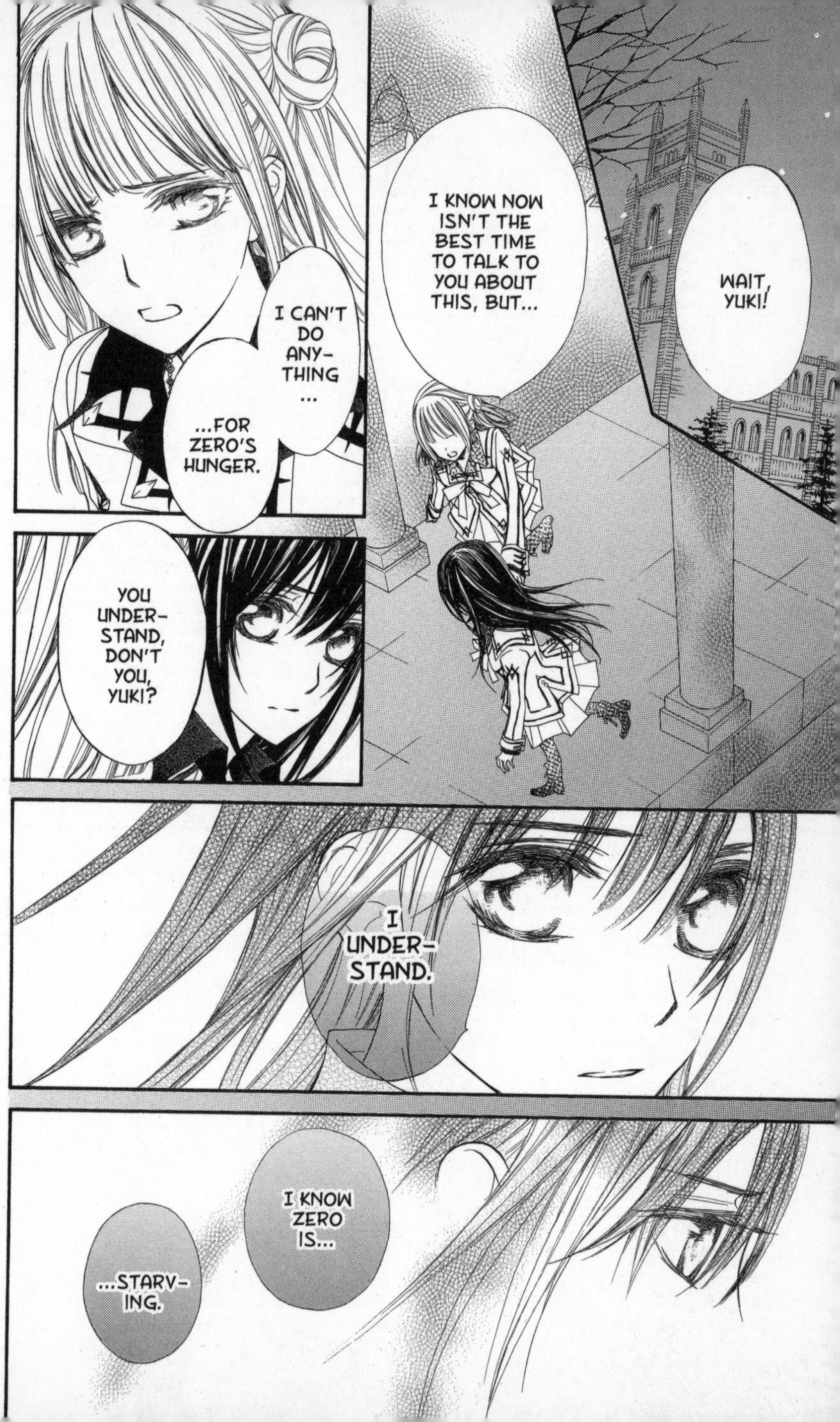
WAIT, YUKI!
I KNOW NOW ISN'T THE BEST TIME TO TALK TO YOU ABOUT THIS, BUT...
I CAN'T DO ANYTHING...
...FOR ZERO'S HUNGER.
YOU UNDERSTAND, DON'T YOU, YUKI?
I UNDERSTAND.
I KNOW ZERO IS...
...STARVING.

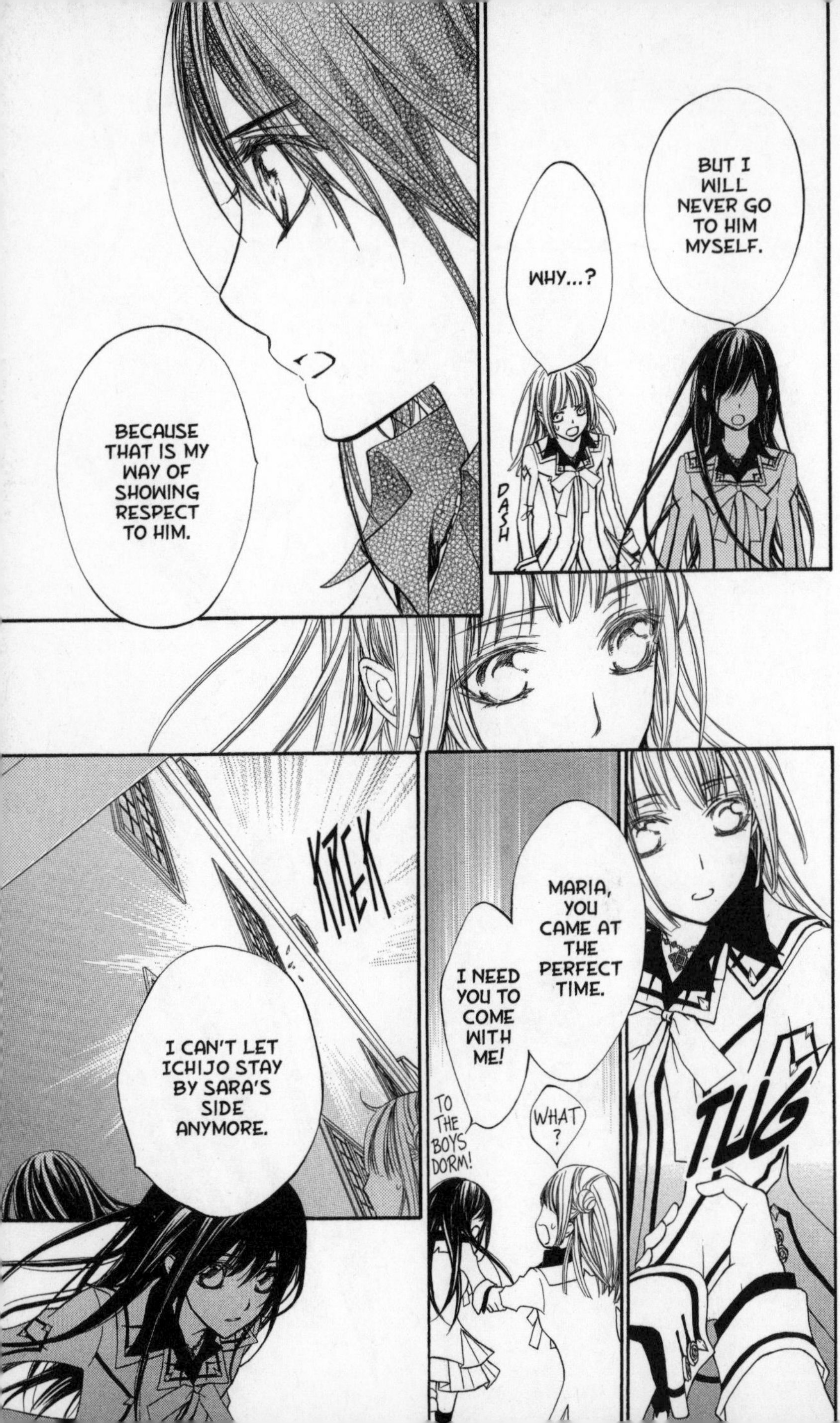
BUT I WILL NEVER GO TO HIM MYSELF.
WHY...?
DASH
BECAUSE THAT IS MY WAY OF SHOWING RESPECT TO HIM.
MARIA, YOU CAME AT THE PERFECT TIME.
TUG
I NEED YOU TO COME WITH ME!
WHAT?
TO THE BOYS DORM!
KREK
I CAN'T LET ICHIJO STAY BY SARA'S SIDE ANYMORE.

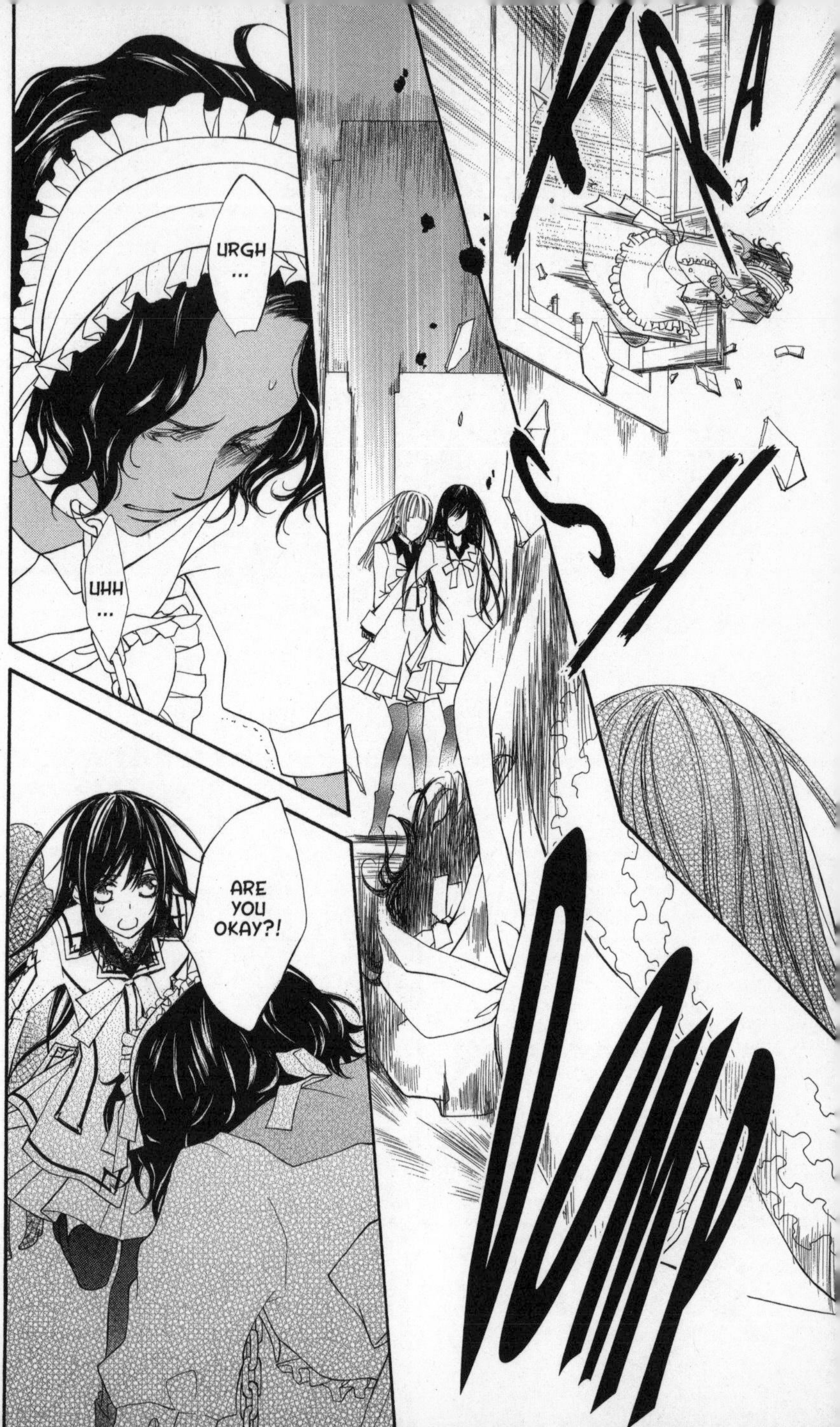
KRASH
WOMP
URGH ...
UHH ...
ARE YOU OKAY?!

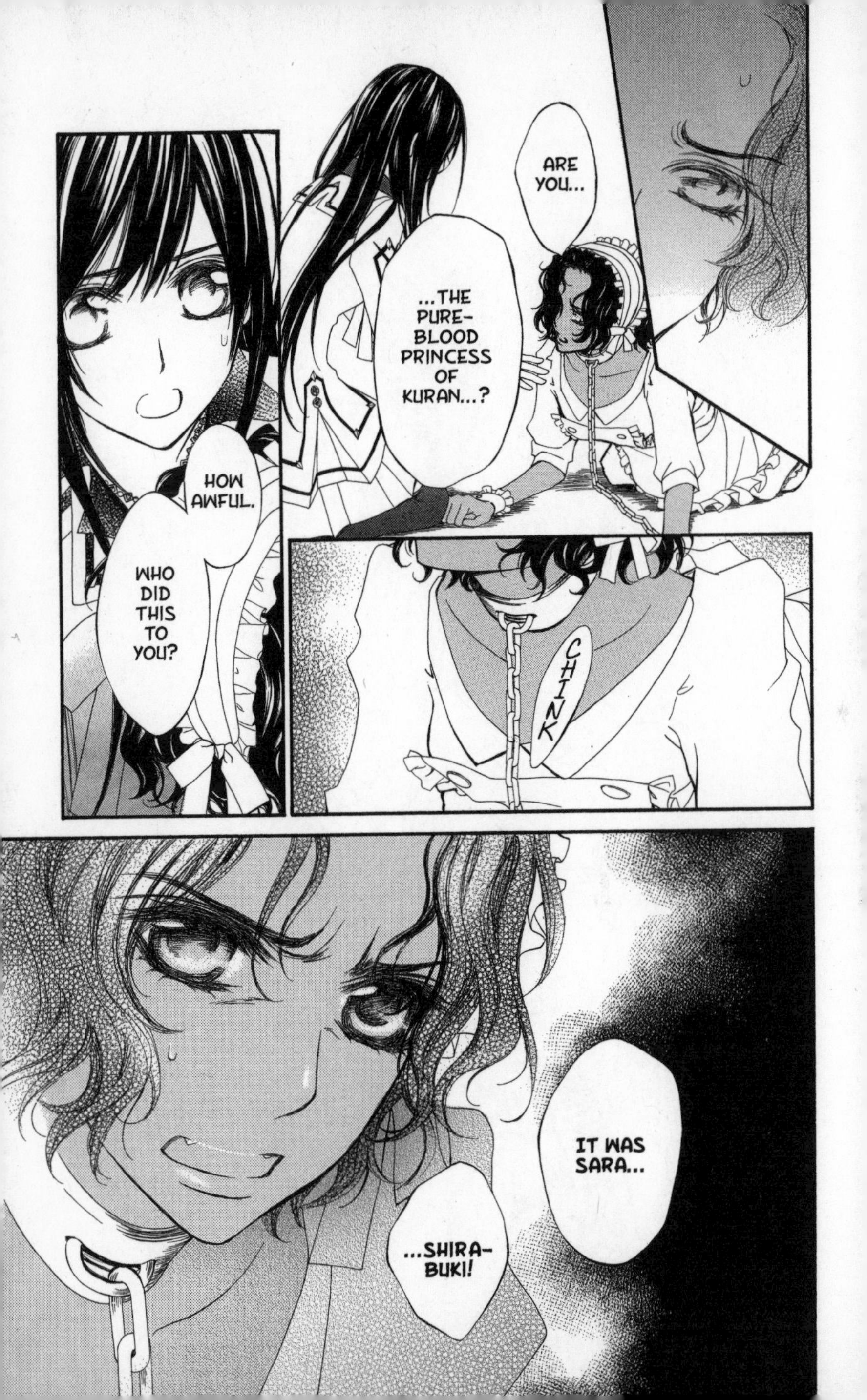
ARE YOU...
...THE PURE-BLOOD PRINCESS OF KURAN...?
CHINK
HOW AWFUL.
WHO DID THIS TO YOU?
IT WAS SARA...
...SHIRA-BUKI!

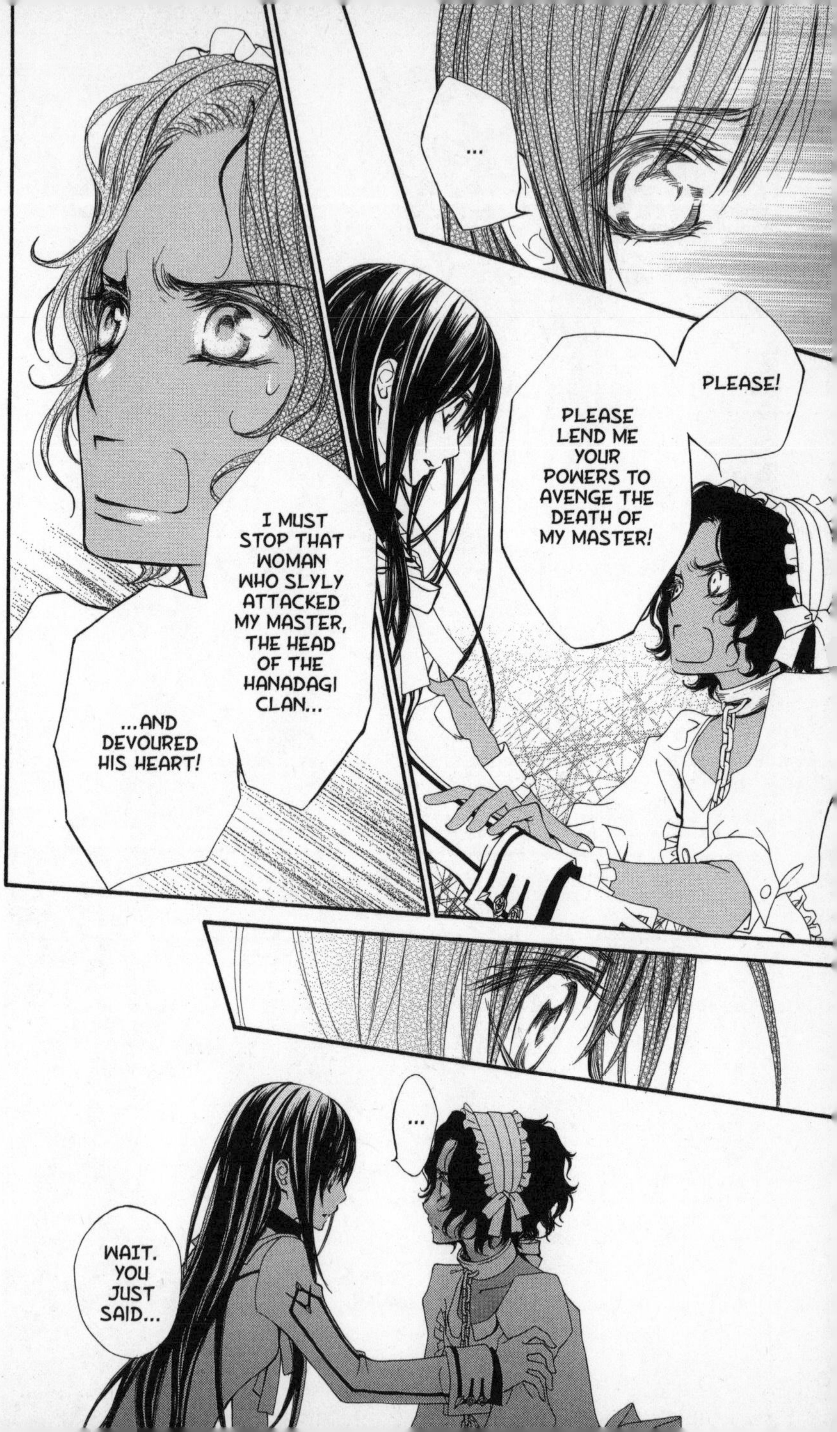
...
PLEASE!
PLEASE LEND ME YOUR POWERS TO AVENGE THE DEATH OF MY MASTER!
I MUST STOP THAT WOMAN WHO SLYLY ATTACKED MY MASTER, THE HEAD OF THE HANADAGI CLAN...
...AND DEVOURED HIS HEART!
...
WAIT. YOU JUST SAID...

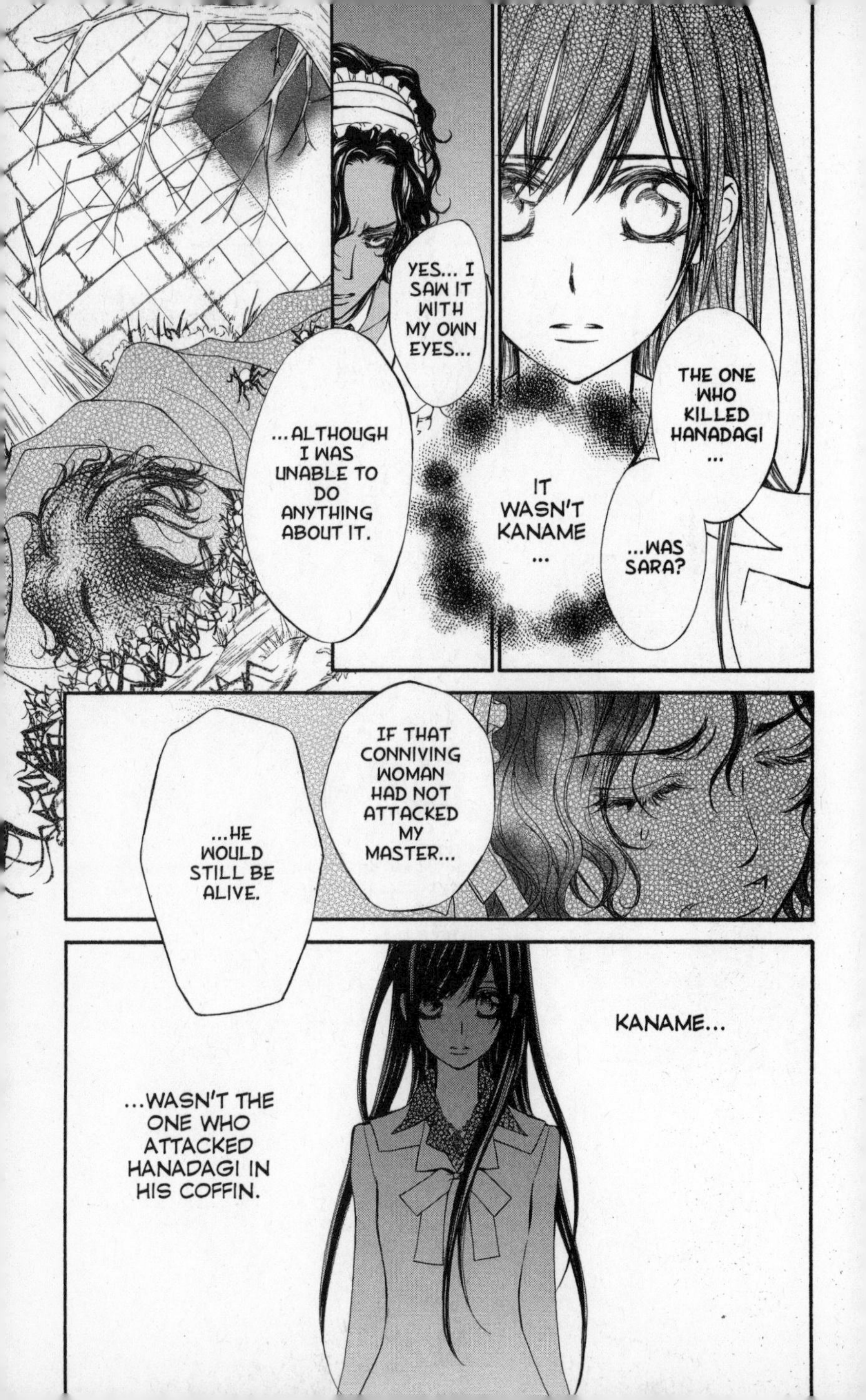
THE ONE WHO KILLED HANADAGI ...
IT WASN'T KANAME ...
...WAS SARA?
YES... I SAW IT WITH MY OWN EYES...
...ALTHOUGH I WAS UNABLE TO DO ANYTHING ABOUT IT.
IF THAT CONNIVING WOMAN HAD NOT ATTACKED MY MASTER...
...HE WOULD STILL BE ALIVE.
KANAME...
...WASN'T THE ONE WHO ATTACKED HANADAGI IN HIS COFFIN.

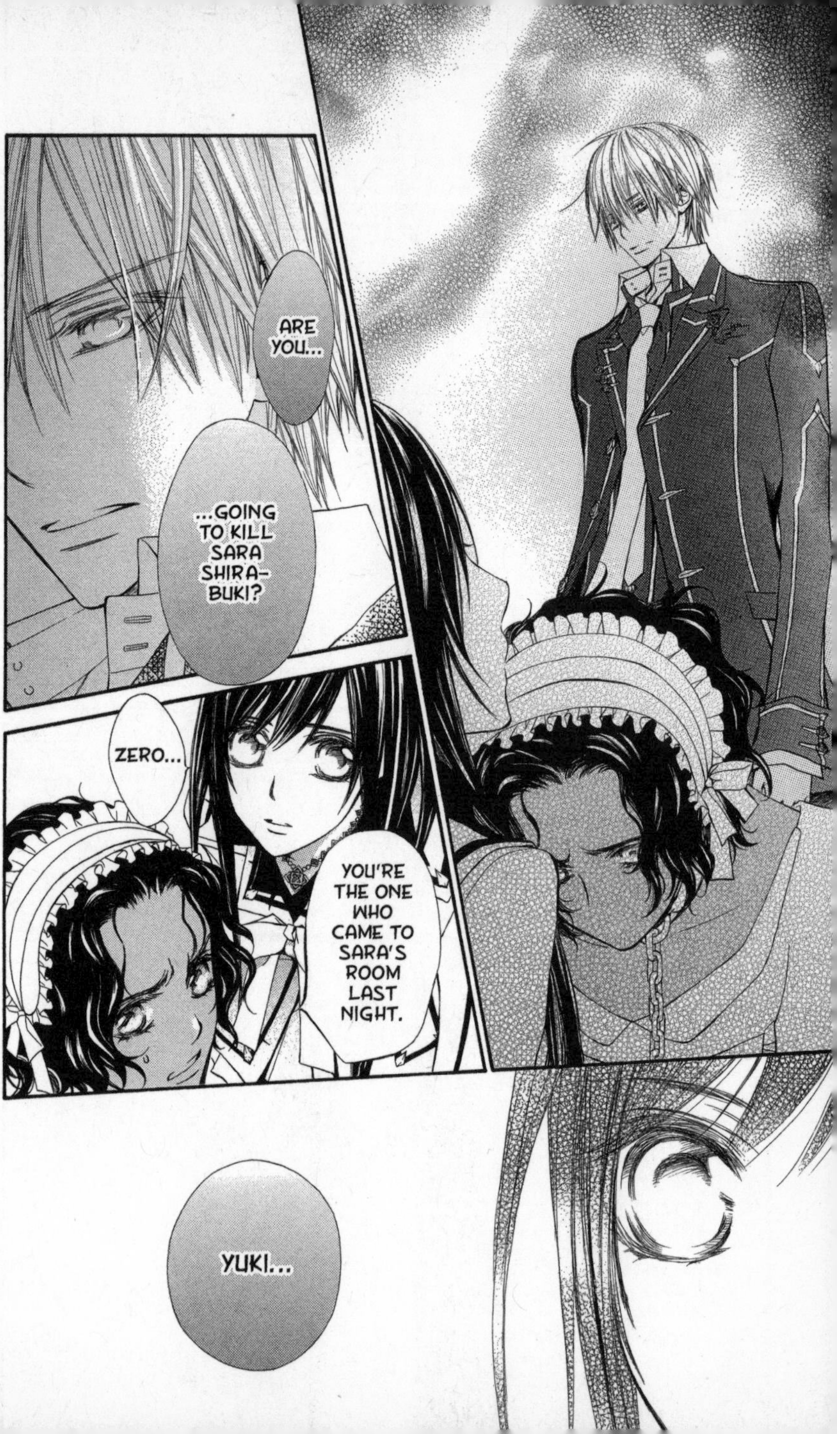
ARE YOU...
...GOING TO KILL SARA SHIRABUKI?
ZERO...
YOU'RE THE ONE WHO CAME TO SARA'S ROOM LAST NIGHT.
YUKI...

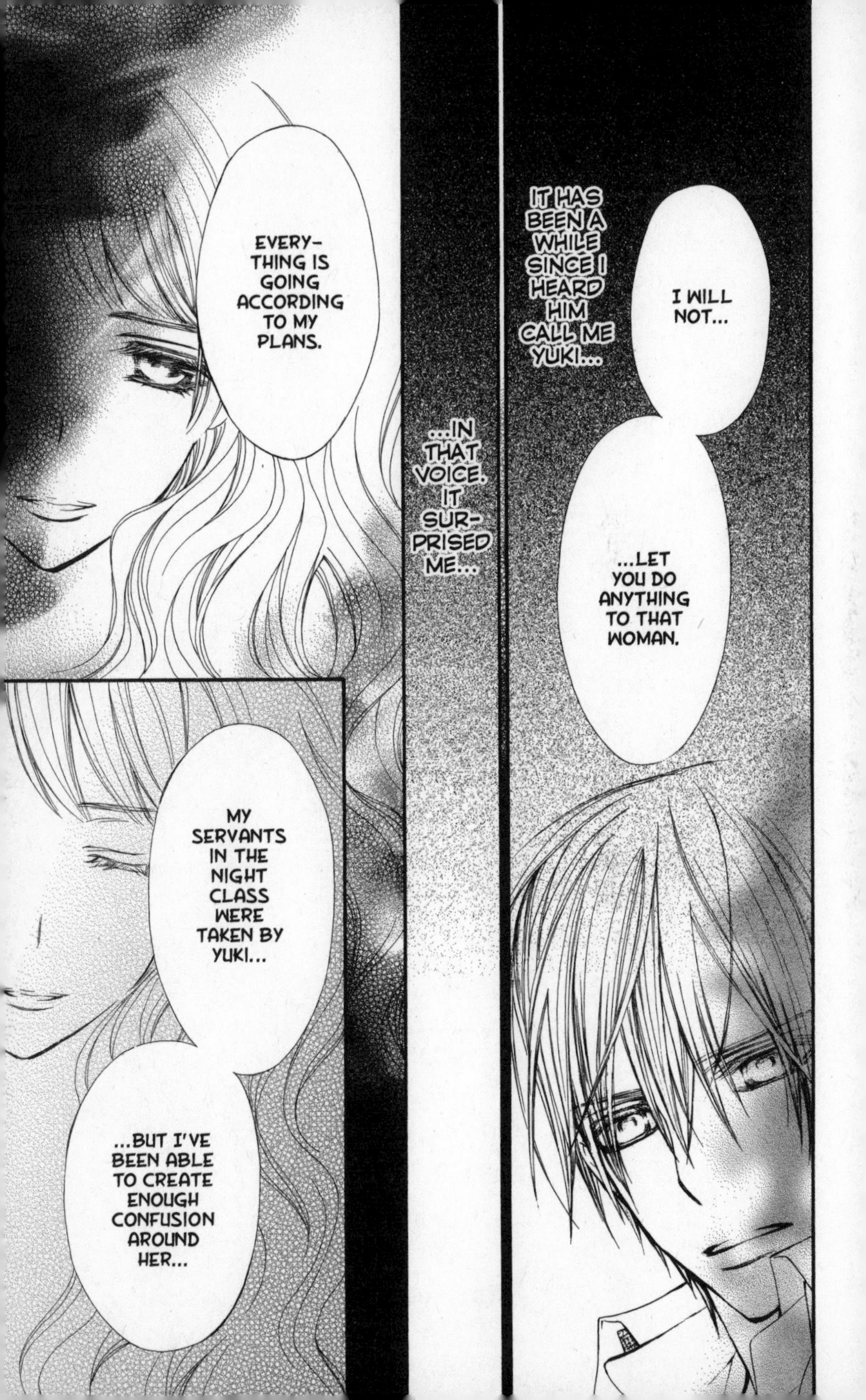
I WILL NOT...
...LET YOU DO ANYTHING TO THAT WOMAN.
IT HAS BEEN A WHILE SINCE I HEARD HIM CALL ME YUKI...
...IN THAT VOICE. IT SURPRISED ME...
EVERY-THING IS GOING ACCORDING TO MY PLANS.
MY SERVANTS IN THE NIGHT CLASS WERE TAKEN BY YUKI...
...BUT I'VE BEEN ABLE TO CREATE ENOUGH CONFUSION AROUND HER...

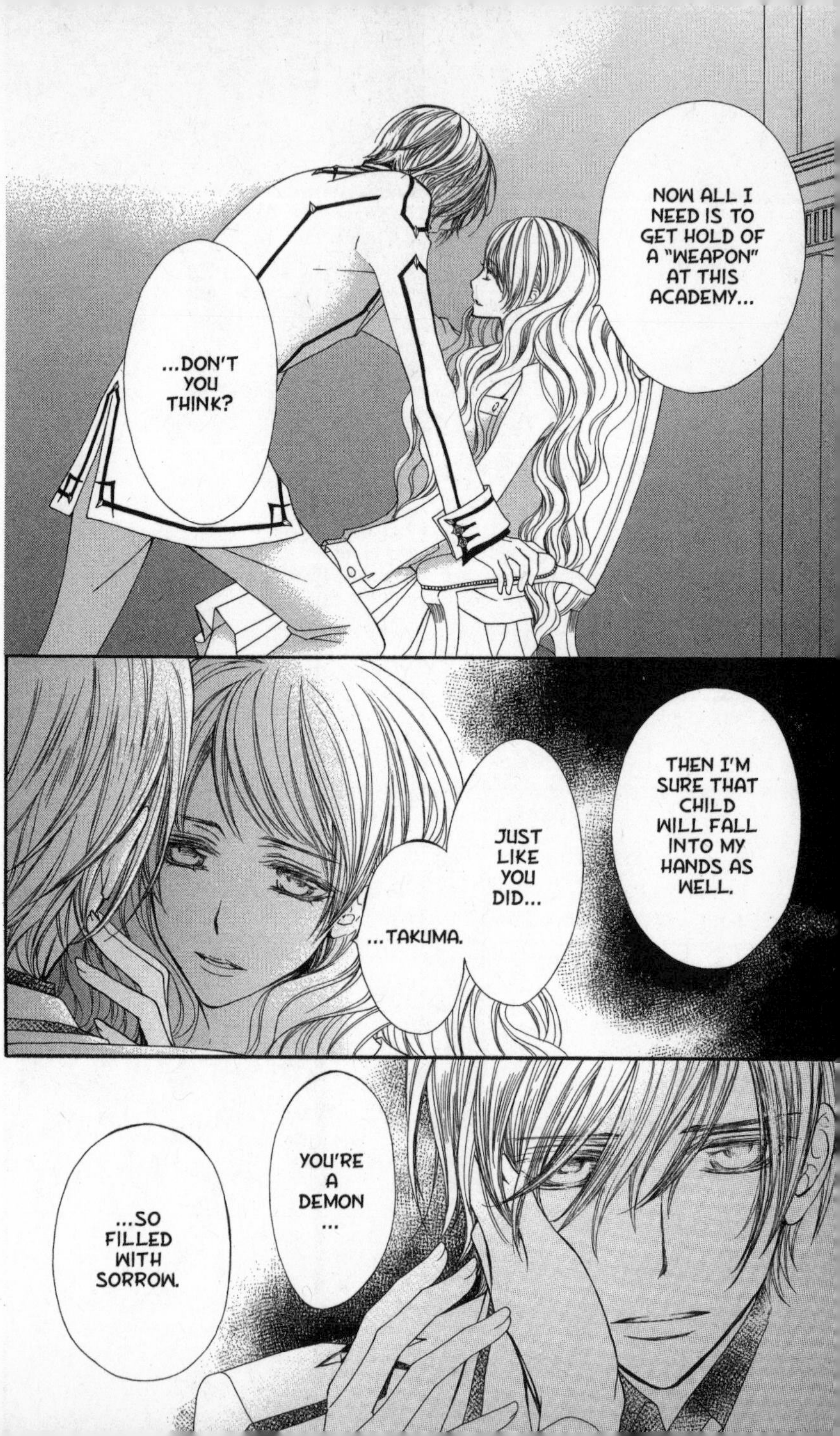

NOW ALL I NEED IS TO GET HOLD OF A "WEAPON" AT THIS ACADEMY...
...DON'T YOU THINK?
THEN I'M SURE THAT CHILD WILL FALL INTO MY HANDS AS WELL.
JUST LIKE YOU DID...
...TAKUMA.
YOU'RE A DEMON...
...SO FILLED WITH SORROW.

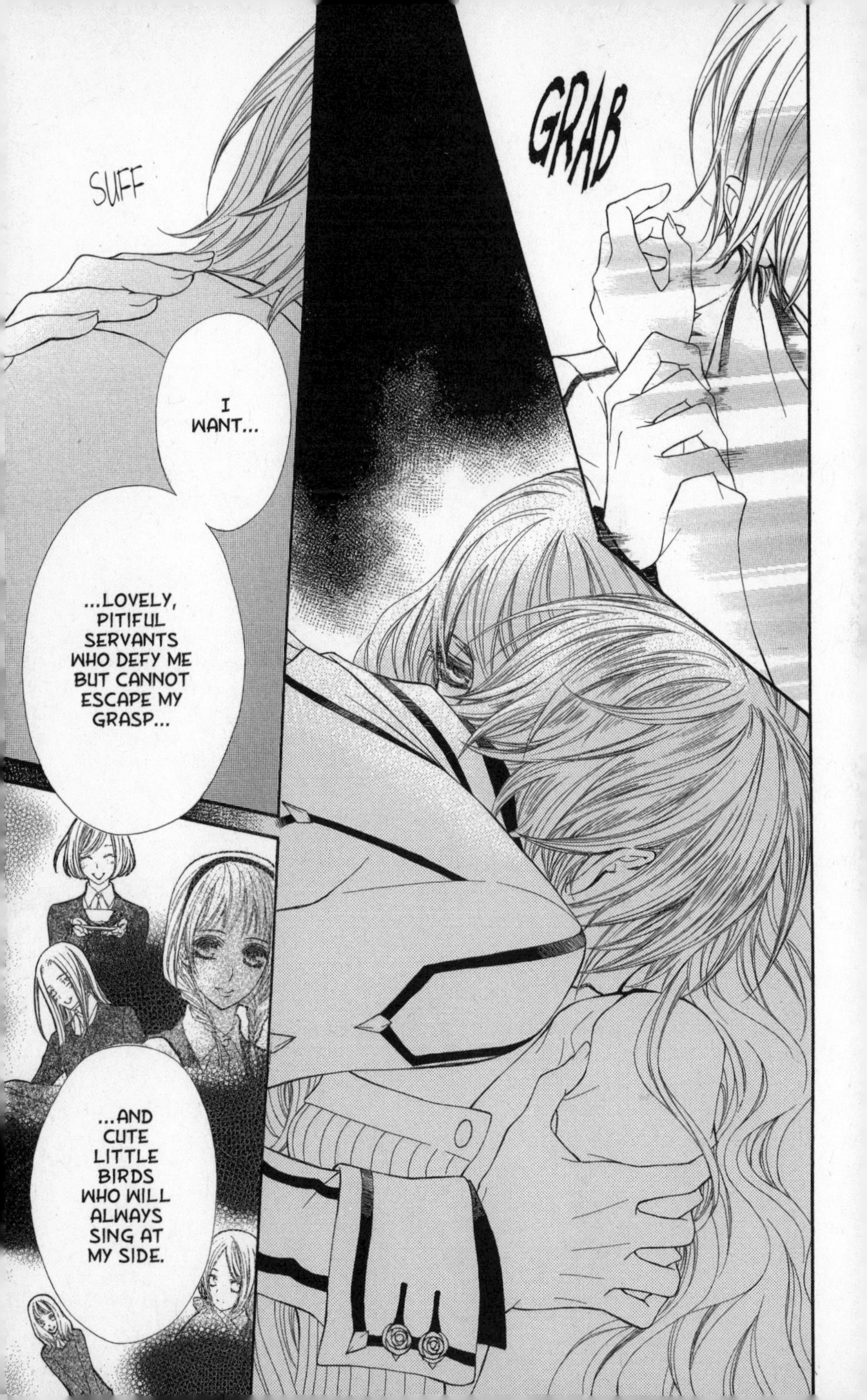
GRAB
SUFF
I WANT...
...LOVELY, PITIFUL SERVANTS WHO DEFY ME BUT CANNOT ESCAPE MY GRASP...
...AND CUTE LITTLE BIRDS WHO WILL ALWAYS SING AT MY SIDE.

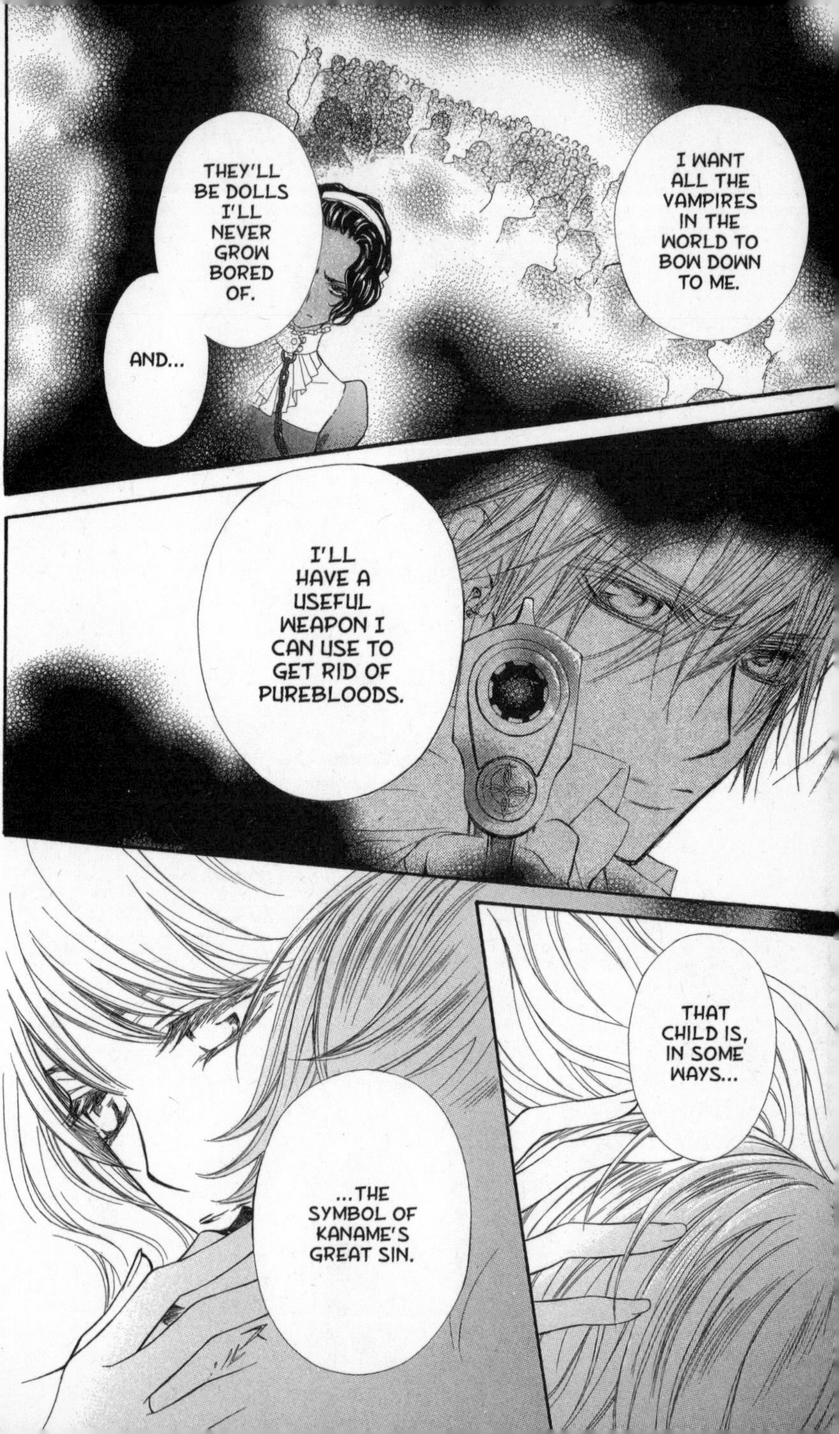
I WANT ALL THE VAMPIRES IN THE WORLD TO BOW DOWN TO ME.
THEY'LL BE DOLLS I'LL NEVER GROW BORED OF.
AND...
I'LL HAVE A USEFUL WEAPON I CAN USE TO GET RID OF PUREBLOODS.
THAT CHILD IS, IN SOME WAYS...
...THE SYMBOL OF KANAME'S GREAT SIN.

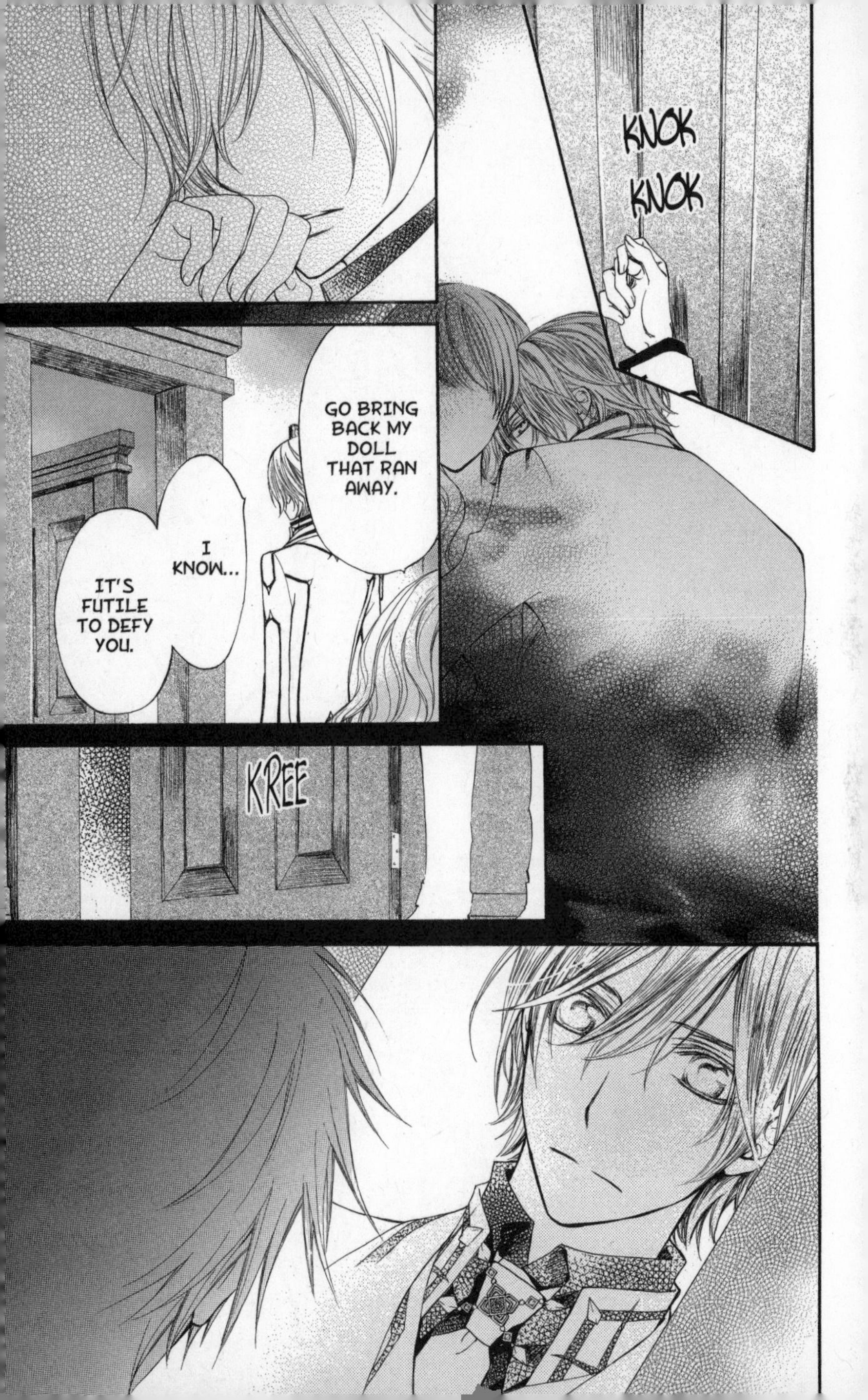
KNOK KNOK
GO BRING BACK MY DOLL THAT RAN AWAY.
I KNOW...
IT'S FUTILE TO DEFY YOU.
KREE

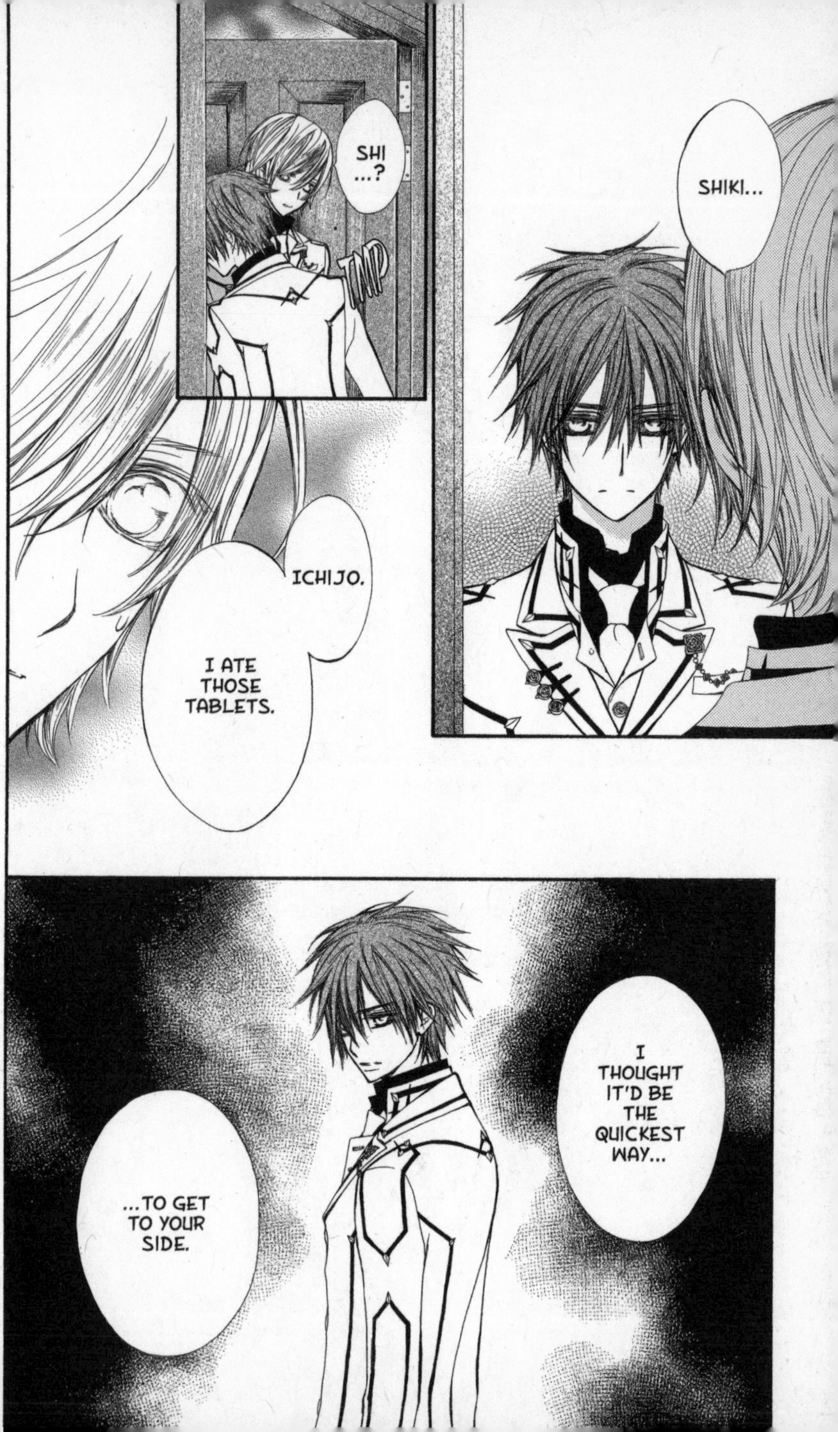
SHIKI...
SHI ...?
TMP
ICHIJO.
I ATE THOSE TABLETS.
I THOUGHT IT'D BE THE QUICKEST WAY...
...TO GET TO YOUR SIDE.

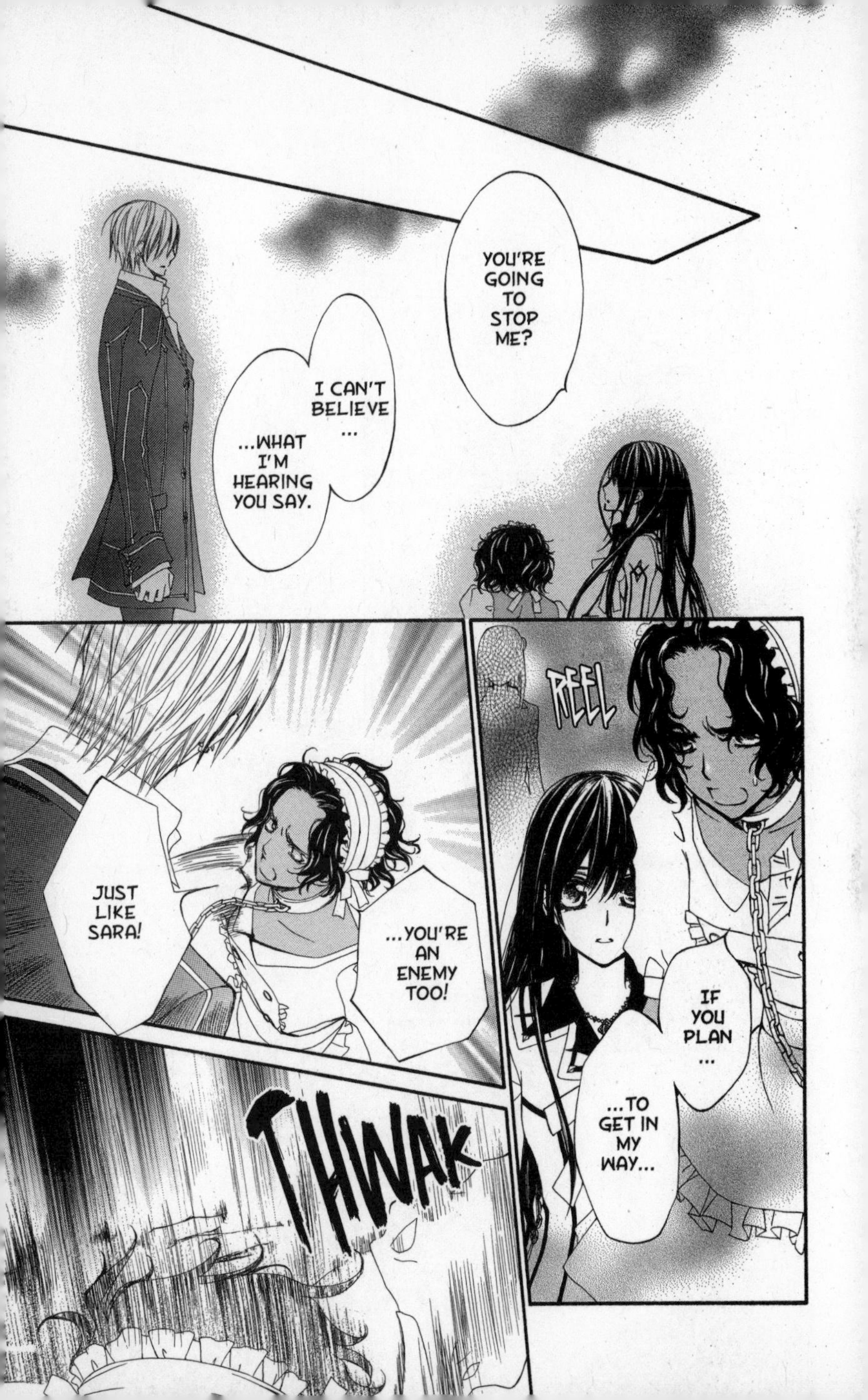
YOU'RE GOING TO STOP ME?
I CAN'T BELIEVE...
...WHAT I'M HEARING YOU SAY.
REEL
IF YOU PLAN...
...TO GET IN MY WAY...
...YOU'RE AN ENEMY TOO!
JUST LIKE SARA!
THWAK

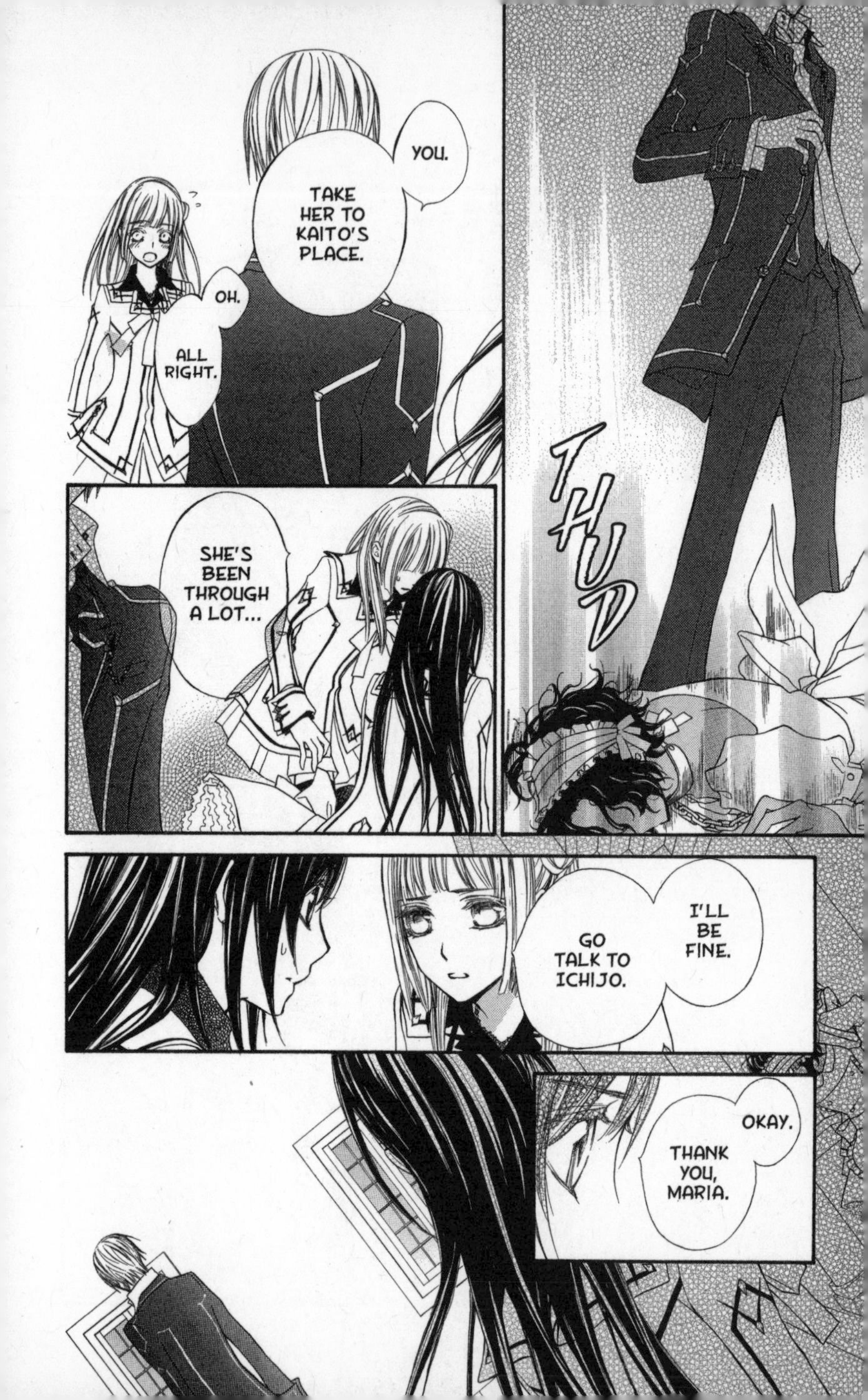
THUD
YOU.
TAKE HER TO KAITO'S PLACE.
OH.
ALL RIGHT.
SHE'S BEEN THROUGH A LOT...
I'LL BE FINE.
GO TALK TO ICHIJO.
OKAY.
THANK YOU, MARIA.

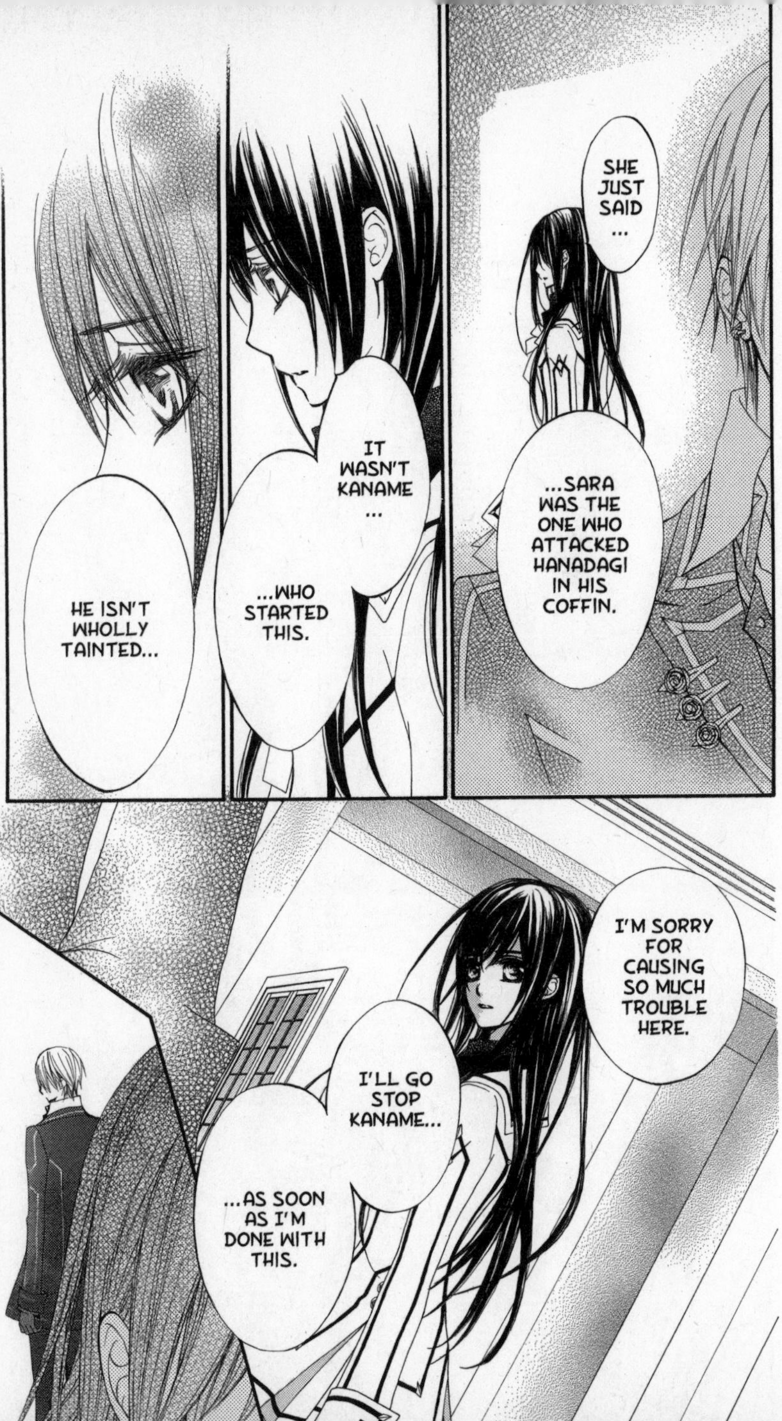
SHE JUST SAID...
...SARA WAS THE ONE WHO ATTACKED HANADAGI IN HIS COFFIN.
IT WASN'T KANAME...
...WHO STARTED THIS.
HE ISN'T WHOLLY TAINTED...
I'M SORRY FOR CAUSING SO MUCH TROUBLE HERE.
I'LL GO STOP KANAME...
...AS SOON AS I'M DONE WITH THIS.

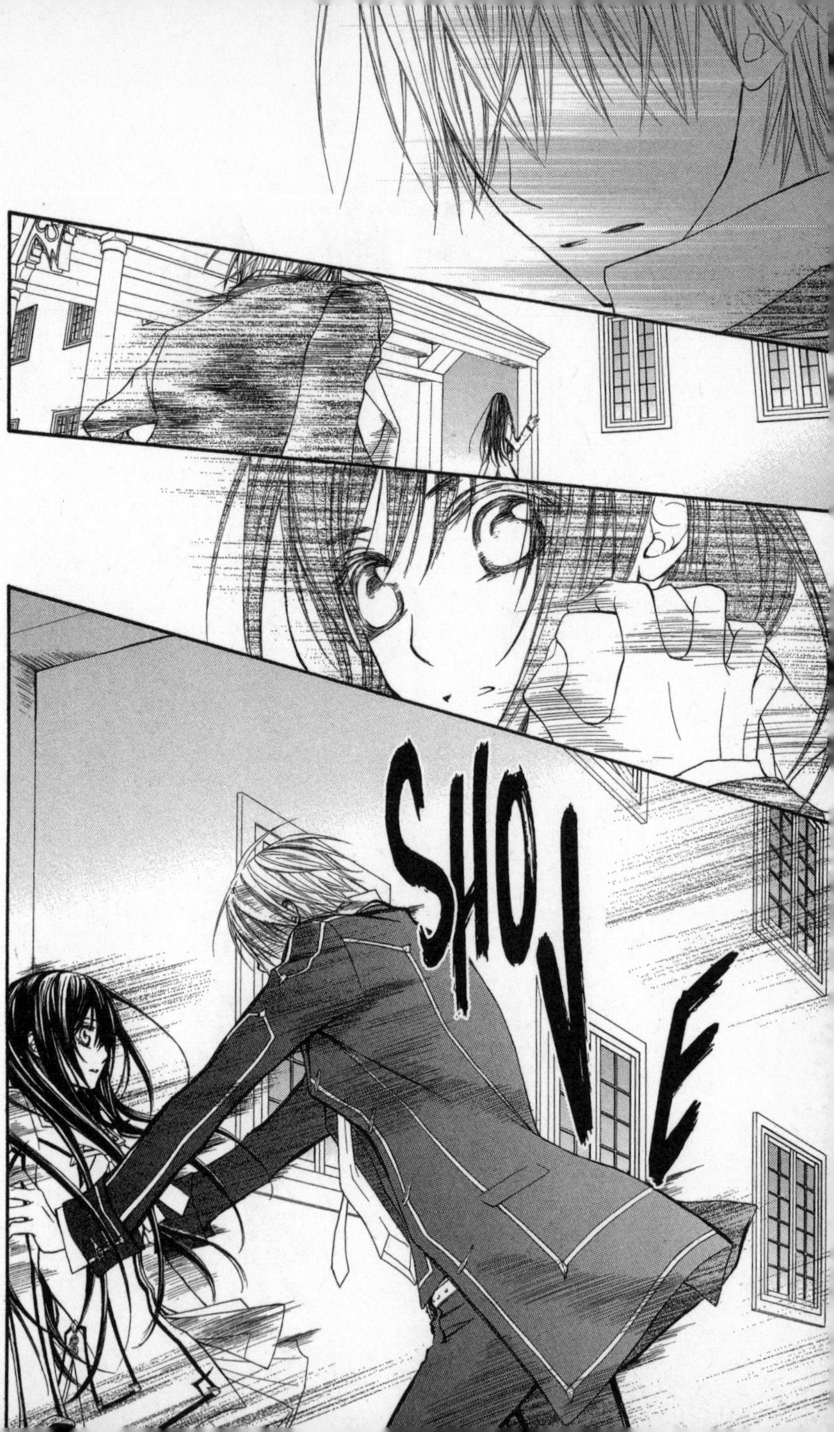
SHOVE

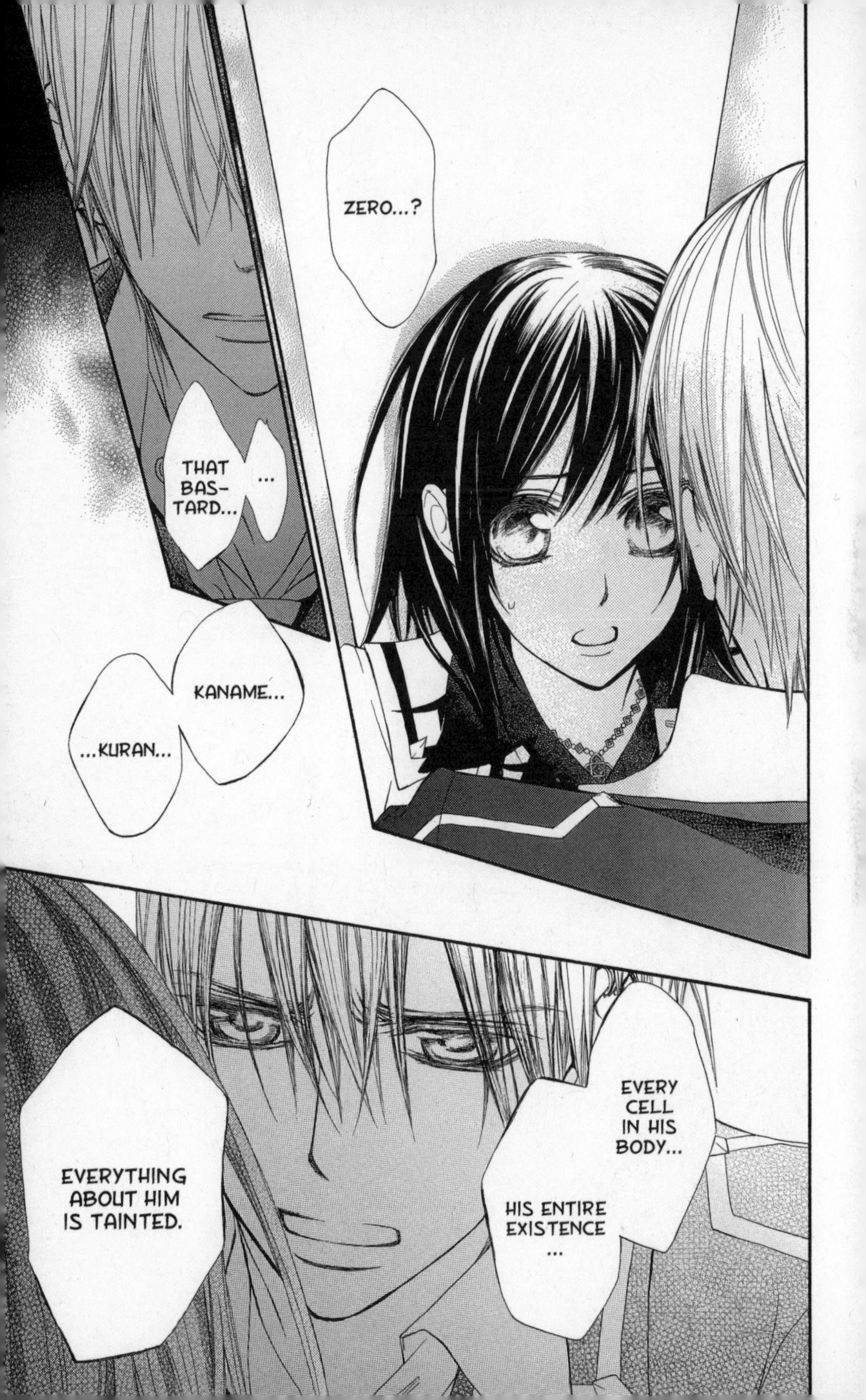
ZERO...?
...
THAT BASTARD...
KANAME...
...KURAN...
EVERY CELL IN HIS BODY...
HIS ENTIRE EXISTENCE...
EVERYTHING ABOUT HIM IS TAINTED.

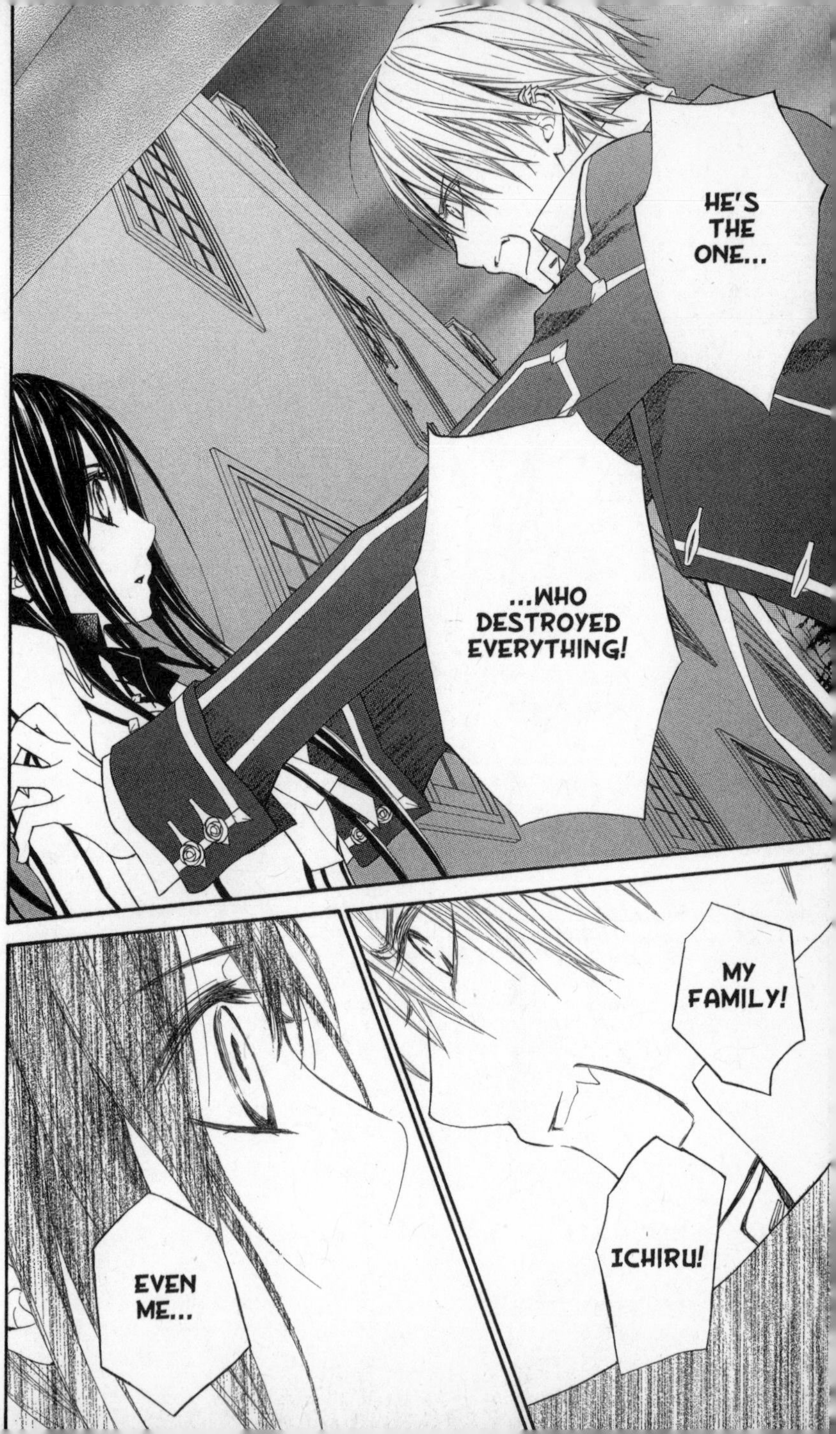
HE'S THE ONE...
...WHO DESTROYED EVERYTHING!
MY FAMILY!
ICHIRU!
EVEN ME...

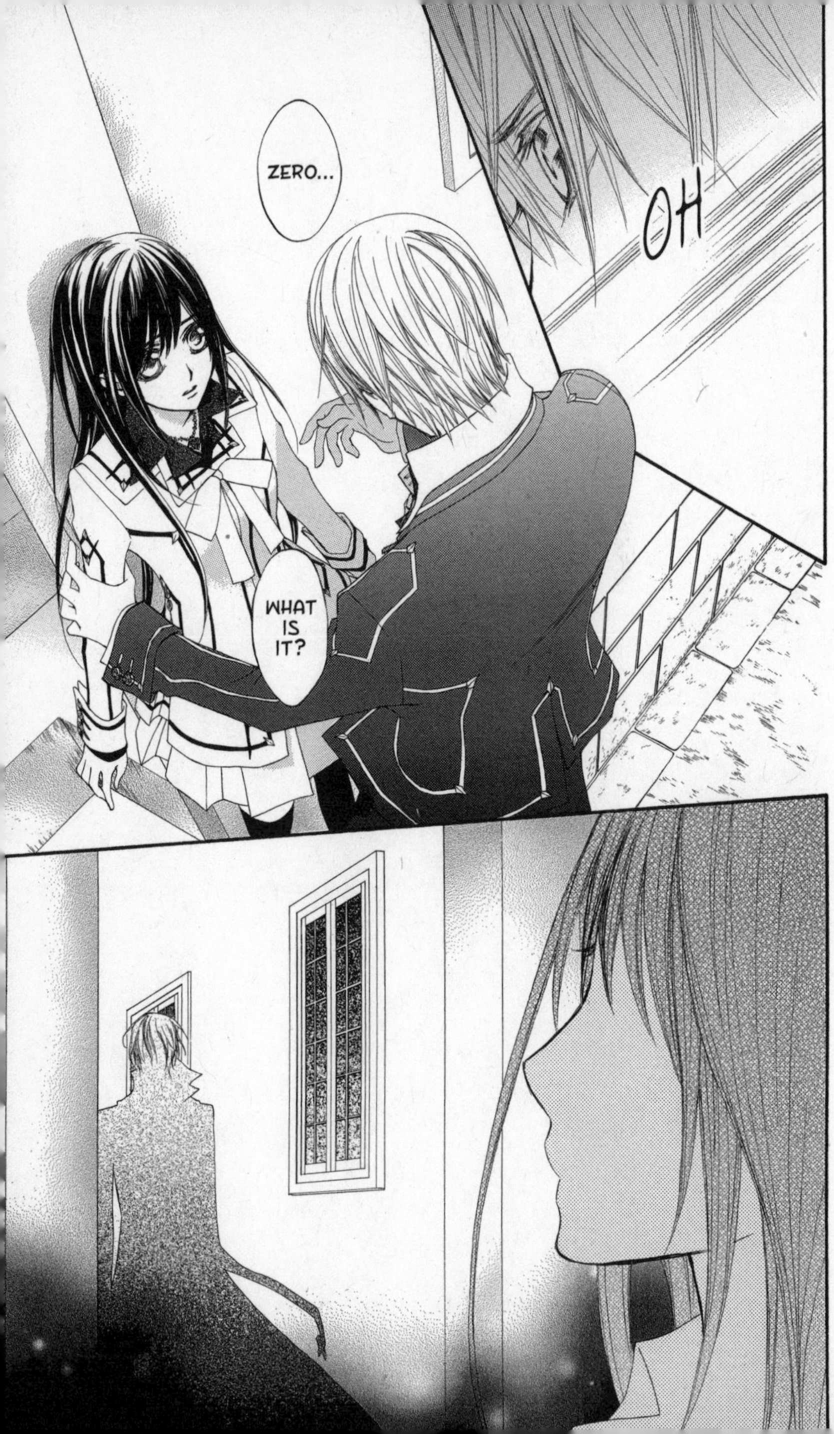
OH
ZERO...
WHAT IS IT?

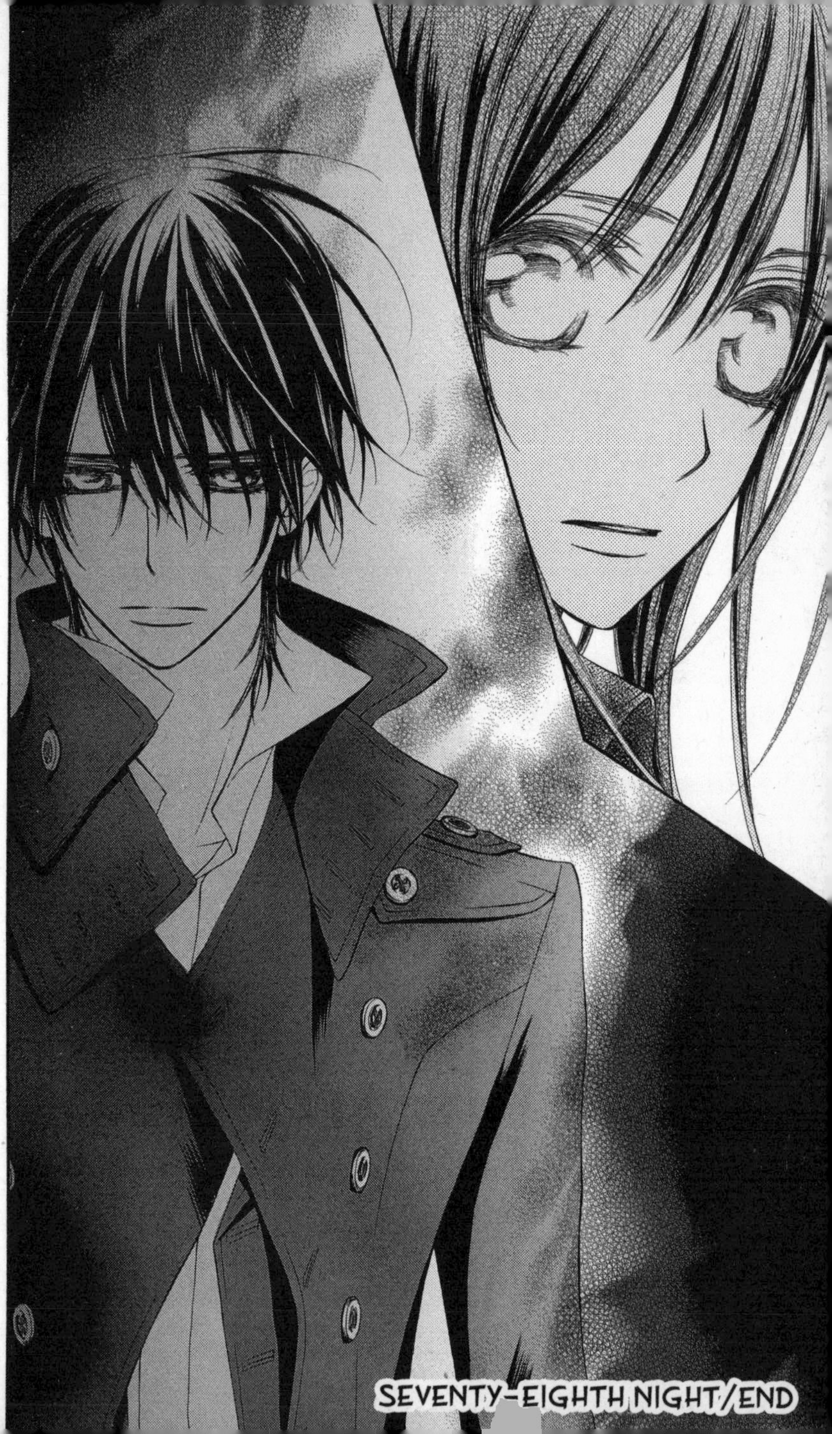
SEVENTY-EIGHTH NIGHT/END

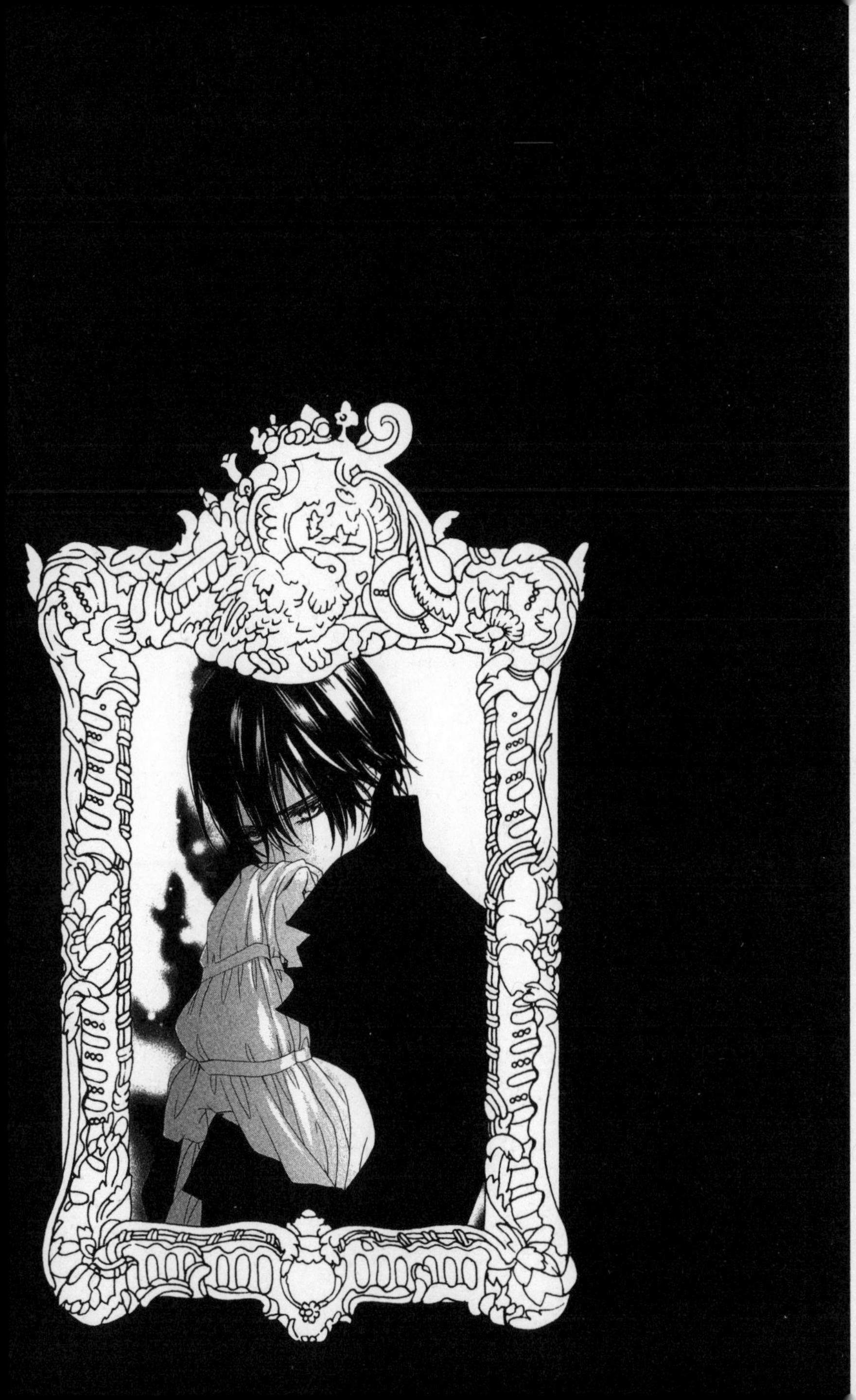

THE NEXT VOLUME WILL BE PUBLISHED
IN SIX MONTHS IN JAPAN.

IT'S BEEN A WHILE SINCE ALL THREE
HAVE BEEN TOGETHER LIKE THIS.

ARE THEY GOING TO STAY LIKE THIS
FOR THE NEXT SIX MONTHS...?

"YOU WANT TO GO GET SOME
TEA TO KILL SOME TIME?"

NO ONE WAS ABLE TO UTTER THAT
SIMPLE PHRASE...

THIS AWKWARD SITUATION WILL BE
CONTINUED IN VOLUME 17!

EDITOR'S NOTES

Characters

Matsuri Hino puts careful thought into the names of her characters in *Vampire Knight*. Below is the collection of characters through volume 16. Each character's name is presented family name first, per the kanji reading.

黒主優姫

Cross Yuki
Yuki's last name, *Kurosu*, is the Japanese pronunciation of the English word "cross." However, the kanji has a different meaning—*kuro* means "black" and *su* means "master." Her first name is a combination of *yuu*, meaning "tender" or "kind," and *ki*, meaning "princess."

錐生零

Kiryu Zero
Zero's first name is the kanji for *rei*, meaning "zero." In his last name, *Kiryu*, the *ki* means "auger" or "drill," and the *ryu* means "life."

玖蘭枢

Kuran Kaname

Kaname means "hinge" or "door." The kanji for his last name is a combination of the old-fashioned way of writing *ku*, meaning "nine," and *ran*, meaning "orchid": "nine orchids."

藍堂英

Aido Hanabusa

Hanabusa means "petals of a flower." *Aido* means "indigo temple." In Japanese, the pronunciation of *Aido* is very close to the pronunciation of the English word *idol*.

架院暁

Kain Akatsuki

Akatsuki means "dawn" or "daybreak." In *Kain*, *ka* is a base or support, while *in* denotes a building that has high fences around it, such as a temple or school.

早園瑠佳

Souen Ruka

In *Ruka*, the *ru* means "lapis lazuli" while the *ka* means "good-looking" or "beautiful." The *sou* in Ruka's surname, *Souen*, means "early," but this kanji also has an obscure meaning of "strong fragrance." The *en* means "garden."

一条拓麻

Ichijo Takuma

Ichijo can mean a "ray" or "streak." The kanji for *Takuma* is a combination of *taku*, meaning "to cultivate" and *ma*, which is the kanji for *asa*, meaning "hemp" or "flax," a plant with blue flowers.

支葵千里

Shiki Senri

Shiki's last name is a combination of *shi*, meaning "to support" and *ki*, meaning "mallow"—a flowering plant with pink or white blossoms. The *ri* in *Senri* is a traditional Japanese unit of measure for distance, and one *ri* is about 2.44 miles. *Senri* means "1,000 *ri*."

夜刈十牙

Yagari Toga

Yagari is a combination of *ya*, meaning "night," and *gari*, meaning "to harvest." *Toga* means "ten fangs."

一条麻遠，一翁

Ichijo Asato, aka "Ichio"

Ichijo can mean a "ray" or "streak." Asato's first name is comprised of *asa*, meaning "hemp" or "flax," and *tou*, meaning "far off." His nickname is *ichi*, or "one," combined with *ou*, which can be used as an honorific when referring to an older man.

若葉沙頼

Wakaba Sayori

Yori's full name is Sayori Wakaba. *Wakaba* means "young leaves." Her given name, *Sayori*, is a combination of *sa*, meaning "sand," and *yori*, meaning "trust."

星煉

Seiren

Sei means "star" and *ren* means "to smelt" or "refine." *Ren* is also the same kanji used in *rengoku*, or "purgatory."

遠矢莉磨

Toya Rima

Toya means a "far-reaching arrow." Rima's first name is a combination of *ri*, or "jasmine," and *ma*, which signifies enhancement by wearing away, such as by polishing or scouring.

紅まり亜

Kurenai Maria

Kurenai means "crimson." The kanji for the last *a* in Maria's first name is the same that is used in "Asia."

錐生壱縷

Kiryu Ichiru

Ichi is the old-fashioned way of writing "one," and *ru* means "thread."

緋桜閑, 狂咲姫

Hio Shizuka, Kuruizaki-hime

Shizuka means "calm and quiet." In Shizuka's family name, *hi* is "scarlet," and *ou* is "cherry blossoms." Shizuka Hio is also referred to as the "Kuruizaki-hime." *Kuruizaki* means "flowers blooming out of season," and *hime* means "princess."

藍堂月子

Aido Tsukiko

Aido means "indigo temple." *Tsukiko* means "moon child."

白蕗更

Shirabuki Sara

Shira is "white," and *buki* is "butterbur," a plant with white flowers. *Sara* means "renew."

黒主灰閻

Cross Kaien

Cross, or *Kurosu*, means "black master." Kaien is a combination of *kai*, meaning "ashes," and *en*, meaning "village gate." The kanji for *en* is also used for Enma, the ruler of the Underworld in Buddhist mythology.

玖蘭李土

Kuran Rido

Kuran means "nine orchids." In *Rido*, *ri* means "plum" and *do* means "earth."

玖蘭樹里

Kuran Juri

Kuran means "nine orchids." In her first name, *ju* means "tree" and a *ri* is a traditional Japanese unit of measure for distance. The kanji for *ri* is the same as in Senri's name.

玖蘭悠

Kuran Haruka

Kuran means "nine orchids." *Haruka* means "distant" or "remote."

鷹宮海斗

Takamiya Kaito

Taka means "hawk" and *miya* means "imperial palace" or "shrine." *Kai* is "sea" and *to* means "to measure" or "grid."

菖藤依砂也

Shoto Isaya

Sho means "Siberian Iris" and *to* is "wisteria." The *I* in *Isaya* means "to rely on," while the *sa* means "sand." *Ya* is a suffix used for emphasis.

橙茉

Toma

In the family name *Toma*, *to* means "seville orange" and *ma* means "jasmine flower."

藍堂永路

Aido Nagamichi

The name *Nagamichi* is a combination of *naga*, which means "long" or "eternal," and *michi*, which is the kanji for "road" or "path." *Aido* means "indigo temple."

縹木

Hanadagi

In this family name, *Hanada* means "bright light blue" and *gi* means "tree."

影山

Kageyama

In the Class Rep's family name, *kage* means "shadow," and *yama* means "mountain."

Terms

-sama: The suffix *sama* is used in formal address for someone who ranks higher in the social hierarchy. The vampires call their leader "Kaname-sama" only when they are among their own kind.

Matsuri Hino burst onto the manga scene with her series *Kono Yume ga Sametara* (When This Dream Is Over), which was published in *LaLa DX* magazine. Hino was a manga artist a mere nine months after she decided to become one.

With the success of her popular series *Captive Hearts* and *MeruPuri*, Hino has established herself as a major player in the world of shojo manga. *Vampire Knight* is currently serialized in *LaLa* magazine.

Hino enjoys creative activities and has commented that she would have been either an architect or an apprentice to traditional Japanese craft masters if she had not become a manga artist.

VAMPIRE KNIGHT
Vol. 16
Shojo Beat Edition

STORY AND ART BY
MATSURI HINO

Adaptation/Nancy Thistlethwaite
Translation/Tetsuichiro Miyaki
Touch-up Art & Lettering/Rina Mapa
Graphic Design/Amy Martin
Editor/Nancy Thistlethwaite

Vampire Knight by Matsuri Hino © Matsuri Hino 2012. All rights reserved.
First published in Japan in 2012 by HAKUSENSHA, Inc., Tokyo. English
language translation rights arranged with HAKUSENSHA, Inc., Tokyo.

Printed in the U.S.A.

Published by VIZ Media, LLC
P.O. Box 77010
San Francisco, CA 94107

10 9 8 7 6 5 4 3
First printing, March 2013
Third printing, January 2016

www.viz.com

www.shojobeat.com

SURPRISE!

You may be reading the wrong way!

It's true: In keeping with the original Japanese comic format, this book reads from right to left—so action, sound effects, and word balloons are completely reversed. This preserves the orientation of the original artwork—plus, it's fun! Check out the diagram shown here to get the hang of things, and then turn to the other side of the book to get started!

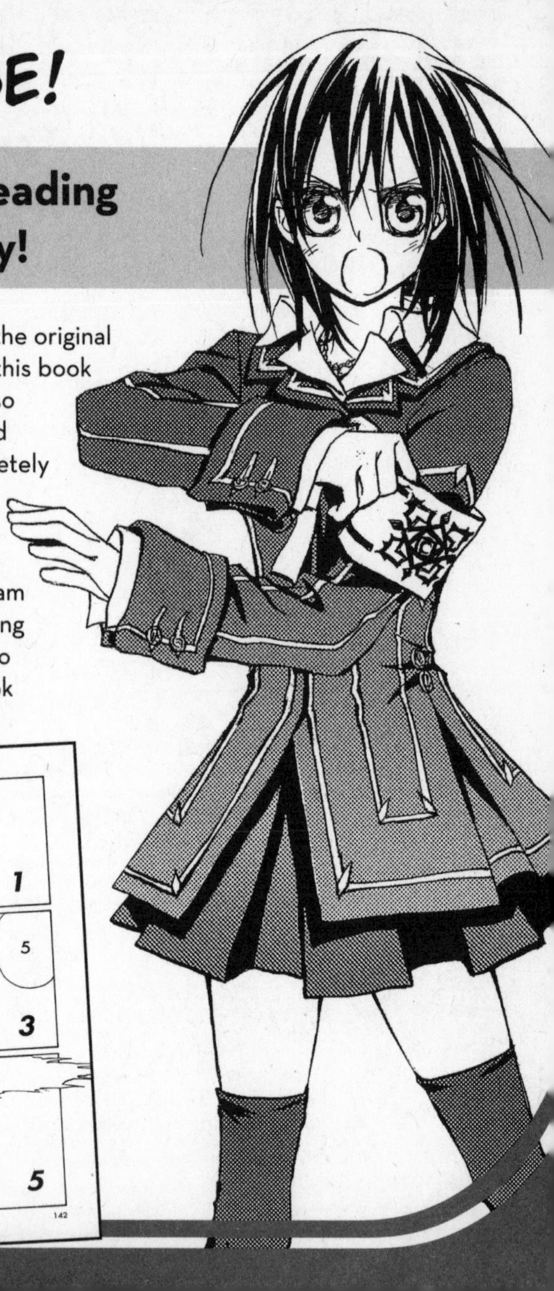

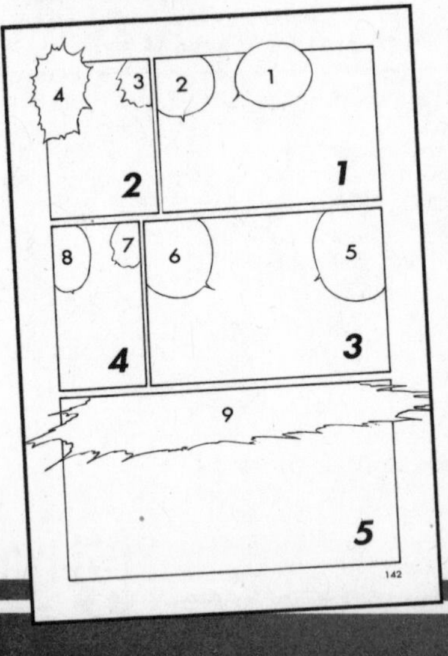
1
2
3
4
1
2
5
6
7
8
3
4
9
5
142